Close to Perfect

Close to Perfect

Tina Donahue

KENSINGTON PUBLISHING CORP.
http://www.kensingtonbooks.com

BRAVA BOOKS are published by

Kensington Publishing Corp.
850 Third Avenue
New York, NY 10022

All Kensington titles, imprints, and distributed lines are available at special quantity discounts for bulk purchases for sales promotion, premiums, fund-raising, and educational or institutional use.

Special book excerpts or customized printings can also be created to fit specific needs. For details, write or phone the office of the Kensington Special Sales Manager: Kensington Publishing Corp., 850 Third Avenue, New York, NY 10022. Attn. Special Sales Department. Phone: 1-800-221-2647.

ISBN 0-7582-1318-2

First Kensington Trade Paperback Printing: December 2005
10 9 8 7 6 5 4 3 2 1

Printed in the United States of America

To Gene and LKB—
"Someone to Watch Over Me"

Chapter One

Nudity—especially his own—had never fazed Josh Wyatt. In the steamy Florida Keys clothing was generally kept to a minimum in public, while stripping down to skin in private was as natural as breathing, and certainly not something Josh had ever thought about.

The last forty-eight hours had changed that. Suddenly his private moments were public thanks to *Keys Confidential,* a popular tabloid.

The latest edition was on his desk, but Josh deliberately ignored those unauthorized photos that captured him from behind as he emerged naked from his very secluded pool. He didn't need to look at that again; those suckers were forever burned into his memory and generated absolutely no sympathy from his staff.

"Lighten up," his secretary had said just a short time ago. Although Peg Mulrooney was in her mid-forties, she seemed closer to Josh's thirty-one given her lingering beauty and flippant attitude. "It could have been worse."

Josh hadn't a clue how, unless that paparazzo hadn't fled before he turned completely around, with those photos being sold from under the counter in brown paper wrappers. "The bastard had no right to break into my private yard and take those pictures of me."

"Of course he didn't, but it's not so bad."

Easy to say since she was fully clothed and still anonymous to the public. Even so, Josh always listened to Peg. They had worked at the same company during his construction days, with Peg being his first employee when he became a developer. She hadn't taken crap from him when he was poor, and wasn't at all impressed with his current wealth.

He trusted her. If she said it wasn't so bad, it probably wasn't. "Why not?"

"The paper named you this year's most delectable hunk, didn't they? They even spelled your name right. What more could you want?"

"Damned if I know. Wait a sec—how about privacy? Or trunks?"

"Give it a rest," she advised. "You look good."

She had said that as her gaze was riveted to those shots of his naked back, ass, and legs.

I'm a dead man, he thought then and now. Proof of it was in the endlessly ringing phones with none of those calls being about business. Oh, no. Propositions from women who had seen him exposed in that tabloid continued to pour in by the hour, and then there were the gifts.

Josh glanced at one particularly lush basket adorned with velvety orchids in varying shades of red, purple, and hot pink. Snuggled within those dewy petals were photos of a young blonde striking the same poses Josh had unwittingly provided for that paparazzo.

Peg assured him that his photos were better.

At least they weren't as obvious. The blonde had a scarlet banner stretched across her bare butt with white print that read: *Bad Boy Meets Even Badder Girl. Yum.*

He closed his eyes.

"Ah, Josh?"

Aw, God. He had momentarily forgotten that his attorney was still in the office. "Yup?"

"You really need to deal with this."

Josh was trying, but not in the way Alan Davis would have

liked. Opening his eyes, his gaze slid to the man. Despite an outside temp of ninety, and punishing humidity that made even an air-conditioned office feel clammy, Alan wore a navy Brooks Brothers suit with a gold tie knotted so tight his thin face seemed paler than usual.

Josh wondered if Alan was about to faint from lack of oxygen, lack of sweating, or the problem *Keys Confidential* had created. "You worry too much."

The man instinctively touched the small bald spot on the top of his head, before smoothing down the rest of his thinning brown hair. He was only thirty-five, but looked older than Peg and seemed suddenly depressed about it. "You don't worry enough."

He had that right. Josh continued to ignore the bundles of that tabloid stacked on the leather sofa and chairs in here. The moment Alan found out about the photos, he had sent his crew to every grocery, liquor, and convenience store to buy all the copies. Rumor had it that the tabloid just printed more since the demand was so great. "I don't want a bodyguard."

"You don't have a choice."

"This will blow over."

"Not before the first wave of lawsuits hit."

"You think Badder Girl would actually sue me?"

Alan looked at her picture.

Josh expected the man's pale cheeks to finally pink up. Didn't happen. If anything, her bare butt made Alan more determined to treat this as seriously as possible.

"I think if you so much as accidentally bump into one of these women while they're after you, they're going to see a golden opportunity to claim that you led them on, you got them in a compromising position, you couldn't take 'no' for an answer, and then—"

"I get your point." Damn. Being poor had sucked, but being rich was not without its problems. The moment Josh hit it big everyone wanted a piece of him with some, even the

ladies, meaning to take it any way they could. He slumped farther into his chair.

Alan rocked on his heels as if he'd gotten his second wind. "That last man you interviewed was just perfect for your needs."

Josh rolled his eyes and swiveled his chair around until he was facing the bank of windows behind his desk. Just past the overhanging evergreens and palms a modest yacht was approaching the dock. Beyond that, the Atlantic stretched into the distance, its bluish waters rustling, restless, offering escape.

Alan sighed from behind. "What was wrong with him?"

"Besides smelling like garlic every time he belched?"

"He's going to protect you, not kiss you. Besides," Alan said, despite Josh's groan, "he was perfect. Big. Strong. No-nonsense and—"

"Stop—you're turning me on."

Again, Alan sighed. "At least reconsider suing the publication."

"And have it all over Court TV, then made into a movie on cable? Aren't you worried about who they'd get to play you?"

Alan muttered something beneath his breath.

"See?" Josh said. "It's not as easy as you think; so no, thanks. I just want this to go away."

"Exactly. And to do that, you need to hire a bodyguard."

Or another attorney. Suppressing a sigh, Josh finally tuned Alan out and concentrated on that boat instead.

It wasn't an exceptional craft by any means. Just a double cabin motor yacht with an upper helm station being piloted by a young guy who kept looking towards this office, rather than the slips.

Was he lost?

"So, what do you think?" Alan asked.

Josh didn't know what to think about that guy. For some reason his grungy hair and sloppy T-shirt seemed vaguely familiar, even though nearly everyone in the Keys dressed like

that. Of course, what really struck a chord was the way he kept dipping his left shoulder as if he was dancing in place. Josh had seen that exact same movement before, though he couldn't quite recall where or when or even if it involved this guy. Did he work around here? Had he been involved in one of the recent developments? Did he own one of the contracting companies?

Was he ever going to look at that damned dock instead of this office?

"Josh?"

"Yeah, sure, right," he said to Alan, then craned his neck to see that guy better, until the guy craned his neck as if he also wanted a better look.

"Right?" Alan asked.

No, that guy's last movement was wrong. Actually, it was bordering on fucking weird.

Who are you?

Josh leaned to the side for a better view, but got squat, since the guy sank to his knees behind the controls. At just that moment, a group of mean-looking clouds blocked the sun.

The windows quickly reflected Josh twisted into a very uncomfortable position, which was probably why that guy had stared and was now possibly hiding.

Straightening, Josh rubbed the side of his neck and looked past his own reflection to the rest of the office. Beyond it was a glass wall that separated his space from Peg's.

She was standing beside her desk as she spoke to a young woman whose back was to him.

Josh's fingers paused on his neck. The pain was forgotten as his gaze drifted down that young woman's thick, dark hair. It fell in gentle waves to her narrow shoulders, all soft and natural.

Nice.

His gaze inched lower.

She was slender and tall and dressed in a suit that Brooks

Brothers never thought to design. Foolish boys. That suit was unbelievably nice. The jacket was fitted, while the slim skirt was slightly above the knee with a side slit to make walking easy and to give a man just a hint of her very nice thigh.

That thigh was currently hidden, but that didn't stop Josh from exploring what he could of her beneath that suit. The fabric appeared lightweight and silky—from here it seemed to be the color of a ripe peach—and hugged her so well that she looked both elegant and sexy.

His thoughts whispered, *Turn around.*

She did.

Without pause, Josh swiveled his chair so that he was facing his desk and her.

Alan immediately stepped into his line of sight. "Then you agree?"

"What?" Josh leaned to the right to look around Alan.

"Then you agree?"

"Sure—whatever—dammit, Alan, stand still, will you?"

The attorney finally stopped pacing. "Why?"

Why else? So he could look around the man to her.

Beneath the harsh fluorescent lights that lovely hair was glossy, the color of an expensive cognac, gently framing her face. Features that were both delicate and exotic complemented her creamy flesh and those lushly lashed eyes that were either a very light brown or hazel.

Josh imagined heat in those eyes, the kind that made a man promise all sorts of things and not regret a one of them. He imagined her in island wear—one of those sheer cotton camisoles and white skirts with a ruffled hem that hung low on her hips, baring her navel.

Something deep within him was stirred as he skimmed the outline of her breasts. Full breasts that would easily fill a man's hands.

Who was she? Why was she turning away? What were she and Peg talking about?

What was Peg doing?

Josh watched as the woman went behind her desk. Each movement caused Peg's beaded hippie dress to sparkle as wildly as the glittery scarf she had wrapped around her reddish curls. There were rings on each finger and too many bracelets dangling against her wrists as Peg reached into her wastebasket, pulled out a copy of that tabloid and showed it to the young woman.

Josh stared as Peg pointed to his buck naked pictures on the cover—as if anyone could miss them—then pointed to the glass that separated her office from his.

The young woman's gaze lifted to where he was seated, then returned to the tabloid as if she just couldn't help herself.

Please don't keep looking at that.

She did.

A moment passed and then another, while heat rose to Josh's chest and throat.

He had to wonder what in the world that young woman was thinking and why he cared. He didn't know her. If she was some weirdo who was here to ogle him in the flesh, so to speak, he would never know her. So, why did he feel so damned embarrassed?

Many women had seen him nude, really nude, his stiffened cock and tightened balls ready for action and not one bit ashamed. So, what was the big deal about this woman seeing his bare ass?

Josh told himself it was no big deal, but didn't believe it, because those pictures hadn't been his choice and certainly weren't something he was proud of.

Of course, try to tell that to Peg or those females who continued to call. Even better, try to explain it to this one. For some reason she seemed different than the rest. She was special, although Josh had no idea why.

He hoped to God she wouldn't laugh.

She did not. After a long moment, she simply lifted her gaze, touching his.

It was a surprise Josh had not expected.

There was understanding in her eyes, but beneath that a female wanting that was so damned honest it touched his core. As embarrassed as he had just felt, he was now as confident. Her gaze gave him that.

So, when was the last time he had needed a woman's approval—a stranger's approval, no less—to feel as if he hadn't been such a bad boy or a fool?

"Yo, Josh, remember me?"

Alan? His gaze drifted to the man. He was still here?

The door to his office opened.

Josh looked in that direction as the young woman came inside, her long legs moving fluidly, like a dancer.

Peg was right behind her, smiling broadly, her expression ordering him to *lighten up*.

Not a chance. Josh had never felt more coiled and aroused in all of his days. Every part of him was stirred by this young woman.

Pushing back his chair, Josh stood, ready for her, ready for anything as Peg said, "Whatever you two guys have been talking about, it can wait."

Tess Franklin couldn't have agreed more, though she hardly got the chance to express it as that pale, overdressed man frowned at Peg.

"No, it can't," he said.

"Sure it can," Peg countered, "just chill for a little bit. That's all I'm asking, Alan."

Alan wasn't convinced. As he whined and Peg refused to be impressed or intimidated, Tess continued to regard Josh Wyatt.

He was taller than she had expected, over six-two, with strong, masculine features and thick, dark-blond hair that was long enough and tousled enough to give him a boyish look.

This was no boy. His creamy brown eyes, his gaze, spoke of a man's experience and need. His lean, muscular frame betrayed those years he had toiled in construction before hitting it big in real estate development.

Despite that wealth, Tess could see that he wasn't at all corporate uptight, not like still-yakking Alan. Josh's choice in clothing was confident and casual—dark beige chinos and a white shirt worn open at the collar with the sleeves folded back to mid-forearm.

That skin was bronzed by the sun, that flesh sculpted by labor.

His gaze was still on her, watching, waiting, while his dark brows were lifting in approval, or was it surprise?

Tess wondered if his surprise was as pleasant as her own. Although she had seen photographs of him in Internet business articles, she never would have believed that he could be even better-looking in person. Or that his male beauty in a business setting could so easily match those bad boy photos in *Keys Confidential,* which was strewn all over this office, even his desk.

Tess warned herself not to look at the tabloid, and certainly not to linger on it, but couldn't resist.

Wow. That cover may have been unauthorized, but it was still amazing—nearly artistic as it showed three large photos of Josh with each building on the last, telling a sensual tale.

In the first, he was emerging naked from his pool. Light danced over the water streaming down his broad, muscular back and that luscious tattoo that ran the length of his shoulders.

Tess suspected he had gotten tattooed during his construction days. It was a geometric pattern, possibly Celtic—tribal, bold, virile. It made her skin tingle.

In the second photo, his ass was finally bared with that flesh as hard and well-toned as the rest of him.

In the third, he was fully out of the pool, his strong legs exposed, his hands lifted to his head as he smoothed back his damp hair, his torso turned to the side as if he finally sensed someone behind him. The muscles in his thighs were powerful and taut, the right side of his chest was exposed showing that hard pec and that dark, silky underarm hair.

He looked like a modern-day *David*. Even the artist Michelangelo would have been impressed.

No wonder he needed protection.

For the first time since Tess had convinced her father that she should come here—despite his vigorous objections—she was honestly glad. And not at all embarrassed by the way Josh was politely clearing his throat to get her attention.

She was behaving unprofessionally, no one had to tell her that, but there were worse things in life than a woman admiring photos of such a beautiful man.

"Yo, miss?"

Tess finished moistening her lips, and flicked her gaze to Alan. His expression was as pissy as that greeting.

Ignoring him, she looked at Josh.

In that moment he forgot what he had planned to say. His gaze dipped to her lush mouth, those freshly moistened lips, before returning to her eyes. A wave of desire so completely consumed Josh that he was unable to tell Alan to shut up.

As the attorney went on and on Josh saw that need again flaring in her eyes. They were hazel, a warm, golden color, as exotic as the rest of—

"Very well, miss," Alan said in his most condescending tone, "you leave me no choice but to warn you."

What the hell? Josh gave him a frown.

Alan ignored that as he continued to address her. "If you're here to throw yourself at Mr. Wyatt so you can turn around and slap him with a lawsuit, it won't do you any good. I'm an attorney and I know the law."

Good God. Josh glared at the man, then looked at her.

A faint blush stained her smooth cheeks, though that had nothing to do with embarrassment as she finally looked at Alan. A moment passed and then another as she took in the attorney's full length, before lifting her gaze. It was as cool as her voice. "Is that right?"

Josh's brows arched. Even the most macho of men would have gone limp in all the wrong places at that dismissive tone.

Not Alan. "Exceedingly so."

"Then you must also know what constitutes slander."

He frowned. Josh smiled. Damn, but he liked her. Her manner was confident, her voice surprisingly musical, lilting, conjuring up images of sheer island wear, sultry nights, and moist flesh.

When her gaze touched his, liquid heat poured through Josh, again.

"I believe you misunderstand," Alan said.

She swung her gaze back to him. "No, I don't think I do."

His voice hardened. "You're trespassing."

"There you go again," she said.

"Now, now, play nice you two," Peg said. "Especially you, Alan. I invited her inside."

Josh smiled. "Thanks."

The young woman seemed momentarily surprised by that response, then returned his smile.

It was so lovely and approving Josh couldn't help but grin.

Oddly enough, that killed the magic. All at once, her expression changed from approving to no-nonsense—watch it, buddy.

Josh fully intended to watch all of it. Didn't she know that?

Her arched right brow said that she did.

Losing his grin, Josh moved around his desk.

"You invited her in here?" Alan asked Peg.

"Yup," Josh said as he bypassed the attorney and went straight to her, not stopping until he was close enough to capture her fragrance.

It was soft and powdery, reminding him of spring air in colder climes; that first hint of warmth scented by delicate flowers.

He smiled.

Her cheeks flushed again.

That and her softening gaze had Josh damned near giddy. "Hi." He offered his hand.

Her gaze remained on his as she slipped her own inside.

Her fingers were slender and warm, her skin deliciously soft, but her grip was as firm as any guy.

She was no pushover; that was for damned sure, which aroused Josh all the more. An easy woman had never been his style. This woman had all the makings of a challenge, out of bed and in.

His cock continued to thicken as he imagined her naked flesh on top of his as he plunged deeply inside her sweet, wet heat. Not that Josh was about to let that arousal creep into his voice, at least not yet. "Josh Wyatt, miss—"

"Tess Franklin," Peg said.

"Tess," Josh said, his gaze still on her.

That faint blush deepened until it was nearly as dark as her silky peach suit. "Mr. Wyatt."

"Josh," he corrected, in an easy, welcoming tone. "What can I do for you?" Please, God, let it be something good.

"Ah, Josh," Peg said, "it's not what you can do for Tess. It's what she can do for you."

Even better. Josh nodded as if he understood, while his fingers gently caressed hers. "And what can you do for me, Tess?"

Although she had come fully prepared to answer that question, and many others, at the moment words escaped her.

He had really beautiful brown eyes that were as dark as his brows and a shadow of beard, which made his hair seem that much lighter. His eyes were also bright with intelligence that was softened with patience and respect. A potent combination in any man. Male was in every part of him, even his clean, masculine scent. It reminded Tess of leather, tobacco, and torrid summer nights when all caution was lost. It drove even more of her good sense away.

At least, until Alan impatiently cleared his throat.

As Josh shot him a look of warning, Tess figured she should pull herself together.

It wasn't like her to behave so foolishly; she had never done such a thing before, especially with a man. Early on, Tess had been determined to be the equal of any guy.

For some reason, Josh Wyatt made her forget everything she had believed was important, while also making her feel more female than she ever had.

His heat, touch, the sound of his deep, rich voice, the power of his male presence was even more intoxicating than the photographs.

Of course, those photographs were the only reason she had come here today. It probably would be best if she remembered that.

"It's all in here," she said, easing her hand from his.

As Josh looked down at that, then to the envelope she was pulling from her shoulder bag, Alan spoke up.

"Don't touch that," he ordered Josh, then frowned at her. "I should have guessed. You're a process server and that's—"

"More slander," Tess interrupted, "or at the very least, another preposterous assumption." She looked at Josh. "I'm a bodyguard."

No shit? His gaze immediately trickled down her, lingering on her heels. They were the same peach color as her suit with a cut out area to expose her toes.

Her nails were polished in a pinkish tint that was so adorable and arousing Josh had an insane urge to drop to one knee so that he could stroke, then lick those lovely toes. A bodyguard's toes.

That brought him back to reality fast as his gaze inched back up her. To his guesstimate, she was probably five-seven or eight, weighed no more than one hundred and twenty-five pounds, though she wasn't skinny—oh, no. Her flesh was ripe, toned, tanned, and looked raring to go.

Even so—a bodyguard?

Josh smiled, unable to help himself, as his gaze settled on the deep V of her suit jacket. "Since when?"

The edges of that jacket moved slightly with her very deep, very pissed breath.

Uh-oh. Josh lifted his gaze and wasn't a bit surprised that her slender brows were drawn together. After clearing his throat, he used his most professional voice. "How long have you been a bodyguard?"

"Since I left the force."

His eyes widened. "What force?"

"The. Police. Force."

She had said that very slowly, as if he was unbelievably dense or an incredibly bad, bad boy.

"You're a cop?"

"Ex-cop."

Not even *CSI: Miami* had cops that looked as good as this.

"You carry a gun?"

"All the time."

Josh struggled for a moment, then let his gaze trickle back down her. Where in the world could she have concealed a weapon in that outfit? The suit fit her nearly as well as skin. As far as Josh could tell, the only thing pushing against that fabric were curves that were supposed to be there.

At last, he glanced at her thighs. Was it possible that she was sporting a gun in a frilly garter? Did bodyguards do that? Did ex-cops?

His brows lifted as he considered that. Maybe that's why she had that slit on the side of her skirt, instead of in the back. Maybe she reached beneath that slit to pull a weapon out when she needed it.

Amazing, but nice. Josh figured even the most hardened criminal would definitely notice that frilly garter and her sleek, tanned thigh, whether she was pointing a fucking cannon at him or not.

"And you have credentials to prove this?" Alan asked.

"Prove what?" Josh asked. Hell, had he spoken his thoughts aloud?

"It's all in here," Tess said. She waved the envelope in her hand as she went to Alan.

Josh followed.

Her gaze noted that, before she looked at him.

Josh looked right back.

Tess's brows lifted before she turned to Alan.

Once the envelope was in his hand, the attorney gingerly pulled papers from it as if they might be hooked to a bomb. After he glanced at the first, he actually smiled. "Ah, well this explains everything."

Josh craned his neck to see whatever had amused Alan. The man rarely smiled, so this was a problem. Already Josh liked Tess far too much to be disappointed by whatever she had brought.

"Your resume," Alan finally added. "How fortuitous that you thought to bring it."

"You know it really is," she said in a surprisingly agreeable voice. "Until I get coverage in a tabloid, I'll just have to rely on my resume, now won't I?"

Joss laughed. Tess looked at him.

He cleared his throat. "Give me that," he said to Alan.

As Josh bent his head to her resume, he again caught her powdery scent. It was on these papers and that envelope; it filled this room.

Inhaling deeply, he forced himself to concentrate. After a moment and some quick math using her dates of employment, he figured she was twenty-eight.

The resume didn't indicate whether she was involved with anyone. Of course, she wasn't married, Josh had already checked for a wedding ring.

"If you'll look at the second page," Tess said, "you'll see I've successfully completed FBI training programs."

No shit? Josh looked at her, then right back down, really reading her resume this time.

It was surprisingly impressive.

She had been a police officer for six years prior to working for Privacy Dynamics, Inc., a firm offering celebrity and VIP protection, private investigations, background checks, and a whole slew of other services, including witness protection and relocation.

Damn. Josh hoped this tabloid thing didn't come to that.

He glanced at her employer's brochure, seeing that the firm had recently been launched and was headed by a man named Fred Franklin.

Josh's gaze jumped up.

Tess's gaze was on his chest. She was moistening her lips again.

Okay, so Fred probably wasn't a current or ex-husband, not with the way she was looking at his chest, and how she had previously looked at his tabloid photos. Could be this Fred was an uncle or her dad.

Josh wondered how the man had known he needed a bodyguard, unless Fred just figured he'd give it a shot by sending his lovely daughter or niece over here to sell him a contract.

Smart man.

Josh returned his attention to her resume, nodding in approval to those commendations she had accumulated during her short time on the force. One was for bravery in the line of duty, several were for civic activities, and others were for her excellence in firearms and other police stuff.

Real stuff. These weren't just honor badges for showing up on time or looking great, they were for honest-to-God police work.

Josh's breathing picked up. He started to shift his weight but thought better of it. Already his rod was so hard it didn't need to be stimulated more by brushing against his clothing.

He continued reading and getting excited. Despite her exotic beauty and quick wit, Tess was skilled in the use of practically every firearm imaginable, not to mention room clearing, building clearing, searching techniques, vehicle formations (whatever that meant), managing the media and bothersome paparazzi, using unarmed defense tactics to ward off not-so-nice fans, protecting individuals in crowd situations, preplanning all itineraries so that nothing bad happened, hostage rescue, and hand-to-hand combat.

Again, Josh looked up. This time Tess was staring at those tabloid photos. "You're skilled in hand-to-hand combat?"

It was a moment before she looked at him, and another moment before her gaze completely cleared. "Yes, sir."

Yes, sir? Damn, he liked her cop talk. "Aikido, karate, jujitsu?"

Her eyes widened. "You know martial arts?"

Only to say the names. He smiled and shrugged. "Not really."

Alan cut in. "Why don't you educate us?"

This time Tess regarded the man for so long Josh was certain Alan wouldn't only go limp, but would start squirming.

When the attorney finally looked uncomfortable, the way only a cop or a woman could make a man feel, she said, "That would take a very long time. Are you certain you want that?"

Alan's face turned a bright red.

Josh suppressed a smile, and was glad he had as she next turned to him.

"I'll make this fast," she said. "Briefly—"

"No need to be fast or brief. Take your time."

Her lips remained parted, her gaze held his as the sound of a boat's motor, the wind, and rustling palms briefly filled the silence.

During it Josh thought about a lot of things, like how fortuitous it was that she had happened in here today, because she was giving him ideas about all kinds of stuff . . . stuff that actually had to do with her work as a bodyguard.

So why did such a luscious woman become a cop? What had convinced her to risk her safety and to compete with the boys? All she had to do was look at a man with those warm, honey-colored eyes and that guy was a goner.

Had she dated a lot of cops on the force? Was she dating one now? Did one of the other bodyguards have his eye on her? Had she noticed? Had she liked it?

"You ready?" she asked.

It was a moment before Josh understood the question, though he immediately noted the mischievous glint in her eyes. "Sure. Shoot."

Peg leaned toward him. "Remember, Josh, she is armed."

He nodded, and again wondered about garters and weapons and her sweet, sweet thighs. "I'll be careful."

Tess looked skeptical. "There are many H2H combat styles, but the—"

"What's H2H?" Alan asked.

"Hand-to-hand," Josh said, his gaze still on Tess.

"Don't interrupt again," Peg warned.

"It's all right," Tess said. "It's best to pay attention since I'll be giving a pop quiz at the end of this."

Josh smiled.

So did she. "You ready?"

"For anything," he said.

She looked briefly intrigued, then got serious again. "The most popular hand-to-hand combat techniques are Jeet Kune Do, Defendo, H2H American Self Defense, Krav Maga, Systema, and Hocks Close Quarters Combat."

Peg chuckled. "Close quarters combat, huh? Now, that one sounds interesting."

Tess smiled. "Remind you of a few dates you've had?"

Peg laughed.

"Which technique do you use?" Josh asked.

Peg looked at him. "Me?"

He arched one brow, then looked at Tess.

Her attention was already on him, her gaze thoughtful.

"You," he said.

Her cheeks and throat flushed. "I like Krav Maga."

He liked the way he could make her blush. He bet none of the cops on her old force or those burly bodyguards she worked with could do that. "Any reason?"

Her gaze traveled his length, then returned to his eyes. "It avoids injury. I can take control of an individual who's far taller, muscular and stronger than me without harming them, even if they have me in a bear hug. With Krav Maga, there are no rules. It uses an individual's vulnerable spots, even a very well-toned and fit individual, so that I can protect myself."

"Good for you," Peg said, then spoke to Josh. "Better remember that."

He would, especially that no rules stuff, and everything else about this very unexpected and amazing young woman. Her cheeks were really rosy now, as if she liked to talk about her work, or had just been thinking of what he had—them engaging in some erotic H2H combat.

Suppressing a smile and the urge to move closer so that he could capture even more of her delicate scent, Josh looked back to her resume and that brochure for Privacy Dynamics. As his head remained bent to those papers, his gaze quickly moved to her thighs, her shapely calves, those long, slender toes peeking out from the openings in her peach-tinted high heels.

She should always wear shoes like that, even in bed. If she shared his, Josh would want her hair hanging loose as it was now, and the rest of her stripped bare, except for those shoes and a garter, with her weapon removed.

He would definitely insist upon that. At least, until she gave him that hard cop's stare she liked to use on Alan, who was still unimpressed.

"Even if your credentials are excellent—"

Josh interrupted the man. "They are."

Tess seemed pleased with his assessment, but also confident as if she knew it to be true.

Cocky and soft. What a combination. But then, what else

could Josh have expected from a delicious ex-cop bodyguard?

Alan cleared his throat. "That may well be," he said to Josh, before addressing her, "but Mr. Wyatt has already decided on another—"

"No, I haven't." Josh looked at Alan, then Peg, "I'd like to interview Miss Franklin now, so if you two don't mind . . . "

Peg nodded. "I'm cool." Because Alan wasn't, she slipped her arm through his to pull him from the room if need be.

"Josh," the attorney said, "I really should stay while you interview—"

"We'll be fine," he said, then asked Tess. "Won't we?"

Now, there was a question that didn't need answering. Tess knew he would be more than fine, the professional in her would see to his safety. The woman in her was another matter entirely. She was far too attracted to this man; he was making her want more than just this job.

Not a chance. Behave like the professional you are.

It wasn't only her future on the line here, it was also her dad's. If she were to act like a silly fool and lose this job or compromise it, his business would be the one to suffer. It probably would be best if she also remembered that. "I'll protect you as no one else ever has."

Josh's expression said he had absolutely no doubt of that as his gaze grew thoughtful and lingered.

If any other man had looked at her as he was now doing, this moment might have felt inappropriate and uncomfortable.

With this man it seemed oddly right, even though Alan and Peg had not yet left. Tess was vaguely aware that they were speaking, but whether it was to each other or Josh, she had no idea.

Only he existed. She saw wanting in his gaze, the kind fueled not only by desire, but admiration and respect. How many times had Tess searched for that look on the faces of other men? How many times had she been so disappointed that she had come to believe what she was now seeing didn't exist.

Her belly fluttered and her body felt deliciously weak. If she hadn't already wanted him, she surely did now.

Not that she would act upon it.

The door closed behind her.

Tess glanced over her shoulder to see that Alan and Peg were now in the woman's office, lingering by the glass wall that separated it from this space. She turned back to Josh.

His gaze was on her heels, before lifting to her eyes. "I believe that."

"Believe what?"

"That you'll protect me as no one else ever has."

Her cheeks and throat got hot. Her heart was beating far too fast. If she spoke now, Tess was afraid her voice would betray what she felt, so she simply nodded.

Josh regarded her for a moment more, then went to his desk. He was lowering her resume and the brochure onto that copy of *Keys Confidential* when his head lifted to the boat outside.

Several moments passed as he continued to watch that boat, obviously forgetting her, and so easily too, unless there was something about that boat that bothered him. "Everything all right?"

Josh looked over his shoulder. His expression and sudden smile said that he had forgotten her. "I hope it will be, but I'll need your help."

Tess nodded. Her heart was really pounding now. He was going to give her this job. She suspected it, of course, but then, there had always been the possibility that he asked Peg and Alan to leave so that he could gently let her down and ask for a date, instead.

Tess had to admit that a date with him would have been very nice, but that had to be put aside now. She was going to get this plum assignment for Privacy Dynamics. She had beaten out all of the really big industry players.

Her father would be so proud just as soon as he finished yelling at her. Tess had given him no end of grief when she became a cop and now that she was a bodyguard, he wasn't all that thrilled about her going after clients like Josh.

Just this morning he had ordered her to stay away from the man.

"I mean it," he had said as he lifted the tabloid in his fist. "He's obviously a pervert."

"Aw, Pop. He was swimming in his own pool in his own yard in a gated estate, not taking a dip in front of City Hall."

"Just stay away from him."

As a rule, Tess followed orders in her professional life, but not today. Something kept drawing her to this man, like the promise of an outstanding contract and those luscious pictures of him and—

"Of course," Josh said, interrupting her thoughts, "you wouldn't be acting solely as my bodyguard."

Just like that, Tess's heart sank, because she knew what was coming. It wasn't uncommon for wealthy clients to expect a bodyguard to also walk their dogs, run errands, and be a substitute maid. Because this man had to work for his wealth, because he kept looking at her with admiration and respect, Tess had expected far better of him. "What?"

"Let me explain." He moved past her.

Where was he going? Tess looked over her shoulder, surprised he was so close. As she turned her back to that bank of windows, he glanced outside again.

"You okay?"

Josh nodded, then spoke in a lowered voice only she could hear. "If you were to act solely as my bodyguard you'd attract all sorts of animosity and probably even more press. However, if you were to pretend to be involved with me romantically, when we're out in public, you'll get rid of the others fast, without bloodshed."

As low as Tess's heart had just sunk, it now bottomed out, making her feel like the ultimate fool.

He didn't want her to be his maid, he wanted her to pretend to be his girlfriend?

Is that why he had turned on the charm? Is that all he thought she was—a pair of boobs and hands and lips that would be all over him in public to keep the rest of the women away? Nitwits like Badder Girl Yum?

Tess's gaze drifted to that basket of orchids adorned with that blonde's erotic photos.

She tried to imagine doing that herself, but could not, unless she loved a man and those pictures were for his eyes alone. If Tess loved a man, there would be no end to her need or what she would do for him. That kind of passion knew no shame or restrictions. She met Josh's gaze.

His brows lifted. "Hey, you all right?"

Tess wasn't sure. He wasn't leering at her as she had expected or looking as if she were no more than a potential employee, a mere staff member paid to do all of his bidding, even if it might be weird.

That same admiration from before, that same respect was in his eyes and expression. That and his concerned manner was turning her brain to mush.

Just stay away from him, her father had advised.

Too late now.

Tess cleared her throat. "What?"

"Are you all—"

She interrupted, "I heard that. I'm still having trouble with what you first said about being romantically involved with you."

Josh appeared surprised, maybe even hurt. When he spoke again, his voice was still lowered, as if he were afraid Peg and Alan might be eavesdropping. "Why?"

Is he kidding? Tess spoke in her normal voice. "I'm not an escort, Mr. Wyatt. I'm a bodyguard."

"No need to shout. In fact, I'd prefer it if you kept your voice lowered."

"Why? Can't you just order Peg and Alan not to listen in on my interview?"

He arched one brow to the snotty way she had said interview. "I'm not worried about them. Besides, they never do what I want anyway."

That was the honest-to-God's truth. Tess had seen the two of them in action.

"It's not funny," Josh said.

She sobered.

"Can I continue?" he asked, his voice still lowered.

"With what?"

"With what I'm asking of you."

Tess told herself to leave. "Go on."

"First of all, it's Josh."

"Whatever you say, Mr. Wyatt."

He inhaled deeply, then sighed it out.

Poor baby. Tess warned herself not to smile.

"As my bodyguard," he finally said, "you will be staying at my place to protect me from intruders, and lawsuits and, well, you know. So, it's only one small step for you to pretend to be involved with me romantically when we're out in public."

This was getting worse, or better, by the minute depending upon how Tess wanted to look at it.

As my bodyguard you will be staying at my place . . . involved with me romantically when we're out in public.

A few seconds ago those public moments had stopped Tess cold; now the private ones were an even greater worry. Stay at his place? Was he kidding?

His place, which Tess had researched for security purposes before coming here, was a Caribbean-style estate with an eighteen-eighties mansion flanked by moss-draped live oaks and cypress trees. The kind of place where heroines in historical romances were deflowered by guys who looked like Josh, after which they spent each day in bed awaiting their lovers, their naked flesh moist from the tropical heat and desire. Was he kidding?

Tess looked from the open collar of his shirt to his eyes.

They still weren't leering. They were honest and looked nearly as vulnerable as she felt.

"It'll only be a little flirting until this blows over." His voice, though lowered, had a reassuring tone to it.

Still . . .

"You do know how to flirt with a man, don't you?" he asked.

Tess arched one brow.

"I'm not kidding," he said.

"That's what worries me."

"Okay, let me prove it to you." He moved so close this time they were almost touching.

Good sense told Tess to step back. His masculine scent, the sound of his deep, rich voice, and his powerful male presence kept her rooted to the spot. "What are you doing?"

"Trying to explain my position without anyone else knowing what I'm saying."

Uh-huh. "You mean someone other than Peg or Alan?"

"That's exactly what I mean. There's a paparazzo outside."

Tess knew she shouldn't have been surprised by that, but she was. No wonder he had been acting so weird. "Where?"

"No, don't look," Josh said.

Tess turned back to him and arched one brow.

Josh sighed, then leaned close and whispered in her ear. "He's in the upper helm station of that boat to the left. I saw him earlier and thought he looked familiar, but couldn't figure out why. That camera and zoom lens in his hand made everything click. That jerk's been following me for days. He's the one who snuck into my yard and sold those photos to that tabloid. For all I know, he's not only taking pictures of us now, but using that zoom to read our lips."

Tess glanced down to Josh holding her wrist. His fingers were calloused from years of labor, his skin warm and dry, his touch exceedingly gentle.

"I'm telling you the truth," he whispered.

Her belly fluttered to his rich voice; his sweet, hot breath tickling her ear.

"I wouldn't joke about something like this," he said, "especially after those humiliating pictures."

Humiliating? Tess's gaze turned inward, remembering each. Until this moment, she hadn't considered that a man as beautiful as Josh would be humiliated by those pictures. They were nearly artistic. Of course, he hadn't asked for that exposure. He hadn't suspected it. It must have really blindsided him, making him look ridiculous to the business community.

Turning her face into his, she whispered, "He shouldn't have done that. I'm sorry."

Josh was so surprised by that response he didn't know what to say. He was far too used to Peg's *lighten up, give it a rest, it could be worse,* or anything else that was all too flip.

But there was genuine understanding in Tess's voice.

There was comfort in being this close.

Her cheek was silky and moist against his; her hair was as soft and fragrant as he had imagined.

She was an amazing woman, and it took all the will Josh owned to ease back.

He was glad he had.

Her gaze was so sincere, seeing only him, not the wealth, not the status, that it stole his breath. "Thanks."

Her color heightened; those delicate nostrils flared.

Without thinking or considering the consequences, Josh touched her cheek.

Her lids fluttered, but she didn't move back. After the briefest hesitation, she lifted her hand and gently stroked the inside of his wrist.

Her touch was thrilling, yet comfortable, and more powerful than sex or all the money the world had to give. It was a caress that touched every part of Josh, and made him want more.

He searched her gaze and saw unexpected trust mingled with a female yearning that hardly needed to be questioned, and could not be denied.

Without pause, he lowered his mouth, gently brushing his lips over hers.

They were velvety, her sigh so soft only he was privileged to hear it, and to feel those lips yielding to his.

He explored that exquisite flesh, he enjoyed it, then felt humbled as Tess parted her lips, inviting him inside.

Josh's first reaction was to seek immediate relief, savage and wild; his second was to be tender, searching, making certain she enjoyed his touch, scent, and unbearable need as he slipped his tongue inside.

She suckled him without pause, as if she had been born for this and him. Her heat and response thickened his cock, making him bold as he drew her closer so that he could deepen the kiss.

Again, she responded, until Josh couldn't breathe, he couldn't think.

He wanted this to last forever, but already she was pulling away, then putting even more distance between them as someone continued to hammer on his door.

Josh ignored that intrusion, following her, instead.

Noting that, Tess gave him one of her hard stares.

This time, Josh wasn't intimidated. Her lips were still moist from their kiss, one she had fully participated in.

"Yo, Josh?" Alan suddenly said from behind.

Fuck. "What?"

The attorney paused to Josh's sharp tone. "Ah, we have business to discuss, and I thought—"

"It can wait," Josh said, his gaze still on Tess. "It'll have to wait."

"Well, I—"

"Later, Alan. And close the door."

The attorney sighed loudly, but did what Josh wanted.

"Please don't leave," he said to her.

Leave? Tess hadn't even moved; after that kiss she wasn't certain she could.

She had responded to this man as if she had known him all her life; she felt that safe in his arms. And yet, he aroused her as if they just met, because they had.

"Do this for me," he asked.

There it was again, that reassuring tone, that respect, that admiration.

If she took this job, where would it lead? Tess had known him less than an hour and already she was letting him kiss her—hell, she had practically begged to taste his tongue. And that wasn't the end of it. Oh, no. She really wanted to kick that paparazzo's butt for humiliating him with those pictures.

"I'll make it worth your while," he added.

Closing her eyes, Tess ordered herself to use her head, not her body or heart. This was a terrific opportunity, one that could easily take her dad's business to the next level and beyond. One she really wanted, and not entirely because of that business.

"I want you," Josh said.

That sounded nice, except all that wanting would only be for as long as he craved it, right? After that, what would happen to her?

Leave, Tess ordered herself. *Run, don't walk, to the nearest exit, and don't look back.*

"Please," Josh said.

Tess opened her eyes and was sorely disappointed that he looked even better than she had recalled. Walking away from him would be hard. Staying for a little while, only to be dismissed a short time into the future, would prove to be even harder.

Taking a deep breath, she finally nodded.

Josh smiled. "Thanks."

Tess's gaze lowered to his sensuous mouth, then returned to his beautiful eyes. "Better wait before you thank me," she said in a voice that was finally professional, one that hardly matched the pounding of her heart. "We need to set up some ground rules before we get started."

Chapter Two

Josh sighed. It seemed the honeymoon was over before it ever got started. Still, he wasn't completely bummed.

Tess hadn't bolted out of here even though it kept crossing her mind. Ex-cop or not, she hardly had a poker face, especially before their kiss.

Her eyes then had been softened with surrender and glazed with desire, the same that Josh felt as her body snuggled into his, delivering her need and trust.

Wow. In that slice of time, she had believed in him, she had wanted him, and as far as Josh was concerned, she'd want him even more in the days to come, despite that skeptical look on her face now.

"Sure," he said, casual as all get-out. "Whatever you want or need."

Tess regarded him until Josh's legs were limp and his cock was rock hard. "A private place to speak would be nice."

Josh followed her gaze to Alan and Peg on the other side of the glass wall, craning their necks to see in, while that paparazzo was probably still clicking away outside.

"Sure. We'll go to the conference room." He took her hand, but didn't get all that far as she decided against surrender and held back like an ex-cop. Josh gave her a moderately hard stare, then inclined his head towards that docked boat.

Tess finally glanced in that direction. Her eyes widened

and then her lips parted to the camera in that guy's hand. It was nearly as big as an assault rifle with the ability to do some serious harm.

Leaning toward her, Josh whispered, "Told you."

Tess turned her face to his.

There was a tiny mole on her right cheek he hadn't noticed before, and a renewed look of wonder in her eyes. They searched his and didn't seem at all disappointed.

At least, until his phone rang.

Just like that, Tess's gaze cleared; she frowned.

"I won't answer it," he murmured.

"Maybe you should. Could be that paparazzo out—"

"Shhhhh."

Her frown deepened. "Why?"

He lowered his voice even more. "Could be he has one of those listening devices I read about on the Net when Nicole Kidman was having problems with the papa—Are you laughing at me?"

Tess lowered her face and breathed hard. "Not at all."

Uh-huh. Curling his fingers around hers, Josh said, "This way." Then he led her into the conference room. Or, at least, he tried as she stopped dead at the door.

"Something wrong?"

Tess figured he had to be kidding. Snuggled against the walls and resting on every chair in this room were scores of baskets with sweetly scented flowers, lewd banners, and pictures of women in provocative poses.

I wouldn't joke about something like this, he had said, *especially after those humiliating pictures.*

Humiliating wasn't the half of it. "Wow." Tess looked at him. "You *are* popular."

His brows drew together. "Believe me, it's not all it's cracked up to be. Actually, it sucks."

"Oh, yeah?" Tess went to one basket that was simply stuffed with pink tea roses and baby's breath. The kind of arrangement one might send to the parents of a new little girl.

Tess lifted the photos that had been included with the basket. This babe was naked as any newborn, but a lot more active, as she went through various contortions in a pool. Tess arched her brows as she looked at Josh, then waited for him to lift his gaze from her butt.

After several seconds, he did. "Sorry. What did you just say?"

"I didn't say anything."

He nodded, agreeably. "Then what were you about to say?"

What else? "I know lots of guys who would give up several decades of their lives for this kind of adoration."

"Like who?" He went to her and whispered, "You're not involved, are you?"

Tess looked down as he again held her wrist. If possible, this caress was even gentler than the last.

Of course she wasn't involved. Would she be here if she was involved? Would she have kissed him as she had? Would she be getting dizzy to the way his thumb was gently stroking her wrist?

Tess couldn't recall any guy doing that as well as Josh. The only men she had seriously dated were cops; macho cowboys whose idea of a great date was beer and pizza with the guys, sack time with her—which they counted as intermission—then back to the guys just as soon as a game or porno came on.

It sucked beyond belief and hurt to her core, but oddly enough, Tess could have put up with all of that if they had also been kind, tender, faithful, the same as her dad had always been with her mom. That's what Tess needed in a lover and an eventual husband.

Hell, no, she wasn't involved. Not that she was about to admit it so easily to this man. "What?"

He whispered the question, again.

Tess's gaze lifted and her brain went right back to mush. A thread of sunlight had broken through the clouds and was touching his hair, turning those thick locks a pale gold, which made his brows and eyes seem even darker, all too male, and downright dangerous to her heart and good sense. "What?"

Josh looked at her mouth. "Huh?"

Okay, time to get a grip. Inhaling deeply, Tess pulled her wrist from him and stepped back. "Why are you still whispering?"

Josh's gaze remained on her mouth as he inclined his head toward the bank of windows in here. Though the angle was different, that boat and paparazzo were still outside with a good view of this room through the wind-whipped palms.

Right. "Don't you have a place more secluded than this?"

"Only the restrooms."

She regarded the windows. "It never occurred to you to get drapes or shades?"

"I've never walked around here in the nude, but if I do," he added as she looked at him, "I'll definitely consider covering the windows."

Uh-huh. Tess glanced around, then went to the intercom on the wall and turned on the music.

A hot Latin number came up with lots of trilling, whooping, and lusty squeals.

She glanced over her shoulder at Josh. "This okay with you?"

His gaze lifted from her heels to her eyes. "What?"

Tess joined him at the conference table. "You okay with the music?"

He seemed stumped for an answer, though slightly aroused. "Sure. Do you like it?"

"I like the fact that the bum outside can't hear us now."

Josh arched one dark brow. "You think I'm being foolish."

"You're being cautious. That's good."

He smiled.

"Is there a phone in here?"

"Why?"

"You need to call building or marina security to get rid of that guy."

His brows lifted as if he hadn't thought of that. Pulling his cell phone out of his pocket, he moved even farther away from the window and made the call in a lowered voice.

Just as he turned back to her, Tess lifted her gaze from his butt.

"Better?" he asked.

Not better—as good—since Tess liked looking at his face as much as she did every other part of him. "Are you involved?"

Just like that, his smile faded into an offended frown. "Would I have asked you to pretend to be my girlfriend in public if I were?"

If he wanted to put the brakes on a currently soured relationship he might. "I don't know, would you?"

"No." He went to her. "Are you involved?"

Tess stepped back. Josh followed. One of those Latin singers moaned and moaned. "Not at the moment," she said, still edging back.

He continued to follow, with both of them moving in time to the music. "Good. That works well with my plan."

She stopped. "About those ground rules."

He stepped back. "What about them?"

"At your place I get my own bedroom and bath, which is off-limits to you."

He looked offended, again. "I thought that was a given."

"Just want to make sure we're on the same page."

"Guess the honeymoon's over, huh?"

Tess stepped towards him again, a smile playing at the corners of her lips. "Don't forget, I do know how to protect myself."

That she did, but she sure as hell hadn't done it during their kiss, nor had Josh felt her concealed weapon while she was that close. Where in the hell did she keep it?

His gaze moved all the way down to her adorable toes before Tess cleared her throat.

Josh looked up. "No matter what you may think, I don't throw myself at women." He gestured to the flowers in this room. "It's actually the other way around."

"Maybe you haven't met the right woman."

Josh lowered his arm and regarded her.

There was a brief moment of quiet before new music filled this room. This number was slow and sensual, the lush sounds of muted trumpets and classical guitars. Music that brought to mind images of a man and woman, their bodies entwined, their passion played out in a timeless dance.

Josh knew that most women might have used this moment to look away or to ease the tension with come-on chatter that wasn't arousing. Not Tess. She returned his gaze; she fucking held it captive, not breaking their silence.

He liked that. "Could be," he said, then softened his voice even more. "So are we through with the ground rules stuff?"

She seemed to be weighing her answer, then moved past him and didn't stop until she was nearly to the other side of the room. "We haven't even started."

Josh wasn't a bit surprised or disappointed. He liked a challenge. It made winning that much more satisfying. He turned to her. "I won't intrude on your privacy when you're at my place." Unless you want me to.

"When we're alone, you do your thing, I do mine."

"Just like a regular marriage."

She arched one brow. "No more swimming nude in the pool, either."

"I don't mind if you do, really I don't."

"Yeah, I know."

He smiled.

She chose to ignore that. "No touching below the waist or above the waist when we're in public."

"Not even your shoulder or your cheek or your hair or—"

"You know what I mean."

That he did. She was talking about her outstanding butt and lovely breasts. Try as he might, Josh couldn't keep his gaze from dipping back down to her creamy throat and the rest of her chest that suit jacket exposed. "I do know how to act in public." He took several steps towards her. "It's the private moments I seem to be having trouble with."

"Not with me you won't."

God, she was sexy when she was authoritative. He moved still closer, wanting to know everything about her. "Did you like being a cop?"

For once, her composure faltered. She seemed genuinely surprised by the question before she lifted her narrow shoulders. "Sure."

"Was vice better than patrol?"

"It paid better."

"Did you face a lot of danger?"

"It wasn't like what you see on TV."

She was talking like an ex-cop again, not giving him straight answers.

Josh recalled the entry on her resume about that commendation for bravery. When he was reading it, that award had seemed exciting and oddly sexy because it was no more than words on paper. The reality, however, was that she had risked her safety, her life, her future.

What was the matter with her?

What was the matter with him? He barely knew her, but suddenly he was worried that she took too many risks? Now, he wanted to protect her? "You were commended for bravery. What happened?"

"Nothing."

Josh frowned. "How can you say that? You were in danger."

"Maybe."

"How much danger?"

"What does it matter? I'm fine now, though you look a little weird. Why?"

Because he was worried about her. Not that Josh was about to say that to a woman who was going to be protecting him. "Why don't you want to talk about—"

"It was nothing." Tess waved her hand in dismissal. "Just a domestic dispute."

Just? "Aren't those the worst?"

She shrugged. "He didn't have a gun."

Josh's brows lifted. "Good to hear. So, what did he have?"

"A lot of nerve for pulling that knife on a bunch of cops."

"A knife?"

"Calm down. It was just a little one, not a machete."

As if that mattered? "You weren't alone?"

"Of course not. I was with my partner. We called for backup."

"Your partner was a guy?"

"Don't tell her that. Look, the brass liked to segregate those cops with mustaches from the ones without. But," she added, when he didn't return her smile, "the backup was all guys."

"What did they do?"

"They hauled the perp away after I cuffed him and read him his rights."

"They let you do all the work?"

Her brows drew together. "I only broke one nail, it wasn't that bad."

"That's not what I meant and you know it."

If she did, she wasn't giving any ground.

Josh liked that, though he was having a bit of a problem with her macho bravery. "Weren't you scared?"

At last, Tess sighed. "Of course, I was scared. I would have been a fool not to be scared."

"Why'd you do it, then?"

Her frown had returned. "It was my job."

"I meant, why did you become a cop?"

"Why not? It seemed right."

Josh wasn't buying that.

Her expression changed. "My dad's a retired cop. He put in nearly thirty outstanding years on the force. It's all in the brochure. Didn't you read it?"

"I stopped on the witness protection and relocation part."

"Sound interesting?"

"Only if it's for the paparazzo. Your dad really wanted you to be a cop, huh?"

She laughed.

It was completely unexpected, so throaty and unrestrained, Josh was unbelievably aroused, even as a wave of tenderness washed over him as he imagined how she must have looked and felt after taking down someone much bigger, someone who was armed. Damn, she was something.

"Pop yelled at me for a week," Tess finally said. "He told me I was nuts for wanting to follow in his footsteps."

Josh nodded, because he agreed with the man. Of course, that was all in the past. Being a bodyguard, especially his bodyguard, wasn't going to be risky, not like being a cop. "What changed his mind?"

"What makes you think his mind was changed?"

"You're here now. You're working for him."

A smile played at the corners of her mouth. "Only because I'm very good at what I do."

"I know. I've read your resume. So, you took down more bad guys than most?"

"I had my share of collars."

"Do you still have your cuffs?"

Those lovely eyes widened slightly; her chest and throat flushed pink. "Think I might be needing them to secure you to your bed?"

"I'm game, if that's what you want."

Uh-huh. What Tess wanted wasn't something she was

about to share with Josh, because already she wanted him on top of her and beneath her and all over her, and if she wasn't very careful there'd be no end to her wanting. "I want a contract."

He ran his thumb over his jaw as he regarded her. "To spell out what we're going to do with your handcuffs?"

Bad, bad boy. "To spell out the particulars of my services as your bodyguard."

"In private. In public, we're romantically involved, remember?"

As if she could forget that? "Exactly. In public."

"Sure you want that in writing?"

"My father will insist upon it."

Josh's expression said that he had momentarily forgotten about the man. "Because he used to be a cop, too."

"That's right." Tess moved toward him. When she didn't stop, Josh instinctively took a step back. "He really liked the life," she said, as she continued to approach and Josh continued to retreat. "He loved taking down perps and collaring bad guys and using his cuffs and muscle, and sometimes he really misses that and looks for excuses to, well, you know, get back into the game if he sees something bad going down."

Like his little girl being hustled by a guy who was exposed buck naked on the cover of a tabloid? Josh sensed the Franklin clan was one hard nut to crack. Of course, her dad wasn't going to be around during those nights she spent in his house as his bodyguard.

Even if they were separated by numerous rooms, Josh knew he was going to enjoy her lingering scent, the gentle slapping of her bare feet as she moved down the hall, that musical, lilting voice as she talked to herself or issued more ultimatums to him. "Let's get you that contract." He headed for the intercom.

Before he could buzz Peg, Tess said, "Wait."

Oh, hell. She couldn't have changed her mind already, could

she? Josh looked over his shoulder at her, ready to argue his case. "Why?"

"We need to figure out how we met, when we met, and other stuff about our romantic relationship, just in case anyone asks when we're out in public. That, I don't want in any contract."

No kidding. "If anyone asks, we could just tell them it's none of their business."

"Yeah, we could, but who's going to take that for a final answer?"

Josh nodded. "You don't want them digging into your private life."

"I don't want my father reading their version of my private life while he's in line at the convenience store."

Josh hadn't thought about that even though he should have. Pretending to be involved with him was going to expose Tess to the tabloid press as more than just his girlfriend, at least until this died down.

Despite his desire to see her again, hell, to see her continually, he just had to ask, "Sure you want to do this?"

She glanced at the windows. The security guys were watching as that boat left the area. "If it's done right."

And if it wasn't? Josh wanted to assure her that everything would be just fine. Knowing he couldn't even begin to do that, he asked, "And if it falls short?"

Tess looked at him. "I'm a big girl. I can take care of myself."

Not to mention criminals and pissy corporate attorneys like Alan. Still . . . "How about your dad? What's he going to think about all of this?"

Her face quickly paled, but then she shrugged. "I'll handle him, too."

Josh wanted to ask if she were absolutely certain of that, but didn't dare. He figured she'd have him pinned to the floor with her knee on his throat in two seconds flat. Besides, she was a grown woman—nicely grown—and could do whatever she wanted even if her father didn't like it. If the man fired her, Josh would just hire her without Privacy Dynamics. "Okay." He went to her and leaned down until their noses just about touched. "We'll do this as perfectly as possible. How did we meet?"

Those delicate nostrils continued to flare with his proximity. "Beats me." Her voice was downright breathless.

Damn, he liked that, and not only because he had caused it.

"How do you usually meet your women, Mr. Wyatt?"

Women? Like he had dozens of them? *Mr. Wyatt?* Like they hadn't gotten well past that? "Usually through business, Ms. Franklin."

She smiled at his formality. Her gaze drifted to his open collar. "I could say I arrested you while I was still a—"

"Please don't."

She lifted her gaze, then looked right back down at his chest. "We could say that you hired me to be your bodyguard and—"

"Please don't."

She looked at him again. Her gaze and voice softened even more. "You don't want a woman watching over you?" Her brows started to draw together. "You don't think a woman can watch over—"

"I didn't say that." And he sure as hell would never think it. Not with this woman. Josh knew he'd fight a fucking war for the right to have her watch over him. Not that he wanted to publicize the fact. "It'd just be a field day for the press given how you look."

She glanced down, then up. "Because I'm wearing clothes?"

He smiled. "You're not the typical garlic-belching, in-your-face goon most people would be expecting. Believe me, I've already interviewed several."

"Did you kiss them, too?"

He laughed. "No—I knew they wouldn't kiss back." He sobered. "Not like you did."

Tess arched one brow. "What do you suggest?"

"That you keep kissing me exactly as you did when I—"

"About our background."

Oh. "We could work it out tonight, at my place. I'll call you in your room from mine."

Where he'd be handcuffed to his bed?

Tess's gaze turned inward to that thought, the vivid images her mind was quickly creating.

There would be a large four-poster bed dominating a room flooded with golden light from the setting sun. The air would be still, steamy, thick with desire. His arms would be lifted above his head, his hands cuffed to one of those posts, his back to her, so that she could run her fingertips over that luscious tattoo.

More, he would whisper.

Not yet . . . not until I allow it.

The muscles in his buttocks would tense as she slowly stroked and licked that bold design. His flesh would be slightly salty and certainly obedient, allowing her exactly what she willed.

She would draw out the pleasure, taking her time, making him wait, making him want.

By God, he would want. She would see to that, pressing close, allowing him to feel her naked breasts, her furry mound that he wasn't yet allowed to touch. Oh, no. What she wanted came first; he would have to endure as her fingers stroked his silky underarm hair, before slipping down to his pecs and nipples. She would linger on those flat disks, running her fingertips over the tiny nubs, before slipping one arm around his waist to hold him close.

Once he was fully imprisoned, she would slide her other hand down his taut belly, briefly circling his navel before she reached that thick hair above his stiffened shaft.

With great gentleness, she would stroke it until he begged for more.

Not yet . . . in time.

She would play with him; her touch would tempt and tease until she, at last, cradled his stiffened shaft, her fingers circling the smooth, blunt head feeling that first pearl of moisture. He would moan in pleasure, a strangled sound that demanded everything, one that came from deep with—

"Change your mind about those separate rooms?" he asked.

Tess looked at him.

His gaze noted her blush and her frown. He lifted his hands in surrender. "Just asking."

"We need to get down to business."

"I thought I was."

Tess ignored that as she went to one of the chairs at the conference table. After removing a large pink teddy bear with a lewd grin, she sat. Her heart was still thudding. *Stop it,* she ordered. "I'm going to need your itinerary, including the route you take to and from work each day. If you're going to a public function that was publicized before this tabloid thing happened, then—"

"Whoa," Josh said. "You don't actually think any woman would go so far as to check past business stories and follow me to a function?"

Tess crossed her legs.

Josh's gaze lowered to that; it lingered.

She drummed her fingers against the conference table until he looked up. "We have to consider all eventualities. You're a public figure." Her gaze drifted to the stack of *Keys Confidential* in here. "Public figures face all sorts of danger. We should put you in body armor."

"I'd prefer clothes."

"Shoulda thought of that before that." She inclined her head to the tabloid.

Josh crossed his arms over his chest. "You're playing with me, aren't you?"

Only a little. Certainly not as much as she would have liked. Of course, this was a job, only a job. She better remember that. Forcing herself to calm down, to be professional, Tess grabbed a yellow legal pad and pencil that were already on the table. "Okay, we'll skip the body armor for now." She slid her gaze to him. "Unless you don't behave."

"In that case you have your cuffs."

Without warning, her mind returned to that fantasy of him and the four-poster. Before Tess got too excited or distracted, she said, "Better call your attorney in here so we can get started on that contract."

In all of his days, Josh never knew that contract negotiations could be so arousing.

Of course, after the first hour he stopped paying attention to the particulars of that contract, focusing instead on Tess as she duked it out with Alan.

Not once did she back down; not once did she lose her cool.

Alan, on the other hand, had never looked more human or vulnerable. By the end of the second hour the man's face had color, he was actually perspiring, and finally loosened his tie.

And not because he was frustrated. Oh, no. Alan was loving this. He was unbelievably turned on and was actually flirting with her.

Tess didn't seem to mind, or maybe it was that she just didn't notice.

She sure as hell noticed when he had flirted with her.

Change your mind about those separate rooms? he had asked, but only because her breathing had suddenly picked up, while her gaze had been blurry with what appeared to be desire.

We need to get down to business, she had said.

Like the kind she was conducting with Alan? They were currently laughing about something as if they'd been friends for years.

And that certainly didn't bother Josh. By nature, he wasn't a jealous man. If a woman wanted him, fine; if she did not, he had always accepted that.

Tess wanted him; he had seen that in her gaze, in her touch, in her voice. Trouble was, they were never going to be alone if Alan didn't get a freaking move on and end this thing.

"So, we about through?" Josh finally asked.

Alan stopped mid-sentence and looked from Tess to him. "You'll have to ask Tess. She keeps tying my hands."

"Oh, yeah?" Josh's gaze moved to her. *I'm hoping mine are cuffed before this is over.*

"What?" Alan asked.

Josh looked at him, then Tess. Her brows were lifted. Her gaze said, *Bad, bad boy.*

Had he spoken his thoughts aloud?

Alan delicately cleared his throat. "Anything you want to add, Tess?"

Josh suppressed a groan. Was there never going to be an end to these damned negotiations? He waited impatiently as Tess carefully reviewed each page of the contract that was nearly as thick as his thumb.

At last, she looked up and smiled at Alan. "Looks good. I've enjoyed this."

His blush deepened. "Me, too."

"Well," Josh said, "now that we've got that out of the way."

"You won't be sorry you hired me or the company," said Tess.

Josh looked at her and spoke from the heart. "I've never been happier."

This time, Alan sighed. "So, I guess we're through here."

Josh could only hope. Already Alan was sounding far too

down. A few more seconds and the man might be seriously depressed.

"For the moment," Tess said, then waited until both men were looking at her. "I still have to run the contract past my father."

Alan stopped tightening his tie. He smiled. "I can stay here if you want to come back after you see your—"

"No need," she said. Her voice was so nice it didn't sound like a rejection at all. "I'm sure he'll agree with everything here." She pushed away from the table and stood.

So did Josh. "I want you at my place tonight."

Color rose in her cheeks; she arched one slender brow.

"To start protecting me," he quickly said, then added, "you can't do that if you're not there."

Unlike that banter with Alan, her voice was now pure business. "I said I'll be there, and I will."

If she wasn't, he sure as hell would find her. "Great." He gave her the access code to get inside his gate. "I'll be expecting you at seven. Sharp."

"Yes, sir."

God, he loved her cop talk and manner. Of course, a little softness, a little banter with him, would also have been nice. "Wait."

Tess paused, then turned back to him.

Josh tossed her a set of car keys, which she easily caught.

She looked up from the keys. "What's this?"

"Is it a bonus?" Alan asked. "I didn't put a bonus in the contract, but I could right now if you want."

Josh glanced at him. "It's just the company car."

"It's a Mercedes," Alan corrected.

Tess looked at him, then Josh. "I have my own car."

"Which can be traced, because of the plates," Josh said. "I don't want you getting any more press than you have to. I want to control that situation, at least. Use the company car." He told her where it was parked. "I'll have one of my staff take your car back to your place or your dad's office, whichever you prefer."

Tess looked reluctant, but finally nodded and tossed him her keys. "My place is fine." She told him the make and model of her car and the license number, then gave him her address.

Josh wrote it all down, then tossed the pen back on the table. "I'll walk you out."

As he took her arm and guided her from the room, she leaned into him and murmured, "Is Alan always that easy to negotiate with?"

It was a moment before Josh understood the question. Her scent and the way she so effortlessly leaned into him, as if she found it comfortable, continued to distract and arouse.

Clearing that from his voice, he murmured, "You're kidding, right?"

"No—why?"

"I thought he was being a real prick."

"You haven't seen the guys I've had to deal with. Actually, he was pretty easy."

Spoken like a true ex-cop. His ex-cop. His bodyguard.

Josh suppressed a whoop of delight, guiding Tess past Peg, who was speaking on the phone as she spritzed herself with perfume.

He'd have to tell Peg to stop that. He didn't want any scent but Tess's filling this space.

Peg wouldn't listen, of course, but Josh figured he would give it a shot. He opened the door that led to the hall. "Seven," he said.

Tess met his gaze. "I haven't forgotten, Josh."

He liked how she said his name, as if it felt comfortable on her lips. "Drive carefully." Sliding his hand down her arm, Josh took her hand and gently squeezed her fingers.

Tess lowered her gaze to their joined hands. To his delight, she gently squeezed his fingers in return.

"Bring all you'll need for our time together," he added.

She looked at him from beneath her lashes. "Behave yourself."

"I haven't forgotten, Tess."

It seemed that she wanted to comment, but then thought better of it. As she backed away, Josh wasn't yet ready to let go, but then, neither was she.

Their hands remained joined, their arms outstretched as Tess continued to step back. It was as if she was testing him or herself.

Soon, just their fingertips touched as their gazes remained locked, captive to each other.

"What's up?" Peg suddenly asked, joining Josh at the door.

She would ask that. In that moment, Tess broke their bond. She moved back and lowered her arm.

Josh lowered his, too, though he did it with great reluctance.

"Did I interrupt something?" Peg asked.

Nothing that wouldn't be continued tonight.

"Yeah, you did," he mumbled as his gaze followed Tess. She moved like a dancer, gracefully, effortlessly, as she turned and headed for the exit.

"Well, excuse me," Peg said, then added in a nicer tone, "I like her."

That didn't begin to address what Josh felt. He scanned that silky, peach-colored fabric hugging all of Tess's curves until she moved out of view. Only then did he look at Peg. "You were right."

"About what?"

He turned back to the exit. Tess was gone, but only for the moment. "This stuff with the tabloid—it's not so bad."

As his mind returned to that last image of his bodyguard, the exceptional woman who would now be living with him, looking out for him, pretending to be romantically involved with him, Josh thought that it was looking pretty damn good.

Chapter Three

On the way to her dad's house Tess had the stereo and air-conditioning pumping full blast. Didn't help. Her thoughts were still tangled, while the backs of her thighs were glued to the seat's buttery leather as she continued to sweat.

So much for being Ms. Cool and enjoying this Mercedes.

Tess eased to a stop at a red light and sagged into the seat. In a little over an hour she'd have to be at Josh's place. She was cutting it close, but getting ready for this new job had eaten up a lot of time. There were clothes and toiletries to pack, a shower to take; she had to wash her hair, give herself a manicure, wax her legs even though they didn't need it, launder the T-shirt and cutoffs she was currently wearing, and figure out how she was going to tell her dad that she would now be living with Josh, while also pretending to be his girlfriend in public, at least until this all blew over.

"It will, you know." Her voice sounded loud even though it had to compete with Christina Aguilera's lusty wails; it also sounded as bummed as Alan's had earlier.

The man hadn't wanted her to leave, but hadn't pushed it because he knew he didn't have a chance with her. If he wanted to see her at all, it would have to be at another meeting to tweak the contract.

Poor guy. After this was all over maybe she would suggest a yearly reunion where they'd share drinks while she pumped him for information about Josh's newest romance, since it wouldn't be covered by any publication if he remembered to stay dressed whenever he was outside.

When he was behind closed doors, however . . .

Uh-uh. Tess wasn't going there, again. That earlier fantasy about him nicely nude and cuffed to a bed would have to be enough, at least until she got aroused all over again as she explained to her dad about the public kissing, touching, and flirting she and Josh were going to share.

He was just gonna love that.

The driver behind her honked his horn.

Tess gave him an apologetic smile, then pulled away more slowly than he would have liked. She didn't have a choice. The only way to control the coming situation with her father was to give it as little time as possible. She'd rush through the good news about the contract, zip through the bad news about Josh, then quickly cut out to meet her seven P.M. deadline. After that, she wouldn't answer her phone for days until her father calmed down and got on board with all of this.

Sure.

Tess sighed deeply wondering how she could have agreed to this even if it was the job of a lifetime. It wasn't as if Privacy Dynamics was totally without clients, though it certainly didn't have any in Josh's league.

Even if it had, Tess seriously doubted she would have kissed those clients, agreed to move into their homes, or pretended to be romantically involved with any of them.

She had done that far too easily with Josh, because even when he flirted with her or teased, Tess sensed a core of honesty in him she had never seen in a player. The guys she had dated would have been burning up Instant Messenger, bragging like mad if even one babe had been sending them naked pictures and flowers.

Not Josh.

And it wasn't only because Alan was getting a new bald spot worrying about potential lawsuits. Tess sensed right off that Josh didn't use women. If anything, he seemed kind of stunned that he was so popular.

Didn't he know what a hottie he was? Didn't he look at those pictures of himself?

Tess couldn't stop. She figured that's how she was going to spend a lot of her time tonight when she was holed up in his guest bedroom.

You are hopeless.

She was also pretty damned scared, because she was falling under his spell faster than the speed of light and had absolutely no excuse.

It wasn't like she was a blushing virgin. And yet, when Josh's mouth had covered hers, all the kisses she had shared with those other guys seemed to be only so much practice for his kiss, which was the real deal.

His initial tenderness, then hesitation before deepening the kiss moved Tess more than all the words or promises in the world. After that, all she could think of was that she wanted a whole lot more, and not only because of passion.

She had felt comforted and protected, which was the greatest aphrodisiac of all. In no way did Josh seem to be taking advantage of her or seducing her, unless he was a very good actor and she had already been deeply conned.

Oddly enough, that possibility didn't bother Tess as much as the feeling that Josh hadn't been acting; he was a really good man, which meant that she was unbelievably screwed.

How in the world was she going to restrain herself tonight and all those other nights when there was nothing to do but watch him and want him?

How in the world was she going to move on when this came to an end?

Why was she even thinking about any of this? She wasn't a romantic fool, had never been a pushover, and even Josh Wyatt was not going to change that.

"This is nothing more than a job," Tess told herself as she turned into the street where she had grown up.

It was a cramped, middle-class neighborhood that still felt like home since nothing here ever changed. The Minelli's front yard was as cluttered with their grandkids' toys as it had been with their kids' stuff.

Tess recalled more than a few afternoons when she had chased Tommy Minelli into his house because he had pissed her off. Didn't matter that Tommy was two years older than she and outweighed her by more than sixty pounds; even then, Tess hadn't taken any lip.

She smiled in memory, because Tommy was now a professional wrestler on one of those awful cable shows. The Minellis thought it was great and couldn't brag enough about their boy no matter how often he got hurt.

So maybe she should tell her father that she wanted to be a wrestler now. Maybe then he wouldn't whine about her being a bodyguard for a man she would soon start living with.

Right. Tess's smile faded, her heart started to race as she finally approached her childhood home, a modest one-story frame crowded by foliage and protected by a white picket fence, which had been her mom's idea.

Her dad had built that fence himself despite the ribbing he got from his friends on the force. But then, Freddy Franklin hardly cared what others thought. Until the day her mother had passed two years before, he would have done anything for his Carlie. The only time Tess heard him address her mom as Carlita, the woman's given name, was when he was really mad.

There hadn't been many of those moments between her parents as Tess had been growing up. Never had she known a man and a woman more devoted to each other. Because of that, her dad rarely dated now, even though her mom would have wanted him to be happy.

Tess turned off the stereo and spoke from the heart. "You need to talk to him, Mama. You need to tell him to get off his butt and meet someone like he met you."

That meeting, according to Carlie Franklin, had been magic, and the reason they had endured.

"It's all in that first moment," she had said for as long as Tess could remember. "In how a man and a woman meet."

Tess wondered if it was all that simple.

How did we meet? Josh had asked just a short while ago.

We could say that you hired me to be your bodyguard and—

Please don't.

You don't want a woman watching over you? You don't think a woman can watch over—

You're not the typical garlic-belching, in-your-face goon most people would be expecting. Believe me, I've already interviewed several.

Did you kiss them, too?

No—I knew they wouldn't kiss back. Not like you did.

What do you suggest?

That you keep kissing me exactly as you did . . .

Uh-huh. Could be her parents' romance and marital success wasn't in how they met, but just pure, dumb luck, which Tess sensed she was going to need in abundance now.

Already her dad was standing in the doorway of the screened-in porch looking at the sleek black Mercedes, then her, then the Mercedes. A bottle of beer was halfway to his lips, but completely forgotten.

Tess felt like she was sixteen years old again and getting home late from a date. Although her father was in his fifties and graying, he was still a man to be reckoned with. The modified crew he favored made his head look bristly and his neck thicker than a man should be allowed, while his flowered sports shirt was barely fluttering in the breeze, his build was that powerful.

Go on, Tess ordered herself, *get this over with.*

"Pop," she said, then smiled broadly as she left the car.

He looked from it to her. "Tessie." His gaze returned to

the Mercedes, which reflected his weathered picket fence in its sleek, flawless body. "Please don't tell me you carjacked someone."

"You know me better than that." Joining him on the porch, Tess gave him a peck on the cheek. "I found that baby in my parking space this morning with the keys in the ignition and a full tank of gas. Is life great, or what?"

Freddy looked at her. His neck seemed even thicker, while that nasty scar on his chin did nothing to soften the moment.

Tess forced another smile. "Okay, if you must know, it's what I'll be using for our new job!" She waved the contract in her hand.

Her father looked momentarily stunned, then frowned. "For that guy?"

"He's more than just 'that guy.' "

"Oh, excuse me. That *naked* guy?"

Now, Tess frowned. "He's a businessman, Pop. A very rich businessman." Before he could snarl to that, Tess told him what they were being paid for this job, a fee that any of those big firms would have probably killed for.

Freddy's pale blue eyes widened. "Did you threaten him with your gun?"

No, she had returned his kiss. Not that that had anything to do with getting a fee that wasn't outlandish, but reasonable. "I negotiated with his attorney."

"Is the man licensed to practice law? Did he just get out of school?"

Tess's eyes narrowed. "He's about forty-five and balding and wanted to throw me out when I first got there. But," she continued, interrupting her father, "I wouldn't let him. I wouldn't back down, just like you taught me. I did great. Go on, say it."

The man screwed up his mouth as if he refused to be chastised. "I'll let you know what I think after I read the contract."

Tess arched one brow.

"Okay, okay, you did good," he finally conceded, then gave her a bear hug that stole her breath, after which he easily swung her around. As Freddy let go, he snatched the contract. When Tess regained her footing and returned to his side, he handed her the beer.

She took a sip.

"No more than that," he warned, then pulled his reading glasses out of his front pocket and perched them on the tip of his nose. "Not if you're driving home."

Tess snuck another sip, swallowed quickly, and mumbled through her belch, "I'm not driving home."

Freddy's gaze remained on the contract. "Good. We can discuss this over supper, especially the part about you going after this on your own after I told you not— "

"Ah, I'm not staying here either, Pop."

He read a bit more of the contract, nodding as if he agreed with it, then finally looked up. "What?"

"I have to meet Josh—our client," she quickly corrected, "at seven."

"Josh?"

"He prefers that to Mr. Wyatt or naked guy."

"And what do you prefer?"

"To be there by seven so I make a good first impression."

Freddy regarded her, then looked at his watch. "You have plenty of time. His office is— "

"I'm not meeting him at his office."

He slid his gaze to her.

Tess lifted the bottle of beer to her lips, but before she could even smell fumes, her father took the brew, placing it on a table to the side. "Where exactly are you meeting this guy?"

"I'm not exactly meeting him."

"You just said you were."

That she had. "Promise me you won't upset yourself."

He pulled off his glasses and frowned. "I won't. I figure you're gonna do that."

"It's business."

"What is?"

"It's nothing to get excited about."

"I'm not excited, *Teressa.* I'm beginning to get worried, *Teressa.*"

Okay, so she was handling this badly; he never used her given name unless he was pissed, like when she decided to become a cop and then a bodyguard. Of course, after he found out about her arrangements with Josh, and finished yelling at her, he'd probably start calling her *that girl who's protecting that naked guy.*

"I'm going to be staying with him at his house—as his bodyguard," Tess quickly added, while also failing to add all that other stuff about being romantically involved with Josh in public. Now was not the time to get into that. Maybe later, after she couldn't hide it any longer. "I have to be on the premises so nothing happens to him."

"To hell with him," Freddy growled. "I don't want anything happening to you."

She gave him a look. "Like it could?"

"I saw that guy's pictures, Teressa. So don't give me that *Pop, you're nuts* look, got it?"

Tess took it down several notches. "Yes, sir—but I can take care of myself, Pop. I'm no fool."

"Being a fool's got nothing to do with this, and you know it. We're talking about a guy who likes to swim in the buff and probably walks around his house in the buff, too."

"Aw, Papa." Tess cradled the side of his face in her hand, gently running her thumb over some of his wrinkles. "People do that all over this state and even this nation, except for the deeply conservative areas, and they got problems I wouldn't even want to get into."

His shaggy brows drew together.

"He'll be a perfect gentleman with me from this moment forward, I swear," Tess said. She pulled back her hand and gave him the Boy Scout salute, which she had taught to Tommy Minelli and a lot of the other neighborhood boys.

Her father's expression said she was nuts. "From this moment forward?" His frown deepened. "Did he make a pass at you already?"

Tess forced herself to look surprised, even as her skin tingled to the memory of their kiss. No matter how many times Tess thought about it, and she was doing that far too much, it still didn't seem like a pass to her, but genuine attraction.

Not that that would lead to anything other than some sexy sack time—if she were to allow that—before this whole tabloid thing blew over and Josh went his way, while she went hers.

She suppressed a sigh. "No. And he won't. I've set up some very strict ground rules."

"If he's such a gentleman why'd you have to do that?"

"I wanted to make it all legal."

Freddy jabbed his finger into the contract. "So your ground rules are all in here, right?"

"My ground rules are what you and Mama taught me."

His expression remained hard, but his gaze was beginning to soften, the same as his voice. "I let you become a cop. I let you become a bodyguard. And now you do this to me?"

"We can't all be dancers like Mama."

"You could try."

Aw, Papa. "I like what I do. I'm good at what I do. I got you that contract, didn't I?"

"That's money. You're my daughter. He's going to respect you, got it?"

"He's a good man, so he will."

"Good men don't pose like he did for a tabloid."

"He didn't pose, he was sucker punched, and you know it."

"I know he's rich enough to buy trunks."

And cover that beautiful body? Now that would be a crime. "I've told him he needs to be dressed from now on."

"Tell him he better be fully clothed twenty-four seven while you're at his place or he'll hear from me."

"He already knows that, Pop. Now really, I gotta go." Tess kissed his cheek, again, murmured a farewell in Spanish as her mom always had, then moved quickly to the car.

"Tessie."

She stopped at his tone, a plea rather than a command, and looked back at him. In that moment, a wave of sadness washed over Tess. He looked so alone, so forlorn when what she always recalled was the lightness in his step, his amazing strength. Despite his stocky appearance, he was getting old. He shouldn't be alone. He should have a woman to watch over him, just as she was going to be watching over Josh—at least for a little while. "Yeah, Pop?"

"You call me when you get there."

"I will."

"And when you go inside."

She arched one brow.

"And when you go to bed."

"Pop."

He screwed up his mouth. "You be good."

Oh, she would, at least in her actions, but her thoughts?

They were going to be trouble what with Josh's scent, his voice, and laughter surrounding her, while memories of his kiss kept playing in her mind tempting her to do more.

Far, far more.

Chapter Four

At five minutes to seven Tess turned into the private drive that led to Josh's gated estate, then slowed the Mercedes to a crawl.

She knew she shouldn't be dragging her feet, not at this late hour, but Tess honestly couldn't help herself. The Internet photos she had seen of this place had not done it justice.

Her gaze swept the lavish vegetation that both surrounded and dwarfed her. Live oaks mingled with moss-draped cypress to create a thick canopy of green, which was momentarily still, then fluttering as the ocean breeze whispered past. Towering banyan trees, with trunks as wide as her childhood home, captured the sun's lowering rays. The air was cooler here, clean, and sweetly scented by all that vegetation and the rich earth.

Wow. No wonder Josh liked to frolic in the nude here. To Tess's way of thinking, the Garden of Eden had nothing on this spot.

She looked to the left and to the right; she even turned as far as she could in her seat to see it all, then finally got a move on. Not that it mattered. The vegetation never seemed to end. After a few minutes, Tess wondered if she had taken the wrong turn and was in a state recreational area. She looked for signs, but instead spotted a red convertible parked to the side.

Again, she slowed the Mercedes to a crawl, then stopped it just behind the convertible.

It was a cute little thing with Florida tags. Tess noted the plate number and expiration, then looked up. Ahead, to the left, was an impressive wrought iron gate that was nicely weathered to a grayish-green, matching the primordial vegetation. Thick vines covered the estate's walls, while several baskets of brightly colored flowers had been left to block the drive.

Oh, she had the right place.

Those flowers were twins to what she had seen earlier at Josh's office. Only this time, the person delivering those goodies was still here. She was young, her hair was dyed a bright red, she was scantily dressed in pale yellow short-shorts and a halter, had a tattoo on her left ankle, and was completely unaware of being watched as she tried again and again to punch in the right access code to get into the estate.

Hmmmm. With her gaze riveted to that tattoo, Tess pulled out her cell phone and dialed Natalie Cruz, her former partner on the force.

After two rings, Nat said, "Cruz."

"Franklin," Tess said, using that same don't-bother-me voice.

"Hey, Tessie," Nat said, quickly warming up. "How you doing?"

"Ask me that tomorrow morning."

The woman chuckled. "Hooking up with Mr. Maybe Could Be Right tonight, huh?"

Ask me that tomorrow morning. "Not exactly. Do me a favor?"

"I won't tell your dad you're not a virgin, I swear."

Tess's laughter was throaty.

"Whadaya need?"

Tess gave her the tag numbers from that baby convertible. As she waited for the computer to finish its search, Tess kept her gaze on that redhead's surgically-enhanced butt while commenting to Nat's gossip.

"Amazing," Tess said, "Stein actually bought that pet grooming place?"

"Yup. He's turning in his badge for that. He told me he needs clients, so if you could help?"

"I'll let Tommy Minelli know. He could use his back shaved."

"You got that right. I saw him just last week wrestling some goon wearing a Schwartzenegger mask. What a way to make a living."

"Hey, I was thinking of telling my father I wanted to do that now."

Nat laughed so hard she started to choke.

"Easy," Tess said, her gaze lifting to that redhead's surgically-enhanced boobs.

"I'm fine," Nat said, then cleared her throat once more. "Okay, here you go."

Tess nodded as Nat gave her the results of that computer search. "Thanks. I owe ya."

"Not a problem. But if my mother happens to ask if I'm still a virgin, you tell her that if she ever doubts my purity, she don't get to visit my kids no more. It's bye-bye, Grandma."

Tess laughed, then said a quick good-bye.

Once she was out of the Mercedes, she slipped the cell into her back pocket and went up to the gate where the young redhead was still trying to crack that code.

"You look busy," Tess said in her friendliest voice.

The girl didn't even bother to look up. "Get lost. I was here first."

"Oh, yeah?" Tess asked, keeping her tone light. "You wouldn't be lying to me now, Libby, would you?"

The girl punched in two more numbers before she realized that Tess had just used her name. Glancing up, she met Tess's gaze, then looked right back down as if she were sizing up the competition.

Libby's quick frown said she didn't like what she saw. "Who are you?"

"I would be the girlfriend."

That frown deepened. "Josh is dating you?"

Josh? My, aren't we familiar. "No, Libby, I'm dating him. That makes it a whole lot worse for you."

Libby backed away. "How'd you know my name?"

Tess followed. She smiled. "Easy. It's on the mail that's delivered to your place. You do still live at Fifty-five Conch Court in—"

"Have you been following me?" She continued to back away, while Tess continued to follow. "How dare you follow me!"

"Well, you are trying to break our access code, aren't—"

"You leave me alone!"

"I haven't even started to bother you yet."

"I'm warning you!"

Tess continued to smile. "Better chill, hon, otherwise you'll give yourself wrinkles. You are pushing thirty, you know. You were born in November, right? The third, I believe. And no way are you only one-hundred-and-twenty pounds. I'd say more like one-forty."

Oddly enough, the weight thing did it. Turning quickly, Libby bolted for her car, fired it up, and zoomed away.

"That was easy," Tess mumbled to herself. Maybe too easy. She hadn't even hesitated when claiming to be Josh's girlfriend. In fact, that was the easiest part of all.

Tess shook her head, simply amazed at how easily she was being sucked into this, then she called the security company that had its little signs posted all over this place. She told them to get one of their people out here to watch the estate's perimeter until Privacy Dynamics took over in the morning. With that finished, Tess decided to be professional and announce her arrival, rather than just showing up.

Trouble was, she got no response on the intercom.

She tried again and got zip.

Tess wondered if the intercom was broken or if Josh hadn't gotten back from work yet. After all, he was a busy man. A popular man.

Her gaze slid to those baskets of flowers hugging the gate. It was possible that even more of those gifts had arrived at his office and he was having trouble crawling through them to get back here.

Unless he was skinny-dipping in his pool, again.

Tess closed her eyes, thinking about the problems that would create, and not only for Josh. Already her heart was racing to the thought of seeing him fully clothed. If he were nude, God help her. Lifting her face to the sky, Tess said to no one in particular, "Ready or not, here I come."

She tossed the baskets to the side, punched in the access code, and returned to the Mercedes as the gate swung open.

The drive to the house was shorter than the one to the gate, but no less spectacular.

Here, an attempt had been made to tame the lush vegetation, though it was hardly subdued. Ferns, squat palms, and tropical flowers nuzzled each other as they competed for space.

Tess again slowed the car to a crawl, turned off the air-conditioning and stereo, then lowered her window. Gone were the sounds of traffic and people. In its place was the ocean's faint rustle, the throaty cooing of birds, and a comforting peace.

She shook her head and spoke in a whisper, "Adam and Eve, eat your freaking hearts out."

Never in her life had she seen such beauty. It was as if she had stepped back in time.

Ahead, weathered statues of angels or fairies held vases that overflowed with thick, green vines. As one tropical garden stopped, another started, until the vegetation finally paused, allowing space for the house that was just ahead.

This time, Tess stopped the car. She got out and stared.

The house had been painted a light peach that blushed

coral beneath the lowering sun. It was two stories, of a Caribbean design with wide verandas and lots of gingerbread. That ornamentation seemed even whiter next to the scarlet bougainvillea that clung to each graceful column. The arched windows were tall; the shutters opened to allow in every bit of light.

Tess moved closer.

On the front porch a pair of white Adirondack chairs awaited guests, or the man and woman who had once claimed this place as their home.

Had those chairs been part of the original estate? Had they been used by the first man and woman who had come here?

What business had he been in? Was she a bride?

Tess imagined she was and could almost feel that woman's awe at these surroundings, her restlessness of what was to come as her carriage clattered to a stop in this exact place more than a century ago.

The horses would have whinnied then and kicked at the dirt path; the servant would have kept his gaze forward, not daring to look at his master.

Tess's gaze turned inward. Her mind pictured that young man with dark eyes, but surprisingly light hair worn stylishly long in the fashion of the day.

She imagined his new wife stealing a glance, only to see that his gaze was already on her.

Had her heartbeat quickened in that moment? Had her breath caught when he boldly placed his hand on her waist? Until that touch there had surely been no intimacy, not even so much as a caress or a kiss.

Tess thought about that, and what a wedding night meant to a young woman in the late eighteen-eighties as she was being carried by her husband to this front porch, the one Tess was standing on right now.

She looked down to the polished wood faintly creaking beneath her weight, and imagined that husband's weight making an even greater noise because he would have been taller than most, with a strong build. His gaze would have been no less potent, remaining on his wife as he opened the door, just as Tess was now doing, and brought her inside.

Again, Tess felt as if she were stepping back in time.

The front entrance was large and airy with high ceilings, Bahama fans, and shiny hardwood floors. To the right, Tess saw a parlor that was not yet fully renovated. Its walls were freshly papered, the floor had been restored, but the marble fireplace looked as if it had seen better days. To the left was another room that had no set purpose, though the windows wore delicate lace curtains and white wicker furniture had been stacked in the corner.

Ahead was a wide staircase leading to the second floor, the master bedroom.

Tess went to that first step. She looked up. The landing was washed in the day's waning light, the doors closed.

Even so, her mind saw a room dominated by a four-poster with lacy linens, mosquito netting, and a fireplace for cool nights.

Had that night, more than a century ago, been sultry and still as the master carried his new bride up these stairs to his room? Tess believed it was. She imagined that man lowering his wife to her feet, so that he might open the French doors leading to the veranda. Fragrant, moist air would have wafted inside. Faint voices of the workers would have been heard.

Not that it mattered. Those men would hardly have dared to come near this house while the master was enjoying his bride.

But she would have known those workers were outside, and that would have added another layer of tension to this night.

Tess imagined the questions running through that woman's mind. Would they hear her moans as her husband aroused her? Would they know she was naked, her flesh bared to a man who would use her as he willed?

Would they guess when his mouth suckled one of her nipples, while his long fingers stroked her hidden lips? Would they imagine her surprise as those fingers so aptly invaded her, driving deep to prepare her for more? That moment when she would no longer be a girl, but a woman. That moment when her husband finally mounted her.

Would she spread her legs widely then; would her gaze be on this man who was muscled and hard above her, while the featherbed was achingly soft below?

Did she gasp as he finally entered, breaking through any barrier that kept them separated, that stopped her from being his?

Did her body at last dance with her husband's as she wrapped her legs around his lean hips, and threw back her head, then opened her mouth as she cried out again and again and—

Will you just stop?

Tess covered her eyes with her hand, breathed hard, and told herself that no eighteen-eighties bride had ever had a night like that. Hell, she had never had a night like that even years after losing her virginity, so what was she thinking?

In those days if a woman couldn't catch her breath, it wasn't due to passion, but because of the corset she was forced to wear and possibly a former bout with TB, while her husband was most likely very old, very demanding, and about as hot as one of her father's middle-aged friends.

In other words, he wouldn't have looked or acted or made love like Josh.

Where is he?

Tess dropped her hand and looked over her right shoulder, then her left as she recalled his words.

I'll be expecting you at seven. Sharp.

It was after seven now, so where was he?

Tapping her foot against the floor, Tess looked back up those stairs and told herself she wasn't going to search the bedrooms, at least not yet. After all, there seemed to be no end of rooms down here with the possibility that some of them were also bedrooms.

As if she needed that kind of stimulation.

Chewing her lower lip, Tess again looked to the right, to the left, then finally gave up and shouted, "Josh!"

"Tess?"

Her heart paused to his shout, then beat wildly. He had been here all along? He was downstairs? "Yeah!" she shouted, then hoped to God he hadn't been watching her panting to that stupid fantasy. "Where are you?"

"Kitchen. It's to your left past the parlor, the dining room, the—"

She interrupted. "I'm on it!"

"Are you sure?"

Tess made a face to that odd question. "Yeah! I'll be there in a second."

A minute later she was about to give up and beg for a map. Each room she went into led to another until Tess felt as if she was trapped in a beautifully appointed maze. The hardwood floors were exquisite, reflecting the delicately flowered wallpaper, Victorian antiques, the occasional rattan furniture, and her mounting irritation.

She turned a full circle wondering if she should take those French doors to the left or the ones to the right.

Since she liked the lace curtains on the ones to the left, she opened those suckers and stopped dead.

The room just ahead was obviously the kitchen as it had a score of appliances from way back when, an ancient sink, a counter with antique bar stools, and Josh.

He was on a ladder, working on a Bahama ceiling fan.

Tess completely ignored it as her gaze crawled all over him. He had changed from his office wear to a navy blue T-shirt and battered jeans that hugged his lean, muscular body. His arms were above his head as he did something to that fan, which hiked up his T-shirt exposing a bit of his flat belly.

Tess moistened her lips as she regarded those silky dark hairs circling his navel before they trickled lower to beneath the waistband of his jeans.

Following that path, her gaze slipped down to that lovely bulge behind his fly.

Josh shifted his weight.

If anything, that made his bulge seem even bigger. So damned big, Tess felt briefly dizzy.

He shifted his weight again.

Looking down, Tess saw that he was barefoot. Her heart beat really hard, which was odd. She had never been into feet, especially a guy's, but his were kind of nice. Large, with long toes.

She wanted to touch them and taste them. She wanted to work her fingers from those toes to his calves to the insides of his thighs to that luscious bulge.

Her gaze lifted to it; her mind paused. Was that an erection?

Tess looked up and wasn't a bit surprised to meet Josh's gaze.

His brows lifted. "Hi."

She moistened her lips, again. Never in her life had her mouth been this dry. "Hi."

He smiled, then frowned. "You're late . . . something delay you?"

Tess thought about the truth, and decided to lie. "Yeah—you."

His expression said that wasn't the answer he expected. "How'd I do that?"

"You're impossible to find."

Josh glanced down at his full length, then looked back up. "What are you talking about? I'm big as life."

Oh, hell, he was way bigger than that, not that Tess was about to give him anything else to be smug about. Resisting the urge to see if his erection had gotten any bigger, or harder, or nicer, she asked, "What are you doing?"

"Screwing."

Her face and throat flushed.

Josh smiled again, as if he were really enjoying this, then

lifted his screwdriver to show her what he had meant. "I'll be done in a few secs."

"Just like most guys."

He murmured, "Bad girl. Now, you be nice or I won't give you a tour of this place."

Like she hadn't had one already? "Yes, sir." Her gaze drifted back down him, again.

After a moment, he asked, "See anything you like?"

Of course she did, and he damn well knew it.

"Okay, be that way," he said to her silence, "but at least tell me you brought your cuffs."

Her gaze lifted. "What?"

Josh gave her an innocent look. "I didn't say anything."

The hell he didn't. "While you finish up with that, I'll get my bags."

And leave him? Not a chance. She had taken too damned long to get here, and Josh wasn't about to let her out of his sight now. Her cheeks were nicely pinked up, her tightened nipples strained against that stretchy T-shirt, and her lovely legs were completely bared beneath those cutoffs. *Mmmm.* "I'll take care of them later. You're not wearing your heels."

Tess looked down at her sandals. "That's because I'm in shorts."

Josh's thickening cock was already well aware of that. Still . . . "I like those heels."

She met his gaze. "They're in the trunk of your car, if you want to wear them later."

Bad, bad girl. Cocky, but also soft. It was in the way he could so easily make her blush. "No, thanks."

"Are you sure?" she asked, using the same tone he had used earlier. "I could get them right now and everything else that I—"

"I'll get it later, really."

Tess shoved her hands into her back pockets and rocked on her heels. "I really need to go back outside."

"Why?"

She looked vaguely embarrassed, then pissed. "I'm not certain I turned off the car."

Uh-huh. "Do you usually forget to do that?"

Tess gave him a look that said he was more of an idiot than she. "When I got here I was kind of distracted."

Josh already knew that; still, he said, "Oh, yeah? By what?"

"Your place. I was overwhelmed by it, okay?"

He smiled. "You like it, huh?"

Her face flushed again. Her voice softened even more, "Very much."

Uh-huh. She wasn't talking about this place any more than he was. Still, Josh figured he better continue this verbal foreplay until Tess gave him a signal that she would be willing to accept something more. "Stay in here and watch me so I can watch you."

A smile tugged at the corners of her mouth. "What about the car?"

"Did you put it in park?"

"Of course I did. I had to get out of it, didn't I?"

Josh held up his hands in surrender. "Hey, I was just asking." He lowered his hands. "Let the damn thing run until it's out of gas."

"Aren't you worried about someone stealing it?"

"Couldn't care less."

Tess arched one brow. "My clothes are in there. Just about every stitch I have."

Okay, now he was hoping the damned thing would be stolen so that she had no choice but to walk around here in skin. "I see the problem."

"I don't think you do." She reached into her back pocket.

Josh's gaze dipped to her pebbled nipples. "Please don't tell me you're going to pull out your gun now and shoot me."

"That comes later."

Why later? "Aren't you carrying a gun now?"

"Sure."

Josh looked at that flimsy T-shirt, those brief shorts, and her sandals that couldn't have concealed anything, then what she had just pulled out of her pocket. "That's your gun? It looks like a cell phone."

She laughed as she punched in a number. "It is."

"Who are you calling?"

"My father."

Josh came down a step. "Why? I haven't done anything."

Tess smiled. "He'll definitely want to hear that little bit of informa—Pop?" she interrupted herself, then turned her back to Josh as she spoke into the cell. "I got here all right, just like I said I—what?" She listened, then said in a lowered voice, "Of course, he's here, he *lives* here, Pop. Huh?" She listened again, then blurted, "You have nothing to worry about. I have nothing to worry about. He's a good man."

Josh's gaze lifted from the backs of her silky thighs. She thought that? She meant it?

She must have, because all at once Tess seemed to realize what she had blurted, and was now turning around to see if he had noticed.

Damn right he had. Josh's gaze touched hers and he wasn't about to look away. There may have been a lot of females after him because of that stupid tabloid, but this woman thinking he was a good man meant more than all of that. It meant the world.

"Thanks," he said.

Her blush deepened, and then she was back on the cell.

"What?" she asked her father, then listened and frowned. "That was Josh. No," she said after listening again, "he was just thanking me for handing him the brochure to your business. That's right," she said after she listened again, "we're talking business so I really gotta go. Night." Tess shut off the phone and shoved it into her back pocket.

"Your dad okay with this?" Josh asked.

Tess looked at him. "I'm here, aren't I?"

That she was, and raring to go, right down to wearing a gun.

Josh continued to look for unsightly bulges in her T-shirt and shorts, at least until she shifted her weight.

He looked back up.

"What?" she asked.

"I didn't say anything."

"Yeah, I know. You keep looking at my clothes—why?"

No way was he ready to answer that. "Same reason you keep looking at mine?"

Tess pressed her fingers to her forehead.

"Please don't get upset—we're still on our honeymoon."

Her shoulders shook with suppressed laughter.

Josh came down the ladder. Tess dropped her hand. He finally stopped his approach. "You're not thinking of shooting me now, are you?"

She laughed, until he crossed the room and captured her hand.

"What are you doing?"

"Escorting you to the pool."

She held back. "The scene of the crime?"

"The scene of our supper—you haven't eaten yet, have you?"

No, she had not. She had been too busy manicuring and waxing and primping and evading her father's pointed questions to even think of food. "Your cook's out there?"

Josh looked at her as if she was nuts, and then he frowned. "Why?" His head swiveled on his shoulders as he glanced past her to the hallway, then to the outside. "Was there a guy here when you came here who said he was my—"

"No." Tess wondered if she should tell him about redheaded Libby at the gate, but decided against it. "I just assumed you'd have one."

Josh looked at her. "Why?"

Because he was a guy. Because he was so rich. "No reason."

"Exactly." He leaned down to her until Tess could see each laugh line at the corners of his beautiful eyes. "I'm capable."

"Well, that remains to be seen."

Josh worked his mouth so he wouldn't smile. "You're supposed to be nice to me, remember?"

"You may have to keep reminding me."

He straightened, then lifted his free hand to her chin, holding it between his thumb and forefinger.

Tess's heart went into immediate overdrive. She felt the heat of his skin clear to her toes, and surrendered completely to his quiet gaze.

A moment passed, and then another. Tess was vaguely aware of the breeze rustling the outside foliage, birds calling to each other, and her own heightened breathing.

If Josh noticed, he didn't say. His gaze remained on her, quiet and confident, before he murmured, "Don't you worry, I will keep reminding you. Come on."

Tess swallowed, then took a much-needed breath as he led her outside to the pool.

Her eyes widened in renewed awe.

This area was as lovely as the rest of the estate, drenched in tropical foliage, and very secluded behind numerous bushes and trees. Stone statues of cranes, flamingos, and other wildlife stood silent guard, while the Olympic-size pool couldn't have been more inviting.

No wonder Josh liked to swim in the nude. No wonder he had felt safe and protected.

Tess looked at the crisp, blue water that made gentle lapping sounds as it hit the sides of the pool. On the bottom was a picture of two dolphins, their supple bodies arched as if they were jumping out of the water.

It caught the waning sunlight, which sparkled back, and made the flickering flames of the outside torches seem downright seductive.

Inhaling deeply, Tess looked over her shoulder to a glass table, two wicker chairs, and a refrigerator.

Josh finally released her hand and went to the fridge. When Tess joined him, he handed her a bottle of chilled beer.

She pressed it to the side of her neck.

"You hot?" he asked.

Of course she was hot, and it had nothing to do with the sultry, close night, and he damned well knew it. "Just a little warm," she lied in her most casual voice. After taking a sip of that beer, Tess kicked off her sandals, went to the edge of the pool, then sat, dangling her legs in the water.

It felt so good that it was a moment before she looked over her shoulder at Josh.

He was sipping his beer as he continued to watch her.

"You coming?" she asked.

He arched one dark brow, swallowed his beer, then pulled a platter of something from the fridge before joining her.

Tess regarded the fresh fruit, vegetables, and four types of dip as Josh rolled up the legs of his jeans, then sat next to her, dangling his legs in the water.

Her gaze drifted from the food to his feet. God, but she liked his toes, and had an insane urge to hold them in her hands, to kiss the blunt tips.

"Go on, try it," he said.

Tess's face got hot, she looked at him, then at the slice of cucumber he held between his thumb and forefinger. That vegetable was drenched in the pinkish dip, but quickly forgotten as he slipped his free hand beneath her chin.

Her lids fluttered and her heart raced.

"Open up," he murmured.

Tess finally did, then held back a moan as he eased the food into her mouth with one hand, while stroking her throat with the other.

"Good?" he asked.

If he was talking about the food, Tess had no idea. A dribble of perspiration wiggled down her temple as she finally remembered to chew.

Using his thumb, Josh eased the perspiration from her cheek. "Is it good?" he asked again.

As far as Tess was concerned, this moment was like nothing she had ever experienced. Her senses were overloaded, and she definitely had to cool it. "Spicy," she said at last, then took a prolonged sip of her beer and swallowed. "But very good."

Josh smiled.

Her gaze drifted to it, she was briefly lost in it, before she said, "I can't blame you for liking this."

Josh was about to pop a carrot, smothered with onion dip, into his mouth, but given her comment, he thought better of it. Lowering the veggie back to the tray, he lifted his gaze to her. "This what?" *You, me, here?*

Tess licked dip off her lips and looked reluctant to answer.

Josh lifted his brows as if to say *Well?* and waited.

"This area," she said at last. "The pool." She gently moved her legs back and forth in the water, until her left foot touched his right ankle.

Josh's gaze lowered. To his surprise she didn't move her foot.

"It's a really nice pool," she said.

He lifted his gaze. "I've always liked it."

"You're really lucky."

No kidding, if she was talking about them being here together. Not that Josh figured she meant that. Taking a sip of his brew, he swallowed, then asked, "Why?"

Tess moistened her lips as she glanced around. "To have all of this. It's beautiful."

It didn't come close to the woman beside him. "Well, it will be once it's fully renovated."

"It's beautiful now. Have you done some of this work yourself?"

Josh suppressed a smile and took another sip of his beer. "You mean besides screwing in screws?"

Tess flicked her gaze at him, then concentrated on the food.

Taking his dip-smothered carrot, Josh popped it into his mouth, chewed, then swallowed. "Actually, I've done all of it."

Tess looked at him. "Shut up." She glanced at the pool, then the surrounding area again as if seeing it through different eyes. "You actually did this and what's inside?"

"I'm capable."

"Obviously." She met his gaze. "But you're also very rich. Rich people don't do their own work. What's the matter with you?"

"Hey, I've been poor. I learned."

"To fix old houses?"

He smiled. "It's called renovation or construction, and that was what I did before I got into real estate."

"You miss it."

"Am I that transparent?"

"You looked really intense while you were working on that ceiling fan."

"Ever have one fall on you?"

"You also looked like you were enjoying yourself."

"I knew you were watching me."

Tess arched one brow.

Damn, she was luscious. Her smooth skin glistened in the light of the torches that also picked up the red highlights in her silky hair. "I miss the physical aspects of construction, which is why I keep my hand in it by renovating this place." He shrugged. "My dad was the same way."

"He was in construction, too? He's retired now?"

Josh looked at the platter of fruits and veggies and chose a strawberry this time. After chewing and swallowing, he said, "He passed away when I was ten in a construction accident."

"Oh, I'm so sorry." Tess rested her hand on his. "I didn't mean to bring up anything bad."

"Who says you did?" Josh turned his hand over until hers was inside, then curled his fingers in a gentle caress. "I have good memories of him."

Tess's head remained bent to their hands. "Yeah, I know what you mean. My mom's been gone for two years now, but at times I still expect her to call me, you know?"

"Yeah, I do."

Tess nodded as if that pleased her, and then she sighed. "Mama was really sick, so I have to say it was a blessing when she passed. Deep down Pop wanted to hang on, so did I, but we let her go. Some of our relatives were upset, but I know it was the right thing to do." She looked at him.

Despite her words, Josh saw uncertainty in her expression and the sting of her relatives' disapproval in her eyes.

For the first time he imagined Tess as she was before she became a cop and then a bodyguard. Josh saw her as a little girl seeking approval, wanting only to please.

Of course, that was before she had to be strong and capable and watching over everyone else—including her father and now him.

"You made the right decision," he said.

She seemed grateful that he thought so. In the silence that followed, she lowered her gaze to their hands and traced his fingers with her own as if they had been doing this forever, as if they hadn't just met.

But they had, and Tess seemed to finally remember that as she lifted her hand from his. "So," she said, her casual tone sounding forced, "is your mom remarried?"

Josh didn't want to talk about that, he wanted her to continue stroking him, but figured he better not press it. "Haven't a clue."

Tess looked up. "You don't see her?"

"Nope."

"Since when?"

"Since she wanted to put me up for adoption."

"Get out—really?"

"Hey, I don't fault her for that. She didn't want to be a mother."

Tess couldn't even begin to hide her surprise. She knew her own mother would have fought to the death to keep her, and that she would surely do that for any child she might have. And yet, his mother hadn't wanted him? How sad for her. "So you were adopted by your dad?"

Josh frowned as if he didn't understand the question. "Is that possible or even necessary?"

"I meant, the guy who raised you, the one you knew as a father, adopted you?"

"No. My biological father found out that my mother was putting me up for adoption, and he decided to raise me himself."

"I'm asking too many questions."

"No. Just the wrong ones."

Tess started to pull her hand from his, but Josh gently increased his embrace, not allowing it.

She looked from that to him.

He smiled. "What would you like to know?"

Everything. Did he ever ask about his mom as he was growing up? Did he wonder what had happened to her? Had his father told him that she didn't want him? Could any adult explain that to a child, while also trying to soften the blow? Did he feel different than the other kids who had intact families? Did he like the women his father dated? Did he want one of them to be his mother?

At last, Tess asked, "What happened when your dad died? You were ten, right? Did you live with a stepmother? Was she nice?"

"She probably would have been if Dad had ever gotten married. He did prefer his women defanged."

Tess arched one brow.

"Gonna shoot me now?" he asked.

"Maybe later."

"I'm looking forward to it. And no, there was no stepmother or even a girlfriend to take care of me, all right?"

Of course it wasn't all right. It sounded awful. "You grew up in an orphanage?"

"Do they even have those anymore?"

"Be serious."

He smiled. "Now, you're beginning to see why nobody wanted me."

"I didn't say that. And you should never say that. Surely someone got you to adulthood. A priest? A parole officer? A bounty hunter?"

He laughed. "My grandparents. On my father's side," he added.

"Thank God."

"Hey, are you actually worried about me?"

Well, sure. Who wouldn't be? Not only was he great-looking and fun to be with, he had a good heart. Not that Tess was going to tell him any of that. "I am your bodyguard."

"Oh, right."

She rolled her eyes.

"But all that other stuff happened when I was ten," he said.

"That's why I was worried. Were you a good boy?"

"Better than I am now." He gave her a sexy grin. "'Course now I have a driver's license and can drink and can—"

"Get your picture in tabloids. What in the world did your grandparents say about that?"

"They don't know yet."

"How's that possible? They don't live in the Keys?"

"They live here, all right, but they've been traveling around the country in this huge sucker of an RV I got them. Looks a little like that weinermobile you see on those commercials. I am not kidding," he said, speaking above her laughter. "Granma complained that they'd need oxygen because the thing's so damned far off the ground, but Granpa took to it right away. Said it kicks butt."

Tess continued to laugh. "They sound adorable."

"They really like me, so what else is there to say?"

Oh, there were volumes, and Tess would have said everything she felt, if she had been his real girlfriend. "You do know how lucky you are, don't you?"

"To have my grandparents putting up with me? Or to be out here with you?"

The latter sounded nice, but he was just being kind. "To have your grandparents and all of this. Most guys would love to be in your shoes with what you have and all those women after you. And don't tell me it sucks, I don't believe it."

"You should." He shrugged. "Sometimes I get lost in all of this."

"Lost?" Tess arched one brow. "You mean in your fantasies?"

"I wish," he mumbled, then shrugged again and regarded his surroundings. "Honestly, it would be nice if the people I meet would like me for me, not my bank account. Sometimes, this is all a woman sees." He looked at her. "The wealth, the stuff, not me."

Tess's smile faded. Although she fully understood what he was saying, that downside of his wealth had never occurred to her until now. "In that case, they're fools."

Josh appeared genuinely surprised. "That's the nicest thing a woman has ever said to me."

"I doubt that."

He looked down, then used his free hand to trace her fingers.

It was a small touch, hardly intimate, but this man's goodness, his scent, his utter maleness made Tess wonder how in the world she was going to make it through the rest of this night. At last, she pulled her hand from his. Before Josh could comment on that or ask anything she might not be ready to answer, Tess said, "We really should decide on how we met and all, just in case anyone asks."

Josh lifted his gaze. Whatever he was feeling was now well hidden behind an expression that was as casual as his voice. "Okay. How'd we meet?"

Tess thought fast. "Anywhere but a grocery store since I avoid going at all cost."

"That's too bad."

She couldn't imagine why, unless he was going to start being like other rich clients and expect her to do errands and stuff, in addition to living with him and pretending to be his girlfriend. "Why?"

"Because that's part of my itinerary. I go once a week."

"By yourself?"

"No. Now, you'll be with me."

Tess nearly smiled. "Where else do you usually go?"

"Nowhere special. Just hardware stores for supplies, junkyards for supplies, and construction sites, but that's just because I like them."

Tess continued to frown. "You said earlier that you usually meet women through business. Are you telling me you've met women at those places?"

"None that look like you."

She worked her mouth around so she wouldn't smile. "Where else do you like to go?"

During the next fifteen minutes Josh told her.

At last, Tess sagged to the concrete, her gaze on the brightest star in the sky, as she answered his last question. "Nope and nope. I don't play golf or go yachting in my free time."

"Better get used to it now, baby; it's part of my itinerary."

No kidding; so where in the world could they have met when it wasn't a part of hers?

Tess turned her head to look at him, to tell him that she was an ex-cop, not an heir of Princess Di, but did not.

Josh was already looking at her, his gaze both tender and aroused. A potent combination that washed everything else away.

Tess said nothing; neither did he, and somehow that seemed right. It seemed enough.

It reminded her of those moments when she came upon her parents as they sat in the backyard. Many times, they'd simply be exchanging a soft smile or gaze because of something they had just shared.

Until now, Tess had no idea how intimate that could feel, how very powerful, though it didn't last.

The sweet silence was finally broken by a bird flying overhead. Tess followed it with her gaze. "Maybe we met at a bird-watching club?"

Josh groaned. "Since you don't seem to enjoy any of the things that I do in my spare time, then—"

"Hey," she interrupted, "I did not say that."

"You didn't exactly do backflips when I mentioned that fixture sale at Home Depot."

"Was that about the time I asked for another beer?"

He smiled. "Come on, what do you like to do in your spare time?"

Oh, that was easy. Tess smiled. "Dance."

Josh didn't look at all surprised. "You move like a dancer."

"Oh, yeah?" She was flattered by his compliment, but also realistic. "You should have seen my mom. She taught the tango and the merengue and all kinds of ballroom dances for a living. That's how she met my dad."

"No kidding? A retired cop actually took dancing lessons?"

"He wasn't retired then, and he did it for his job."

"It was some kind of anger management course?"

Tess laughed. "No, of course not, he had to go undercover for one of his assignments, and he had to learn how to tango for it. I know it sounds weird," she quickly added, "but that's how they met and fell in love."

"Then we'll say we met dancing."

Tess opened her mouth, then closed it without saying a word.

If Josh noticed her surprise, it wasn't obvious in his expression. After a moment's pause, he reached out and gently touched her cheek.

Tess swallowed. His fingers were hot and dry, his gaze intent. She expected him to kiss her; she had been expecting that all night.

He did not.

There was need in his gaze, but he restrained it as he gently stroked her cheek.

Tess inhaled deeply, luxuriously.

His expression said he liked giving her that small pleasure. He next traced her lips with his finger, then smiled as he wiped a bit of dressing from the side of her mouth.

Tess smiled, too, then without thinking captured his hand and licked the length of his finger, before swirling her tongue over the blunt tip.

It was only then that she realized what she was doing. The ground rules she was breaking. Ground rules she had insisted upon.

Pulling in her tongue, Tess released his hand and started talking about dancing. The clubs she frequented most, the music she liked, the kind of moves she preferred.

Josh listened without comment.

At last, Tess asked, "So, you want to use that?"

"Sounds good."

She nodded.

"You still hungry?"

She was, but not in the way he meant, unless he wasn't talking about food. "I don't want you to go to any trouble to make anything."

"I made it earlier, so it's no trouble."

"Then, yes, I'm very hungry."

Josh pushed to his feet and offered his hand.

Once Tess was standing, he let go, then spoke over his shoulder as he moved toward the kitchen. "While we eat, we should discuss tomorrow's itinerary."

Chapter Five

The food was surprisingly good and included a chilled shrimp salad served in a creamy dressing, then tortillas stuffed with chicken, bacon, avocado, and numerous cheeses.

"Very impressive." Tess licked a bit of Monterey Jack from her lips.

Josh's gaze followed her tongue. "Thanks."

After that, their conversation focused on business. Their exchanged glances were another thing entirely.

A few times when Tess looked up, she saw that Josh was already watching her. Although he was busted, he didn't look away.

Nor did she. Their gazes lingered, the silence grew, but it didn't feel uncomfortable, although Tess knew it should have.

This was just a job.

It would last only as long as it took the Libbys of this world to get lost. So, no matter how attracted Tess and Josh were to each other there were far too many nights to get through to be so aroused on the first.

Already Tess had kissed him and look where it had led. If she slept with him now there would be no end to the complications.

What if they started to fight like regular couples, instead of the pretend one they were supposed to be? What if he only wanted her physically?

Oh, sure, he respected and even admired her, but that wasn't love. And even good men slept with women they had no intention of sharing their life with.

Josh was no saint. He was a young, healthy male—very male—and he needed sexual relief as much as she did. Trouble was, if things didn't work out after their sex fest, Tess knew she just couldn't walk away.

She'd have to stay here and live with him, work with him, kiss him in public, then possibly even watch over him as he met someone else, someone he might eventually love.

Uh-uh. No way was she going there. Closing her eyes, Tess sighed.

"Tired?" Josh asked.

More like depressed and kind of scared, not that she could admit it. "Yeah." Opening her eyes, Tess flicked her gaze to him, then stared at her empty plate. "Guess we should turn in."

Josh reached for his beer. "Whatever you say."

Tess looked at him, and only then realized she had said *we,* instead of *I,* and that it was too late to take that back now.

Whatever you say.

He was letting her decide, the bum. Of course, she was his bodyguard, so maybe he figured she should be running this show. "I need to check out the grounds before I turn in, but if you're tired, you go ahead."

"I'm not. I'll go with you."

Tess shook her head. If they were to stroll these moonlit grounds hand-in-hand, no telling how long her resolve would last before she decided to play out her earlier fantasy of that virgin bride and her new husband. "That's my job."

"It's dark out there."

Huh? Tess lifted her gaze. "Yeah, I know; it's night."

Josh rolled his eyes. "There's a lot of vegetation out there. Someone could be lurking around."

Not if that security person was making passes at this place as Tess had asked. "So? I'm armed."

Josh didn't look all that relieved as his gaze dropped to her T-shirt and then her cutoffs.

Tess pushed back in her chair and stood. "Could you get my bags?"

He continued to regard her feet. "And turn off the car?"

"It's probably out of gas by now, with a dead battery to boot, but you might want to get the keys. That is, if you're finished making fun of me."

"I'm not making fun."

Right. "Gotta go," Tess said, then didn't dare look back.

She went to the gate first and was pleased to see that the security company had followed through. After giving the guard some firm instructions, Tess waved him on his way, then went back up the drive, at least until she saw Josh coming down it.

"You okay?" he called out.

Not really. Shadows from moss-draped cypress trees and enormous banyans played across his clothing and face, making him look like a brooding hero on the cover of a romance novel.

He moved closer when she didn't answer. "Tess?"

"I'm fine." She cleared her throat. "What are you doing out here?"

Josh planted his hands on his lean hips, and sounded slightly pissed. "I live here?"

Tess went to him. Moonlight skimmed his hair, turning it a paler blond than she recalled, while shadows continued to play across his handsome face. "I thought you were going to get my bags."

"I will. If the car's still there."

"It is. I saw it."

"Where are you going now?"

Tess spoke over her shoulder as she moved past him, "To check out this place. You stay here."

"In this spot?" he called out.

Tess turned around and walked backwards as she talked. "No. Get my bags! Please."

To her surprise, he finally headed in that direction.

Turning, Tess moved quickly down the path, focusing on business. Once her heart stopped thudding, she heard leaves rustling in the breeze, crickets chirping, and unknown animals scurrying about.

Suppressing a shiver to that, Tess walked the perimeter of these grounds, her gaze searching for whatever might be out of place.

A half hour later, everything was as it should be; she was the only thing that didn't belong.

Lifting her face to the moonlit sky, Tess searched for the brightest star and called herself a fool. It was only her first night here and already she was wishing on stars, hoping that when this was all over she could easily move on.

Sure. Sighing deeply, she turned to go back to the house, but then paused.

The master bedroom doors that led to the veranda were open; Josh was inside the room.

His head remained bent to a clock he was setting.

Tess's gaze touched his tousled hair, his broad shoulders, his powerful chest.

As if he felt her watching, he slowly looked up and turned to those open doors. His gaze searched the darkness, then seemed to touch hers.

In that moment, warmth flooded her chest, her belly, the insides of her thighs. Her heart raced out of control.

Could he actually see her in this darkness? If he did, was he as awed by this moment as she?

Tess ached to know, but wasn't about to ask. This was only a job. She was here for as long as he needed her professional services, and not one second more. She had to remember that.

Lowering her gaze, Tess went back to the car and saw that Josh had gotten her bags.

She returned to the house, but stopped at the bottom of the staircase, not certain if she should go up.

A minute passed and then another. At last, Josh walked across the landing, then looked down, noticing her.

"Everything all right?" he asked.

Not even close. Blood pounded in her ears as Tess imagined what it would be like to have Josh waiting for her each night as he was now. To know that she would be protected in his embrace as she slept. That her aching need would be filled with contentment and peace.

"Fine." She cleared the catch in her voice.

"Are you coming up?"

She was now. "Sure." She climbed the stairs.

Josh waited for her on the landing. "I should show you which room is yours."

Given her current state, Tess didn't think that was such a good idea, but obediently followed him down the hall to a room that was so close to what she had imagined earlier, she was briefly dizzy.

Josh asked, "Is this all right?"

It was beyond lovely. There was a four-poster dressed in clean, white linens; a cheval mirror and other Victorian furnishings; lacy curtains, a pink marble fireplace, two ceiling fans, and mosquito netting. The open door of the bath showed a darling, claw-footed tub and antique fixtures.

"You did all this?" Tess asked.

He sounded amused. "I had a professional decorator provide the furniture and other stuff, but yeah, I restored the fireplace, floors, and the rest."

"It's the loveliest room I've ever seen."

"You haven't seen mine."

Tess looked over her shoulder at him. Josh regarded the bed for a moment more, before glancing up.

There was neither shame in his expression, nor a foolish effort to hide what he had been thinking. Even his voice was casual. "Night, Tess." He left the room and was ready to close the door when she followed.

Josh looked at her.

Maybe she should explain. "I need to check out the rest of the house before turning in. You go to bed, though. Please."

He didn't seem all too enthused about that. "You'll be careful?"

"I always am, Josh."

"Out there," he added.

Right. After all, wasn't she being very, very careful in here? "If you'll recall, I do know H2H."

"And you like Krav Maga the best," he said. "Don't you worry, I remember."

But that's why Tess was so worried, because he did remember; he did listen to her. When was the last time that had happened with such a virile, good-looking guy? Never, that's when. Josh was so damned different, so damned worthy of all the love a woman could give and yet Tess realized that even for him—perhaps especially for him—that was so hard to get.

Honestly, he had said, *it would be nice if the people I meet would like me for me, not my bank account. Sometimes, this is all a woman sees. The wealth, the stuff, not me.*

A wave of tenderness mixed with need so quickly consumed her, Tess could barely think as Josh finally moved down the hall to his own room, then stopped at the doorway and looked back one last time.

"Night," she said.

It sounded so final, Josh nodded his farewell, closed the door, then pressed his forehead against it as he listened to her moving down the stairs.

He liked her, really liked her, and couldn't do one damned thing about it during these private moments, unless she gave him the green light, which didn't seem likely as long as she was in his employ.

So, how in the hell had he gotten himself into this mess? Oh, right, he remembered now, he had decided to hire her, have her pretend to be his girlfriend in public, then kissed her in his office.

Thank God for that since he was about to enter one very long, dry spell—at least while they were in this house.

Damn. How in the world was he supposed to get through tonight with Tess driving him fucking nuts? Her scent, that lilting voice, the graceful way she moved, the fact that she wore a damn gun; God, he just couldn't stand it.

Not only was she the most capable female Josh had ever met, she was sharp, and funny, and brave.

Too fucking brave. Josh rolled his forehead over the door as he listened to her moving around downstairs looking for the bad guys, or in this case, the bad girls.

She needed to be more careful.

Dammit, she needed to be in here, stripped bare, and bent over the dresser with her sweet little ass inviting him closer.

That was what Josh wanted, that was what he needed, to hear her sharp intake of breath as he rested one hand on her plush buttocks, while the other lazily explored her moist opening, her erect clit until her breathing picked up and her head hung on her shoulders.

Only then would he be satisfied. Only then would he lift his stiffened cock, then plunge into her heated depths to be willingly imprisoned by her flesh.

Once he was and had given them both pleasure, Josh knew he would have been willing to simply hold her, to keep her close, to keep her safe.

She might have been his bodyguard, an ex-cop, and a kick-ass Krav Maga expert, but she was also a woman who still missed her mother, and wanted so to please her father.

Josh's shoulders slumped at the thought of that man. Tess sure as hell wasn't going to be pleasing Mr. Franklin anytime soon by sleeping with her employer, a guy she just met.

Swearing softly, he pushed away from the door and went deeper into his room

It's the loveliest room I've ever seen, she had said.

You haven't seen mine.

As Josh's gaze swept the billowing lace curtains, the black

marble fireplace, the ivory embossed wallpaper, the gold Persian rug, and the king-size brass bed, he hardly felt awed.

No matter how nice this stuff was, no matter how expensive, this room was empty without her inside.

He padded to the bed and lay faceup on it, arms above his head, fists clenched as he listened for her movements downstairs. Her security check seemed to be taking forever, but when Josh glanced at the clock on the nightstand, only a few minutes had passed.

After what seemed another eternity, the stairs finally creaked beneath her weight as Tess moved to the second floor. Josh pulled in a deep breath, then held it as he heard her coming down the hall to this room.

He pushed to a sitting position as she paused just outside his door. Easy, he warned himself, but his heart wasn't listening. It continued to hammer against his chest as he wondered what she was doing.

Was something wrong? Had she seen something downstairs she hadn't liked?

Had she seen something in this room that she did?

Before Josh could work it out in his mind, he heard Tess moving back down the hall.

Why? What had changed her mind?

Josh pushed off his bed and went to the door, fully prepared to go to her room to demand some answers, which she certainly wouldn't provide.

His hand fell away from the knob as he recalled how good she was at evading answers; how much like a cop she seemed during those times.

Josh really hated that, and having to restrain himself, but he would because he wanted her to trust him.

He's a good man, she had told her dad.

He would be with her, because she was special. He wouldn't push it, he wouldn't rush her.

She wouldn't allow it.

Shaking his head, Josh heard her moving around her room, and then the faint sounds of her voice. After a moment he figured she wasn't talking to herself, but to someone on her cell.

Her dad? Probably.

That man didn't want her here; that was painfully obvious. Not that it made a bit of difference. No matter how hard it would prove to be, Josh was determined to win Tess over—and her father, too. Whatever it took.

She was definitely worth it.

The following morning, Tess felt like the living dead. She had never been good at sleeping over at someone else's house, and the fact that she knew Josh was just down the hall, in bed, surely naked, hadn't helped matters.

Every time she heard the slightest noise, her heart had jumped to her throat, because she thought he might be coming down the hall to her room.

A part of her didn't want that, while an even greater part of her did.

By midnight, Tess had been so tightly wound she shut off the air-conditioning and opened the French doors. Her veranda was next to his, but the lights in Josh's bedroom were off so Tess couldn't see a thing past his open doors, not even when she hung over her railing.

Returning to her room, she put on the ceiling fans, stripped to skin, then lay on her bed and listened to the sounds of the night. Wind rustled through the trees, the ocean murmured against the shore, insects buzzed, she sighed again and again as she pictured Josh padding into this room, coming to this bed, watching her as she continued to explore her nudity, fondling her breasts, caressing her belly, then finally stroking her clit until she was breathless.

Only after Tess brought herself to completion for the third

time was she able to catch some sleep. By then, it was nearly dawn and she felt like hell now as she sat in the kitchen.

Gulping her second cup of coffee, Tess swallowed hard, then bit into an English muffin slathered with butter and strawberry jam. At just that moment she caught movement in the corner of her eye. Looking up, she saw Josh.

Her brows lifted, while a dribble of that jam slipped over her bottom lip to fall on her chin.

Tess forgot to wipe it off as her gaze caressed Josh's broad, naked chest, those well-toned pecs, and his strong arms that were lifted as he pushed his fingers through his hair, while yawning loudly.

Her nostrils flared to his unrestrained manner. Her gaze drifted over his impressive morning stubble, then down to the waistband of his black pajama bottoms and lower—his long, hard shaft pushing against that silky fabric.

Tess swallowed her food, forgetting to chew. Her gaze lingered on his erection, it adored, before moving back up.

Josh was no longer yawning. His fingers remained in his hair, while his expression said he just now noticed her. Glancing down to her mouth, he next looked at that jam on her chin.

Tess swiped at it with the back of her hand.

Josh warned himself not to smile even though he had never seen a woman look more adorable or inviting. Her hair was bed-mussed, her features still plump and dewy from sleep, while the smear of jam that remained on her chin just begged to be licked off.

Not that she would allow him to do that. Still, that didn't mean he couldn't join her. Josh lowered his hands and was crossing the room when a shrieking alarm went off.

"Holy shit!" he hollered, stopping dead. His hands flew to his ears. "What in the fuck is—hey!" he shouted to an older man who just came inside, "Who in the hell are you?"

Ignoring him, the man reached past Josh to a keypad on

the wall where he easily punched in a code that stopped the alarm.

Despite the blessed quiet, Josh's ears were still ringing. "Damn."

"Watch your mouth," the guy ordered. "There's a lady present."

"I've heard worse," Tess said, serene as could be.

Josh turned his head to her.

"I'm sure you have," the old guy said, "but you won't from him."

Huh? Josh looked at the man who was now glaring at his naked chest.

"You don't own clothes like normal people?" he asked. "You never think to get dressed?"

This couldn't be her dad. If it was, Josh figured he'd be dead by now. He glared back. "Not in my own home where you haven't been invited." He looked at Tess. "You know this guy?"

She lifted her gaze from his chest. "Yup."

"Yup?" he asked when she added nothing more.

Tess lifted one finger, asking for a moment, as she finished chewing her food. After swallowing, she moved her finger between him and the old guy. "Hank Rogan, Josh Wyatt. Josh Wyatt, Hank Rogan."

Josh looked at the man. Despite his fifty or so years he was a freaking tank with a barrel chest, fists as big as grapefruits, dyed black hair, a full mustache, and a broken nose.

"Josh," Tess said, "where are your manners?"

He looked at her. "What?"

She mouthed, *Shake Hank's hand.*

Josh frowned. "You expect me to shake his hand?"

Hank leaned over to Josh and said in a normal voice, "I don't think she wants you to give me a kiss." He straightened and looked at her, "Right, Tessie?"

Tessie?

She lifted her shoulders in a *who-cares?* shrug. "Up to him. Josh?"

He pressed his fingers to his forehead. "Who in the— " He abruptly paused before he swore, inhaled deeply, then dropped his hand as he turned to Hank. "Who exactly are you?"

"Hank's a retired cop and a friend of my dad," Tess said.

"A really devoted friend to both Freddy and Tessie," the man added.

Figures. Josh put out his hand. "Nice to meet you."

Hank muttered, "Uh-huh," which sounded more like *drop dead,* then took Josh's hand and really squeezed.

Fuck that. Josh squeezed right back.

"Ah, guys," Tess finally said, "play nice."

Hank grunted out his words. "Don't you worry. I won't break his fingers."

Josh clenched his jaw as he tightened his grip.

"I'm not worried about his fingers," Tess said. "Josh used to work in construction. He's very strong."

He looked at her. Her gaze was on that tattoo between his shoulders, before moving to his ass. Her delicate nostrils flared as she took a very deep breath.

Josh figured if she kept doing that with Hank in the room, she'd get him killed for turning her on.

At last, Josh loosened his grip and yanked back his hand.

Hank's chest continued to pump as if he was in real pain, though he kept that out of his voice. "Didn't hurt you, did I?"

"If we don't count your alarm puncturing my eardrums, then no."

"Alarms are supposed to be loud." Hank rolled his eyes as if Josh was a moron. "That's what makes them alarms."

Tess giggled.

Josh looked at her, then back at Hank. "Did you install a new alarm system in my house?"

"You needed a better one," Tess said, then continued

when Josh frowned. "Hank came out here very early just to upgrade it. You should thank him."

"For roaming around my house and changing everything while I was out cold?"

"Tessie put you in your place last night, huh?" Hank asked.

Josh swung his head to him.

"He was a perfect gentleman," Tess said.

Josh turned to her. His expression said it all—she sure as hell better not get used to his being a perfect gentleman, not when she looked so fucking luscious. He wasn't that good of a man.

She knew. Her cheeks flushed pink.

Josh was pleased, but hardly finished. His gaze traveled her silky throat and chest to that unbelievably sexy camisole. It was a delicate green, there were tiny bows on each of the thin straps, and best of all, she wasn't wearing a bra.

Her nipples were as hard as his cock as they pressed against that stretchy fabric.

Josh smiled, then frowned as Hank punched his arm.

"Don't hit me again," Josh growled.

"Then pay attention," Hank growled.

Josh flicked his gaze at Tess, before addressing Hank. "To what?"

"Your new code." He jabbed his thumb towards the keypad, then punched in the numbers five, four, three, two, one. "There. Got it?"

"You might have to write it down."

"We could put it on your chest," Tess said.

Josh turned his head to her.

"So you don't forget it," she added in a strangled voice as her shoulders shook with suppressed laughter.

Josh arched one brow at her making fun of him, but couldn't have been more pleased. That suppressed laughter was causing her breasts to quiver very nicely.

He looked lower, and immediately approved of her silky boxers that were also a delicate green.

Her arms and legs were bare, her skin moist with the morning heat and desire. Josh saw that in her eyes as her laughter finally wound down and her gaze became slightly glazed.

Hank punched him in the biceps again.

Damn. Josh glared at the man. "*What?*"

Hank worked his jaw as if to say—*What else? Keep your damn eyes off of her.* At last, he opened his left hand and held it out to Josh, palm up.

Josh looked down and saw a black piece of plastic, no bigger than a key chain alarm.

"Take it," Hank ordered.

Not a chance. "What is it?"

"A panic button," Hank said, his tone dry. "It transmits a panic alarm."

Josh looked at him.

Hank arched one bushy black brow. "Just in case you need my help in fighting off the babes."

Tess made a strangled sound from behind.

When Josh looked, he noticed her shoulders were really shaking as she tried not to laugh.

Hmmmm. He turned back to Hank. "Why do I need that—or you—to fight off the babes? I have Tess for that. You should have been here last night. She did a great job when Libby—"

Tess interrupted. "What?"

Josh noticed she wasn't laughing now. In fact, she seemed kind of stunned. Still, he gave her an innocent look. "Huh?"

She frowned. "You heard?"

"Libby?" he asked, then shrugged. "Well, yeah, that's why I have an intercom out there."

"Really." Tess's brows continued to draw together. "You didn't answer when I announced *my* arrival."

"Why not?" Hank asked.

Josh ignored him so that he could play with her a little more as she was always playing with him. "Tess, you know why. I was busy scr—" He was about to say *screwing,* but thought better of it. "I was busy," he repeated, then pointed to the ceiling fan, the screws he had put in. "Remember?"

Tess took a sip of coffee as her gaze remained on him.

Josh gave her a sweet smile, then turned to Hank. "I don't think I'll be needing you."

The man crossed his arms over his chest. "That's for Freddy to decide."

"Aren't I the customer here?"

Ignoring him, Hank spoke to Tess. "About those intruder sensors in the lawn, I—"

"Whoa," Josh said. "You want to put sensors in my lawn?"

Hank took a deep breath, then leveled his gaze on Josh. "You want to be safe, right?"

"Safe, not paranoid. Sensors in my lawn seem a little extreme."

"Land mines are extreme," Hank countered. "Traps are extreme, especially those with metal teeth that clamp down as soon as you—"

"I get the picture."

Hank turned to Tess. "About his car."

"What about it?" Josh asked.

Hank lifted his gaze to the ceiling as if his patience was really being tried. "We're thinking about putting a safety release inside your trunk." He looked at Tess. "Just in case one of those babes wants to kidnap him."

Tess lifted her brows.

Josh frowned.

Hank ignored him as he talked to Tess. "You want anti-passback for any of the employees?"

She swallowed her sip of coffee, then shook her head. "No

need. I've already checked out the maid service, and Josh doesn't have a cook or a chauffeur or even a pool person, just an intercom he doesn't answer."

He lowered his head and shook it.

Hank continued, "I've set up five zones to make this easy."

Easy? Josh was getting dizzy as Hank went on and on about access controls, arming levels, video motion detection, and whatnot. The guy was making it sound like he was arming Fort Knox against an inva—

"Whoa," Josh said, interrupting Hank and his own thoughts. "Did you just say closed-circuit TV?"

"That's right. You want me to explain to you what that is?"

Josh frowned. "No. I know what it is. You've got cameras in here?" His gaze darted around this room looking for those cameras that were probably being monitored at her father's place to see if big, bad Josh was doing anything naughty to little Tessie, who knew Krav Maga and just about everything else to make him non-ambulatory so that he behaved.

"On the outside," Hank said. "Around your pool, where you seem to be having the most trouble with paparazzi, because you don't swim dressed."

So much for his plans to someday go skinny-dipping with Tess. Holding back a sigh, Josh glanced at her.

She was still regarding him as she sipped her coffee.

"This place is as tight as a drum," Hank said.

"Or a prison," Josh said.

"It's whatever you make of it." Hank clamped Josh on the shoulder so damned hard his knees briefly bent. Satisfied with that, Hank strolled outside.

Josh kneaded his shoulder and looked at Tess.

Her gaze, this time, was on his cock, which was suddenly blossoming beneath his pajama bottoms because of her attention.

Okay, so he was no longer pissed and neither was she. Taking that as an invitation to move closer, Josh started across the room, then stopped, waiting to be ambushed by another alarm. When it didn't happen, he went around the counter.

Tess continued to sip her coffee as she watched him move to her side. When he casually walked behind her, trying to determine where in the hell she was hiding her gun in that outfit, she asked, "What are you doing?"

His gaze jumped up.

Her cup was on the counter, her gaze on him, those lovely eyes narrowed.

Josh talked fast. "I should've acknowledged you last night, when you said you were here."

She didn't comment.

He wiggled his brows. "I like the way you handled Libby."

Tess glanced to the side, then looked back at him, again.

"You really did seem like my girlfriend."

She arched a brow.

One tough nut to crack. Josh held back a sigh and finally asked, "So where is it?"

That brow lowered. "Where's what?"

He looked down. "Your gun." He met her gaze. "You said you always have one on."

"I do."

Uh-huh. He leaned to the side to get a better look at her back, though not for long. Tess turned around on the stool. Once she was facing him, with her left knee so close to his groin that Josh took a cautious step back, she reached behind herself, and after a moment pulled out a gun.

It was smaller than Josh had imagined, with a short barrel, but it was an honest-to-God real gun.

"Satisfied?" she asked.

Actually, Josh was getting really turned on. Damn, but he liked the fact that she was an ex-cop, even if she evaded all of his questions. After clearing his throat, he asked, "Do you ever wear it in a garter?"

Tess stared at him, then slipped the gun back to where it had come from. "Huh?"

"In a garter." Josh stepped closer to explain the concept, until her gaze stopped him. He retreated a step. "On your leg, actually your thigh," he corrected. "You know, a garter, one of those frilly things women wear sometimes."

Her eyes kept getting wider and wider.

Josh wasn't certain if she was playing dumb or not, so he continued to explain. "I've seen it on TV—surely you've seen it on TV—where those TV cops, at least the female ones, have garters that hold guns and—are you laughing at me?"

She was actually bent over the counter, her head resting on her arm she was laughing so hard.

"What's going on in here? Everything all right?"

Josh looked up to see an older woman hurrying inside. She was about the same age as Hank, built like him, too, though much shorter, with close-cropped salt-and-pepper hair, and really bad frown marks.

Was that Hank's wife?

"Hey, you okay?" the older woman asked Tess as she rubbed her back.

"I'm fine, Sammie." Tess looked at Josh. "Sorry."

Sammie gave him a hard stare. "What's Tessie got to be sorry for?"

"She keeps laughing at me."

"Not at you," Tess corrected, "at what you said." Her shoulders continued to shake with laughter.

"Oh, yeah?" Sammie said, then shot Josh a nasty frown. "Whadya say?"

"It wasn't anything bad," Tess explained. "He just wanted to know if I ever carry my gun in a garter."

"A garter? What kind of a garter?"

"The kind women wear," Josh said, then moved his hands to illustrate while he explained. "With lace and maybe some sparkly stuff, and—"

This time Sammie's laughter interrupted him. She asked Tess, "Why would you do that?"

Josh sighed. "It's done on TV all the time."

"Oh, yeah?" Sammie continued to laugh. "Everyone on TV is gorgeous and rich and miserable. How real is that?"

"Well, you know," Tess said to Sammie, "I bet you could carry a derringer in a garter."

"Don't you carry a thirty-eight special?"

"Well, yeah, but I'm just saying, a derringer might work."

"For what? It's only got two rounds."

Tess nodded. "That's true. It wouldn't keep *all* the babes away, that's for sure."

Josh rolled his eyes.

Both women ignored that.

"No matter what you're carrying," Sammie said, "think of how hard it would be to pull that sucker out of a garter if you needed it. You'd have to hike your skirt halfway up to your navel."

"I hear you," Tess said. "And if you're wearing panty hose, that'd be a real killer."

"Run city. Might as well kiss those babies good-bye."

"You got that right."

"Now, for me," Sammie said, "I like an ankle holster. Easy to get to, no muss, no fuss. And what about those pocket holsters. Damn, those are nice."

Tess quickly nodded. Her eyes sparkled as if she was getting excited. "Have you seen those new ones they're advertising on the Net?"

"From Keep the Peace dotcom?"

"No, that other dotcom, the one that just came online recently. They got stuff that would curl your hair."

"It's already curled. So impress me."

Tess readjusted her butt on the stool and talked fast. "There's this new purse holster that's really outta sight—nice, slick leather, smooth as a baby's bottom, with release features that make it always ready to go. And then there's this holster that looks like a pair of briefs, for the guys I would imagine, but it— "

Josh loudly cleared his throat.

Tess paused and looked at him with an expression that said she had forgotten he was here.

So did Sammie, until she suddenly noticed his naked chest and silky pajama bottoms, before she looked at his naked chest again.

Josh's brows were lifted as her gaze finally met his. "Hi. I'm Josh Wyatt."

"Yeah, I know. Sammie Tufts here." She put out her hand.

Josh took it and wasn't a bit surprised that she squeezed his fingers nearly as hard as Hank had. He, on the other hand, restrained himself. "So, I take it you're not Hank's wife."

Sammie looked confused. "Hank who?"

"Rogan."

"Him?" Sammie laughed so hard, she started to wheeze.

"Sammie's a retired cop," Tess said. "She's also a friend of my dad."

"A devoted friend of him and Tessie," Sammie added, just as Hank had.

Josh nodded, not at all surprised, then sighed as Hank came back in.

"Hey, Rogan," Sammie said. "You show this boy how to use the new alarm?"

Boy?

Hank's gaze slid to Josh's chest, before returning to Sammie. "Yup." He scratched the back of his neck. "Don't know if he got it or not."

"Maybe we should write it down for him."

"Tessie already suggested that. She thought we should use his—"

"That's enough," Tess finally interrupted. "Mr. Wyatt understands what he needs to do." She looked at him. "Don't you, Josh?"

He arched one brow. If she was talking about hauling her into his arms and kissing her until they both were breathless, then, yeah—he knew exactly what to do, just as soon as he got rid of these guardian angels her pop had sent over. "I'm getting a fair idea."

She smiled.

"Have a seat," Josh said to Hank and Sammie. If he couldn't beat them, then he was just going to have to join them. "I'll make all of you breakfast."

Chapter Six

Despite Josh's best efforts, including changing into a T-shirt and jeans before he made everyone a huge breakfast, Tess knew the meal wasn't going to be a walk on the beach, unless that beach was littered with nuclear warheads.

When his comments were kind, Hank twisted their meaning so that Josh looked like a fool. When he said something neutral, Hank wanted to know why Josh didn't have an opinion.

The poor guy couldn't win.

Sammie didn't make it any better. She saw to it that *the boy,* as she kept referring to him, didn't get anywhere near Tess.

It was awful. Oddly enough though, Josh didn't fire the lot of them right then and there. He responded good-naturedly, even laughing at himself, when Tess knew she would have come out swinging.

Could be he was just punch-drunk from all those insults, or raring to get started on their first day as employer and bodyguard, not to mention pretend lovers. They would kiss, touch, and hug in public, then come back here to sweat out another celibate evening, until the next day when there would be more of the same.

Uh-huh. Why in the world was she feeling sorry for him?

"What are you doing?" he asked.

Tess lifted her gaze from the Mercedes, which was in the same spot she had left it last night. Breakfast was now a bad memory; Hank and Sammie were currently out of earshot, but it was also time to go to work. Maybe that's why Josh was frowning? "I'm getting into the car."

His frown deepened. "On my side?"

"The driver's side," she corrected, in a tone much nicer than Hank would ever use. "Technically, it's not called Josh's side."

He lifted his face and breathed hard.

At last he was acting pissed and Tess was glad. It gave her a chance to admire how dolled up he was for today's press conference to publicize his newest development.

Josh was freshly shaved and shampooed, though his hair was still deliciously tousled. He wore a beige sports coat, brown dress trousers, an ivory shirt, silk tie, dress shoes, and a *fuck this* expression as he looked at her.

"My car, I drive." He went around the front of it.

As he did, Tess backed away and held up the keys. "Not without these you don't."

Josh stopped. Planting his hands on his lean hips, he looked down and growled, "Don't make me fight you for them."

"I won't. I don't want to hurt you."

He lifted his gaze. He looked like he wanted to spit.

Too bad. Tess got tough. "I'm your bodyguard. I'm driving you, Josh, and that's final."

He dropped his hands and continued to approach.

Tess walked backwards down the drive as she talked fast. "You don't know anything about defensive driving or vehicle formations, or anti-ambush, or counteractions, or— "

"The hell I don't," he interrupted as he continued to advance, while she continued to retreat. "I danced around the insults from those two friends of yours this morning, didn't I?"

"They're my dad's friends," she corrected, "and from where I was, you weren't doing so good."

Josh stopped, shook his head, then advanced again. "I'm the man, so I'm— "

"Oh, *please,*" she interrupted, "you're the man so that makes you the better driver?"

"Fine. Have it your way. You're as good as me."

"Tell me something I don't already know."

"Tess, you are going to give me those keys."

"Not a chance." She continued to retreat.

He continued to advance. "If I apologize for being a man will you give me the— "

Her laughter interrupted him. "Like I'd believe that?"

"Ah, so you're glad I'm a man. Well, that's good to know."

"Like I hid it during our kiss?"

Josh smiled. "That was nice wasn't— "

"It'd be nicer if you did what you were told."

"Sure you really want that?"

"I am not giving you these— "

"Oh, Josh! Over here!"

Both he and Tess stopped at that shout.

It came from a young woman on the other side of the gate, which was just ahead.

She wore a red bikini bottom, while her long black hair clung to her naked breasts. Josh frowned, not believing this. She looked as if she had just stepped out of a pool, unless that was baby oil glistening on her tanned flesh. As she regarded him, her forefinger ran up and down one of those iron bars, stroking it, fondling it as she probably wanted to do to his cock.

"Let's take a swim," she said.

Josh's gaze continued to follow her forefinger. "That Libby?" he asked Tess.

"Nope."

"You mean this is a new one? Aren't your friends supposed to be guarding my gate?"

Tess didn't answer.

Josh looked over his shoulder, then shouted, "Hold it!"

Tess did not. She was already on her way back to the car, moving more like a world-class sprinter than a dancer, despite her heels.

Did she honestly think she could outrun him? Without breaking a sweat, Josh easily caught up, took her arm, pulled her away from the driver's side door and into himself.

Tess's eyes and mouth widened in surprise.

Josh used the moment and his body to so quickly back her into the hood, Tess lifted her right leg until her pale yellow skirt was hitched more than halfway up her thigh.

God, that looked nice.

Tess didn't seem to notice. Her gaze darted to his hand as Josh cradled the side of her face, keeping it still, then leaned down to her and murmured, "Now's a good time to prove that we're romantically involved to get rid of that lunatic at the gate."

Tess arched one brow. "She can't see us from here."

Who the fuck cares? "You owe me," Josh murmured, then covered her mouth with his own. This time there was no hesitation or restraint. He plunged his tongue inside and took what he wanted, what he needed, making this kiss as wild and savage as he felt.

Now, he was in charge, and Tess didn't seem to mind that one bit. She surrendered immediately, completely, suckling his tongue until a moan escaped the back of Josh's throat, and his cock strained against his clothing. He ground his hips into hers until Tess knew the pain she was putting him through. As if that pleased her, Tess wrapped her leg around him, pulling him even closer. Josh moaned again, and deepened the kiss.

Tess allowed it. She encouraged it. There was no stopping her now. She didn't care if that young woman, Hank, Sammie, and her father were all nearby watching. This moment belonged to her and Josh.

Lifting her hands, Tess drove her fingers through his silky hair, keeping his head still so that he wouldn't dare lift his mouth from hers. Pushing his tongue aside, she drove hers into his mouth, then pressed her hips into his until she could feel every inch of his impressive rod.

Even that wasn't enough, nor was this kiss, though they were both finally breathless.

As Josh rested his forehead against hers as they both heaved air, a car honked.

Tess flinched, hitting her cheek against his nose. Rubbing it with his fingers, Josh quickly backed away from her and swung his head to the side.

"Oh, hell," he whispered, "don't tell me."

"You two ready to get started, or what?" Hank shouted. He was leaning out the window of his car that was edging towards them.

"Yeah," Tess shouted to him, then murmured to Josh. "Okay. I won't tell you."

As she went to the driver's door, Josh said in a voice only she could hear, "We're not through, Tess. Not by a long shot."

She looked at him, but already Josh was moving to the passenger side, yanking the door open and sinking into the seat.

On the drive to the office, Tess kept her gaze on the road, while Josh pouted.

Here he was, a grown man, but being treated like a freaking little kid as Tess chauffeured him to work, while that psycho Hank brought up the rear, and possibly used this trip to think up more insults.

That hadn't been part of this deal. Nowhere in the contract did it say he had to accept this extra, snotty protection. That wasn't something Josh was going to pay for.

And he'd tell Tess that, too, just as soon as he figured a way to get his point across without pissing her off or hurting her feelings. Josh didn't want her pissed or hurt. She might just hold out on him in public rather than giving him another great kiss that they wouldn't be sharing in private.

Swearing beneath his breath, Josh looked out the passenger side window, then stared at Sammie who was already staring at him from her car, which was in the next lane.

He wondered if this was only a coincidence, a chance encounter, then figured it wasn't, since she kept pace with this car rather than passing.

Great. He was surrounded by Pop's *very* devoted friends who were all armed to the teeth.

Well, screw that.

"This has to stop," he said, then looked at Tess to make his point, which he quickly forgot.

Her lips were still bruised from his kiss, although she didn't seem to mind. She wore a lingering smile and an expression that said she hadn't heard him at all; she was reliving that moment in his arms.

As she inhaled deeply, luxuriously, sunlight rippled over her suit. This one was almost as nice as the one she had worn yesterday, though it had a back slit in the skirt, rather than one on the side.

And why not, since she didn't carry her weapon in a garter.

Josh arched one brow, then looked at her shoes. They were the same ivory shade as his tie and hiding her toes.

He frowned. What was the matter with her? He liked those other heels.

"Was this your idea?" he asked.

It was a moment before Tess seemed to hear him. She lost that lingering smile, before meeting his gaze. "Was what my idea?"

"To have us chaperoned by Bonnie and Clyde."

She laughed.

Josh turned his head away before Tess saw his smile. He was supposed to be pissed—hell, he was pissed, but he was only human. As far as Josh was concerned, there wasn't a man alive who wouldn't be moved by Tess's laughter. It was as musical, as intoxicating as her voice.

Inhaling deeply, he glanced out his window. Sammie was still in the next lane, only this time she was frowning as if she was really pissed.

Why? His hands were on his thighs, not Tess's. She was driving his car, and he was allowing it. Hell, he was being an unbelievably good boy, even though Tess was now leaning toward him, delivering her soft, powdery scent.

Turning his head towards her, Josh inhaled as deeply as he could.

Tess looked at him, then back to the radio. Once it was on a station she liked, with that music fairly loud, she said, "Better be careful what you talk about."

Was she kidding? "Why? Are you wearing a wire?"

"Sure."

Uh-huh. "I don't believe it. Pull the car over, I want to frisk you."

Tess gave him one of her cop stares. "In your world that would be called foreplay."

"You have a problem with that?"

"My colleagues might."

"You're evading my question, just like you always evade—"

"They can hear what you're saying, Josh."

Huh? "What do you mean?"

"We've modified your car's communication system so that Hank and Sammie can hear what's going on in here—just in case anyone tries anything and you need the truth to fight a future lawsuit."

Josh sagged farther into his seat. This was worse than prison. There, a man wasn't tempted by a woman as luscious as Tess—just by folks who looked like Hank and Sammie. He sighed.

"It's for your own protection," Tess said.

He looked at her. "And I guess yours doesn't have anything to do with it, huh?"

Okay, so maybe it did a little; maybe her dad was glad that Hank and Sammie were listening in. Even so, it was in Privacy Dynamics' protection package. They weren't treating Josh any differently from other clients, except for Hank's constant criticisms, of course.

"Can it be turned off?" Josh asked.

"Sure you want that?"

"I trust you, Tess. The question seems to be, do you trust—"

"There," she said, reaching under the dash. "It's off."

"Thanks. I enjoyed our kiss this morning, how about—whoa, watch it," Josh interrupted himself, "you nearly sideswiped that guy."

She mumbled, "I was giving him a warning. He was staring at you. Could be another fan."

Josh rolled his eyes.

Tess muttered an oath in Spanish.

"What was that?" Josh asked.

She pretended not to hear.

Josh regarded her a moment more, then lifted his hands to the back of his head and got really comfortable. "As I was saying about our kiss, I—"

This time he was interrupted by a prolonged honk from behind.

Tess's gaze moved to the rearview mirror. Hank was gesturing and mouthing that the communications device wasn't working.

Tess looked at Josh. "Hold that thought." She leaned over and turned the device back on.

Josh lowered his hands, then drummed his fingers against his thighs.

"It won't be so bad, really," she said.

"You got that right. They're not coming into my building or my office."

"Well, not your personal office," Tess said. "There, you can be alone."

Josh frowned. Who said he wanted to be alone?

Who said he could? The moment they got inside his building there were people all around. Not that Josh noticed anyone but Tess, while she noticed every single woman who passed by, as if they might cause trouble.

Josh knew they wouldn't. They could have been buck naked and doing jumping jacks and he knew he wouldn't notice them or care.

None of them were Tess. None of them would have gotten away with a tenth of what he was putting up with, with Tess.

Suppressing a sigh, he followed her through the building until they reached his office suite. Peg was already in the doorway of her office, dressed in more hippie finery, and spritzing herself with perfume.

"'Bout time," she said, then looked from Tess to him and smiled. "What kept you two?"

"Never mind," Tess said as she passed Peg and went into his office.

Josh stopped by the woman's side. "Don't worry, you'll probably get a chance to read about it in a tabloid."

Peg's reddish brows lifted. "Kissed her, again, huh?"

Damn right he did. "Don't you have work to do?"

"I'd rather hear about the kiss."

Josh moved past her.

She called out, "Don't forget, the press will be here at eleven!"

Josh nodded, then stopped and turned around. "If you see anyone new, check them out. If they're not from a legitimate publication or station, call the cops. And not Bonnie and Clyde, either, but cops who aren't retired and definitely ones who aren't devoted friends of Freddy."

Peg frowned. "Huh?"

He didn't have time to explain. He didn't want to waste one second of what could be some quality time alone with Tess, just as soon as he got her into the conference room.

Once he was in his office, Josh paused, then looked over

his right shoulder, his left, before turning a complete circle to see that those stacks of tabloids had been removed, there were no new baskets of flowers, and Tess wasn't anywhere in sight.

Where is she?

Josh went into the conference room, which had also been cleared of all those unwanted gifts. He was grateful for that, but still looking for Tess.

He went through all the other offices, greeting his staff as he did, then asked one of the older women to check out the ladies' rooms to see if Tess was inside any of them.

Maybe she needed to freshen up. Maybe she needed to adjust her gun.

"Sure thing," the woman said. "What's she look like?"

"She's younger than me," Josh said, "but not that young, not that old either, twenty-eight, at most; she's tall, five-seven or eight in her bare feet, so probably five-nine or ten now, and a hundred and—it doesn't matter how much she weighs," he quickly said. "She's wearing a yellow suit with a skirt that has a back slit, instead of one on the side, since she doesn't wear garters, but she does carry a—well, that's not really important, either," he said. "She has on high heels that are covering up her toes, and her hair's long." He put his hand on his own shoulder to show its length. "It's the color of an expensive cognac, and her eyes are kind of golden with—"

"Be right back," the woman interrupted, then went to check out the johns.

Her head was shaking as she came back. "Not in any of them."

"You're sure?"

"Given the way you described her, she'd be hard to miss."

Damn. "Right. Thanks." Josh finally went to the meeting room that was being prepared for the press conference and the celebration that would be held afterwards.

Catering staff were setting up the area for the food and booze, but still there was no Tess.

Where is she? Josh looked over his shoulder, then faced the series of windows when he saw her outside by the dock.

The edges of her suit jacket, skirt, and hair were fluttering in the breeze; her gaze was on those docked boats as she spoke on her cell.

Josh moved to the windows, watching her in a way he hadn't been able to since they first met. Was it only yesterday? Amazing. It was hard to remember what it had been like before she was protecting him.

His gaze followed her skirt's back slit as it lifted briefly in the wind. He regarded her shapely calves as she strolled to the right, paused, then strolled to the left, moving like a dancer as she concentrated on that call.

Josh smiled, then lifted his gaze to her narrow shoulders, that long, slender throat, her reckless joy as she laughed to whatever had been said by the person on the other end of that call.

Was that person as aroused as he by her musical laughter, her cocky attitude, that soft, yearning gaze? Was that person able to make her blush as he so easily could?

Josh honestly doubted it. He had stirred her as deeply as she continued to move him, with Tess using very little effort to accomplish that.

She didn't need to be in a string bikini with water dripping over her half-naked flesh to get his undivided attention. That's what those other women didn't seem to understand. It wasn't raw sex Josh was looking for, it was a reason to engage in that sex, to continue it beyond one night.

Tess gave him that in abundance.

Seeing her gaze on him at unexpected times, feeling the warmth of her fingers covering his, experiencing her in his arms during a kiss was far more powerful than any come-on.

Even when Josh had been poor, before romance got all too complicated and litigious, the women he had dated had not returned his kiss as Tess had.

She seemed to require his mouth on hers as much as she

needed to breathe. His tongue wasn't an intrusion, it was welcomed and cherished as she gave it a home. And when he became so lost in the moment that nothing else mattered, Tess took that journey with him as his willing companion.

She was his equal in every way. She would really be amazing in bed.

Tell me something I don't already know.

Josh smiled to her remembered words. She was so damned cocky, but he was no slouch, either. He would win her over, along with all of her friends, relatives, and neighbors, too, if necessary, no matter what it took. He wouldn't rush her, he would wait for her to come to him, and she would definitely come.

There would be a night, sometime soon, when Tess would face him with all of the old barriers gone.

She wouldn't be patient, because that just wasn't her style. She would strip herself bare, and if he wasn't keeping up, she would strip him, too, then crawl on top and give Josh what he most wanted.

A woman who celebrated his maleness, who adored his hard cock, and who was genuinely interested in him, not the money or status, making him feel like the most important person in her world.

It was a need Josh hadn't noticed until now. He had been too busy with work to realize that he was actually lonely.

Not anymore. Not with Tess in his life.

Trouble was, she was still outside, when Josh wanted her in here. He had a slice of time before the conference and needed to relax. She could help him with that.

But only if she wanted to.

Josh lowered his fist before he knocked on the window to get her attention.

If he asked her to come inside to hold his hand, and a whole lot more, she'd be insulted because he was keeping her from doing her job. If he didn't respect that, he'd lose whatever chance he had with her, not to mention pissing off Hank, Sammie, and Freddy.

As if he needed that. Already the unholy trio wanted to crush every bone in his body.

Sighing, Josh turned away from the window only to come face-to-face with one of the catering staff.

She was in her early twenties, heavily made up, and wearing a hungry expression that had nothing to do with the food she was supposed to be putting out.

"Mr. Wyatt," she said, moving closer, "so nice to meet you."

Josh had already backed away. Although her gaze and voice were probably meant to be seductive, he found them downright predatory. "Excuse me," he said, then turned to leave.

She so easily stepped to the side, blocking him, it seemed almost an afterthought on her part. "We'll be finished setting up in here in no time at all. Of course, if you have any special needs, I'd be happy to take care of them . . . just let me know what you want and— "

"Excuse me," Josh said once more, then turned back to the window and pounded on it with the heel of his hand.

Tess's cell was still to her ear as she looked over her shoulder, then turned completely around.

Josh gestured for her to get in here, now. If ever there was a moment when she should pretend they were romantically involved, this was it, and Josh wasn't about to miss out on a chance to get her into his arms, again.

Tess frowned as if she didn't quite get that, until she noticed the young woman behind him. Tess's frown faded; she mouthed *be right there.*

You better be. Josh turned, then nearly collided with the young woman who had edged even closer. It was as if she wanted him to touch her in all the wrong places, in public no less.

And hadn't Alan warned him about that?

If you so much as accidentally bump into one of these women while they're after you, they're going to see a golden opportunity to claim that you led them on, you got them in a compromising position, you couldn't take "no" for an answer, and then—

Josh didn't even want to consider the rest. "I said, excuse—"

"Not until you hear me out," she interrupted, then smiled. "I can stay after the rest of the staff to—"

"No, thanks." Josh went around her.

She followed, touching his sleeve. "But you haven't heard what I was going to say. Now, I could—"

"Excuse me, Mr. Wyatt?"

Josh looked over his shoulder. A middle-aged man in a tropical shirt and cargos was frowning at the girl.

"Robyn, don't you have work to do?" he asked.

"Well sure, but—"

"Then do it," he said, his tone allowing no argument.

As she finally moved away, the older man spoke to Josh. "Sorry about that, Mr. Wyatt. She's my sister's second cousin, and she gets kind of stupid sometimes, but I'm sure she meant no—"

"You're right. I'm sure she didn't." Josh patted the man's shoulder, then looked past him to see Tess watching the exchange.

Josh went to her. He kept his voice low. "Where were you? Didn't you see that girl practically wrestling me to the ground? I thought you were supposed to be protecting me. I thought you were supposed to be pretending to be romantically involved with me."

She leaned close and whispered, "You never gave me the chance, Josh. In fact, you did so well yourself, I have to wonder if you need me at all."

As she straightened, Josh looked at her. "You want to cancel the contract?"

She didn't miss a beat. "Would you let me?"

He smiled. "Hell, no."

Her expression was smug. "That's what I thought."

"Cocky, aren't we?"

She returned his gaze for a long moment, then lowered it to his fly, as if she just couldn't help herself. "You tell me," she murmured.

Damn, this woman. "Just wait until we're alone."

Tess's gaze finally lifted. Her cheeks, throat, and chest were flushed. "And when might that be?"

"Soon."

"There you are," Peg said.

His shoulders slumped. *Please, go away.*

She slipped her arm through his instead, then pulled him away.

Tess lifted her brows as Josh looked over his shoulder at her. Poor guy. Absolutely nothing was going the way he would have liked. Not only was Peg shaking Josh's arm to get his attention, she was talking a mile a minute about some business problem that he just had to solve.

Josh finally said something that got Peg to shut up and to stop, without pissing her off.

Smart guy.

Tess's brows lifted again as he looked over his shoulder at her.

"No matter what happens between now and eleven," he called out, "I want you in this building, not outside."

Oh, yeah? Tess crossed her arms over her chest.

"Please," he added. "Be here, in this room, at eleven for my thing."

The tone of his voice, the look in his eyes turned her resolve and brain to mush. "I'll be here."

Satisfied, Josh went his way, while Tess went hers.

She spoke with building security to make certain they kept an eye on the dock, just in case that paparazzo decided to return. She got today's amended guest list from a member of Josh's staff, and checked out everyone's credentials. When more flowers and photos arrived from Josh's fans, Tess refused those deliveries and made arrangements with the area florists to deliver all future gifts to retirement homes, instead.

"With the photos, too?" one of the male florists asked.

"I'll leave that up to you," Tess said, then continued with the rest of her business.

At ten minutes to eleven she returned to the meeting room. Members of the press were already inside along with the people who helped make this newest development happen.

To fit in with the rest of this crowd, Tess grabbed a press kit and a bottle of Perrier, then smiled blandly and kept milling about so no one would ask her any questions.

Like who she was, where she had come from, what she was doing here, and how long she had been romantically involved with Josh. Tess finished half that bottle of Perrier as she considered the answer, since that wasn't something she and Josh had talked about. Instead, they had held hands, kissed, and chased each other around his car.

They really needed to get their act together.

"Hi. You're new."

Tess lowered her bottle of Perrier and smiled blandly at the young man who had just said she was new and seemed to be waiting for a response.

"This is really something, isn't it?" she asked, moving away from him to the model of the retail, residential, and commercial development Josh had succeeded in putting together. If the conversation circulating this room was true, he had succeeded where many of the other developers had failed, since the local politicians, citizens, and even the environmentalists had finally gone along.

Maybe they realized what Tess already knew in her heart—he was an honorable man, who instilled loyalty in his people. Peg might have given him a hard time, but she adored him, while the others treated Josh with genuine respect.

"Yeah, it is something," the young man answered, since he had followed her to the model. "So, are you press or staff?"

Tess put up her forefinger as she faked a minor cough, took a prolonged sip of her designer water, then turned to the flurry of activity as Josh entered the room.

Despite the applause, maybe because of it, he seemed kind of embarrassed, and gestured for it to stop.

As it did, Tess saw his gaze searching this room. A lot of the young women flashed him welcoming smiles, though Josh didn't seem to notice.

At last, his gaze saw what it wanted, his bodyguard.

Tess's heart fluttered.

Josh winked.

It was more intimate than a caress, because it was meant for her alone, even though they were surrounded by a roomful of people.

Tess smiled. She put the press kit under her right arm and gave him a thumbs up.

He grinned, then turned to an older man who had just clamped him on the shoulder. As they exchanged a handshake and conversation that had them both laughing, that persistent young man asked, "So, you know Josh?"

Tess made her voice light even though she wanted to shoot this guy. "Doesn't everyone?"

He seemed surprised by her evasive answer. "I guess. How do you know—"

"Hold that thought," she interrupted, then pointed to the podium. "I think it's starting."

"Oh, yeah. So," he persisted, "you're a member of the—"

"Do you have a pen?"

He looked down at the one he was holding. "Only this one."

"Could you get me one?" Tess asked. "And more water, too?" She stroked her throat. "I have this tickling, you know?"

The guy's gaze followed Tess's fingers to the base of her throat where she was drawing lazy circles. "Sure. Be right back."

She smiled. "I'll be here." The moment his back was to her, Tess moved to another part of the room, glanced at her watch, then looked up at the microphone's feedback.

Josh was finally at the podium. As the others moved closer, Tess retreated toward a wall, leaning against it as this thing finally got under way.

Josh first thanked everyone involved in this project, encouraging the crowd to applaud each individual. After detailing the stages of construction, which was accompanied by a video presentation, and offering a dizzying array of facts and figures, Josh finally wrapped things up and asked if there were any questions.

A young male voice from the back immediately called out, "Did those naked photos of you in *Keys Confidential* hurt your credibility with the investors?"

Tess swung her head to that guy. She frowned. How dare he ask such a thing.

Before Josh even had a chance to respond, a female reporter asked, "Were you behind those photos being published, in a misguided attempt to gain publicity for this project?"

On the heels of that was another question, "If this wasn't a publicity stunt orchestrated by you, do you plan to sue the tabloid?"

After that, everyone seemed to be talking at once.

Tess looked from the crowd to Josh as he remained at the podium, saying nothing, his expression unreadable. Even so, she sensed his anger and his hurt.

After all he had done for the Keys, after all he had accomplished, these ghouls were only interested in those tabloid photos?

Well, to hell with that.

Moving quickly through this crowd, Tess went to his side. Before Josh could ask what she was doing, Tess leaned toward the microphone and said, "That's enough!"

Her voice was loud and cop hard.

Some shut up; others did not.

Tess addressed them personally, asking if they were having trouble hearing or just didn't understand English. "I can say it in Spanish if that'd help," she said, then did.

That shut them up.

Tess seized the quiet to address everyone. "Josh was as surprised by those photos—no, he was more surprised—than the rest of you. It wasn't your privacy that was breached—it was his. Do you have any idea how terrible that is? As to your question," she said to the woman who asked if this was a misguided attempt to gain publicity, "didn't you do your homework before coming here? Don't you know what this man has done for the Keys and this state? Do you really believe he'd need a tabloid, of all things, to promote his projects?"

Before the woman could answer, Tess looked at the young man who asked that first, stupid question. "And you—do you really believe that with Josh's track record, investors would question his credibility? Is anyone really that naïve? And you," she said to another, taking him to task for his idiotic question.

Moving from him to the next and then to the next, Tess vented as she never had, until she had said it all.

In that moment, silence greeted her, along with more than a few raised brows.

Well, too bad. She wasn't about to keep her mouth shut when they were attacking Josh. If they wanted a fight, then she'd give them one.

"Who are you?" a reporter finally called out.

Josh grabbed her wrist, as if warning her not to say anything else. Leaning toward the microphone, he said, "This press conference is over."

As he tried to lead her away, Tess held back.

Josh gave her a hard stare, which she ignored.

"Tess Franklin," she said into the microphone.

Josh hissed, "Tess."

"It's okay," she said to him. She wasn't going to tell these nitwits that she was his bodyguard, which would just bring everything right back to that tabloid stuff. She wouldn't embarrass him that way. Turning to the crowd, she said, "Josh and I have been seeing each other for some time."

He looked at her as if she was nuts, or as if he'd forgotten the pretend relationship was his idea.

"Where did you two meet?" a reporter called out.

"When?" another shouted.

Tess put up her finger, asking for a moment, as Josh pulled her away from that mike and whispered in her ear. "What are you doing?"

She turned into him and whispered, "Figuring out when we met."

"Are you kidding?" he whispered. "This is a press conference. Those are reporters."

"They're ghouls," she corrected, "and we both knew we'd be asked about our relationship."

"Not at a press conference."

"Let's get it all out right here and now. Unless you've changed your mind and want me to just be your bodyguard in public."

Straightening, Josh met her gaze, then moved toward the microphone. "We met a while back through Tess's dad, Fred Franklin. He owns Privacy Dynamics. Fred's company did all the security upgrades for my estate and will soon start on the security for this building and the others I own."

Tess tried to hide her surprise. That wasn't the history they had agreed upon.

Didn't matter. During the following minutes, Josh raved about her dad's business, giving the man publicity he couldn't have hoped to get in several years.

At last, Josh scanned the crowd and said, "Peg, see to it that all of these good people get a copy of Privacy Dynamics' brochure before they leave."

"What's next for you two?" another reporter called out.

As the other reporters laughed and smiled, Tess considered that question.

No matter how much she enjoyed being with Josh, even at a stupid press conference, this couldn't last forever. It was just a job. And even if he was promoting her dad's business, even if he respected her and wanted her physically, that didn't mean that he would ever love her.

Tess finally went to the microphone and said the only thing she could. "That's between Josh and me."

Chapter Seven

The moment those words were out of her mouth, Josh knew Tess had made a mistake. Not as big as disclosing their relationship to the freaking world, of course, but a definite no-no. If anything, the reporters now seemed determined to find out all that they could.

There were more questions about the romance, then ones about her age, where she had grown up, where she lived now, what she did for a living. It quickly dawned on Tess that their pretend relationship should have been assumed when they showed up at various functions, not spelled out at a media event. Even so, she dug in her heels, answering all of those questions with ones of her own, just like a former cop.

That only made the press more persistent.

Josh figured this couldn't get any worse until he noticed Sammie and Hank in the back. They were staring at Tess, then frowning at him, rather than taking control of this crowd, especially that guy to the right. He had tabloid written all over him as he kept snapping pictures.

Sammie finally pulled out her cell, punched in a number, then talked until her face was red. Josh figured she was reporting this newest wrinkle to Freddy.

If that wasn't bad enough, late in the day, Hank, not Tess, showed up to drive him home.

Josh wondered if she had been summoned to her dad's or was still hiding out. After the press conference, Josh had seen her only once, and that was when she was talking to Peg. From what Josh could overhear of that conversation, Tess admitted to losing her cool, something she never did.

"I just had to protect him," she said with absolutely no regret in her voice, which got quickly ballsy, "and I'd do it again in a second, so shoot me."

Josh would have hauled her into his arms and apologized for this mess he created, if not for Peg frowning at him to get lost before Tess noticed that he was eavesdropping.

After that, everything went downhill fast, which brought Josh to this moment with Hank. "Why are you driving me? Where's Tess?"

"She's got stuff to do."

"Sounds important. How long will this stuff take?"

Hank's expression hardened. "Let's just say there's no need for you to wait up for her."

"No need at all," Sammie said as she came into his office.

By ten P.M. Josh started to believe that. He could only imagine what had happened at the Franklin house. It wasn't every day that a father learned that his daughter was romantically involved with a client she had met less than forty-eight hours before and had announced that at a press conference. Of course, Tess surely told her dad that the romance was just pretend, and that she had willingly lied about it to the press.

Josh guessed Freddy Franklin wasn't exactly doing backflips, and had probably explained how she was hurting herself, him, and the business with press that could turn ugly, fast. Could be Tess had finally listened to cold, hard logic, which explained why she wasn't here now; and might not be here tomorrow or any other day, for that matter.

He had to fix this, and not only because he wanted her back in his life. He had to tell her dad that what happened today was his fault, not hers.

After twisting the arm of a phone company exec, Josh finally got Freddy's unlisted number, punched in the first few digits, then hung up.

What if Tess had already gotten the situation under control and was on her way here, now? Getting her father worked up all over again, and at this late hour, wasn't going to help matters.

He should wait to call. If she wasn't back here by one, he would bite the bullet, wake Freddy, and have a man-to-man.

After all, he was still the client—unless Freddy had already torn up the contract.

Don't let him do that, Tess. Come back.

By eleven she still had not.

Josh finally went into his office to lose himself in work. An hour later, he was deep into construction costs for another project, and had just finished calling an overseas client, when the phone rang.

Tess? "Yeah?" he said, answering the call.

There was a momentary pause, before the caller asked, "Is Tess there?"

Josh frowned to the question and that voice. It was male and young, possibly a teenager. "Who is this?"

"Is Tess there?"

Josh's voice hardened. "Who wants to know?"

"I'm a friend of hers."

Was that right? So, how come all of the other people in her life seemed to be hard-assed ex-cops? Given this kid's lightweight voice, he wouldn't have made it as a hall monitor. "That's your name?"

"She knows who I am."

Uh-huh. "I don't. So, you better tell me, buddy, if you want to speak to her."

"So, she does live with you."

Josh pushed out of his chair. "Who is this?"

The boy's voice got smug. "Just tell Tess we're looking forward to seeing her pictures everywhere, even on the Net. She is *so* hot."

"Who are you?"

The kid had already hung up.

Josh sank to his chair. He recalled that man taking pictures at today's press conference. Surely those photos wouldn't be considered hot. So, was the kid talking about the ones the paparazzo took while Josh had been kissing her, or had someone pirated images of Tess walking around in her PJs—or even less—from the dumb security cameras Hank had set up around the pool and possibly in the rest of this place?

Was something like that even possible?

Oh, hell. Josh's heart continued to race as he pulled up Google, keyed in Tess's name and came up with fifteen hits.

He rubbed his temple as he quickly scanned the first, then the next, then the rest.

He lowered his hand. This stuff was press from her police days, not any of that other junk.

After taking a moment to calm down, Josh pulled up the first article and started reading about the act of bravery that had gotten Tess a commendation.

It was nothing, she had said. *Just a domestic dispute. He didn't have a gun.*

According to this report, the guy did have a ten-inch butcher's knife, which in Tess's world was considered little, not a machete. Josh rolled his eyes, then read that the man had used his wife as a hostage to make the cops back off.

Tess hadn't. She talked the guy into letting her be his hostage, even offering him money and safe passage, if he'd just let his wife go.

The man finally did, taking Tess instead, until she worked her magic.

At least, that's the way this article made it sound. They downplayed the fact that Tess had been banged up pretty bad as she wrestled the weapon away from that guy.

Josh shook his head. No way was he going to let her do stuff like that again. Having her pictures in tabloids and on the Net was bad enough. If he had to cuff her to his bed to make certain she was safe and was behaving herself, then he damned well—

The sound of a car approaching, then its headlights bleeding into this room, interrupted his thoughts.

Josh glanced at the time—half past twelve. He turned off the computer and moved through the darkened office to the window.

His Mercedes was pulling up. He hoped it was being driven by Tess, and not being returned by one of her dad's very devoted friends.

An eternity seemed to pass before Tess finally got out of the car.

She didn't look sad, but then, she didn't look like she wanted any company, either; especially his.

Before she came inside, Josh left his office and went up to his bedroom. It was only then that he realized Tess might have returned for her things.

When he heard her come up the stairs, then go to her room and close the door, Josh knew she was staying, at least for a little while longer.

But if things got worse than today?

Uh-uh. He wasn't going to allow that. No matter what it took, he was going to protect her from the paparazzi and everyone else. He was going to keep her here.

It wasn't a matter of choice, anymore, but something that his heart simply demanded.

The following morning, Tess made no mention of the press conference, nor did Josh. Instead, he kept bringing up the work he had done last night while she had been out, then waited for her to say what she had done.

Not a chance.

Tess sensed they had come to a crossroads in all of this, and that Josh might be questioning the wisdom of their contract. Having to fight for it at her father's weekly poker game with Sammie, Hank, and Vic, another retired cop, in attendance was not one of Tess's better memories.

The moment she had walked into the house, Sammie yelled, "Freddy, she's here!"

"Gee, thanks," Tess muttered.

"You got some explaining to do," her father said as he came out of the kitchen.

"Okay," Tess said.

He frowned. "That's it? Okay?"

"Maybe you should tell her what this is about," Sammie said.

"She already knows what this is about," Freddy said, then spoke to Tess. "You actually like that guy enough to lie for him in front of all those reporters?"

"Of course she likes him," Sammie said, then looked surprised when Tess gave her a hard stare. "I don't blame you," Sammie quickly added. "He is very cute. I'd lie for him, too."

Tess moved past them to the kitchen.

Her dad followed with Sammie and Vic bringing up the rear. "Are you gonna answer me or not?" her dad asked. "Do you like this man?"

If she allowed herself, Tess knew she'd be falling in love with Josh, and not getting over it any time soon. Not that she was about to hold a press conference on that. "He's a nice guy, Pop." She dropped her purse on the counter. "It would be hard not to like him. Didn't Sammie tell you what he did for your business? All that free publicity? All these new jobs setting up the security for his other properties? You should be thanking me. You should be thanking him."

"I'd be serving a life term if I thanked him the way I want. No, you listen to me," Freddy said, interrupting her. "After knowing this guy for two minutes, you agree to move in with him? After knowing him for five minutes, you agree to start lying for him at press conferences? What's gonna happen after you know him for ten minutes?"

Tess figured that wasn't something she would ever discuss with her father. "I never said I was a saint, Pop. Besides, telling those reporters that I was his girlfriend was my idea."

"Have you lost your mind?"

Apparently, given the fallout here and from the press. "So now I'm a nun? I can't date men anymore?"

"You just met him! You don't know him!"

"The reporters don't know that and they won't know that. He was in trouble and I just had to help."

"She just had to help," Freddy mumbled, grinding the heel of his hand into his forehead. "If the guy wanted you to rob a bank to help him out, would you do that, too?"

"Better not," Hank said, as he came in the back door, "not with me around."

Tess arched one brow. "Did you get Josh to his house without incident?"

"You see any bloodstains?"

"Hank, did you threaten him?"

"I'm leaving that up to your dad."

Tess cried, "What is the matter with you people? Josh is paying big bucks for this contract." She turned to her father. "I know I should have told you about pretending to be his girlfriend in public, but," she interrupted him, "it just never came up until the press conference. And it's only to help him out with those women who are after him."

"Guy's got a real problem fighting off the babes," Hank said to Vic, bringing him up to speed.

"He is very cute," Sammie added.

Tess swung her head to them both, then turned back to her father. "I'm not giving up this job, Pop, just in case you were thinking of asking. I got it for the company and I'm seeing it through. That's my right."

"What about mine?"

Aw, Papa. "I swear I won't do anything really bad."

"How about moderately bad?" Vic asked.

Tess looked at the man. He was older than the rest, in his

mid-sixties, wrinkled and gray, and wearing dark-rimmed glasses with trifocal lenses.

"We don't do anything bad, period," Tess said. "So all of you, please back off."

Didn't happen.

In the following days, Hank and Sammie always seemed to be around, not that that was entirely necessary as Josh had already severely curtailed any contact with the public and with her.

Tess endured his hands-off approach until she couldn't stand it any longer. She missed the possibility that they might have to kiss or hug to keep the babes away. It was grasping at straws, sure, but it was all that she had. Their private moments were still off-limits, and would be, because of the contract. No way did Tess think she could honor it if their relationship turned sexual, then tanked.

At last, she cornered Josh in his office. "What's up?"

He followed her gaze to his groin. "Huh?"

Tess lifted her gaze. "Why do you keep canceling all of your business functions? No, don't tell me," she said before he could answer, "you're afraid I'm going to hold another press conference, right?"

A smile played at the corners of his sensuous mouth. "I don't blame you for that."

"You didn't thank me for that, either."

Josh came around his desk, but stopped well short of her. "Thanks. I appreciate how you came to my—"

"Did Hank threaten you?" Tess went to him, then paused when he stepped back. "Is that why you're not going to any of these functions and why you keep backing away from me?"

"Hank has nothing to do with this." Josh continued to move around his desk. "You and I just need to cool it."

Tess's heart fell so fast she could barely breathe. Even so, she kept her voice casual, professional. "Sure." She turned to leave his office.

"Tess, wait," Josh said, then quickly added, "I didn't want to have to tell you about this."

About what? Oh, God. Was he seeing someone? Did he hook up with an old girlfriend while Tess had been defending him to her dad and his friends at that weekly poker game? Was he going to use that old girlfriend to run interference for him now, rather than—

"Tess?"

She warned herself not to lose her cool, something she kept forgetting around this man. Well, no more. "Then don't tell me," she said, turning to face him.

Josh's expression changed. "Don't tell you?" He frowned. "I have to. It's for your own good."

Now, she frowned. "My good? I know you're popular, Josh, but bragging about that would be for your benefit, not—"

"What are you talking about?"

Tess wasn't certain anymore. He looked as confused as she felt. "What are you?"

"Keeping your picture and your personal life out of the tabloids and off the Net, what else?"

Tess wasn't about to answer that. He wanted to cool it because he wanted to protect her? Was that sweet, or what? Tess was about to smile, when she considered something else. She looked past him to the dock. "Did you see another paparazzo out—"

"A kid called the night you were out—doing whatever it was you were doing. Anyway," Josh said to her expression, "he asked to speak to you, and somehow in the conversation I confirmed that you're living with me."

Her brows lifted. "Were you bragging?"

"Of course I wasn't bragging. It just came out. And he said you were hot and that your pictures are going to be all over the Net."

Her brows lowered. She frowned. "What pictures are those?"

"I don't know." Josh shoved his fingers through his hair. "Could be ones from the conference. I just hope to God they're not ones from the security cameras." He dropped his hand and went to her. "There aren't any cameras in your bathroom, are there?"

"Are you kidding?"

"Maybe you should wear a robe around the house."

"In this heat?"

"You want your pictures on the Net?"

"I don't care. I was fully dressed at that conference when I was shouting at those reporters. I have nothing to be ashamed of, unless I made an obscene gesture. I didn't, did I?"

"I didn't notice. What about our kiss?"

Tess touched his arm. "Which one?"

Josh looked down at her hand, then curled his fingers around her wrist. "The one the paparazzo took pictures of that first day you were in this office. The one that might be circulated on the Net."

"I was fully clothed then, too. Weren't you?"

Josh gently tightened his fingers around her wrist, then used that to ease her closer. "You're playing with me, again."

Not as much as Tess would have liked, given that Hank and Sammie had just come into the outer office and were looking this way.

Josh swore under his breath and released her wrist.

"We can't avoid them or the public forever," Tess said. "No matter how many kids call and tell you I'm hot."

He looked at her. "Public appearances and displays of affection could make this worse."

Not to Tess's way of thinking. "But that was the plan, to drive all those other women away."

"It doesn't seem to be working. Eight called this morning."

"Then we'll just have to try harder." Tess lowered her gaze to his cock—that lovely bulge was definitely blossoming—then looked back up. "Unless you've changed your mind."

Josh's eyes grew hooded. "You could come with me tonight."

"To protect you?"

"And pretend you're my girlfriend."

God, she was loving this. "Where?"

"Grocery shopping."

Tess's smile paused. She curled her upper lip.

"It won't be so bad," he said.

"It's grocery shopping, Josh."

"With me."

Okay, so Tess was on board and Josh knew it, because he took care of too damned much business before he was finally ready to go.

Tess lifted her head from the desk and forced her eyes to open. "We're going now? It's after midnight."

"It's an all-night market. This way we could avoid the crowds."

They were back to that? "What about vampires? Don't they go shopping in the dark?"

"Hank and Sammie don't."

Josh saw Tess's mind running around that concept, the same as his had earlier. It was so late, the place was so public, they could essentially hide in plain sight, just like a normal couple.

"Come on." Josh took her hand and played with her fingers, pleased that he didn't have to keep his distance any longer. Besides, she was right; those photos from the conference couldn't be bad. "I'll get you something good."

"Oh, yeah? Like what?"

For starters, one of those scooters that really old people used to zip around the store because their legs were bad.

Tess took to that little sucker right away, driving it to the right, the left, forwards, and backwards. She giggled. "Cool. Buy me some candy on the way out and I might just go home with you."

Josh quickly backed up before she ran over his foot, then

looked at an older woman frowning at them. "Kids," he said to her. "Give them a permit to drive and see what happens?"

Tess laughed so hard she was soon hanging over the left side of that thing.

The older woman shook her head and left the aisle.

"Will you behave?" Josh asked in a lowered voice.

Tess's laughter turned to giggles, then a lusty sigh as she stretched. "Sure you want that?"

Not when she was this radiant. Josh was aroused by every inch of her, yet humbled by what he felt. Making her happy after so many awful days meant more to him than closing a zillion dollar deal. So far as he was concerned, from this moment forward he would be making everything right for her. Lifting his hand, Josh gently ran his knuckles down her cheek.

Tess swallowed. Her gaze and voice got soft. "Now I can see why you like shopping."

He smiled. "We haven't done any yet."

"Oh. How bad can it be?"

For him, it was magic, and Josh could see that Tess was feeling it, too. They behaved like teenagers, giggling at the dumbest stuff; then, they acted like an old married couple as they argued about which brand of detergent to get.

By the time they got to the checkout counter, Josh was in a contented haze, while Tess was devouring a package of strawberry licorice. "I want a candy bar, too," she said with a full mouth as she waved her finger at the rack nearest his shoulder.

Josh grabbed the whole box and tossed it on the conveyor belt. "How about gum?"

Tess didn't say.

He looked over his shoulder at her. That piece of licorice was suddenly forgotten and hanging over Tess's bottom lip as she stared at the rack.

Josh followed her gaze, then actually took a step back. A competitor of *Keys Confidential* had run a double photo spread on the cover of this week's edition. To the right was one of those buck naked photos of him, while to the left was a picture of him kissing Tess.

The headline read: *One Long, Hot, Sexy Summer for Keys Developer and Mystery Babe!*

"It's okay," Tess said.

Josh looked at her.

She forced a smile. "I look good, don't you think?"

Josh pressed his forefinger and thumb into the inside corners of his eyes. Of course, she looked good. As far as Josh was concerned, that was one picture he wouldn't soon forget. In it, Tess's face was lifted to his, causing her hair to flow in a thick, shiny mass halfway down her back, which had thankfully been to the paparazzo when this photo had been taken.

Her face hadn't been exposed in this shot. But who knew about the next and the next?

"You want me to talk to your father about this?"

She continued to regard his buck naked photo. "Talk?"

"Okay, apologize."

"For kissing me?"

"Hell, no, and you know it."

Tess met his gaze. Her expression was oddly serene as if she were in denial or shock. "It's okay, Josh. I'll handle my father."

Chapter Eight

"This is how you get us a contract?" Freddy shouted the following morning. "By kissing the clients during the interview?"

Tess remained calm. "Josh is the first."

"What?"

"Was the first," she amended. "He'll also be the last."

"You disappoint me, Teressa."

"Pop, I'm only human."

Her father hardly cared. He told her he was increasing Hank and Sammie's role in this.

"That's hardly necessary."

"It's in the contract," he said. "Your naked guy wants protection? Well, by God, he's going to get it."

After that, Hank and Sammie stuck to her and Josh like superglue. They were just outside the gate now, waiting for Josh as she was, so they could all start the procession to work. The morning was muggy, her heels hurt like hell, and it felt like she was getting a zit on her chin.

"Let's go," Josh said.

Tess looked up as he strode to the car. Gone was the tenderness and carefree delight he had shown her at the market. Now, he waltzed by without a glance.

Well, fine. It gave Tess a chance to look at him.

His finger-combed hair was still damp from his shower, his

cream shirt was unbuttoned at the collar with the sleeves rolled up, while the rest of his attire was also business casual. He tossed a gym bag into the trunk, then got in on the passenger side.

The last time he had been in this much of a hurry was when he had been trying to pull her out of that press conference.

Sinking into her seat, Tess asked, "What's in the gym bag?"

"Stuff."

Okay, be that way. Tess started the car, then looked at his legs. They were bouncing up and down, while his fingers were drumming against his thighs. "You all right?"

Josh looked at her. "Shouldn't we get going?"

"Yes, sir."

His legs really started bouncing.

Tess drove the Mercedes past the gate, then glanced at Hank who pulled out in front of her, then Sammie, who brought up the rear.

They were two miles into the silent, funereal ride, when Josh said, "Hey, look."

Tess glanced at him, then followed his gaze to the cross street they were approaching. Yeah, so? It looked no different than yesterday. She glanced at him, again, then his thumb. He kept jabbing it to the right, below the window, as if he wanted her to make a turn into that street.

She did.

Sammie must have been daydreaming, because when she finally saw that turn, it was too late to follow. The last image Tess had of the woman was her car shooting through the intersection as Sammie looked over her shoulder and frowned.

Josh must have seen it, too, because he turned back in his seat, patted Tess's thigh, then pointed ahead, and gestured for her to take a left.

Why not? This was getting interesting. Tess moistened her

lips and took that left. As she worked the Mercedes into the rest of the traffic, she asked, "Where are we going?"

Josh frowned at her, then looked over his shoulder at what might be following.

"They're ex-cops, not stunt drivers," Tess said. "No way can they catch up with us now, not in this traffic, and," she added to his frown, "the communications device isn't working. Hasn't been since yesterday evening when I accidentally busted it."

Josh's eyes narrowed. "And you were going to tell me that when?"

Tess smiled. "Now, I guess." Her smile faded. "You haven't exactly been easy to live with since those photos came out. Where are we going?"

"You'll see. Just drive."

Tess did, following his directions, until they finally reached the ornate entrance of a private country club that was closed. "What now?"

"We go inside."

"It's closed."

"Only to the rest of the world."

She laughed. "But not to you?"

"Not to us." He fished an access card out of his shirt pocket. "Stick this into that metal box over there. When the gates open just drive on in."

She took the card. "You're a member of this place?"

"Don't need to be."

Tess finally got it. She blurted, "You actually own this place?"

"Someone has to. It'll open in a couple of weeks, but for today, it belongs to you and me."

She looked at the gates, then at him. "You're going to play golf?"

"We're going to play."

Tess regarded her beige suit and heels.

"Unless you don't want to," Josh added.

She looked up. Her heart started to race. "You know there's going to be hell to pay."

Josh's gaze slipped down to the low-cut V of her jacket, the skin that exposed. "How much time do you think we have before Bonnie and Clyde figure out where we are?"

"A couple of hours."

He met her gaze. "And the paparazzi?"

"Maybe a little less."

"Then we should get going."

"Yes, we should."

Tess felt like a kid at Christmas, or one out on parole, as she slipped the access card into the metal box, then eased the Mercedes through those parting gates.

A long, shaded drive flanked by palms and exquisitely manicured bushes greeted her. Beyond that Tess could see towering live oaks and a carpet of grass that was so perfect, it didn't look real.

She swallowed.

"Like it?" Josh asked.

Who wouldn't? She nodded, then continued to drive, passing a group of tennis courts and what seemed to be stables, until they reached the main building that was two stories and of a Spanish design with stark white walls and a red-tiled roof. The arched windows faced a body of water with five strategically placed fountains that were just spraying away.

"Wow."

Josh patted her thigh. "You ain't seen nothing yet."

Tess looked at him. "It gets better?"

His eyes grew hooded, his voice mysterious. "You'll see. Let's go."

Tess was so on board with this, she was out of the car before Josh could even get out of his seat belt.

She lifted her face. Clouds crowded the sky, allowing only momentary glimpses of the sun. When it broke free, those rays glittered on the pond and the fountains, while a lazy breeze sprayed that water even farther, creating mini rainbows.

Tess inhaled deeply and almost moaned, the air was so sweetly scented with the fragrance of flowers and newly cut grass. She might have stayed in this spot forever if not for the sound of Josh closing the trunk.

Lowering her face, Tess saw that he was holding that gym bag in one hand, while offering her the other.

It was an invitation she readily accepted, lacing her fingers through his. If they had no more than this moment, Tess knew she would have been grateful, then greedy, because she would want still more.

"Ready?" Josh asked, his voice still mysterious.

Her heart skipped a beat, then continued to race. "For what?"

"You'll see. Come on."

Hand-in-hand they walked across the parking lot to the building. The tapping of her heels mingled with the sound of Josh's footfalls, breaking the exquisite silence. It was only then that Tess believed they were truly alone.

Once inside, her gaze swept this expansive area that reminded her of a hotel lobby in one of those old Hollywood movies. There were casually arranged leather sofas, chairs, low tables, lovely lamps, lush plants, and expensive rugs. The only thing missing were the rooms.

If they had been here, too, Tess wasn't certain she could have honored her ground rules. She wanted Josh as she had never wanted another man. She needed him on top of her, inside her, filling a need that grew with each passing day.

As he led her to the right, Tess willingly followed, looking down as her heels clacked against Mexican pavers, then up to an area where the country club staff would answer questions from its guests.

Passing that, Josh turned into a hall that opened up into a pro shop. At last, he released her hand.

Tess made a face at that, but only because he couldn't see. He had already moved to a counter and was now pulling a pale green Polo shirt and a pair of beige khakis from that bag.

"Here you go." He tossed her the bag.

Tess caught it easily and looked inside.

"Those all right? he asked.

She lifted her white sleeveless top and white cotton shorts from the bag, then looked around them to him. "When did you get these?"

"Pulled them out of the dryer while you were outside waiting for me. I didn't think you'd mind."

She didn't. She looked back down. "Did you pack my running shoes, too?"

"I thought you'd play in your heels."

Tess kept her head lowered, but did lift her gaze.

"Not going to work for you, huh?" Josh asked, then inclined his head to the right. "Your dressing room's over there."

Tess looked from it to him.

"Go on," he said. "We don't have all day."

That was true. Hugging the bag to her chest, Tess went to her dressing room as Josh went to his, then changed into her shorts and top. Once her heels were in the bag, she padded out of the room.

Josh was already leaning against one of the counters, arms crossed over his broad chest, obviously waiting for her.

As her gaze trickled down him, his did the same to her. "You still armed?" he asked.

"Always."

His nostrils flared. "Bring your cuffs, too?"

Tess looked at him from beneath her lashes. "Wouldn't leave home without them."

"In that case, I better be careful."

Tess figured it was the other way around as Josh pushed away from that counter and came to her. The man was turning her heart inside out and driving away every bit of resistance as he slid his hand down her forearm, before working his fingers through hers.

She moistened her lips and looked up. "What now?"

"You'll see."

Tess followed his lead until they reached the area with shoes. "Go on," he said. "Sit."

"Shouldn't I pick out a pair first?"

"That's my job."

Tess sank into one of the chairs.

"Okay, then." Josh rocked on his heels as his gaze prowled all over her, then finally settled on her chest. "What are your measurements?"

Tess crossed her legs, then swung her right foot in the direction of his groin. "Shouldn't you be asking for my shoe size?"

"Not if you hurt me."

Uh-huh. "I wear a size eight. And that's all the information you're getting."

"It'll do for now." He went to the shoes, then picked out a really ugly black-and-white pair.

"Don't you have anything else?" she asked.

Josh looked over his shoulder at her. "We still have your heels."

No wonder only old people played golf. Tess gestured for those black-and-white suckers. "Bring 'em here."

Josh did, but instead of giving them to her, he went to one knee and ran his fingers up her left calf to the back of her knee.

Tess felt that clear to the top of her head. Her breath caught. She arched her back.

Josh scolded, "Now, keep still."

Was he kidding? It felt like a lifetime before Tess was able to catch her breath and speak. "You like your women tame, huh?"

His answer was to run his fingers over the back of her knee.

Tess sagged into the chair. Her head was thrown back, her eyes were closed, and she was breathing hard.

"Only at the right time," he said.

Tess licked her lips. She didn't have the strength for anything else as Josh continued to stroke the back of her knee and calf until she couldn't stand it any longer. She actually moaned.

That only encouraged him.

As Josh's stroking grew lazy and prolonged, it was all Tess could do not to slide out of this chair and onto his lap, straddling his lean hips so she could grind her buttocks into his rigid shaft and tightened balls.

She was actually whimpering when he finally slipped the right shoe on her foot.

"How's that?" he murmured.

Tess cleared her throat. "How's what?"

"The shoe."

"It's ugly."

He laughed. "That's not what I was asking."

No? Tess inhaled deeply as Josh anchored her foot against his flat belly, then tied the laces.

She felt the solid strength of his body and each breath that he took. She imagined her hands—and surely her mouth—being in that location.

She saw her tongue circling his navel, then moving lower to that thick, dark hair above his shaft. She imagined pressing her face against his stiffened cock, adoring it with her tongue, before she guided it to her opening so that he could plunge inside, stretching her, filling her.

"So, it fits?" he asked.

"Oh, yeah," she said. "It'd be perfect."

"What?"

Tess's heart continued to race, then started to slow as she finally understood his question. With great effort, she lifted her head, opened her eyes, and looked at him.

Josh's expression was thoughtful, his right brow arched.

Tess cleared her throat and tried to be casual. "It's perfect."

Josh didn't comment. He didn't have to. Her eyes were still glazed with the same longing that he felt.

It'd be perfect, she had said.

Call him crazy, but Josh knew she hadn't been talking about any damned shoe.

With his gaze still on her, he eased her right foot down, then lifted her left and ran his fingers over her long, slender toes.

Tess giggled and squirmed.

"Uh-uh," he said, holding her calf as he continued to stroke. "You need to keep still."

Tess breathed so hard her delicate nostrils flared. "Yes, sir."

Josh smiled to her crisp cop voice that was completely at odds with that soft surrender.

Her head was already lolling on her shoulders as her eyes fluttered closed; her chest lifted and fell with her now lazy breathing as he traced her toes with his fingers, stroking each, before lowering his head and kissing the tips.

She whimpered, then moaned.

Josh closed his eyes, savoring those sounds that would be only the first of many, when the time was right. He had to keep reminding himself of that before he got too damned excited. This was Tess's day. He would show her a good time, erasing all the bad, to prepare her for the wonderful moments to come.

Josh kissed her toes again, then her arch.

When she was, at last, breathless and weak, he slipped on the other shoe and tied the laces. Pushing to his feet, Josh bent forward at the waist, planted his hands on the arms of her chair, and murmured, "Ready to play?"

Tess's eyes fluttered open. He was so close she felt his male heat and was surrounded by his clean scent. As her gaze traveled his face, Tess saw a small scar near the edge of his right brow that she hadn't noticed before. She liked that scar . . . she loved him. It was foolish, of course. Even this moment hadn't changed their reality. This was just a job. Jobs never lasted forever. They always came to an end.

But for today, Tess decided she would dream. Today she would hope. "Yes, sir."

The corners of Josh's eyes crinkled with his pleased smile. After he straightened, he offered his hand, then pulled Tess to her feet and into himself.

Because this was a day of dreaming and hope, Tess softened even more, and was quickly rewarded as Josh pressed his mouth to her neck.

She fisted her fingers into his shirt, needing it as an anchor. She buried her face in his shoulder so that she wouldn't cry out as he left a trail of kisses on her neck, her cheek, her ear.

It was only then that Tess heard tapping sounds in the hall. Someone was here? Someone was coming closer?

"Do you hear that?" she whispered, then moaned as Josh wiggled his tongue in her ear.

"Hear what?" he whispered, while Tess was still trying to catch her breath.

"Those tapping sounds," she said, then swallowed. "Listen."

He did, then pulled her right back into himself. "It's just a worker. He won't bother us."

That was the God's honest truth. Tess heard those footfalls coming to a sudden stop as the guy neared this room, then the sound of that person beating a hasty retreat.

Tess stroked the bottom button on Josh's shirt. "I thought we were going to be alone."

He pressed his lips to her temple, then murmured, "There'll be even less of them outside on the course. Want to go there?"

"Okay."

He whispered in her ear, "Aren't we tame?"

"Only at the right time."

She proved it, too, a short time later, when they were outside.

As Josh stood with his arms crossed against his chest, Tess drove one of the carts around him in smaller and smaller circles as she shouted, "I'm driving—I'm here to protect you, remember?"

Josh looked over his shoulder at her as he shouted, "But who's here to protect you?"

Laughing, Tess zipped that cart past him, turned, then came right back, stopping at his side. She lowered her gaze to his fly and asked, "You coming?"

If she kept looking at him like that, he might. Already his cock and balls ached with frustrated need.

"You're asking for it," Josh said as he got in on the passenger side.

"That's okay." She leaned close and murmured, "I can protect myself."

Before Josh could comment on that, Tess took off down the course. After a moment, she looked to the right, the left, then finally at him. "Where to?"

He gave her an easy smile. "Away from the trees would be nice."

Tess followed his gaze, then made a sharp left to avoid the trees. "You need some clearly marked lanes here."

"You've never played golf before, have you?"

"I've never been to a country club before, not even on a police call." She looked at him. "My thing is dancing, remember?"

That wasn't something Josh was likely to forget. The thought of her succulent body moving in time to the music and into him had fueled many a fantasy that Josh had every intention of seeing come true. "Yes, I remember. Go over there."

Tess looked to where he was pointing, a broad expanse of green flanked by trees on the right and a pond on the left.

She stopped the cart and viewed the lush surroundings. "What now?"

"We tee off."

She leaned back in her seat and regarded him.

"What?"

"You like doing this, huh?" she asked.

He did now, with her. "Everybody conducts business this way. It's the law."

"Yeah, I know. But why?"

Josh shrugged. "All that swinging, swearing, and sweating wears them down before the negotiations?"

"Maybe I should have tried that with Alan."

"You didn't have to. He was a goner the moment you threatened him with slander." Josh got out on his side, came around to hers, and took her hand. "Come on."

Tess's fingers played with his. "Yes, sir."

After he handed her a driver, then took his own, they went to the tee. "Okay, here's what you do," Josh said, then explained how to make that first shot.

Tess pulled her wind-whipped hair away from her face as she listened intently and nodded frequently.

"That's all there is to it," he said. "You want to try?"

"You go first."

Josh did, making an excellent shot. "That's all there is to it," he repeated, looking over his shoulder at her.

Tess's gaze was on his ass.

Josh cleared his throat.

She ignored that as her gaze lingered on his ass, then moved to his back, and finally his shoulders, before she lifted her gaze to his. "What?"

Josh suppressed a smile and pointed to where his ball had landed. "That's what you need to do."

Her brows lifted. "I need to look at that ball?"

He laughed. "You need to hit the ball so that it lands where mine did."

Tess turned to him. "Not farther?"

His laughter paused.

"So," she said, "that's all I have to do?"

"You might want to also keep your ball out of the pond." He pointed. "And the trees." He swung his arm in that direction. "And if you don't hit me with it, that'd be great."

Tess's gaze dropped to his groin as she gently swung that driver back and forth. "I'll try my best."

Josh stepped back.

Tess winked. "Relax. I'm just playing with you."

Before Josh could respond, she rested the head of her golf club on the ground, took up the same basic stance that he had, and got ready to swing.

"Ah, Tess?"

She paused and looked over her shoulder at him. "Yeah?"

"Don't you want to play with one of my balls?"

Her gaze dipped to his fly, her cheeks turned a bright pink, and her shoulders started to shake with suppressed laughter.

"You know what I mean," he said.

She let out a low, throaty laugh.

Josh rolled his eyes. "Maybe you should just take a few practice strokes, first."

She pressed her face into her shoulder and continued to laugh.

"The pros do it all the time!" he said.

She bent forward at the waist, one hand on her knee, she was laughing so hard.

"I give up," Josh said, then put a ball on a tee. "Go on, hit it."

Tess nodded, but continued to laugh.

"If you can," he added.

Her laughter slowed, then stopped. She straightened and looked at him.

She wasn't so smug now, though she did look amazing. Her eyes sparkled, her cheeks were flushed, and her hair was mussed. If Josh hadn't known better, he would have thought she just finished having some great sex.

Of course, she also looked challenged by his comment.

"Oh, I can," she said, then got into position, lifted the club, swung, and actually hit the ball.

As it arched in the air, then came back down, Tess squealed and swung that club above her head as if it were a lasso.

Josh hunkered down, protecting his head with his arms. "Tess!"

She looked over her shoulder at him, then up at that swinging club. Bringing it back down, she said, "Sorry."

Josh straightened. "It's okay."

She turned to him. "What do you mean it's okay? That was a great shot. This is *so* easy."

Easy? "Okay," he said, "let's see if you can do that again."

"Let's see if you can. We'll make it the best two out of three."

Josh laughed. "That's not how we play."

"You wouldn't be making up the rules as you go along, would you?"

"Not any more than you're making up the ground rules for when we're alone, right?"

Tess regarded him, then put out her hand. "Give me one of your balls."

Josh grinned. "Sure you really want that?"

Her chest flushed. "I'm a big girl. I think I can handle it."

Josh had no doubt about that, which made him crave her all the more. As he kept his gaze on her, he pulled a golf ball out of his pocket and tossed it.

Tess easily caught the ball, then turned her back to him as she bent at the waist to put it on the tee.

Josh's gaze dropped to the backs of her seamless thighs. A wave of desire so quickly hit him, he was briefly dizzy. His voice sounded far away as he said, "Now, be gentle."

Tess's shoulders trembled briefly with suppressed laughter. Shaking it off, she straightened, got into position, swung hard, and completely missed the ball.

"Not that gentle," Josh said.

She looked at him.

He smiled.

Tess arched one brow, turned back to the ball and swung at it again, then again, and again, but kept missing. At last, she swore in Spanish.

"Now, now," Josh said, trying hard not to laugh. "Is that any way for you to behave?"

Tess studied the club as if there was something wrong with it. "This is a stupid game."

"Not if you do it right."

Her voice got downright frosty. "I did exactly what you did."

"The first time. But during the next fifteen times? I don't think so." He moved behind her. "Lower the club."

Tess looked over her shoulder at him and murmured, "I'm here to protect you, Josh, not beat you up. If I wanted to floor you, all I'd have to do is use my hands."

Not to mention her mouth and the rest of her body. "Good to know. Now, lower the club to the ground, to the right of the tee so I can show you how this is done."

Men. Always having to show off. Not that Tess really minded. This could get interesting.

And quickly did as Josh placed his hands on her biceps.

His touch was unexpected and so damned gentle, Tess let the top of that club fall to the ground.

"Good girl," he murmured.

Her mouth went dry when his hands lingered, hugging her flesh as if he was in absolutely no rush.

"Now, pay attention," he said.

She nodded.

Josh waited a moment, as if to be certain he had her full

attention. Only then did he run his fingers down her arms until he reached her hands, which he then covered with his own.

Tess lowered her head to that. Her breathing picked up, and then her heart raced as Josh eased into her, his stiffened shaft pressing against the seam of her buttocks until there was absolutely no doubt about his arousal.

She swallowed, then lifted her head as Josh rested his chin on her shoulder and turned his face to hers.

"You with me so far?" he asked.

Her gaze slid to his. She nodded.

"Good. Now, here's what you do." Moving his powerful body into hers and with hers, Josh lifted the club off the ground and completed the swing.

Tess heard the ball being whacked, but had no idea where it had gone. Her eyes were already closed, her lips parting as Josh's chest pressed into her back with each deep breath.

"Want to do it again?" he asked.

"Maybe we should."

His voice sounded pleased. "Whatever you want."

What Tess wanted would have been against the law if they had engaged in it out here. Even so, there was no denying the moment as they practiced the swing again and again, until she was dizzier than hell and Josh finally murmured, "Think you have it?"

"I don't know if I'll ever have it."

He laughed, then unexpectedly eased away. "Go on, swing."

Yeah, right. She was having enough trouble just standing and catching her breath. Frowning, Tess looked down at the ball and swung the club just like Josh showed her, but still missed.

"I did that right," she quickly said.

"Looked good to me."

Tess glanced over her shoulder to see that his gaze was on

her butt, the backs of her thighs, her calves, her back, then her butt again.

She rolled her eyes, repeated the swing, then growled, "I did that right."

Josh nodded. No way was he going to complain. Each time she swung at that ball and missed, her supple, toned flesh tightened or quivered.

He might have watched her forever if not for the first drop of rain that hit his cheek.

As Josh looked up, another drop smacked his nose.

"Dammit," Tess said, swinging again.

"Easy," Josh said, "it's an itty bitty ball, not an ax murderer."

Tess paused, glared over her shoulder at him, then cursed the ball and continued swinging.

At any other time, Josh would've just let her duke it out with that ball, but not today. Already those two drops had turned into a steady drizzle.

Tess hardly noticed as she studied the ball, then the club, then tried swinging it again, and again, and—

"Tess," Josh said as it started to pour, "that's enough, let's go."

She continued swinging.

"Tess!"

"It's only rain. There's no lightning or thunder. This happens all the time."

"Yeah, I know, but we're getting soaked."

"So? It'll be over in no time. Just give me a few more minutes."

"You've got one second," he said, then went to her, grabbed the club, tossed it to the side and said, "Time's up. We're going. Now."

Her head swung to that club, then snapped back to him as Josh leaned down and threw her over his shoulder.

"Hey!"

"Quiet," he warned, then headed for an oak with a wide

canopy of leaves. By the time Josh got them under it and put Tess on her feet, they were both drenched and breathing hard.

She arched one brow. "Quiet?"

"That's what I said." He crowded her with his body until she had to step back. "You're through arguing with me. Now be nice."

Her gaze dropped to his mouth, then lifted to his eyes. In that moment, the world surrounding them grew very quiet, even the pounding rain sounded muffled, far away. The damp air was cooler now and perfumed with the pungent smell of earth.

Her flesh was scented with female need as she moved into him, wreathing her arms around his neck, kissing him, while driving her fingers through his damp hair to keep him from lifting his head.

Josh had no intention of doing that or ending this savage kiss. Tess's need seemed endless, as greedy as his, as she drove her tongue more deeply into his mouth and ground her hips against his, giving his body a taste of pleasure.

Josh wanted more.

Holding her to him with one arm, his free hand covered her right breast, then worked that flesh.

Tess pulled her mouth from his so that she could kiss his throat, his jaw, his cheek, before Josh captured her mouth, thrusting his tongue inside, then deepened the kiss even more.

It was a moment to dream, to hope, to—

"Tessie!"

Her thoughts paused to that faint, aged voice, while her mind tried to understand how that voice could be here, now.

"Tessie!"

This time, Josh heard that faint cry. He pulled his mouth from hers and backed away.

"Oh, hell," Tess muttered.

Josh looked at her, then back at a really old guy with white hair, dark-rimmed glasses, and a huge umbrella he was using to protect himself from the shower as he slogged across the course to this tree.

"Tessie!" the man called again, then waved.

"Let me guess," Josh said, "that's Bonnie and Clyde's dad?"

Tess pressed her fingers to her forehead. "Nope. That's Vic Lopez. Another devoted friend of my father."

Chapter Nine

On the way to the office Tess drove, while Vic rode shotgun, and Josh got to sit in the back.

Like a little kid he pressed his face against the window, watching the rain, as Vic lectured Tess on good police procedure.

"Your client should never be in the front seat," Vic said. "You're making him a target. You put him in the back. That way, if anything happens, he can sink to the floor and be out of sight, while you take care of business."

Josh frowned. As if he would actually allow Tess to put herself into danger to save his sorry ass? Biting back a comment, Josh looked over his shoulder and met Tess's gaze in the rearview mirror. Her brows lifted.

Vic adjusted his trifocals. "You listening to this, Tessie?"

Her brows lowered. She returned her gaze to the road. "Yes, Vic."

"Good. Now in a case like this, the one we have right now, if anything was to happen, I could put down my seat and shield the boy with my body to protect him."

Josh turned back to his window as he tried to imagine that, but just could not. Each time his mind saw Vic scrambling over the seat to drape that aged body over his, that nightmare evaporated into something far more pleasant. The sweet scent of Tess's breath before he had captured her mouth, then the heated fragrance of her skin. The weight of her breast, its aching softness in the palm of his hand. The way her right leg had wrapped around his so that he had no chance of escape. The way her—

"What was that?" Vic asked.

Josh's head snapped away from the window to the old guy, then to Tess.

Her gaze remained on the road. "Josh was just sighing. Right, Josh?"

He hoped that's all he had done. "Uh-huh."

"We boring you with our shop talk?" Vic asked.

"No, sir."

Vic leaned into his door, then looked over his shoulder and past the headrest at Josh.

He could see the traffic behind them reflected in those thick lenses. "Really," he said, "I enjoy police talk." To prove that, he threw in a smile.

Vic regarded him for a moment more, then turned to Tess. "Now, here's what you need to do in the future."

As she endured that lecture, Josh stared at the scenery passing by, barely listening, until Vic said, "I thought we told you all of this at the last game."

Last game? What game? Josh worked his mind around the events of these past weeks and knew that Tess hadn't been out of his presence long enough to go to any game, unless it was after that press conference.

He leaned forward in his seat. "Did you just say game?"

Vic swiped his handkerchief across his nose, then looked over his shoulder at Josh. "That's right. Me, her dad, Hank, and Sammie all play poker every week, except last week when we couldn't all make it. Tessie always sees to the food—at least since her mom's been gone—don't you, Tessie?"

She sighed. "Yup."

"Tessie cooks?" Josh asked.

She shot him a look in the rearview mirror for the nickname and the comment, then gave Vic a hard stare.

The old guy finally stopped laughing. "Let's just say Tessie tries her best."

"Really." Josh spoke to her. "And you actually go grocery shopping for that food? You've been holding out on me."

Vic muttered, "Not from what I saw on that golf course."

Tess looked from Josh to Vic, then decided to play it safe and keep her gaze on the road.

Josh sank back in his seat and very nearly smiled, because the mystery was solved. While he had stayed home, alone, that night worrying about her, she had simply been at a poker game with her dad and all of his very devoted friends.

Friends Josh really wanted to get off his ass and hers so that what happened today at the golf course wouldn't be repeated.

Josh knew he could simply ask them to back off, but figured they'd just give him some cop double-talk. Demanding that they leave him alone was probably what Freddy wanted most. The man could then say he was running this show or they weren't doing it at all, then tear up the contract.

But what if the unthinkable happened? What if they got to know him and started to trust and like him, especially Freddy?

Even that guy had to have a soft spot, other than the one he reserved for Tessie. And Josh thought he just might know the way to reach the guy's heart, give him something to think about, something to do, other than making life miserable for him, of course. Suppressing another smile, he asked, "Hey, Vic, at these weekly games of yours, you play for cash?"

The man turned around as far as he could in his seat. "No, we play for passes to Disney World." He made a face that gave him a dozen more wrinkles. "Hell, yes, we play for cash. Why? You gonna call a cop?"

Tess mumbled, "I think Josh is kind of tired of cops."

"I'd like in on the game," he said.

Tess looked over her shoulder at him, then back to the traffic when someone honked.

I'd like in on the game?

Okay, that blindsided her. "You're kidding, right?"

"Never been more serious in my life," Josh said to her, then spoke to Vic. "You guys looking for some serious action?"

Tess growled, "They're retired."

"Retired," Vic admitted, "but not dead." He looked from her to Josh. "What do you have in mind?"

"Depends on whether you guys play like girls or like men."

Tess stopped at a light that was only yellow and endured the honking of the car behind her as she turned in her seat and glared at Josh.

He was oblivious. So was Vic.

"Five card draw is for little girls?" the old guy asked. "Five card stud is what nuns play?"

"I wouldn't know," Josh said. "I don't play with nuns. Look, if you guys can't keep up, then maybe I'm wasting my—"

"Hold it right there," Vic growled. "You think you know it all? Well, let's see if you do. Impress me."

"Fine." Josh leaned up in his seat. "You ever play variations like DogButt and Monkey Love?"

Vic didn't miss a beat. "I've heard of them. They don't interest me."

"Really?" Josh arched one brow as if he just couldn't believe it. "How about Don Juan?"

Vic snorted. "I thought that was your game. Looks like you've been trying it a lot with our Tessie."

Oh, hell. She lowered her head and breathed hard.

Josh wasn't even fazed. "Trying, maybe, but hardly succeeding. Nobody gets anything past Tessie. Now you and the other guys? I think you're gonna be real easy."

Tess tightened her fingers around the steering wheel as Vic said, "Oh, yeah? Well, prove it."

During the following minutes, Josh did, talking about poker games Tess was certain Vic had never heard of. She sure as hell hadn't. Of course, she never participated in those weekly games. She just tried her best at cooking stuff for those goons to eat, then listened to them moan about it as they played regular poker. Nothing like Josh was talking about now. There was Pick a Partner, Caribbean Stud, Omaha Hold'Em, Golf, and Howdy Doody.

As he ticked off the rules of each, Tess was certain he was making that stuff up.

By the time he got to the particulars of a game called Bloody Sevens and one known as The Good, the Bad, and the Ugly, Tess was ready to drive the Mercedes into the ocean.

Vic, on the other hand, was actually warming up. "That one sounds interesting. We ought'a try it."

"No way," Tess said. "You know Pop likes his poker clean and neat, none of this fancy stuff."

"It's not fancy," Josh corrected, his voice patient as all get-out. "It's challenging. That's what guys need. Of course, there's even a game you might like."

"Oh, yeah?" Vic said before she could. "Tessie doesn't like to play. She usually just walks behind us, looking at our cards, with her face giving away our hands."

"I do not do that," she muttered.

"If you play with us, you won't get a chance," Josh said.

Play with us? Already he was a part of the group, inviting her inside? "What'd you have in mind?"

"Let me tell Vic first."

Tess came to another stop—at a red light this time—then looked in disbelief as Josh whispered to Vic, with that guy quickly laughing.

"Don't tell her," Vic said. "She'll kill you."

"In that case," Tess said, "you should definitely tell me."

Josh gave her a patient smile. "No need to get upset. Remember, you are driving."

Not to mention tightening her jaw. "You going to tell me or not?"

"It's no big deal," Josh said. "The game's simply a variation of stud poker. High and low hands split the pot. You have a showdown after a round of betting." He shrugged. "I could go on, but you have to be playing it to really know what I'm talking about."

"Tell her what it's called," Vic said, then snickered.

"Oh, I don't know," Josh said. "Maybe I really shouldn't tell—"

Tess interrupted, "What's it called?"

"The Price Is Right."

So? "I don't get it," she said.

"No kidding," Vic said. "In poker circles it's known as Grocery Shopping. You don't get that, either."

The old guy howled and so did Josh.

As those two goons had a good laugh at her expense, Tess pulled away from the light.

When the laughter finally died down, Josh asked Vic, "Think I should apologize to her?"

"Don't know if it'd do any good. When Tessie gets mad, there ain't much you can do about—"

"I am still in this car," Tess said. "I am still driving it. So, if you want to arrive safely, you better wait to discuss me after we get to where we are going."

"See?" Vic said to Josh.

Tess rolled her eyes and got real. "Josh, you're not going to that game. I won't allow it."

"I'll ask Freddy," Vic said to Josh. "I'm sure he'll say it's all—"

"This isn't a good idea!" she cried.

"Why not?" Josh asked. "You're supposed to be protecting me, which means we should be in the same place at the same time, not me in my house, while you're at your dad's, during those weekly poker games. Actually, I think it's perfect."

Vic looked at Tess. "He's got a point, hon."

He's got a screw loose. Why was he doing this? Tess

looked at his reflection in the rearview mirror. "You really want to play poker with my father and all of his friends?"

"I'm looking forward to it," Josh said to her, then spoke to Vic. "Next game, Tessie and I will be there."

Uh-uh. No damned way. Not if she had anything to do about it.

Once they returned to the office, Tess was determined to get Josh alone to ask him why in the hell he was doing this. She was fully prepared to listen patiently, then no matter what he said, shake some sense into him, threaten him with her weapon if need be, or kiss him senseless so he'd see things her way.

She never got the chance.

Suddenly, Josh was a *very* busy man.

He spent what remained of the morning, then the rest of the day, on the phone or in meetings, which he must have suddenly called, since he hadn't planned on being at work at all today.

The only time Tess saw him was when he was with Peg, or Alan, or a staff member.

The only time Josh actually spoke to her was when another female fan slipped past all the security, because she was posing as a postal worker. Unfortunately, she wasn't delivering any mail, only herself.

Once Tess was finished escorting the young woman off the premises, did she get Josh's gratitude? Did she get so much as a smile?

Hell, no.

When she returned to his office to tell him the matter had been resolved, Josh was already with yet another staff member, this one a young guy who eyed Tess as if he had seen her tabloid picture.

Before Tess could think to give the guy one of her nasty cop stares, Josh said, "You should really pay better attention to these matters so what happened just now, with that young woman, won't happen again."

Right. Tess wanted to slug him. Since she couldn't, she decided to wait until she got him alone that night.

Didn't happen.

At eleven P.M. Josh was still in a business meeting and Hank told Tess to go back to the estate, that he would see Josh safely home.

"Give him hell," she muttered, then gave up on seeing him alone that night.

The following day was no better. They were never alone; he was always busy, and definitely avoiding her.

Well, fine. Tess decided to take matters into her own hands. She called her dad.

"Hey, Pop," she said when he answered the call, then got straight to the point. "Vic talk to you about Josh yet?"

"You mean naked guy?"

Exactly. Before his love fest with Vic in the car, where those two goons had bonded, Tess would have vigorously defended Josh, calling him by his given name, or referring to him as the client, or even Mr. Wyatt. No more.

"Yup, that's who I mean."

"Yeah, Vic mentioned him. Why? Do I need to wear a disguise to the grocery store again this week? You two got more photos coming out on—"

"Nope. That probably won't happen again," Tess said.

"Probably?"

Well, yeah. No way could she be more specific than that. Who knew what photos had been taken of her and Josh before he decided to ignore and avoid her.

"I'm just trying to tell you that I'm behaving myself."

"About time."

Tess hesitated a moment, then asked, "Don't you want to know if Josh is behaving himself?"

"Sure. That's why I get those daily reports from Hank, Sammie, and Vic."

Right. "Then you do know he wants to come to the

weekly poker game." Tess forced a laugh. "I told him he was crazy; that you'd never allow—"

Freddy cut in. "What are you talking about? I can't wait till naked guy is here. I'm really looking forward to meeting him, in the flesh, so to speak."

Tess covered her eyes with her hand. It was going to be a bloodbath. "Pop, please," she said, using all the sincerity she could muster. "Just let it go. Tell him he can't come. I swear, I'll behave myself."

"Until I find out you haven't, right?"

He knew her too well. Tess figured she needed to be far more careful in her romantic adventures with Josh—if and when they happened again—not to mention more persuasive with her father.

Despite all of her pleas, she didn't come close to changing his mind. He wanted to be in the same room with naked guy.

That left only one thing, sweating it out until the night of the game, and enduring Josh's new attitude toward her. One of a boss to an employee.

The day before the game, he suddenly announced, in Peg's presence, that he was going to a business luncheon and that Tess was to accompany him.

She glanced at her watch. It was already eleven-thirty and she had already devoured two candy bars as an early lunch. "When are we leaving?"

"Now."

Tess met his gaze. "Thanks for giving me so much time to prepare."

Josh ran his gaze down her full length, lingering on her heels, before he looked up. "Your shoes look fine. Not as cute as the ones where your toes show, but not ugly by a long shot."

Tess gave him a sweet smile. "Maybe that's because we're not going to play golf. Or are we?"

"As long as we avoid a press conference I'll be happy."

Before Tess could respond, Josh said, "Let's go," and led the way to the car, where Alan was waiting.

The moment the attorney saw her, he smiled. "Hey, Tess."

"You're going, too?" she asked.

His smile wilted to her tone. "Yeah. That's okay, right?"

"It's fine," Josh said, before Tess could answer. "Peg's going, too."

She is? Tess looked over her shoulder, surprised that the woman had been following them.

"Let's go," Josh said. He got in the backseat with Alan, while Peg got in on the passenger side.

During the drive to the hotel, Josh and Alan discussed an upcoming contract, while Tess tried to figure out how Josh had gone from unrestrained passion to treating her like a neglected wife in two seconds flat.

She glanced at Peg who was pulling a bottle of perfume from her beaded purse. "So, you looking forward to this?" Tess asked.

Peg spritzed her right wrist with that perfume, then rubbed it against her left wrist before looking up. "You mean the game?"

"Huh?"

"Oh," Peg said, her eyes widening as she finally got it. "You mean this luncheon?"

Right now, Tess wanted to return to what the woman had said about the game. "What game are you talking about?"

"Peg," Josh suddenly said, "did you bring those stats on Trent Howard?"

"You bet." Peg pulled them out of her briefcase and handed them over to Josh.

"This all of them?" he asked.

"Let's check," Peg said, then ticked off every single solitary page.

The moment that exchange was finally finished, Tess asked, "What did you mean when you said *the game*?"

Peg gave her a blank stare. "I'm sorry, I'm not following."

Like hell. Josh had obviously discussed the game with her. Could be he had even bragged to her about going to the game where he was going to do . . . what? Win against her father and all the other old guys and take their money? Then what? Give them a new security contract so they could earn back the money he had won from them?

This was nuts. Tess glared at his reflection in the rearview mirror.

He ignored her.

Once they got to the luncheon it wasn't much better. There were more than two hundred businesspeople in attendance and Josh seemed to know them all. There were handshakes, smiles, slaps on the back, and his always generic, "This is Tess Franklin," after which he moved quickly to the next person before the last could ask any hard questions.

Like did he enjoy their kiss that that tabloid had captured? And did he thank her for defending him at the press conference? And did he love her and have plans to build a life with her?

Josh seemed to want no part of that mess, and neither did she.

At last, Tess sat alone at the table. Peg had already gone to the ladies' room to fix some loose beading on her blouse, while Alan and Josh were still working the crowd.

Let 'em. Tess told herself she wasn't going to give Josh so much as a glance, and didn't, until she heard young female laughter that sounded both pleased and aroused.

Turning in her chair, Tess scanned the crowd and immediately saw Josh. In that moment, she recalled what she had told him that first night at his estate—that he was impossible to find.

What are you talking about? he had asked. *I'm big as life.*

He was impressive enough to stand out among hundreds of other people. He was simply beautiful in his Sunday best—a pearl gray suit, pale blue shirt, and a striped blue-and-gray tie.

Despite his male beauty, that female laughter hadn't been for him. Josh and Alan were speaking to an older man, but the women were still watching.

Tess saw those wistful gazes and interested smiles. She had to wonder if it had always been this way for him with women, with those tabloid pictures only making it worse.

She had to wonder if it would always be this way for him with women, then called herself a fool. Didn't matter how many women chased Josh after the contract was over. He was a big boy, and what he did with his life once she was out of it was up to him.

The time for dreaming, the time for hope, was long gone. It had ended on that soggy golf course.

Suppressing a sigh, Tess turned back in her chair to see two younger men lifting their water glasses to her in a kind of toast.

When the one to the left winked, she frowned. When the one to the right, grinned, Tess averted her gaze, figuring they had seen her tabloid photo, because she sure as hell didn't look all that great today.

"Keeping busy?"

Tess looked up as Josh suddenly pulled back his chair and sat.

"Just fighting off the guys," she said.

Alan sank into his chair. He looked worried. "Men are after Josh now, too?"

"I think Tess is referring to herself," Josh mumbled, then draped his napkin across his lap. "Because of that photo, right?"

She slid her gaze to him. "Couldn't be because I look so hot today, right?"

Alan cleared his throat and looked like he wanted to run.

Josh, on the other hand, started talking business with Peg, who had just returned to the table. He kept it up, too, throughout the meal, right to the speaker's presentation.

As that guy just went on and on about all the people who

kept the Florida Keys afloat, Tess studied Josh's broad shoulders, his firm jaw, the way his hair curled around his ears, and finally that female server who came to his side.

Tess arched one brow as that young woman bent at the waist, leaned really close to him, and murmured, "Hi, can I get you—"

Tess interrupted, "No, you can't."

The young woman's gaze jumped to her. So did the gazes of everyone else at the table, while Peg and Alan exchanged a glance.

Well, screw that. Tess returned their stares, then looked at Josh.

His eyes were widened in surprise. Well, screw that, too. He was the one who wanted her here. He was the one who insisted that she make certain no fake postal workers tried to deliver themselves to him. Who knew what this server was willing to offer? If he didn't want to find out, then he'd just have to accept her protection, and not only as a bodyguard.

Tess leveled her gaze on the server, then wiggled her finger between herself and Josh. "He and I are together."

The young woman frowned.

"If you don't believe it," Tess said, "just look at one of those supermarket tabloids."

"Do you want another drink or not?" the server asked Josh.

"No, thanks."

The server hurried away, shaking her head.

Josh looked at Tess.

She looked right back.

He hesitated a moment, then leaned toward her and whispered, "You okay?"

Would she be acting so stupid if she were?

She whispered, "I was just about to ask you the same thing, for the last several days, in fact, but you haven't given me a chance, now have you?"

Josh mumbled, "Maybe I should get that drink."

"You better be really tanked when you show up at that poker game."

His gaze lifted to hers. He smiled. "That's not until tomorrow night."

"Keep grinning like that and you might not live until then."

He leaned close again, and whispered, "I like it when you're mean."

Tess was not going to smile. It was too late now for him to be flirting with her. He should have thought of that when he started to treat her like an employee.

Leaning back in her chair, Tess behaved like the bodyguard she was supposed to be and regarded the other women in this room. These ladies—unlike the fake postal worker, and Libby, and that other girl who had shown up half-naked at Josh's gate—were legitimate. They had something to offer him.

More than a few probably wanted him. Hell, Tess wanted him, but she wasn't going to get him, especially after he played poker with her dad. *Is he seriously nuts?* Her father was going to grill him like he was a suspect in a gangland murder; then, when Josh was limp and sweaty and babbling "I'm sorry, man, I'm sorry!" her dad was going to toss him to Bonnie and Clyde and Vic to finish him off.

After which her father would probably fire her from this job, and then she wouldn't have an excuse to stare at Josh at boring functions like this.

Tess thought about that clear to the time this thing was finally over.

As everyone else jumped out of their seats like they were ready to conquer the world, Tess sighed.

Josh helped her with the chair. "Tired?"

More like depressed. "Couldn't be better."

"Really? You look like maybe your gun's a little too heavy."

Three people near them turned around to look at Josh.

Tess lifted her brows as if to say she had no idea what he was talking about, then leaned into him and whispered, "So now I'm through being just your girlfriend in public? Now you want me to also be your bodyguard? Should I rough up anyone?"

"Just me."

"Don't tempt me."

He seemed genuinely surprised by her snotty tone. "Believe me, I'm just trying to behave myself."

Aren't we all? Tess straightened before his heat and scent made her forget her latest good intentions. "You should'a thought of that before you started swimming in your birthday suit."

At just that moment, Alan strolled up.

Tess looked at him.

He edged back. "Trouble in paradise?"

"Don't you worry," Peg said, joining them, "Josh has everything under control."

He gave her a look.

"Oh, sorry," she said. "I won't say another word."

"About what?" Tess asked.

"Let's go." Josh took her arm.

Tess looked down. It was the first time in forever that Josh had actually touched her, and it felt so right, so comforting her knees went briefly weak.

Girl, you are such a fool.

The man had ignored her since their morning at the golf course, and she was ready to forget all of that with one simple touch?

Maybe.

What is the matter with you?

Tess had never let a guy treat her bad, not even the first ones she hung out with in junior high.

She had never chased a guy, either. If she liked someone and he didn't return the favor, Tess just figured to hell with it.

She admired the honesty of her parent's marriage, the fact

that they were so goofy with need that the rest of the world didn't matter.

She wanted that for herself. She wanted that with Josh.

Glancing at him, Tess was surprised they had reached the elevator. She went in first, followed by Josh, who quickly turned to the others. "Take the next one down," he said to Alan and Peg.

As the doors closed on those two, Josh looked at the buttons for the floors. He pressed the one for the lobby, but the moment the elevator started its descent, he hit the stop button.

Okay, that wasn't something Tess had expected. She lifted her gaze from that button.

Josh turned to her.

In that moment, Tess didn't stop to think of the consequences; she didn't even consider her hurt pride. All that mattered was that she was alone in here with him.

Moving across the small space, Tess wreathed her arms around Josh's neck and kissed him with all the passion and love that she felt. She couldn't help herself. She didn't want to help herself. She missed him more than she would have believed possible, and wasn't about to let him go until he was breathless.

Several minutes later, they both were.

At last, Tess pulled back and tried to catch her breath. "Thanks."

"You're welcome." Josh pulled her right back into himself, and didn't hold back, nor did he come up for air.

He kissed her as if he meant it, as if he had missed her even more than Tess had missed him, because there was yearning in this kiss, a lingering tenderness that hadn't been there before.

Of course, bad boy that he was, Josh soon went back to savage and wild, but Tess didn't mind. She stayed with him from beginning to end.

Even when they were both finally breathless, Tess just

couldn't keep away. Resting her head on his shoulder, she ran her fingertip over his ear, tickling him.

Josh's chest quivered with his quiet laughter.

"I like it when you're bad," Tess said.

"Oh, yeah?"

She was about to nod, but didn't get the chance as Josh backed her into the wall, then cupped her buttocks, pulling her up until Tess was straddling him. He held her to himself with one arm around her waist, as his other hand cupped her breast, fondling it, while he kissed her until she had no resistance left.

Only then, did he allow her a moment's peace.

"Oh, yeah," she said, then sighed.

"Oh, yeah, what?"

"I like it when you're bad."

Josh grinned, then kissed her neck until she moaned. Satisfied, he eased Tess to her feet, then whispered in her ear. "You're sure?"

"About what?"

"That you want me to be bad."

Tess released all of her weight into him. "You bet."

"Then you're going to love it when we're at that poker game."

"I can't wait—what?" Tess lifted her head, then pushed him away. "What do you mean?"

"Don't you worry." He followed her to the other side of the elevator, and when he had her cornered, Josh held her chin between his thumb and forefinger. "I've got everything under control."

"Are you seriously nuts?" Tess slapped his hand away from her chin. "You don't have anything under control. First, you make up that junk about those poker games and then—"

"Nope, that's not true," he interrupted. "Learned some of it from Grandpa, the rest from my friends in construction. It's totally real and legit."

"Who cares?" Tess said. "If you haven't yet noticed, we're kissing in an elevator."

He smiled. "Oh, I've noticed."

Tess lowered her head and breathed hard. "If you haven't yet noticed, we *have* to kiss in elevators, because if we kiss out there," she flung out her arm, "a bunch of psychos are ready to take our picture or every retired cop in the Keys is ready to ride posse for my dad." She lifted her head. "Hank and Sammie and Vic are probably calling the building people right now about you hijacking this elevator."

"Let them. It won't stop me. Only you can do that."

He was putting it on her, again. Tess closed her eyes, too tired to fight. She rested the back of her head against the shiny metal wall, then trembled as Josh first kissed the base of her throat, then worked those kisses lower as he unbuttoned her blouse. At last, he lingered on the swell of her breasts just above the cups of her bra.

She sighed. "Better hurry before the firemen break us out of here."

"Believe me, that won't happen."

No? Tess inhaled deeply as Josh eased the right cup below her nipple. That small nub tightened quickly to the cool air and his forefinger as he gently circled it.

Tess bit back a moan, then paused, because she just understood what he said. "The firemen won't break us out of here because you own this elevator—that is, because you own this hotel?"

"Had to buy it to get the elevator. We can stay in here as long as you want."

Oh. *Ahhhh*. She moaned as Josh rolled her nipple between his thumb and forefinger even as he suckled her neck.

Tess was a goner, except for one thing.

They couldn't stay in here as long as she wanted, because that would be forever, and that wasn't something Josh was giving to her.

"Wait a minute," she said.

Josh didn't. He continued suckling her neck, then the swell of her breast.

"Josh. Stop."

He finally did, but kept his head lowered and breathed hard as if he was frustrated.

And she wasn't?

"Why?" he asked.

Because this wasn't going to last forever, that's why. No way was Tess going to have sex with him in this elevator or at his house, not while they had the contract. It would make things too damned hard.

Not that she could tell him that.

"Why are you going to that poker game?"

He lifted his head and looked at her. "You want to talk about that now?"

It was either that or the brutal truth about not having sex with him until the contract ended—or maybe not even then if things got too damned complicated. "Yeah. So, why?"

Josh straightened, then shrugged. "If you can't beat 'em, Tessie, then you just gotta join 'em."

"Uh-uh—hold it," she said, then literally kept him at arm's length when he tried to kiss her again.

Josh's gaze slipped down to her hand on his chest. Her forefinger was stroking his tie. He smiled.

Tess stopped stroking. Her mind continued to work around what he had just said.

If you can't beat 'em, Tessie, then you just gotta join 'em?

How twisted was that? So were they now going to spend all of their free time with her father and his friends, because Josh figured there was no other way around it?

Tess could see it now—their evenings filled with lively discussions about who had the baddest aches and pains and all that bitching about how young cops could run a computer, but could they get down and dirty with a perp—hell, no.

She pulled back her hand, pressing the heel of it against her forehead.

"Trust me," Josh said.

Despite all of her worries, Tess did. It was the countless women who would always be after him that Tess didn't trust. No man, not even a saint, could resist temptation forever.

And even one slip from Josh, one minor indiscretion, would kill the love she felt for him. Better not to get involved in that sorry mess.

"Tess?"

She dropped her hand and shook her head.

"You don't trust me?" He sounded genuinely hurt.

Oh, hell. Tess cradled the side of his face in her hand, gently running her thumb over his smooth cheek. "You I trust. Now, your judgment?" She muttered an oath in Spanish.

"I heard that," he growled, then pulled her back into himself and silenced her surprised gasp with his mouth and tongue.

Tess pulled her mouth free. "Josh."

He had just pressed his lips to her cheek. "You want me to stop, again?"

Yes. No. Maybe. Tess placed her hands on either side of his head, lifting it until he had to look at her and she could look at him.

"What?" he asked.

"Forget it," she said, and kissed him fast and hard, slipping her tongue inside.

He moaned, returning her kiss as he eased her blouse off her right shoulder. Pulling his mouth free, Josh kissed her shoulder, her biceps, the swell of her right breast, and was about to suckle her nipple when the emergency phone rang.

Josh's head snapped up. "What was that?"

Tess looked past him to the still-ringing phone.

He looked over his shoulder at it, then back at her. "Want to just let it ring?"

"There's going to be hell to pay."

"How much time do you think we have?"

"Two minutes. Maybe three."

"Right." He lowered his head to her breast and gently flicked his tongue over her nipple.

Tess moaned.

At just that moment, Sammie's voice suddenly filled the small space, "Tessie! You okay?"

Josh's head snapped up again. He lifted his gaze to the ceiling as if he expected Sammie to be up there.

Since she wasn't, he looked back down and whispered. "Are you wearing a walkie-talkie?"

"No. Of course not. Her voice is coming from the emergency speaker. It's right below the phone. We can hear her, but she can't hear us."

"You're sure about that?"

"Relatively."

"Then you better start moaning in Spanish."

Tess laughed so hard she sagged into him, then whimpered as Josh ran his hand down her back.

"Tessie!" Sammie shouted, "Hank's gonna call your dad—Freddy'll know what to do if something's wrong, if you're not all—"

"I'm fine," Tess said. In one second flat, she had pushed Josh out of the way, went to the emergency phone, and was still holding the receiver to her ear as she tried not to sound too breathless.

Not that Josh was helping. He had regained his balance and was now pushing her into the wall, his hands on her breasts.

Tess lowered the receiver to her left shoulder. She moaned.

"Tessie?" Sammie shouted. After a brief pause, her voice was fainter, as if she was talking to someone on her side. "I hear moaning."

Josh's hands dropped away from Tess's breasts. He whispered, "Fuck."

Tess pressed the receiver into her shoulder so Sammie couldn't hear. "You behave," she whispered to him, "unless you want to leave here in traction." Sidling away, Tess turned her back to Josh, and spoke into the receiver. "Sammie, hi, it's me, I'm fine. Josh had to take an important business call, very private, so I stopped the elevator." Tess looked over her shoulder at him.

His hair was still a mess and the right tail of his shirt was pulled out of his trousers.

Tess pointed. "Put it back in."

"What?" Sammie asked.

Crud. "Josh is still on the phone," Tess said to the woman, keeping her voice very low, as if she were afraid to disturb him. "He's still talking to that important client, so I can't talk right now."

"We don't want you to talk, hon. We want you to come down."

"Josh is finishing up right now. Be right there. Bye."

Tess hung up the phone and made certain the speaker was no longer on, then started buttoning her blouse as she backed away from Josh.

"Come here," he said, giving her a sexy smile.

After that call he still wanted to play? "I'm warning you," Tess said, "stay where you are. Remember, I'm armed."

His eyes grew hooded. "Yeah, I know, I finally felt your weapon."

"I felt yours, too, but," she said, continuing despite his quick laughter, "we gotta get this show on the road. We don't have a choice, not if you still want to go to that game tomorrow night."

That got him to stop chasing her around the elevator. "Okay."

Okay? Getting his cooperation was that easy? All she had to do was threaten to take away his poker night with a bunch of old ex-cops? "What are you planning to do?"

Josh hit the elevator button to get the little box moving. As it started its descent, he tucked in his shirt and ran his fingers through his hair.

"Just trust me," he said.

Chapter Ten

What choice did she have but to trust him?

There was no stopping that dumb game, unless a business emergency came up.

None did, though Josh did spend a lot of the next day in the conference room with a guy Tess had never seen before. He was probably in his mid-twenties and looked more like a gigolo than a client.

What he and Josh were doing was a mystery, because each time Tess tried to find out, Peg escorted her away from the area, guarding that room as if Josh's life depended upon it.

Maybe he was brushing up on his poker skills. Maybe he and that guy were devising new games. Who knew? Not only was Peg keeping Tess in the dark, but ever since the paparazzi problem, that area, and most of the others, now had blinds.

Still, Tess strolled outside hoping to sneak a peek into that room, just like the young woman who was currently bent forward at the waist, butt in the air, with her hands cupped around her eyes as she tried to see past those tightly drawn blinds.

Tess regarded the girl's snug pink capris and even snugger top. And what about those three-inch heels? Tess figured Josh would have loved those if he could have seen them. Suddenly, she was grateful for those blinds.

"You look busy," Tess said to the young woman, just as she had to Libby that first day at the estate.

This girl wasn't as snotty. Without so much as a backwards glance, she took off in those spike heels, not once losing her balance.

"That was easy," Tess mumbled to herself, knowing that tonight certainly wouldn't be.

It was decided that Josh would be driven to the game by Vic, since they had planned this stupid event, and since Tess needed to arrive first to prepare the food that everyone would bitch about.

"Is that really necessary?" Peg asked.

Tess didn't think it was, but then she knew Peg wasn't talking about that bitching. She leveled her gaze on the older woman. "What do you mean?"

When Peg didn't answer, Tess next glared at Sammie and Hank, who were also in the reception area. Had they already said something nasty about her cooking?

Sammie wasn't fessing up, while Hank was too busy eating a candy bar to talk. Once he had swallowed his bite, he glanced at the wall clock. "Better leave now," he said. "That way if your stuff doesn't come out, we'll still have time to order a pizza or something."

"Is that really necessary?" Peg asked again.

Tess swung her head back to the woman. "What do you mean?"

"Maybe Josh would know," Peg mumbled.

"Know what?" Tess asked.

Peg looked at her and smiled. "Nothing, hon, just trying to participate in the conversation."

By being cryptic and insulting her? Tess shoved her purse under her arm and went to Hank. "If you don't like my food, you don't have to come."

"I wouldn't miss this for the world," he said.

"Me, either," Sammie said.

On that happy note, Tess left the office. Tonight was going to be brutal.

The truth of that was in the way her father came out to the Mercedes even though Tess had parked it down the street, rather than in the front of the house.

"You're not coming in?" he asked.

Tess was still thinking about it. "Sure."

"When?" he next asked. "You've been sitting out here for five minutes."

No kidding? It seemed longer. "Just checking to see if I've been followed."

He quickly straightened; his head swiveled on his shoulders as he searched the narrow street. "By who?"

Babes, paparazzi, needy clients, young guys who looked like gigolos—anyone who might stop the coming events.

"Just kidding," Tess said, then hauled her ass and the groceries inside.

When her father looked inside the bags he had been carrying, he made a face. "Oh, shit."

Ignoring that, Tess started to unpack her bag.

"Teressa," he said, "we need to talk."

"Sorry, Pop, but I'm not going to stop making the no-fat dogs. You and the others don't need grease clogging your arteries and giving you high blood pressure. Once the other stuff's on them, you won't notice the diff—"

"Are you in love with Wyatt?"

Tess so quickly turned to her father, she dropped the can of sodium-free sauerkraut, then watched it roll across the floor into the utility room.

When she started to follow, Freddy blocked her. "Leave it."

"Can't," she said, trying to get around him. "That stuff's expensive. I'm not going to waste my money or yours by letting it go to—"

"Teressa, I'm serious, are you in love with Wyatt?"

She looked from where that can had stopped to her father.

No way could she get past his bulk, that expression, or his question.

Of course, she was in love with Josh. Wasn't it obvious? Hell, everyone but Josh seemed to know it or want confirmation of it. "I can take care of myself."

"To hell with that, you're a woman."

Tess stepped back. She frowned. "Excuse me?"

"I didn't mean that in a bad way and you know it."

"I don't think I do."

"You're changing the subject," he said.

"About my being incapable of taking care of myself, because I'm a woman?"

"No, about me worrying myself into a stroke, because you're my little girl."

Oh, Papa. "I know I'll always be your little girl, and I know you worry, but if you stick to a no-fat, no-salt diet you won't get a stroke, I swear."

He didn't appreciate her levity. "Just tell me one thing and I'll leave you alone."

Tess didn't want to tell him anything, not if it concerned Josh, but knew she had no choice. "Sure. What?"

"Tell me that even if you've fallen for that guy you're not going to do anything that will break your heart."

"Okay."

Freddy lowered his head. "Oh, my God, you are."

He made it sound as if she had a terminal disease. Of course, loving a man who didn't feel the same, a man who only wanted to sleep with her was pretty damned terminal. Not that Tess wanted to give her father any more stuff to worry about. "I'm no fool, Pop, okay? The last time I believed in a happy ending with Prince Charming was when you and Mama got me that Cinderella tape when I was five."

He lifted his head. "What's that supposed to mean?"

"I know there's not a chance in a billion of having a future with Josh. He's very rich and great-looking and—"

"What is *that* supposed to mean? Are you saying you're

not good enough for him? That bum would be lucky if you let him get down on his knees each and every day of his life so that he could kiss your feet!"

Tess wondered if she should tell her father about that morning at the golf course when Josh did just that.

What a sweet moment that had been. How very hopeful. She smiled.

"Glad to see you agree," Freddy said. "Glad to see you want that from a man."

She wanted it from Josh. Not that she was about to admit that to him or her dad. "I'm a realist, Pop, and so is Josh. He's in his world and I'm in mine—we're not about to forget that."

"And what is that supposed to mean? Did he say you're not good enough for—"

"He hasn't said anything, Pop, except to praise your company and to get you new jobs, which you should thank him for when he gets here."

He swore in Spanish, just as her mother used to do.

Tess rolled her eyes. "Pop, I know what you're saying."

His face turned a bright pink.

"No need to apologize," she said. "I am a big girl."

"You're my little girl and jobs or no jobs you shouldn't be staying at his place. I ought'a cancel the contract, I ought'a—"

"What you ought to do is calm down," she quickly said in a lowered voice. Someone had just come in the front door, and Tess was afraid it might be Josh. "Please. And no more talk about canceling the contract. That's your future—it's my future since I work for you. So be nice, okay?"

He growled, "I'll do my best."

Josh Wyatt, you are a dead man.

"Yo, Freddy, you here?" Hank called out.

"Of course, he's here," Sammie said. "He lives here."

A very dead man. Tess mumbled, "Wait till he gets stuck in this small space with Bonnie and Clyde."

Freddy looked at her. "What?"

Tess shook her head. "Nothing." Planting her hands on his shoulders, she turned him around, then gently pushed him toward the living room. "Go on, greet your guests."

Freddy stopped in the doorway and looked over his shoulder at her. "Them, I will. Him, I'll—"

"Pop."

"Let me finish," he said. "I might be busy eating when he comes in. I might be in the can. I might be—"

"I don't care if you're on Mars. You'll go to wherever he is, shake his hand and thank him for the contract and everything else he's done for your business. Please."

Freddy shook his head as if he couldn't believe what she was asking, then left the room.

Hank immediately greeted him with, "Hey, Freddy, where's loverboy?"

"Hopefully buying some clothes."

On that happy note, Tess went to the refrigerator and rested her forehead against it.

"He is cute," Sammie said.

"Not cute enough or good enough for my daughter."

Sammie quickly agreed. "No way."

"He's okay for a regular girl," Hank said. "You know, like the one who used to work in records."

"Wanda," Sammie offered.

Tess rolled her forehead against that cool surface. No matter how many years had passed, each time this group got together they always talked about Wanda, who was probably in her sixties by now, but in her day had made a lot of cops rock hard.

"Wonder what Wanda's doing now?" Hank asked.

"Wonder who she's doing now?" Sammie asked.

They all laughed.

At just that moment, the doorbell rang.

"Vic forget how to open a door?" Hank asked.

"Probably can't get to it," Freddy said, "not if he's got naked guy in a choke hold."

Tess pushed away from the refrigerator thinking if Vic were foolish enough to do that, Josh could just flick the old guy off like a pesky mosquito. Unless, of course, Vic pulled out his gun.

Tess got into the modest living room just as Hank opened the door.

"Well, hi, there; do I have the right house?" Peg asked.

Tess's gaze zipped over the woman. As always, Peg was dressed in beaded vintage wear that sparkled wildly, only this wasn't what she had been wearing at the office. Tonight's outfit was a low-cut coral blouse and silky pants that matched the color of her hair.

"Oh, Tess, hi," Peg said. "I am at the right place. Good."

Tess exchanged a glance with Sammie, who also seemed surprised, then looked at her dad. The poor man must have been getting dizzy, his eyeballs were zipping up and down Peg so much.

Tess finally lifted her hand in greeting. "Peg." She frowned. "What are you doing here?"

"Looks like she brought us some supplies," Sammie said, then broke with all formality. "I'll take that." She grabbed the twelve-pack of beer Peg had in one hand and the plate of munchies she had in the other.

Tess arched one brow and thought back to when she and the others had been discussing the crappy food she would be making tonight.

Is that really necessary? Peg kept asking.

Apparently not.

"There's more in my car," Peg offered.

"Sammie'll get it," Hank said as he continued setting up the poker table.

Freddy nodded in agreement as he remained rooted to the spot, staring at Peg.

"Wow, it is hot tonight, isn't it?" she asked, delicately touching her neck with a lacy, vintage handkerchief.

Freddy slowly nodded, his gaze following the ends of that handkerchief as it fluttered above Peg's low-cut top.

When she spritzed herself with perfume, Tess rolled her eyes. There might as well have been drugs in that perfume or the aroma of a thick sirloin, given the goofy expression on her father's face. "Pop."

He looked at her, then right back to Peg.

Tess was about to frown because of how foolish he was behaving, when she told herself to lighten up. It had been a long time since her dad had looked this interested in a woman; too damned long.

The man deserved some happiness. Josh probably thought so, too, since having Peg come here, in that outfit, had certainly been his idea. "Pop, you haven't met—"

"Fred Franklin," he said before Tess could finish, then went to Peg and offered his hand. "Mrs. . . . "

"Mulrooney," Peg offered, "but it's Miss, and has been Miss going on six years now." She slipped her bejeweled hand into his and smiled. "But since I like you, I'm going to let you call me Peg."

He grinned. "In that case, you can call me Freddy."

"Give me your number and I'll call whenever you like."

They both laughed.

Uh-huh. Although Tess wanted her father to be happy, she didn't want to have to watch it.

She had just turned to go back to the kitchen, when her father asked, "So, how do you know my little Tessie?"

Tess looked over her shoulder at Peg. The woman's gaze was briefly on her, before she easily said, "I work for Josh."

Tess turned around, waiting for the fallout.

To her surprise, her father actually seemed intrigued, rather than pissed. "So, you're protecting him from the babes, too?"

Peg nodded. "I also take care of the guys, if they get to be a problem."

Freddy's smile faded. "Guys are after him now?"

"Of course not," Tess said, before this got completely out

of hand. "Peg's not talking about the kind of protection we're providing; she's his executive secretary. She makes his appointments, takes care of his schedule, and keeps people out of his office when he doesn't have time to see them."

"That's right," she said to Freddy. "Did you think I was a bodyguard, too?"

He shrugged as if embarrassed. "You sure don't look like a secretary."

She gave him a sexy smile. "You sure look like a cop."

"Ex-cop," Hank said, as he continued setting up the table.

Freddy looked from him back to Peg. "That guy good to you?"

Her smile faded. "What guy?"

Here it comes. Tess wondered what Peg would do when her father called Josh the naked guy or the bum. Given how tight those two were, Tess figured Peg would come to Josh's defense, and her father was definitely not going to like that.

At last, he said, "Your employer."

Tess arched one brow.

Her father ignored that as he continued to speak to Peg. "He good to you?"

"He better be." She winked.

They were both laughing, again.

"Will you look at this?" Sammie asked as she came back inside holding several trays. "We got enough here to last clear through to tomorrow."

"Oh, goodie," Tess mumbled.

"Any of it look normal?" Hank asked. "It's not that diet crap that Tessie makes, is it?"

She turned completely around so she could glare at him.

"Nope," Sammie said. "This is the real deal."

"Josh only prepares the best," Peg said.

Freddy looked surprised. "You mean he made all that? He can actually cook?"

"Boy's a whiz in the kitchen," Hank said.

Sammie nodded. "Makes a mean breakfast."

Freddy's eyes continued to widen, then quickly narrowed as he looked at Tess. "Why didn't you tell me that?"

"Why should I? Did you want him to make you breakfast, too?"

"Quit changing the subject. Why didn't you tell me the boy likes to cook and likes to do stuff in the kitchen?"

"Ah, Freddy," Peg said, before Tess could answer, "Josh cooks, sure, but he is just a regular guy. Real regular. Believe me, he likes the ladies. Don't you, Josh?"

Tess's heart caught, her belly fluttered as she looked over her shoulder and saw him in the front doorway.

He was such a tall man, he made this already-cramped house appear far too snug.

And yet, he seemed to fit here as much as she did. Gone was his business attire. Instead, he wore battered jeans, mocs, and a black T-shirt that hugged his powerful chest.

He was also blushing badly. Even the tips of his ears were pink as he stared at Peg.

"He does like women," she answered for him, before she spoke to Freddy. "I've even met some of his old girlfriends. Haven't I, Josh?"

He wasn't about to answer that question, either.

Why was Peg taking this moment to convince everyone of his sexual preference, especially Freddy? The man should have already known where Josh's mind, heart, and body were, given that tabloid picture of him kissing Tess. Of course, maybe that's why Freddy wanted to be convinced otherwise.

Josh wasn't about to help him out on that one as he looked past Peg and finally saw Tess.

The screen door made a loud whack as Josh came inside. His gaze swept Tess's thick, dark hair, that soft gaze, those plush lips. They were slightly parted, the same as his as he continued to regard her with wonder. Since leaving the office Tess had changed into cutoffs and a gray T-shirt that bore the emblem of her old police force. Her feet were bare; she was curling her toes.

Josh liked that. He sensed she would do that when he was finally within her, his cock giving pleasure.

His gaze lifted. "Hi."

Tess moistened her lips. "Hi."

"Yeah, hi from me, too," Freddy said, then moved in front of Josh, blocking his view of Tess. "I'm Fred Franklin, Teressa's father."

Teressa? Josh liked that, too, but kept his face expressionless as he met the man's gaze. Thank God Tess looked like her mother. Freddy's face was nothing but hard angles interrupted by that nasty scar on his chin.

"Sir," Josh said, offering his hand, "Josh Wyatt. Nice to finally meet you."

Freddy looked down at Josh's offered hand, then over his shoulder at Tess.

She narrowed her eyes.

Freddy rolled his, turned back to Josh, then finally took his hand and squeezed, just like Sammie and Hank had. "Likewise, I guess. You don't look so bad with clothes on. You should plan on doing that all the time."

Tess lowered her head, while Sammie and Peg snickered.

Josh shot Peg a look. He didn't ask her here to be a part of the problem. "Yes, sir," he said to Freddy, then finally squeezed back, showing this man his strength, that he was no pushover, that he couldn't be scared away from Tess.

Freddy's eyes narrowed. "About kissing my daughter."

"Pop!"

He ignored her and squeezed even harder. "I'm not supposed to mention that even though it made the cover of those tabloids. I'm supposed to thank you for the contract."

Josh put even more strength into his grip. "No need."

"That's what I told my daughter."

Tess finally joined them. She looked from those squeezing fingers to Josh. "Why don't you help me in the kitchen?"

"Too late for that," Hank said. "Even if he recooks what you made, he ain't gonna be able to make it taste good."

Josh laughed.

Tess frowned at him, and then her dad who was also laughing.

"Unless you two intend to start dating, you can let go now." She smacked their joined hands, then took Josh's. "Help me in the kitchen."

They hadn't taken two steps towards the room when Vic asked, "Hey, Freddy, you want me to go in there, too, and keep an eye on them?"

Josh stopped; he looked over his shoulder at Freddy. The man immediately stopped rubbing his squeezed hand and spoke to Vic. "You made Tessie frown again."

Josh looked at her. She ignored him as she continued to glare at her father.

"Now, Tessie," Vic said, "you know that's the way cops are. They stick together. They protect their own."

"So, is that where you got that mean scar on your chin?" Peg asked Freddy. "During your cop days when you were protecting one of your friends?"

Tess spoke before he could. "Actually, he tripped over one of my toys when I was three and banged his chin on the kitchen counter. Mama had to revive him after he passed out. Right, Pop?"

He gave her a hard stare, then actually smiled at Josh. "So, I hear you can cook."

They were back to that? "You bet," Josh said, facing the man, even though Tess was trying her best to pull him into the kitchen. "Just a sec," he said to her, before he looked back at Freddy. "Learned it when I was in construction and between jobs. Had to; I like to eat."

"You are a big guy," Sammie said.

He gave her a wink.

Freddy crossed his arms over his chest. "You worked in construction, huh?"

"Yes, sir." He moved closer.

Tess growled, "Josh."

He looked at her, then back at her father. "One of the first houses I worked on was a lot like this one."

"You really screw that one up?" Hank asked. "Is that why they chased you out of construction?"

"He wasn't chased out of anything," Tess said. "He left on his own to do real estate development, but he still keeps his hand in construction. You should see what he's doing to his own house."

"Yeah, we should," Freddy said, "before we read about it in a tabloid."

Josh gave Tess a look that said, *Really walked into that one, didn't you?*

A blush stained her chest and throat. She spoke to her father. "He's restoring it to the way it looked in the eighteen-hundreds when the first guy who owned it brought his bride there for their wedding night."

Huh? "Where'd you hear that?" Josh asked.

Tess looked at him, then seemed to realize what she had just said. "Read it on the Internet."

"While you were looking for more photos from those tabloids?" Freddy asked.

Tess lowered her head and shook it.

Time to change the subject. "So, your house was built by the Sanger Company?" Josh asked.

"Maybe." Freddy shifted his weight. "That the company you used to work for?"

"No, sir. But their work is similar to this."

"So, how much damage did you do to that house that looked like mine?"

Josh grinned. "Not much. That sucker's still standing—made it through the ninety-eight hurricane."

"No shit," Freddy said, then quickly blushed and looked at Peg. "Sorry."

"Not a problem, hon. I'm no Girl Scout."

He smiled. "Believe me, I'd be a Girl Scout if they had members like you."

Peg laughed.

Josh held back a sigh as those two continued to flirt. Although that's what he had hoped for when he thought to invite Peg here, he still had a lot to do to make Freddy like him. He spoke to Tess. "I saw construction material to the side of this house as Vic and I pulled up. Someone thinking about doing a few repairs?"

"That would be me," Freddy said.

"For over a year now," Tess said.

He shot her a look. "I got a life."

"Exactly," Peg said to him, then spoke to Tess. "Those repairs can wait if your dad's dating some—"

Freddy interrupted, "I'm not dating anyone."

Peg pressed that dainty handkerchief to her neck. "No?"

Josh held back another sigh as they started flirting again. He needed to get the man back on track and the best way to do that was to focus on Tess. "So," he said to her, "what's your dad thinking of repairing?"

"Like she would know?" Freddy asked.

Tess made a face. "Excuse me?"

The man seemed to have no clue why she was pissed. "Well, do you?"

Of course, she didn't. But that hardly excused his rude behavior to her and Josh. "He was only asking me, because you refuse to tell him." Tess spoke to Josh. "Could be that Pop just doesn't know what he's going to repair."

"The hell I don't." He left Peg's side and went to Josh. "I'm gonna upgrade the kitchen and the bath and do some repairs on the roof, if that's any of your business."

"It's not, though I would like to know where you got your materials."

"Why? They're not good enough for you?"

Tess frowned.

Josh took it in his stride. "I think you might have paid too much if you bought them at Taylor's."

Freddy looked surprised. "Their prices are high? That's not what I heard."

"Then you heard wrong. You want rock bottom prices, you go to Robard's."

"Where's that?"

"I'll give you the address before I leave. You need anything there, you ask for Tommy Bell and tell him Josh Wyatt sent you. He'll pull down those prices faster than if you used your gun."

"Oh, yeah? Think old Tommy can get me a cheap hot tub?"

"What?" Tess asked. "You're going to put in a hot tub now?"

Freddy's gaze slid her. "I might." He looked at Josh. "So, can he?"

"Let me know when you want it and I'll have it delivered. What else do you need?"

Freddy told him. Josh nodded to some of that junk, but shook his head at others, telling her father that he should use another type of bolt or nut or something.

As the two of them got into an animated discussion about studs that Tess found boring as hell Peg pulled her aside.

"What?" Tess asked.

Peg leaned close, keeping her voice low. "I just wanted you to know, I think your dad's very nice."

"He can be when he wants to." She shrugged. "He's ruder than usual tonight, but that's only because Josh is here."

"Forget Josh," Peg said, her expression serious. "Your dad's a nice man. And I'm nice, too, really. So, don't you worry."

Oh, Peg. She touched the woman's arm. "Josh trusts you and so do I."

"Then you don't mind if we maybe have dinner sometime—me and your dad?"

"Not at all." Tess wished they'd do that right now as she

noticed Josh and her dad leaving this room. "Hey," she called out, "where you two going?"

Josh spoke over his shoulder as he followed her dad down the hall. "We're going to see where the hot tub should go."

Tess didn't believe it for a minute. She was afraid the moment her father got Josh outside, he was going to lay down the law and tell him that if he so much as touched her again he was a dead man.

"I'll go, too," she said.

To her surprise, it was Josh, not her father, who stopped dead and frowned. "You'll just get in the way," he said.

"Yeah," her father said, "you stay here."

"I'll make sure she does," Vic said.

Tess swung her head to him, then looked back to her father and Josh as they turned the corner, disappearing from view. Damn.

"Where you going?" Vic asked.

Tess stopped at the hallway entrance. "The bathroom, all right?"

"Fine with me. But I expect to hear water running."

God. As he, Hank, Sammie, and Peg went to the poker table to enjoy the munchies Josh had made, Tess went into the bathroom and sat on the edge of the tub worrying about tonight and the future.

Ten minutes passed before Vic apparently remembered her and shouted down the hall. "You okay, Tessie?"

She rolled her eyes, splashed cold water on her face, dried off, and came out. "Fine." She moved past him to the kitchen, then stopped to Josh lying on the floor, looking at something under the sink, which her father was trying to illuminate with a flashlight.

"No," Freddy said, "it's over to the left. You see it now?"

"No—uh—wait—move the light a little more to your left," Josh said, "yeah, that's right, got it."

Tess lifted her gaze from his fly. "Got what?"

Freddy looked at her. "Never mind. You wouldn't understand."

"Oh, right. I forgot. I didn't inherit your plumbing gene."

Josh laughed.

"You say something?" Freddy asked him.

"Got it," Josh repeated, then slid out of the cabinet, and propped himself up on one elbow as his gaze lifted from her naked feet to her naked legs to her eyes.

At least, until her father directed the flashlight beam into Josh's eyes.

"Pop."

"What?"

Tess took the flashlight from him and turned it off.

Her father looked as if he hadn't any idea why she was pissed this time, then spoke to Josh. "Let's have the wrench." He put out his hand.

"I'll take that." Tess snatched it from Josh before her dad could whack him over the head with it. Josh may have fixed whatever it was under the sink and he may have given her dad some good pointers on how to fix the stuff that was falling apart in this house, but he wasn't out of the woods yet—not by a long shot. "You go on and play poker."

As Josh pushed to his feet, he was still blinking from having that flashlight beam in his eyes. "What are you going to do?"

"You don't have to cook," Freddy said.

Tess looked at him.

"Okay, okay," he said, "I'll be in there if you need me." Instead of moving in that direction, he frowned at Josh. "You coming?"

"In a minute," she answered for him, "he has to tell me how to heat up this stuff he brought."

"I can tell you that. Use the oven or the microwave."

"Pop."

His eyes narrowed. "I'll be in there with my friends. We'll hear you if you call."

Once he was out of earshot, Tess mumbled, "They'll hear us if we breathe."

Josh leaned close and whispered, "What was that?"

She looked at him, then quickly averted her gaze before her thoughts got tangled and her heart made her do something stupid. Keeping her voice low, she asked, "What happened when you were outside with my dad?"

"What?"

Tess hesitated, then finally looked at him, and repeated her question.

Josh shook his head, then touched his ear as if he couldn't hear her.

She leaned closer and whispered, again, "What happened when you were outside with my dad?"

"Nothing. You smell good."

Tess stepped back.

He mouthed, *You do.*

She spoke in a normal voice. "How can you tell with all this stuff you brought?" She gestured to the serving plates. There were two kinds of burritos, three dips, beans smothered with cheese, rice smothered with hot sauce, several pizzas, marinara sauce, and lasagna. She lowered her voice, again. "Is that how you plan to get them off your back? You're going to cholesterol them to death? And don't you dare say that you can't hear me."

He murmured, "I like it when you're mean."

Tess closed her eyes. He was picking now to flirt with her?

"Not to mention unreasonable," Josh said, then quickly added in a lowered voice, "all the stuff I brought is healthy and low fat."

Tess opened her eyes and looked at it. "Wow, you're good."

"You're just now noticing that?"

Of course not. The first day they met, Tess knew he could kiss like nobody's business, while his touch could revive the dead. Even when he was clear across the room, she could feel his male power and heat.

"Yo, Wyatt," Hank called out from the other room, "you gonna play or what?"

"I'd like to," Josh said in a voice only Tess could hear.

"I think Hank means with them, not me."

"Not what I had in mind."

"You do like to live dangerously, don't you?"

"Don't you worry, Teressa, I have everything under control." He shouted to Hank, "Be right there! I have to write down the heating instructions for Tess so she doesn't mess up this food!"

She arched one brow as he looked at her.

"Well, I do." He smiled.

"Teressa?" she asked.

"Beautiful name." He held her chin between his thumb and forefinger, then lifted her face to his.

Tess was a goner. She whispered, "Josh, I really don't want to live this dangerously."

"What do you mean?"

Her gaze drifted to his rich mouth. Her eyes fluttered closed as he gently brushed his lips over hers.

Tess inhaled sharply.

Josh murmured, "I better go before your dad sends out a search party."

"Like he'd even care if you're gone with Peg here?"

Josh straightened and got serious. "Are you pissed that I invited her?"

Tess opened her eyes, but kept them lowered. "No." Not only was her dad going to benefit from Peg's company, Tess figured when this was all over, she could at least grill the woman about Josh's romances that no longer made the tabloids.

She sighed.

"You're sure?" Josh asked.

"Very," she said, her voice still lowered. "Thanks for asking her. My dad's been very lonely."

"You're welcome." Josh cradled her face in his hand, until Tess smacked it away.

He frowned, but kept his voice low. "That's the way you treat a guy you've just thanked?"

"Yeah, when that guy's trying to get himself killed in my father's house. Believe me, I'm on your side. I'll even call nine-one-one if you need it."

"I won't. Just you wait and see."

"Uh-uh. I'm staying in here."

"Chicken." Josh playfully patted her butt, then headed for the living room to continue winning over her dad and the rest of this crowd so that they'd finally trust him, leaving him and Teressa alone.

It was going to be a piece of cake. Already they were attacking the second plate of munchies, while Freddy was still making eyes at Peg. If the man needed even more convincing after that, Josh had an ace in the hole . . . all those helpful hints on how to fix up this place.

Oh, yeah.

Feeling ready for anything, Josh pulled back his chair. "So, we going to play, or what?"

Freddy was the first to look up. Gone was the smile he had just shared with Peg. Now, his expression was asking what right Josh had to even pose such a question when it was his first time in this house.

The others weren't any better. They had all stopped midchew to exchange glances with each other, before lifting their gazes to him.

Josh suddenly knew what a cornered felon felt like.

He looked over his shoulder at the kitchen. Tess was leaning against the doorjamb, arms crossed against her chest, head lowered as she slowly shook it.

"Well, guys," Freddy said, "are we going to play—or what?"

One after the other said they were ready as their gazes remained on Josh.

"Then, let's play," Freddy ordered.

Josh sank into his chair.

An hour later, the crowd was enjoying the main courses he had prepared, and the poker game, and making him the butt of every joke.

Peg had tried to defend him, for about three seconds. After that, she switched sides and gave this group even more ammunition by bringing up his past.

"I kid you not," she said now, after a lengthy story that had everyone howling, "Josh actually did that on his first job."

"Not the brightest jewel in the crown, huh?" Hank asked.

"Oh, shut up," Sammie said, then patted Josh's hand. "He's cute. He doesn't have to be smart."

"Lucky he didn't become a cop," Vic said, "can you imagine him with a gun?"

"Not even one that shoots glue," Freddy said.

They all laughed, again, after which Peg revealed yet another stupid mistake in his past.

Shit. Josh hadn't been treated this badly on that first construction job when he was eighteen. Then, Peg had been the only woman around to see everyone laughing at him. Now, he also had Tess to consider.

Forty minutes ago, she had padded into the room, sprawled on the sofa, then became quickly engrossed in a paperback police procedural that couldn't have been as gory as what was happening to him.

"Aw, he didn't do that," Freddy suddenly said to Peg, then laughed so hard he actually got up from the table and bent over at the waist. "You're making it up!"

"I kid you not," Peg said, as she stared at the man's ass.

Josh rolled his eyes, then finally slid his gaze to Tess.

She was already looking at him.

It was so unexpected Josh lowered his beer to the table without tasting it. It was so welcomed, he could hardly breathe as her gaze drifted to his mouth and lingered, before she, again, met his eyes.

In that moment, her expression was filled with such honest regard, Josh finally understood what it meant to be a man. All the sex in the world couldn't give him a tenth of what Tess was providing now—the approval of a woman who was his equal in everything that mattered.

If she had found him lacking, no praise on earth could have made up for that disappointment.

It was a feeling that humbled and awed, making Josh realize something he hadn't until now. He was falling in love with her, and probably had been from the moment Tess had first walked into his office, moving like a dancer.

Josh wanted to smile at that memory, but did not. Love was serious business. It was an endless responsibility he had never been faced with before, and he really didn't need the extra pressure tonight, considering Hank was suddenly kicking his foot under the table as he sagged in his chair and just laughed and laughed.

Freddy continued to howl as he inclined his head toward Josh. "That one's a real—"

"That's enough," Tess finally said. Her voice was surprisingly gentle, which gave it that much more power.

"What?" Freddy asked.

Sammie cleared her throat. "She said, that's enough."

Josh looked at the woman.

"Aw, hell," Hank said, "we were just having fun with this one. Don't get all—"

"His name is Josh," Tess interrupted.

He looked back at her.

Her gaze was still on him. She seemed not to care that her father was frowning. She seemed indifferent to everything but him.

"He's an amazing man," she added in that same gentle voice. "Shame on all of you for saying otherwise."

It got so suddenly quiet in here, Josh could hear the fridge kicking on and Peg's bracelets jangling.

Didn't matter to Tess. Her gaze remained on him for a

long moment before she casually looked back to her book, as if what she had just said was the most natural thing in the world.

I just had to protect him, she had told Peg after that awful press conference, *and I'd do it again in a second, so shoot me.*

Josh wanted to thank her and hug her, though he wasn't crazy enough to do that now.

He hoped to God Freddy wasn't going to ask Tess what in the hell she was doing by defending him in front of everyone. Josh didn't want to know that she was only doing it because of the contract, because she wanted to help her father's business; that she was acting solely as his bodyguard; that her feelings for him stopped there, with the exception of some future sex.

He wasn't ready to hope that she might be falling in love with him. He sure as hell wasn't man enough to ask.

"We gonna play or what?" Freddy finally asked in a subdued voice.

"I'm in," Hank mumbled.

"Me, too," Sammie said, after which Vic chimed in that he was also still playing.

Josh looked at his cards, then returned his attention to Tess.

Her head remained lowered to that book, her expression unreadable.

"Hey, hon," Peg said in a quiet voice, tapping his hand.

Josh looked at her. "What?"

"You in?" she asked.

He looked back to Tess knowing that whether he was in her life or out was completely up to her.

Chapter Eleven

The rest of the evening went smoothly, if Josh counted hard stares, rather than emasculating comments, as the measure.

At least the letup in insults gave him a chance to win a few hands, using moves preferred by serious poker players.

That seemed to do the trick for Hank. When it came time to leave, the man actually clamped Josh on the shoulder as if they were buddies, not like he was trying to injure him. "You're all right."

Freddy muttered, "Not as bad as some."

"Careful," Peg said, "or he'll stop cooking for you."

"Oh, yeah?" Freddy shot back. "Then maybe you'll just have to start."

"Only if you're nice, mister."

As those two huddled and shared a private laugh, Josh looked at Tess.

She had fallen asleep on the sofa more than an hour ago and hadn't stirred since. The paperback was draped over her eyes, that lush mouth hung open, and there was a smear of marinara sauce on her chin.

Men had fought wars to protect scenes like that, hoping to come home to it. Josh couldn't imagine a better reward. He smiled.

"Hey, cutie." Sammie slipped her arm around his waist. "Whatcha doing?"

Falling in love. "Just seeing if Tess is okay."

"Looks to me like she's in for the night."

Not a chance. Josh wanted her home with him where she belonged.

Freddy must have known it, too, because the man asked Peg to get him another beer. As she headed for the fridge, he joined Josh and Sammie.

The woman immediately tightened her embrace as if warning Josh to make a run for it.

No way. He wasn't about to leave Tess, not even if that meant a fight with Freddy.

The uncomfortable silence grew, before the older man said, "Tessie's been like that since she was a toddler."

Josh looked at him. All the hard-ass cop talk and male blustering couldn't erase the love in his eyes as he looked at his little girl; nor could it erase the fear that another guy wanted to replace him as the most important man in her life.

Josh knew if he had a daughter he would feel exactly the same. No guy would be worthy of her, not even if he loved her completely, because that jerk would surely want her in his bed and that wasn't something any father could abide.

God, men were fucked up. "I don't know what you mean—been like what?"

Freddy slid his gaze to Josh. "The way she is now. You've only known my daughter for a very short time, I'm her father." He looked at her again, and smiled. "She's a light sleeper unless she feels really safe. When she does, like now, even gunfire won't wake her."

Josh tried to work his mind around that pleasant image.

"She sleep like this at your place?" Vic asked.

Freddy frowned at his friend. "I would hope he wouldn't be able to answer that."

"You're right," Josh quickly said. "I can't. Believe me, sir,

I've given you nothing to worry about. Tess has given you nothing to worry about."

Vic asked, "What about those pictures in that tabloid?"

Josh resisted the urge to swear. "She wasn't asleep then."

"No kidding," Vic said.

"We have separate rooms," he mumbled.

"Keep it that way," Freddy said.

Josh suppressed a sigh, and not only because of that directive.

Although he had never actually witnessed Tess asleep at his house, he certainly saw her every morning. With the exception of the first, she was always bent over the counter, head resting on her arm, while her other hand cradled a cup of coffee strong enough to dissolve paint.

It had never occurred to Josh that she wasn't getting enough sleep because she felt uncomfortable in his house or uncomfortable with him. He simply thought she wasn't a morning person.

He looked at her now and had to wonder if she'd ever feel this safe with him, especially after that tabloid stuff. What woman would want to willingly be involved in that, unless she was after her own publicity or simply wanted to enjoy his status and wealth?

Tess surely wasn't looking for any press and she was as unimpressed by his lifestyle as her father was. Not that the tabloids cared. They would hound her; first, because of him, then, because of her beauty. And that would give stupid kids—like the one who'd called that night—pictures to drool over.

Pictures that were private; moments that were no longer sacred or safe.

Fuck, why did it always have to keep coming back to that? Why couldn't the world just leave them alone?

"You gonna have her stay here?" Vic asked Freddy. "You want me to take the boy home?"

Before Josh could argue that he wanted Tess to do that, Freddy grumbled, "Why you asking me? She's the one making that call."

Josh looked at the man, surprised Freddy was already frowning at him.

"Go on," he said to Josh. "Ask her."

"Okay. Thanks."

"Don't thank me," he complained, "you don't know my daughter when she gets really pissed. You think tonight was bad? Believe me, I've seen worse. When she told me she wanted to be a cop and I said not a chance, she didn't back down, not even when I started hollering. She told me flat out that I couldn't stop her. Hell, if the possibility of getting shot on duty couldn't stop her, how could I? So I let her be a cop. When she wanted to be a bodyguard, I had to let her do that, too, which brings us to you." Freddy swore beneath his breath in Spanish, then sighed. "She could've been a dancer, but oh, no, she had to do all this other stuff." He gestured to her. "She's a grown woman. Where she sleeps tonight is up to her, not me—not you. Go on."

"Yes, sir." Josh moved closer and lifted his hand to nudge Tess out of sleep, but didn't know what part of her to touch; not with her father, Vic, Hank, Sammie, and now Peg watching. At last Josh bent at the waist and murmured, "Tess?"

"Oh, for God's sake," Freddy said, "you'll have to do better than that."

Josh looked over his shoulder at the man, then flinched as Freddy hollered, *"Teressa!"*

Jesus. As Josh pressed his fingers against his aching ear, Tess finally moved in a slow, sensuous stretch that had the book falling from her face, and liquid heat shooting straight to his groin where it lingered, making him too damned hard for this crowd.

"Teressa!" Freddy shouted again.

This time, her eyes fluttered open. She squinted at Josh, then smiled.

His cock and balls simply ached with frustrated need. Before they ached from something far worse, he slid his gaze to the side, her dad.

Tess's smile paused. She looked at her father, then all of the others. After running her tongue around her mouth, she asked, "Party over?"

It would be, if she didn't go home with him. "Yup."

Tess looked at him. "You win?"

He would, if she went home with him. "At times."

She yawned, then asked, "Time to go?"

"Uh-huh . . . unless you want to stay at your dad's."

Tess didn't even hesitate. "Just give me a minute and we can leave."

Josh wanted to smile to that *we,* but didn't dare. His gaze slid to the side just in time to see Freddy crossing his arms over his chest.

"Will you look at that?" Peg asked.

Josh didn't want to, but figured he should. He followed the woman's gaze to see that Tess had already closed her eyes and had fallen back to sleep.

What now? Rather than screaming her name, again, Josh looked over his shoulder and said to Freddy, "I'll just carry her to my car."

Vic spoke up. "Unless Freddy wants to."

"With his hernia?" Sammie asked.

Freddy shot her a look, then stole a glance at Peg.

She gave him a wink. "Sunday, right?"

His face flushed. "It's a date."

"Maybe I should give you my address now," she said. "So you don't get lost."

He looked at his daughter, then Josh, then finally gave up the fight. "I got a pen and a piece of paper in the kitchen," he said to Peg.

"I'm right behind you."

As they left the room, Josh made his move before anyone's

mind was changed. Slipping one arm around Tess's waist and the other beneath her knees, Josh lifted her off the sofa and into himself.

Just like that, her body molded to his, fitting perfectly as her face snuggled against his chest and her breath warmed it.

Vic moved closer. "Want me to open the door for you?"

"Please."

Once he had propped both the door and screen open, he asked, "Want me to open the car door for you?"

Josh smiled. "I would be forever grateful."

"Getting heavy, huh?"

It was a burden that felt needed and completely right. "What do you think?"

Vic gave him a sly smile.

Before the old guy got too involved in this adventure, Josh inclined his head toward the sofa. "Keys are on the cocktail table."

"I'll get her purse and shoes, too." He moved faster than his age would have allowed, then hurried outside, but stopped dead in the front yard as he looked down the street. "Looks like she parked way down there."

"Uh-huh."

"Wonder why she did that?"

"We can ask her after I drop her."

Vic looked over his shoulder at Josh, nodded quickly, then hurried to the car.

Once Josh got Tess that far, he lowered her to her feet, but kept his arm securely around her waist.

She took just that moment to lift her arms and stretch, hitting him in the jaw with her closed fist.

Damn.

"Did I just hit you?" she asked, then yawned and stretched again, rubbing her body against his.

"Bet that hurt, huh?" Vic asked.

Josh inhaled deeply to that sensual stretching and nodded.

"Better get her inside," Vic said, "before she has you on the ground."

Josh figured he didn't have that far to go. Every part of him had already surrendered to this woman. Trouble was, she was all arms and legs and body parts he couldn't touch, not in front of Vic.

And then there was another problem.

Josh kept his voice lowered as he asked, "Where's she have her gun? I didn't feel it around her waist."

Vic lifted her purse. "That's because it's in here."

"Put it in the backseat," Josh said, then added, "gently."

As Vic did that, Josh finally got her into the passenger side of the car.

"Hold it," she suddenly said, then yawned again. "I'm supposed to be driving."

"Uh-huh."

"So I will?"

"Uh-huh."

"Good." Her head fell to the side. Her eyes were already closed.

Josh waited a moment to see if she had really fallen back to sleep or was faking. Could be she just liked to play with her dad's head and now his. Licking the tip of his thumb, Josh gently rubbed that sauce from her chin, then brought back his thumb, sucking it clean.

Despite his enjoyment and arousal, Tess did not move. She was completely out of it just as Freddy had said, but not because she finally felt safe with him. Josh figured those beers she had tonight had helped, along with pure exhaustion. Even so, there wasn't any telling how long it might last, so he was extra gentle as he put on her seat belt.

"Everything all right here?"

Josh flinched at Hank's voice, hitting his head on top of the door frame before he turned around.

Despite their previous camaraderie, Hank's meaty arms were now crossed over his broad chest, his eyes narrowed.

Josh rubbed his bumped head. "Everything's fine."

"I'm driving," Tess said in a sleepy voice.

Josh looked from her to Hank. "See?"

The man's eyes remained narrowed.

"Tell you what," Josh said. "If we have any trouble, I'll just use my panic button to get you. Night."

As Vic laughed and Hank continued to frown, Josh got into the car, quickly started it and pulled away.

When those two were finally no more than tiny objects in his rearview mirror, Josh stole a glance at Tess.

Her head was still resting on her left shoulder; her eyes remained closed as she slept.

Looking back to the street, Josh had to wonder what it would be like to wake up during the night, in their bed, and see her as she was now. To know that each morning her warm, soft body would be molded to his, because that's where she just had to be—no other place would do.

No other man would be able to give her what she needed.

It was a heady fantasy that kept Josh occupied until he pulled into his estate and faced the brutal truth. What began as sexual attraction, pure and simple, was becoming increasingly complicated and potentially painful.

Not that Josh would have even minded some future pain if he thought there'd be lots of joy preceding it.

Oh, shit, you're a dead man.

His heart was already lost, there was no getting it back, and he wasn't certain she even wanted it.

During the following minutes, he sat in the car in front of his house watching Tess as if she might disappear. As if this might be the last moment that he saw—

Uh-uh. No way was he going to allow himself to dwell on that because it wasn't going to happen; at least, not tonight. Tomorrow and the next day, who knew? Not him, that's for damned sure, because he wasn't going to think about or face that right now, either.

He had to get her inside and upstairs.

Josh murmured her name several times, but Tess continued to sleep. He finally pulled her out of the car, carried her into the house and up the stairs to her bedroom.

It wasn't until he had her on the bed that her lids fluttered open.

She recognized him, immediately, as if he had always been in her life. The room, however, did give Tess a momentary problem. Her brows drew together as she regarded this moon-washed space. "We're not in Kansas anymore, are we?"

God, he loved her. Not that Josh was willing to admit it now and scare her off. So, he kept his voice casual. "No. We left some time ago."

Tess nodded; she yawned lustily, then at the last moment decided to be delicate as she draped her hand over her mouth. It muffled her next question. "Did I drive?"

"Of course you did. You're my bodyguard." She rolled over on her side, facing him, then said in a sleepy voice, "I protected you tonight at the game."

That she had. She stood up for him. It was a moment Josh would always hold in his heart. It was a moment that changed this slice of time.

If she had been any other woman, he would have used all the charm he possessed, all the seduction he knew to get inside of her. To feel her tight heat holding him, imprisoning him, protecting him.

If she had been any other woman.

But she was Teressa Franklin, an ex-cop who moved like a dancer, a bodyguard who protected him with words, a woman who stirred him as no one else had.

She deserved his respect and would get it even now.

Especially now.

As Tess wriggled her body into a more comfortable position that soon had her left arm dangling over the edge of the mattress with her left leg quickly following, Josh told himself he couldn't touch her. If he did, there would be no turning back, at least for him.

He went to the other side of the bed, fisted his fingers into the linens, and gently pulled until she was fully on the mattress again and completely undisturbed.

The picture she created aroused Josh more than he was able to bear.

Without a backward glance, he left her room and gently closed the door.

Chapter Twelve

It was the tempting aroma of coffee that finally stirred Tess from the best sleep she had had in days.

Forcing her right eye to open, she made a face to all that damned light, surprised it was morning. Given the height of the sun, it had to be past eight. Crud. Time to get up.

Closing her eye, she snuggled back into bed, then paused.

The last Tess recalled she had been on her father's sofa reading a book, but now she was in a bed?

Forcing her head off the mattress, Tess saw that she was back at the estate in her bed and it was unbelievably messy. The comforter and sheets had been pulled clear off the left side of the mattress. She looked down at herself seeing that she wasn't quite as messy, though she was still wearing what she had on last night.

Odd.

Even though she slept like the dead when she was really exhausted, she had never awakened in a different place than where she had started, while also wearing the same clothes.

She got out of bed and went downstairs to the kitchen.

Josh was at the counter already showered and dressed in business casual. The collar of his pale yellow shirt was open, his sleeves were folded back to mid-forearm, while his freshly washed hair looked really thick and blond.

Tess spoke without thinking. "Wow, you're beautiful."

His gaze lifted from the real estate newspaper he'd been reading.

She stopped scratching her butt and tried to sound less horny. "You're up?"

His brows lifted.

She frowned at his plate. "You've already eaten?"

"Not everything."

Tess lifted her gaze. He was staring at her feet. She stopped curling her toes. "Why didn't you wake me?"

His gaze inched up her legs to her breasts before he took a prolonged drink of his coffee, then said, "I tried."

"When?"

"Every fifteen minutes since seven."

"What time is it, now?"

"Way past seven." He pushed the coffee pot and a cup across the counter to her.

"Thanks."

"Welcome." He lowered his head to the paper, but Tess could see his gaze was on her legs.

She quickly drained the cup. "How'd I get here?"

He seemed confused by the question. "On this planet?"

Tess rolled her eyes. "This house. After last night's game."

"Oh. Usual way."

She supposed that meant his car. "Did I drive?"

"You kept insisting on it."

Her gaze turned inward as she tried to recall that, but could not. "After we got here, did I just go to bed?"

"Uh-huh."

"What did you do?"

He inhaled deeply, then sighed it out. "Not much."

Whatever hadn't happened last night really had him bummed. Despite that, his head remained lowered to the paper as his gaze roamed her chest.

Since when had he been so bashful? Last night he had wanted to neck in her father's kitchen.

Oh, hell. Had her father finally threatened him?

Wait a sec. If he had, why was she here?

Oh, damn. Had she threatened him?

Tess patted her body looking for her gun.

Josh noticed. "Lose something?"

"My gun. I can't find—"

"It's in your purse in the hall."

Thank God. Tess poured herself another cup of coffee and drank it so quickly, she belched. "Excuse me. Did Pop threaten you last night while I was asleep? Is that why you're pretending to read that paper when you're really looking at me?"

Josh's expression went from aroused to embarrassed. Clearing his throat, he folded the paper and tossed it aside. "Nothing was said. And nothing happened. The truth is, you were so tired last night that I carried you to the car, drove you here, carried you up to your room and put you on the bed. End of story."

Not entirely. How did her bed get so messy? "Wait. Where are you going?"

Josh lifted his plates, showing them to her, before he put them in the dishwasher.

"Where are you going after that?"

"Work."

"Uh-uh." Tess went around the counter and blocked him. "Not without me. I won't allow it."

He arched one dark brow. "You'd actually try to stop me?"

"Sure. But I wouldn't actually hurt you when I did."

"Oh, really? You punched me in the jaw last night."

Her eyes widened, then narrowed. "I did not."

"Sure you did. You were yawning and stretching and I got in the line of fire. Now, be nice." Before Tess could comment, Josh put his hands on her waist, then lifted her to the counter, out of his way.

Her gaze drifted to his hands still on her waist. "Exactly how nice?"

"Lift either knee and we're through talking."

Tess used her sweetest voice. "Well, you would be." She wrapped her legs around his lean hips, pulling him closer.

Josh eased his hands from her waist to her thighs. "What are you doing?"

"Making sure you don't go to work without my protection."

"But who's going to protect you?"

Tess frowned, then squealed as he tickled her. When she was sprawled across the counter, he easily backed away.

"Before you get your gun," he said, "I was going to do some work in my office down the hall, while you get ready."

Tess extended her right foot to touch his chest. Trouble was, he kept backing away and she kept sliding forward until she was about to fall off the counter.

At last, Josh cradled her foot in his hands, kissed the tips of her toes, then released her.

As that seemed to be the extent of his passion, Tess wiggled back onto the counter and pushed to a sitting position. "You really need to go right this minute?"

His gaze lifted to hers. "I'd better."

I'd better? Oh, come on, he was avoiding her, again. This was what—the third time he was avoiding her since they met? Only now he wasn't trying to protect her from the paparazzi or trying to avoid talking about a poker game she had never wanted him to attend. This time it was because something had been said while she had been asleep at that game. Not that he was going to admit to it this morning. "In that case, guess I'll get ready."

Josh turned to leave the room.

"You'll really wait for me?" she asked.

He stopped in the doorway. "Always." He looked over his shoulder at her. "Now, go on."

On the drive to the office for Josh's business meeting, Hank and Sammie were visibly absent.

Tess finally asked, "Did Bonnie and Clyde get tired of

waiting for me to wake up or did they retire while I was out?"

He smiled. "They have other jobs."

"Jobs you gave them?"

Josh shook his head no, but offered nothing more as he pulled out his cell and made a call that lasted clear through the ride to his office.

After that, the only time Tess saw him was at the conclusion of his business things that continued over the weekend.

Suddenly, she was nothing more than his chauffeur. But each time Tess asked why he didn't need her to be his date in public or on hand as a bodyguard, Josh explained that it was an all-male business meeting or an all-boys club event, or something women didn't attend.

Tess finally understood why Hank, Sammie, and Vic were no longer on hand to protect her virtue. Of course, a few days ago their absence would have given Josh license to seduce her in an all-male elevator or a golf course used by ultraconservative clerics.

Now, he was suddenly a monk?

By Monday she was tired of his latest attempt to avoid her.

As Josh went into his office and closed the door before she could follow, Tess cornered Peg. "What happened at that poker game after I fell asleep?"

"I won a few of the—"

"I'm not talking about that."

Peg stopped spritzing herself with perfume. "Your dad asked me out." She looked worried. "You're not going to give him any trouble about it, are you?"

"Of course not. He should have gone out and had some fun long before now."

Peg's expression and voice became very cool. "If he had, I wouldn't be going out with him, now would I?"

"You know what I mean." Tess glanced over her shoulder at Josh's office. The back of his chair was to this room as he talked to someone on the phone.

She leaned down to Peg and spoke in a very low voice. "Did Pop say anything to Josh while I was asleep?"

"He told him to ante up a couple of—"

"Did he threaten Josh about me?"

Peg slowly shook his head. "Your dad was the one who told Josh that where you spent the night was up to you. When you finally woke up, you chose Josh's place over your dad's."

That was news to Tess. "Before that, did Josh promise Pop anything?"

"Like what?"

"Like never to kiss me again or touch me or anything like that. Because of the paparazzi," she quickly added.

"The subject never came up."

Tess couldn't believe it. Josh wasn't making any moves on her when he finally could?

Sex had seemed such a small thing to hope for; it surely wasn't as monumental as love. But even that wasn't going to happen?

Why?

Days later, when Josh told her they were having lunch at an ultra-private club Tess figured it wasn't because he needed her presence as a public girlfriend or bodyguard. No way could paparazzi or the Libbys of this world sneak into that sacred domain.

This was it. That's why he'd been acting so strange. The abuse at that poker game had convinced him that no sex was worth that, especially if he had plans to cut out after the sex. Better to tell her he didn't need her anymore, the contract was over, and he had chosen a public place with the protection of other diners to drop that bombshell.

Tess knew she should have been prepared for this eventuality, but wasn't.

When they were finally seated at their table she stared at the menu without really seeing it, while Josh studied his as if the lines to a great *you're fired* speech were written there.

At last, he cleared his throat.

"What?" Tess asked, just wanting to get it over with.

Josh looked up at her sharp tone, then returned his gaze to the menu. "You might want to try the mahi-mahi. It's good here."

Tess looked back at her menu. A few more minutes of this unbearable suspense and she'd be totally nuts. "Mahi-mahi, huh?"

"Yeah. It's good. So is the shrimp. You might like that. I have this formal dinner to go to."

Tess lifted her gaze. Her mouth went dry as Josh looked back at his menu. He had been talking about seafood and suddenly decided to change the subject to a formal dinner he had to attend?

"It's this gala event," he said.

Tess's heart started to pound as he explained that it had been planned for mouths, he just had to go, and finally added, "You don't have to go if you don't—"

"Are you going with someone else?"

Josh looked at her and frowned. "What? No." He shook his head. "Of course not."

Of course not? Like she was an idiot for even asking? Tess frowned. "But you still don't want me to go?"

Josh looked at the waiter who took just that moment to arrive at their table.

"Give us a minute," Josh said.

"No, stay, we're ready. In fact we might be finished," Tess said, then spoke to Josh. "We're supposed to be romantically involved. That was the plan, right? Yet, you don't want me to go to this—"

"I didn't say that."

"Then what were you say—"

"You'll go—we'll go, of course."

Tess's heart soared, then fell right back down as she recalled how he'd been avoiding her these last days and before that, too many others. Suddenly, that was forgotten? The show was back on the road, *again*? For how long this time? And where would it end? "Was the poker game really that bad?"

"I'll come back," the waiter said.

Josh followed that young man with his gaze, before looking at her. "What?"

"Haven't you noticed Bonnie and Clyde aren't tailing us like they used to?"

"There is a God."

Tess frowned. "Why are you acting like this?"

"Like what?"

Like he had no intention of ever kissing her again, not even for the public's benefit. Like he was still getting ready to cut out, maybe after that gala event. Tess looked back at her menu.

"Hey, you okay?" he asked.

Of course she wasn't, but at least she hadn't completely lost her mind as he seemed to be doing. A moment before he was all too casual, even distant. Now he looked concerned, his voice was tender, and he was even covering her hand with his own. Of course, they were out in public. Maybe he finally recalled that he wanted them to be romantically involved as long as it was for everyone else's benefit, who knew?

"Tess?"

There it was again, that tender worry that made her forget pride and how badly she was going to be hurt when this was over.

Turning her hand so that his was inside, Tess curled her fingers in a gentle caress. "This dinner thing . . . we'll go?"

Josh's gaze remained lowered to their hands as he nodded.

"Together?"

He looked at her. "You'll even be driving."

"Not that night," Tess quickly said. "I don't want to mess up my heels and clingy gown."

His gaze turned inward as if he were trying to picture that. "A red gown?"

"Sure, if that's what you want."

"You have more than one, in different colors?"

Tess laughed. "I haven't got any, but I do know how to shop for that . . . and whatever I need to wear beneath it."

Josh leaned toward her and spoke in a voice that was downright husky. "A garter for your gun?"

"If that's what you want. I'll even let you pick it out."

He seemed surprised. "You want me to come along?"

"I'm insisting upon it . . . so I get what you want. If you're not too busy."

"Let me free up some time on my calendar."

That's my bad, bad boy. Tess lifted her hand and gently smoothed the hair near his ear. "A lot of time." She ran her fingertip down his cheek to his mouth, then gently traced it as she murmured, "I'm warning you, I don't shop fast. I like to feel the fabric against my skin and see how well it drapes my body."

Josh's eyes fluttered closed. His nostrils flared as he inhaled deeply. "You'll model each gown for me?"

"Whatever you want."

He wanted to be with her, pure and simple. He wanted to tell her he loved her; but it wasn't that easy.

Maybe after that formal dinner. If Tess told him then that she didn't feel the same, Josh knew he would have at least enjoyed their night together and even today's shopping trip.

They were in Kiki's, a cavernous warehouse that Tess swore by, possibly because it was stuffed with billions of gowns and every other kind of female apparel.

The place was so damned big it was twenty minutes before Josh realized that except for little boys with their mothers he was the only guy here.

The ladies certainly noticed. Josh saw more than a few of them sneaking glances at him, then Tess. She was so consumed with rifling through a rack of gowns, she didn't even see those two young women who were whispering to each other and now coming over.

Oh, shit.

The young brunette with close-cropped hair spoke first. "Hey, Josh."

Tess finally looked up.

Before she pulled out her gun, Josh blocked her view of the girl and grabbed one of the gowns. "I like this one," he said, lifting it by the skirt.

Tess's gaze followed the hanger as it fell off the dress to the floor.

"I'll get it." The second Josh bent over, there was a hand on his ass.

He straightened and turned.

The brunette was licking her lips, while her blonde friend was wiggling her fingers as she said, "Hey, Josh."

He stepped back, then quickly looked over his shoulder at Tess. "Sorry." He pulled her out of the rack of clothes he had just pushed her into, then felt a hand stroking his arm.

"Do I know you?" he asked, his voice hard as he turned to the blonde whose wiggling fingers were still trying to touch him.

She moved closer. "We know you. We saw your picture on the Net. Mmmm."

"Take off your shirt," the brunette ordered. "Let's see that yummy tattoo on your—"

"Go away," Josh said, his voice even harder. "I'm with someone." He slipped his arm around Tess's waist, pulling her close.

"Hey, there," the brunette said to Tess, then gave him a wicked smile. "Now, come on, take off your shirt. I want to see that bad-ass tattoo on your—"

"Okay, that's it," he interrupted. "I'm not interested in what you want. I will never be interested in that. If you have anything else to say, it better be an apology to this lady—my lady."

The young women looked at each other, then laughed.

Josh's voice got frosty. "We're waiting for that apology."

"Screw you," the brunette said.

"Bite me," the blonde said.

As they walked away laughing, the brunette looked over her shoulder and shouted, "Old fart!"

"Hey, watch your mouth!" Tess shouted at that girl, then spoke to him. "You're not that old."

He looked at her.

Her eyes widened. "You still have a way with women."

"You think?"

"I didn't say it was a good way."

"And what is a good way?"

Tess turned into him, pressing her fingers against his chest. As Josh stroked her back she lifted her face to his. "What you're doing, for starters, unless you're looking for my weapon."

"I have to." He leaned down to her and murmured, "Yours is always far more concealed than mine."

Tess pressed her face into his chest, suppressing a throaty laugh.

Josh hugged her as hard as he dared, then swung her out of the way of three older women who needed to pass.

"Thanks," the third one said and smiled.

Josh gave her a wink, then spoke to Tess. "Better get that gown."

"Whatever you want." She eased out of his embrace and headed down the racks studying the gowns, while he studied her.

After a moment, Tess looked over her shoulder at him. "See anything you like?"

She knew he did. Arching one brow, Josh joined her. "I was just about to ask you the same thing."

Tess's gaze slowly rode him. "Maybe."

"That's it? Just maybe?"

"I haven't even begun to look at everything I need." Seeing

that they were alone, Tess flicked her fingers over his fly, then spoke above his strangled gasp. "Come on."

Any damned where she wanted.

An hour later Josh had gowns draped over his arms and shoulders as he backed into a dressing room followed by Tess and the salesgirl.

"Now, take your time, you two," the girl said to them both, then spoke to Tess. "You need anything, just holler. I'll bring it to you." She looked at Josh. "Have fun."

He smiled as she closed the door. "This is turning out much better than I thought."

"No kidding," Tess said. "You're finally getting to sit."

Josh looked over his shoulder to the chair, then sidled to it and took a load off. "That's not the only reason and you know it."

"You bet." Tess lifted the gowns from his right shoulder and arm and hung them on a hook. "You were really getting tired of carrying this stuff, huh?"

"I'd rather see it on you, than me, and you know it."

Tess flicked her gaze at him, then lifted the gowns from his left side and hung them up. "Why, Mr. Wyatt, are you actually asking me to model these for you?"

Josh tried not to sound too enthused. "I believe that was the plan, Officer Franklin."

Tess faced him. "Whatever you want."

His gaze dropped to her hands as she quickly unbuttoned her shorts, then lowered the fly, exposing her navel and that silky skin beneath it.

Josh swallowed; he adjusted himself in the chair. Tess moved her hips gently to the right and back to the left as she eased those shorts over her hips and thighs, then straightened allowing them to skim past her legs to the floor.

She stepped out of them.

Josh stared at her white thong, a scrap of silk and lace so brief it just barely covered her dark, furry mound. In fact, a few of those hairs had escaped, curling around the lacy edges.

He adjusted himself again, then looked at that series of mirrors reflecting her plush, naked ass from every angle imaginable, especially as Tess bent at the waist to pick up her shorts.

Josh's heart slammed into his chest at the scene that created.

Tess lifted her head.

His gaze followed her hair swaying back and forth above that gap in her top that exposed her breasts.

"Hold these." She tossed her shorts.

They hit Josh in the mouth.

"Sorry," Tess said.

Josh held them against his chest. "Not a problem."

Tess straightened, then looked down as she unbuttoned her top.

Josh pressed the shorts to his face, inhaling deeply of her soft, powdery scent.

Tess's gaze lifted. He lowered the shorts. She undid the last button, then removed her blouse.

Josh put out his hand, ready to take it.

Tess dropped it over his arm.

He pushed forward in his chair as his gaze settled on her lacy bra. It was as white as that thong with tiny satin straps that must have had a hell of a time holding up her full breasts. That soft flesh strained against those cups, her tightened nipples pushed against the silky fabric, until she unsnapped the front, opened, then removed it.

Josh stared.

"Here," she said, tossing her bra.

He didn't move quickly enough; hell, he could barely move at all.

"Sorry," Tess said, again, as the bra landed on his head.

Josh left it there as his heart paused, then hammered out of control, because Tess was now running her fingers beneath her hair to pull it off her shoulders, which served only one purpose—to give her breasts full exposure.

The areolas were a deep pink and as tight as the tips.

There was a small mole on her left breast and a stray white thread on her right.

If Josh were to live fifty years past today, he would never forget how the end of that thread wiggled gently with her breathing as it clung tenaciously to her naked flesh.

"Josh."

His gaze lifted to hers, then went right back to her breasts.

They looked even bigger than just a second ago. "Yeah?"

"I'm ready."

His gaze jumped to hers, then shot to the door, before he looked back. "What?"

Tess gestured to the gowns, which caused her right breast to quiver.

He really liked that.

"Josh." When he finally looked at her, Tess continued. "Which gown do you want me to try on first?"

He flicked his gaze at them, then looked at all those reflections of her bare ass. "The red one."

Tess planted her hands on her hips, which caused her breasts to jut out.

Josh liked that, too.

"They're all red," she explained.

No kidding? He looked at them, then pointed to the first.

"You're sure?" she asked. "You like that?"

She was curling her toes again. He smiled. "Oh, yeah."

Tess turned her back to him as she went to get that first gown.

Josh didn't waste a second as his gaze prowled her silky back, her naked buttocks, those seamless thighs, then back to the thong that rode her hips.

He was about to adjust himself again, but then simply spread his legs to give his boys a chance to breathe and his cock somewhere to go since it just kept getting thicker and harder.

Tess knew. As she finished unzipping that gown, she looked over her shoulder at him. "You doing all right?"

"Never been better." He followed her gaze to his groin, then suddenly realized something. "Bad girl. You're not wearing your weapon."

"It's in my purse." She regarded the outline of his erection for a moment more, before meeting his eyes. "Want to hold it?"

God, she was killing him. "Bad, bad girl."

Tess smiled, then returned to him, standing between his legs as she slipped that first gown over her head.

That silky fabric skimmed her naked breasts before fluttering to her waist and then tumbling over her hips to mid-calf.

Josh looked up as she turned to the side, holding her hair above her head.

"Zip me," she said.

He dropped her clothes and leaned forward. Placing his left hand on her hip, he eased the zipper up with his right, then ran his forefinger over the edge of the fabric that skimmed her breast.

Tess arched one brow, as if he needed to behave himself, before she turned to face the bank of mirrors. "What do you think?"

He really liked the back of that thing. It dipped very close to the top of her buttocks, but also had thin ribbons crisscrossing that section to keep her decent.

"Nice," Josh said, running his forefinger over those ribbons.

Tess inhaled sharply.

Josh looked at her reflection. Her gaze was already on him, her expression an invitation.

He took it. Moving his hands to her hips, Josh wrapped his legs around hers so Tess had no choice but to remain.

"Put your arms over your head."

She did. It made her look like a dancer, it made her his as Josh moved his hands beneath that gown to her breasts, supporting their weight in his palms, flicking his forefingers over the taut nipples before he roughly fondled her, unable to stop himself.

Tess's moan told him she didn't mind his rough touch. Her quick intake of breath told him she wanted more.

The knock on the door stopped it.

Josh quickly brought back his hands and opened his legs.

"Hey, you two doing good?" the salesgirl asked as she poked her head inside.

Josh nodded so vigorously the bra fell off his head.

Tess spoke in a voice thick with desire. "Uh-huh."

"Good." The girl really smiled as she looked at the gown. "Oh, hey, that one looks great on you. Don't you think?" she asked Josh.

He had to clear his throat before he was able to speak. "Uh-huh."

"You really should get that one," the girl said to Tess.

"I'd like to see the others first," Josh said.

The salesgirl nodded agreeably. "Oh, sure; don't mean to rush you guys. Take your time. I'll be by in a bit to see how you're doing." She shut the door.

Josh looked at Tess.

Her gaze was already on him. "Want to see the next one?"

He wanted to see her. He wanted to touch and taste all of her, but that wasn't about to happen here, not with that salesgirl popping in to see if they were doing all right.

At last Josh took a deep breath that didn't calm him at all, and said, "Yes, please."

Chapter Thirteen

By the time Tess had finished modeling the gowns—with all those stripteases in between—Josh could barely think.

She wasn't any better. Once her purchases had been made and they were back in the car, she looked at the keys as if she didn't know what to do with them; then she moved across the seat to him at the same moment Josh moved towards her.

They had barely started necking when his cell rang.

Shit.

Tess pulled away.

Josh followed. "Come back here."

"Your cell's ringing."

"I don't hear—"

"Go on, answer it." Her hand was on his chest, her gaze moving to the women in the parking lot who were watching them. "It might be important and those two might be gone by the time you're finished."

"I'll make it fast." He brought the cell to his ear and growled, "What?"

"Ah, it's me . . . Alan," the attorney said, then quickly added, "I thought Bonnie and Clyde were giving you a break."

"They are, but then, you're still bugging me, aren't you?"

"Well, excuse me, Josh, I don't mean to be such a bother. It's just that I caught something of interest and thought you would like to—"

"If it's a new property or lawsuit, I don't care. Either make an offer or get rid of it."

"You misunderstand. I don't want to get rid of it."

"Alan, quit being so cryptic. Why did you call?"

"Now that I think of it, I shouldn't tell you over the phone. This is something you really have to see."

"Fine. Send it to my cell—"

"Let's meet at your office. I'm headed there now."

"My office? Why? Why can't you just—" Josh abruptly paused as Alan hung up on him.

"We need to go to your office?" Tess asked.

It surely sounded like it. What in the world could have gotten Alan excited enough to insist on a meeting and then hang up, unless . . .

Oh, no. A paparazzo couldn't have gotten pictures of Tess just now when she was trying on clothes. How could that be possible? Was the salesgirl involved? Is that why she kept popping in? Had she taken pictures with her cell, then forwarded them to someone who had already put them on the Internet? Not that, *please.* "Ah, yeah, we should go back. Sorry."

"Not a problem." Tess started the car. "I can show my gown to Peg."

"Who?"

"Your secretary."

Oh, my God, another problem. "She's dating your father now, right?"

"You got a point. Maybe I shouldn't show the gown to her. I'll show it to Alan."

"Maybe he's already seen it."

"What?"

"Shouldn't we be heading for the office?"

"Sure." Tess pulled out of the lot.

Josh drummed his fingers against his thighs.

"I'll get us there as fast as I can," Tess said.

He bounced his legs.

"Josh, what's wrong?"

He stopped drumming and bouncing. "Nothing."

"You're sure?"

"I'm fine. I enjoyed the shopping trip. I'm glad we got that first dress you tried on. And those shoes. And the other stuff. Did we get the garter, too?"

"Ah, no, we forgot—"

"We forgot that? Hell." He sighed. "We should have gotten that garter."

Tess figured that was the least of their worries as she drove to the office.

Josh stared out his car window like death or another paparazzo was after him. When Tess tried to grill him about that call from Alan, all she received was an occasional grunt or a blank stare.

Once they were back at the complex, Josh was walking so fast Tess could barely keep up with him.

"Hey, do you mind?" she finally shouted.

Josh was already at the door to his suite. He looked over his shoulder at her. "Mind what?"

"That I'm way back here and you're already there."

"Sorry." He went into the suite.

When Tess reached Peg's office, Josh was already in his own with Alan.

"What's up?" Peg asked.

"You don't know?"

"Not yet, but you'll tell me when you find out, right?"

"Sure." Tess went into the office.

Josh immediately shook his head and pointed towards Peg's space. "Stay out there."

Tess frowned. "Why?"

"Because I said so."

"Not good enough." She crossed her arms over her chest.

Josh tightened his jaw. "You don't want to be here."

"Well I didn't a few seconds ago, but now I definitely do."

He muttered something Tess didn't hear, then turned to Alan. "She's not leaving, so let's see it."

"See what?" Tess asked.

The attorney's face got pink. He leaned toward Josh and spoke in a lowered voice. "I really should show it to you first and then —"

"Show *what*?" Tess asked.

"Screw this." Josh grabbed Alan's briefcase and opened it.

"Hey," Alan said. "That's my—"

"Holy shit." Josh lifted the tabloid from the briefcase.

Tess uncrossed her arms and backed away, wishing she had followed Josh's order to get the hell out of here, because no way was she ready to see what was on the cover of this week's edition.

Oddly enough, it lightened Alan's mood. He was actually rocking on his heels. "Told you that you needed to see it."

Josh whistled. "Any fallout from this yet?"

"Bigger than those photos of you."

Huh? Tess's heart started beating wildly. "Exactly whose photos are on—"

"Steve Zilenski's."

She worked that around her brain, then frowned. "Am I supposed to know him?"

"Not if you don't watch football," Alan said.

"And you do?"

"All the time."

That was a surprise.

"He's a football star," Alan explained, then clamped Josh on the shoulder. "And you, apparently, are yesterday's news, not to mention the Keys dethroned hunk."

"Hot damn!" Josh threw his free arm around Alan, hugging him.

Tess watched in stunned silence. A football star? Yesterday's news? Dethroned hunk? Just like that her time with Josh was over?

It was a moment before Tess could catch her breath, another before she could think. She had to be cool; she couldn't show her feelings; not now, not in front of Alan. At last, she joked, "Would you two like for me to leave?"

"That's next," Alan said. "Josh doesn't need you to be his bodyguard anymore."

A bullet in her heart couldn't have been more effective or more painful.

Tess looked at Josh. He was happier than she had ever seen him as he read that tabloid.

He really didn't need her anymore. He didn't even notice her anymore. It was truly over.

Tess told herself to leave, but her heart wouldn't allow it.

She moistened her lips; she rubbed the back of her neck. At last, she asked, "Is that true, Josh?"

He finished reading the article before lifting his gaze. "I'm sorry, what?"

Tess felt as if she were dying, but kept her voice even. "Alan said I don't have to be your bodyguard anymore."

"What?" Josh frowned at the man.

"Well, she doesn't," Alan said. "You're yesterday's news. No one's bothered you for days."

"Oh, yeah?" Josh said. "I was practically assaulted by two lunatics when Tess and I were shopping."

Alan dismissed that with a wave of his hand. "They probably haven't seen this edition of the tabloid yet. Give them time. In a few days this'll all be over. We can all get back to normal."

Tess's heart sank even lower, but she kept that sorrow out of her voice. "Great." She looked at Josh. "Just what we all wanted."

His expression changed. "It hasn't happened yet, all right?"

"It will," she said. "We always knew it would end."

Josh tossed the tabloid on his desk and went to her. "Everything ends, but this isn't over yet, which means you'll still be accompanying me to that formal dinner. The plans have been made and you will attend, is that understood?"

That's all he cared about, that stupid dinner? She frowned. "You couldn't have made it any clearer, Mr. Wyatt."

Josh lowered his head and breathed hard. "Look, I'm sorry, I didn't mean to snap at you." He lifted his gaze. "Please go with me, okay?"

Tess told herself to say no; she ordered herself to just get the hell out of here so she could be alone and cry.

"Tess?"

At last, she nodded; she had no choice. That dinner would be the last time she would see him. Alan was so right. In a few days Josh's need of a bodyguard and a public girlfriend would all be over. The moments they shared would be quickly forgotten by him. He would go back to his regular life.

All she had left was that coming night.

It was a reality that remained with Tess the rest of that day and the ones that followed, right up to the evening of the dinner.

As she got dressed, Tess knew she had to make these final moments ones Josh wouldn't soon forget.

Smoothing her gown, she looked at her room's reflection in the cheval mirror.

She would miss it. Never had Tess felt more at home than she had here.

Her gaze lingered on the bed, then moved to the gentle rapping on the door. A moment later, Josh opened it and came inside, not bothering to ask if she was decent. What did it matter when he had seen nearly all of her at Kiki's?

Tess smiled at that memory and how awesome he looked now.

The bad boy had been momentarily tamed in a black dinner jacket and trousers that complemented his white shirt and pearl gray tie.

How beautiful he was. How she would miss him. Not that Tess could tell him that, so she teased, repeating her father's words. "You don't look so bad dressed. You should plan on doing it all the time."

Josh's expression was playful, his voice deep and soft. "You really want that?"

"Ask me after the dinner."

He started to nod, then stopped. His gaze lifted from her gown. "What's after the dinner?"

"No more ground rules."

Josh's eyes widened, then closed as Tess worked her fingers through his hair, guiding his head to hers, his mouth to hers, keeping it there as she kissed him longer than the law allowed.

There was no reason to hold back anymore.

She wanted to taste him, to rub her scent on him and to take his in return.

She wanted to make him hers tonight, their last night together.

When Josh was finally breathless, Tess pressed her cheek to his. It was smooth, hot, and scented with aftershave that reminded her of tobacco and leather. She whispered, "Let's go."

Before she could ease away, Josh pulled her right back into himself, wrapping his arm around her waist. "We don't have to.

We could stay here. We could take a swim in the pool and then—"

"No." She pulled away. "Then it would be over. I don't want it to go fast."

Fast? Was she kidding? Josh wanted to tell her they could make love from this moment clear to the end of tomorrow, then take a rest and start all over again, but was afraid to push too hard. If he pissed her off, she might just change her mind. So, like a good boy, Josh simply went with the flow as Tess got her purse, took his hand, then led him out of the house to the car.

"I almost forgot." She tossed him the keys.

"You sure you want me to drive?"

"You are licensed, aren't you?"

"What would it matter when Vic's not going to like this? He's going to tell you this is no way for a bodyguard to act."

"Things change."

That they did, and Josh was afraid to ask what she meant by that. Ever since Alan made those stupid comments in the office Tess hadn't been her usual cocky self. Dammit, Josh wanted that woman back.

"Sometimes for the better," he said.

She regarded the house and the grounds for a moment more before meeting his gaze. Her eyes sparkled in the moonlight. "We should go."

Josh didn't want to, and once they were there, he couldn't wait to leave.

No more ground rules, she had said back at the house and obviously meant that to include here.

As the man across their table said something, Josh nodded agreeably even though he hadn't a clue what was being discussed, because his attention was still on Tess.

The moment they were seated, she had wrapped her leg behind his, then leaned toward him so that he couldn't miss her powdery fragrance or the way her gown gapped in front, showing him quite a bit of her right breast.

For the next twenty minutes, Josh endured that sweet torture until the event's speaker said something that had everyone turning in their chairs and looking at him.

At just that moment, Tess ran her fingers down the inside of Josh's right thigh.

Holy shit.

He lowered his head, breathed hard, then slid his gaze to her.

Her attention, like the others, was still on the speaker. Her fingers, however, were creeping back up his thigh. Just as she stroked his groin, Josh wrapped his fingers around her wrist.

Although Tess's gaze remained on the speaker, she did lift her brows.

Leaning close, Josh whispered, "No more ground rules?"

She turned her face to his and whispered, "None."

"Starting when?"

She gave him a wicked smile, then whispered, "Let go of me and you'll see."

"Uh-uh," he whispered. "When are we leaving this stupid thing?"

"In a little while."

"And then?"

"I'll tell you when you let go of me."

He finally did. "What happens after this?"

"You see my world. Excuse me."

My world? Excuse me? What was she talking about? Where was she going?

Josh left his chair, then watched as she crossed the room to a balcony. When he finally reached it, Tess was facing the railing.

Her hair and gown fluttered in the breeze that brought the faint strains of music from another party and the rustling of the ocean below.

He joined her at the railing. "What are you doing?"

She lifted her face to the night sky, the nearly full moon. "Just getting some air."

Josh ran his hand up her bare arm. "We could get even more back at my place."

Tess turned until her back was to the railing, her hands on each side. The breeze lifted the edge of her gown away from her legs. "That's your world."

Josh looked at her nipples pressing against that silky fabric. "And you want me to see yours?"

"You're going to." She moved her knee up the inside of his thigh to his stiffened cock.

He looked down at that. "When you were a cop?"

"I wasn't always a cop."

Josh had no idea what she was talking about, but his voice was thick with excitement. "Okay. So, what were you?"

"I'll show you. In time," she added, then pushed away from the railing and went back into the ballroom.

She had just reached a group of empty tables near the servers' entrance when she stopped and looked over her shoulder.

Josh was still in the doorway of the balcony.

She asked, "You coming?"

Like a good boy he went to her, then slipped his arm around her waist, pulling her out of the crowd's sight and into his stiffened cock. "Just try to stop me."

Tess rested her fingers on his tie. "Bad boy."

"Just wait until I get you alone."

"In time." She eased away.

"Not so fast." Josh caught her wrist, gently holding it. "Where are you going now?"

"The table."

He kept his voice lowered. "We eat and then we cut out. No arguments. That's final."

"Only if you want to rush it."

He laughed. "Rush *what*?"

"You'll see."

He pulled her back into himself, showing her his strength and determination. "I want to know now."

"I want to surprise you." Tess lifted her face to his. Her gaze was as soft as her voice, "Let me surprise you . . . please."

She was already doing that as she eased away and returned to their table. There, she engaged in conversation with the others, again charming the men.

No more ground rules, she had said. *None.*

Josh kept hearing that promise in his head as they ate and Tess played the perfect dinner companion. A little too perfect for his taste. She delicately touched the back of his hand or gently rested her fingers on his jacket sleeve, when she damn well knew that wasn't enough to satisfy a monk, much less him.

Josh needed her hands on his cock; he wanted her mouth on each part of him, but only after he had tasted her.

He imagined drawing her nipples into his mouth, suckling that precious flesh until it couldn't get any tighter; then lifting her gown to remove her thong so that he could see her dark triangle of hair that pointed to pleasure; her swollen lips; that womanly moisture sparkling on those delicate curls and her clit.

He needed to lick that, to taste it, to become a part of her so that he no longer knew where he ended and she began.

Only not now; not yet. As the band started to play a slow ballad, an older man pushed to his feet. "May I have this dance, Tess?" Before she could respond, he looked at Josh. "You don't mind, do you?"

Fucking A he did. He wanted to leave now.

Tess, on the other hand, wasn't in such a rush. "Of course Josh doesn't mind." She looked at him. "In all the time we've known each other, Josh has never once asked me to dance."

"Well, don't start now," the old guy joked.

Tess smiled. "He won't. Will you, Josh?"

You are so going to pay for this. "Guess not."

"In that case, the next one's mine."

Josh looked at the man who had said that. He was in his late thirties and couldn't take his eyes off her gown.

"Then it's my turn," another said.

"I'm looking forward to dancing with all of you," Tess said. She took her partner's arm, allowing him to lead her to the dance floor.

Josh leaned over the left arm of his chair so he could watch her, while she looked past that man's shoulder to look at him.

The guy in his late thirties asked, "How long have you and Tess been dating?"

"Not long enough."

"If I were you, I'd learn how to dance."

Yeah, yeah, yeah.

I want to surprise you, she had said. *Let me surprise you.*

By the time Tess was dancing with that third guy, while also keeping her gaze on him, Josh had decided on a surprise for her.

All it would take was one call.

As he left the table and pulled out his cell, Tess immediately stopped dancing.

"Oh, sorry," her partner said, "did I step on your foot?"

She looked at him, then back at Josh. He had left the table to take a call? He was conducting business, now?

"Tess, did I hurt you?"

She looked at her partner and shook her head. Josh was going to hurt her, but not tonight. By God, she was going to have that.

Tess was about to leave the dance floor when she remembered her partner. He stood there with his arms out, waiting for her.

"Sorry," she said, then danced with him as she kept her gaze on Josh.

During the entire number he talked on his cell. At last, the music ended. As he went back to the table, so did Tess.

"Why, dear," one of the older women said, "you must be exhausted."

More like pissed and depressed. "I'm fine."

"I'm afraid I'm not," Josh said. "I have a long night ahead of me; we're going to have to leave."

Her heart fell. "You have business to conduct?"

"You know I do." Josh took her hand, lacing his fingers through hers. "We discussed it before we came here, remember?"

Ah, so she hadn't lost him to regular business, after all.

Tess gently squeezed his fingers. "Yes, I do. You're right, it's time to leave."

Chapter Fourteen

No more ground rules . . . none.

It had been too much to hope for and Josh couldn't wait any longer. As they reached his car in the parking structure, he saw that they were alone. There was no public, no paparazzi, only a man who craved a woman and wanted her to need him in return.

He met her gaze. "Come here."

A smile played across Tess's lips as she moved into him, her hands sliding over his shoulders.

It wasn't enough. Pulling Tess close, Josh tightened his arm around her waist. The back of her head was cradled in his free hand as he kissed her savagely, not allowing her so much as a whimper. His tongue silenced that. His hips ground into hers so that she felt every inch of his erection.

That only fueled her passion and made her wild, taking exactly what she wanted until they were both temporarily sated.

Breathing hard, Josh rested his forehead against hers. "You know, I should be pissed."

Tess swallowed. "Because I kissed you back?"

He laughed. "No. You've made me wait too damned long for tonight."

She rolled her forehead over his. "It hasn't even started." Slipping her hand beneath his jacket, she stroked his left pec. "And you made me wait, too."

"I didn't dance with every man in that place."

"Did I thank you for that?"

Josh laughed again, until she worked her other hand into his trouser pocket. "What are you doing?"

"Looking."

"Yeah, I know. For what?"

Her answer was to stroke his erection through that pocket.

Josh inhaled sharply.

"Now, be nice," she said, then continued to stroke his rod.

"Aw, shit. *Tess*!"

"Relax. I'm just looking for your keys."

Josh lifted his face and breathed hard as she checked the other pocket, stroking him through that, before finally pulling out her hand.

"Got 'em." She slipped her free hand beneath his chin. "And from the looks of it, not a minute too soon."

Josh swallowed, then frowned. "Now, you're driving?"

"You'll get your turn later. Take off your tie."

"What?"

"That's okay," she said, "I'll take it off for you."

Before Josh could ask why she was doing this, Tess was already unknotting and pulling the tie from his collar, then stuffing it in his trouser pocket.

When her fingers again searched for his cock, Josh's shoulders bunched. "Damn, you're mean."

Tess gave him an innocent look. "You think this is mean?"

"Yeah. One more stroke out here where I can't do anything about it and you're going to kill me."

"Sorry." She pulled her hand out, then eased away. "Take off your jacket."

Josh continued to catch his breath as he glanced around the deserted lot. "Are my trousers going to be next?"

"Only if you want to be cited for indecent exposure and spend the night in jail instead of with me."

He looked at her. "You're stripping me and it's got nothing to do with your no more ground rules stuff?"

"Those are my conditions. You break state law and you're on your own."

He pulled off his jacket and tossed it to her. "Now, it's your turn." He planted his hands on his lean hips. "What are you going to take off?"

"Nothing . . . yet. Unbutton your collar and roll up your sleeves."

He arched one brow.

She ran her fingertips over his cheek. "Please."

Hell. He did as he was told. "What now?"

Tess moved into him; she kissed and licked the hollow of his throat before easing back. "In the car. No arguments."

At the moment Josh could barely breathe.

"Please?" she added.

"Whatever you want."

After tossing his jacket into the backseat, she also got in, and took off.

Josh looked at the scenery whizzing by—all those bed-and-breakfasts, hotels, and motels she kept passing. "Where are we going?"

"You'll see."

"Not if you keep driving so fast." He looked at the speedometer. "You're going to get a ticket. You might even get this sucker impounded."

Tess stopped at a red light. Turning in her seat, she ran her fingertips over his upper lip, then gently traced the contours of his mouth. "I'm an ex-cop, I don't get tickets."

It was a moment before Josh could concentrate on anything other than that stroking. He felt it clear through the back of his mouth. At last, he asked, "By the way, where's your weapon?"

Tess traced his left ear with her fingertip. "Let's just say it's more concealed than yours." She lowered her hand to his fly, then drew lazy circles over his thickened shaft.

Josh moaned.

"Oh, sorry," Tess said, pulling back her hand. "I'm being mean again."

He opened his eyes and continued to breathe hard. "Are you kidding? We're in the car now. Why'd you stop?"

"Had to." She pointed. "Light's changed."

She zipped away from it, driving them down one darkened street after another, taking turns here, there, everywhere, until she finally reached a building that looked like a warehouse, but was surrounded by late model cars.

As the pulsing sounds of Latin music washed over them, Josh looked at her. "Your world," he said. "Dancing."

"Foreplay," she corrected. Her eyes were bright, her expression a promise of what was to come. "If you're up to it."

"Would you like to check?"

She giggled. "Later. Right now I should teach you the moves you'll need in there. We can use that area to the left." She pointed to a darkened part of the lot. "Or that one over to the—"

"Tess, I know how to dance."

She laughed. "The merengue? And the tango? And—"

"Salsa," he added, before she could.

Her brows lifted in surprise, and then she frowned. "How could you know— Wait a sec," she interrupted herself. "That's who that guy was?"

Not only was she beautiful, but sharp. Even so, Josh decided to play with her as she was always playing with him. "I haven't a clue what you're—"

"Don't give me that. The young guy who came to your office that day and disappeared with you into the conference room; he was a dance instructor, right?"

"Actually, he's my auditor."

Her brows lifted. "No kidding. I thought he was a gigolo."

"Aren't those for women?"

"Usually. But you did have the blinds drawn."

"You're going to keep grilling me on this, aren't you?"

"Only until you tell me the truth."

Josh crossed his arms over his chest. "Fine. I took dance lessons, so shoot me."

"Oh, no," she quickly said. "I should thank you. But why did you hire someone? You could have asked me to teach you."

He looked embarrassed. "I wanted it to be a surprise."

It was. Tess couldn't imagine any of the other men she had known going to such trouble for her, especially if it meant spending their hard-earned money or risking their macho image.

Why Josh did it wasn't entirely clear. Could be he had wanted to add some meat to their original story that they had met dancing. Could be he had wanted to convince those persistent women and the paparazzi that he and she were romantically involved by going to a place like this.

Could be he was even falling for her.

Sure.

Tess told herself to get real. Learning to dance wasn't a promise of forever, unless it was in her mother and father's world.

"I'm very impressed," she said.

"Wait'll you see me dance."

"We could leave now if you want."

He laughed good-naturedly. "Not a chance. I'm looking forward to this." He reached out and brushed his knuckles over the swell of her right breast.

Tess murmured, "No more ground rules."

"None."

"I think you're ready," she said.

Josh knew he would certainly do his best as they entered the club.

Its nondescript exterior hardly prepared him for what was inside. There were softly pulsing lights and a glass roof. Beneath countless stars, hundreds of young couples moved sinuously against each other, keeping time to the music.

It was outrageously erotic, the strains prolonged, provocative.

Tess was immediately seduced. Working her fingers through her hair, she lifted it off her shoulders, then swayed her hips. Soon, her eyes were closed, her body undulating as she raised her face to the sky, becoming fully lost in this world.

Josh watched transfixed; there was nothing else he could do.

Never had he seen a woman dance like that. Tess was as free as he was captive and somehow that felt so very right.

When that number finally ended, Tess released her hair, but kept her arms over her head, like a dancer. Her body moved slowly, seductively as the new music quickly began. When she at last met his gaze, her eyes were hooded, those delicate nostrils flared. She spoke above the music, "Dance with me."

Nothing could have kept Josh away. He slipped his arm around her waist, then pressed his hips to hers, moving with the beat.

Tess held his gaze; she owned it. He was in her world now, and her voice became quickly playful. "So, they tell me you can dance."

"Not like you, but then, who could?"

She laughed. "You don't even want to try?"

"Sure. Lower your arms."

The moment she did, Josh wrapped his fingers around her right wrist, while Tess wreathed her left arm around his neck.

As they moved to the music, Josh actually felt that this was almost as good as sex. "How am I doing?"

"Very good. But this is such an easy step. What if it gets complicated?"

"I'll do my best to keep up."

Tess worked her body into his as the music demanded. "We should keep it simple. You need to take baby steps before you can run."

"Point taken, but I have been practicing." He turned her in

time to the music, their hips pressed close. "And you could at least try to follow my lead."

Tess glanced down to their swaying hips, then met his gaze. "Only if it takes me where I want to go." She so quickly changed steps, Josh couldn't follow and was soon two feet away from her.

Hands on her hips, chin held high, Tess said, "I thought you wanted to dance."

Josh arched one brow and moved right back into her.

Her smile was wicked. "You're certain you took lessons for this?"

Before he could respond, she was spinning away from him, then coming right back, pressing her body to his. "Think of an answer yet?"

Josh laughed. "Yes, I took lessons. Over several days, in fact."

"Then those business things you had to go to were really dancing lessons?"

"Maybe."

She gave him a patient smile. "Poor baby. You're not sure?"

"It's not something I would forget, all right?"

Tess glanced down to their bodies. "Not if you danced like this with that guy." She ran her fingers over the soft hair at the nape of his neck. "Did you enjoy that, Josh?"

Oh, she was bad. "Fuck that."

"So you do like women?"

"Depends." He ground his hips into hers, letting her know what she did to him. "Are they as beautiful as you?"

Her eyes widened in surprise. "So now you think I'm beautiful?"

"From the moment you walked into my life and begged to be my bodyguard."

"Begged?" Tess laughed; she gasped in delight as Josh turned her around, then pulled her close, his hand just above the seam of her buttocks, his forehead to hers.

"Yes, begged," he said as he moved to the beat of the music. "Admit it."

"You kissed me."

"You fucking responded."

"Oh, no, Josh, this is responding." She put her hands on either side of his face, angled his head so that his mouth met hers, then didn't let go.

Josh stopped dancing. He couldn't even breathe. Her mouth was relentless, her tongue probing after she thrust it inside.

When she finally pulled back, Josh was still slightly dizzy.

She, on the other hand, casually swayed her hips against his in time to the music. "Poor baby; I didn't hurt you, did I?"

He lifted his brows.

"Maybe you should sit the rest of this one out." She eased away.

"Come back here." He pulled her close, then captured her mouth.

His kiss was filled with urgency and male power, demanding that Tess follow.

She did.

The dance was quickly forgotten; the music, the people, this place no longer existed. His scent, his heat, his strength became her world until Josh pulled his mouth free.

The music came back slowly, as did the noise of the others. Not that any of it mattered. She and Josh remained as they were, undisturbed, until he asked, "Had enough?"

Not even if he had promised her a lifetime. Tess knew she would always want more. "We haven't even started yet, have we?"

His eyes were hooded as he lowered his hand to just above her buttocks, then pushed her into his erection. "You want more?"

Tess wanted tonight to last. She didn't want it to ever end. "Please. Keep dancing with me."

His expression changed. "Really?"

"Please."

He looked as if he wanted to argue, but at last gently pressed his lips to hers, then danced through the number and those that followed. He carefully matched her every move in the tango, the merengue, and salsa until their flesh was heated and moist.

Through it all, their gazes remained locked, their bodies obedient to the music and each other's need.

It was an intoxicating moment that no liquor or drug could match.

As the last dance ended and the other couples whistled and applauded, Tess remained in Josh's arms, her gaze on his.

"Enough?" he asked.

"Only of this."

It was exactly what he had been waiting to hear. His expression was all male, intent and definitely dangerous.

Tess's skin tingled. "Where do we go from here?"

"Back to my world," he said. "Now, I have a surprise for you."

Chapter Fifteen

This was definitely getting interesting.

Josh was driving even faster to his surprise than Tess had to the club. He was so intent, he didn't seem to notice her fingers running down the side of his leg.

Maybe if she unzipped his fly he'd notice that.

Tess restrained herself. Before this night was over she was going to taste and touch him as much as she wanted. There was no turning back now.

As her gaze traced his handsome profile, his strong jaw, his shoulders and legs, she wondered if they were going back to the country club. Maybe there were guest rooms there, after all. Not that it mattered. Tess wanted him so badly, she was prepared to enjoy him in the backseat of the car if that's what he wanted.

At last, she asked, "Are we getting close?"

He kept his gaze on the road, but did smile. "It's just ahead."

Tess looked over her shoulder and couldn't have been more surprised. "We're going to a marina?"

"That's the only way to get to my yacht."

"Get out." She turned to him. "We're making love on your yacht?"

Josh finally looked at her. He seemed confused. "We're going to be making love?"

Tess laughed. She slapped his arm, then quickly sobered. "We better be."

He grinned. "If you insist."

Tess could hardly contain herself as they entered the private marina. Her gaze swept the largest of the boats that only movie stars or drug lords could afford; many of the names suggesting their owners' occupations. One baby was called *The Idol*, another *Addiction*. Then there was *Over the Rainbow*, *Shameless*, and *Lady Lust*.

Josh parked close to that one.

"Thanks," Tess said as he opened her door and helped her out. "What did you name your boat?"

"You'll see." He led her away from *Lady Lust*.

To the left, lively music and loud laughter came from the marina restaurant where a party was in full swing despite the hour.

Here, a few couples were still up and talking quietly on the decks of their boats, while others were in the cabins below, with those muted nightlights dancing across the water.

As she and Josh walked hand-in-hand, Tess lifted her face to the scant breeze. The night was surprisingly clear, yet steamy; the air sweetened by the sea and the scent of their bodies.

At last, Josh gently squeezed her fingers. "There she is . . . the very last one."

As Tess looked, her lips parted. The boat was a startling white with a dark blue line running along its side. It was possibly a hundred feet long, but sleek and sensual, its curved lines designed for superb performance, just like its owner. "Wow."

"I like her."

"Who wouldn't?" Tess tried to make out the letters on the back but they were still too far away. "What did you name her?"

There was hesitation in his voice. "*The Dreamer*."

Tess looked at him. "What the guys called you after your first job in construction?"

Josh seemed embarrassed. "I wanted to show them and myself that I wasn't a complete idiot."

"Believe me, you have. Let's go."

He laughed as she pulled him to the boat. Finally, Josh held back. "Not so fast, remember?"

How could she when he was pulling her into his arms?

Tess pressed her mouth to his ear and whispered, "How do we get on it? Do we jump? Is there a rope we can climb?"

Josh's chest rumbled with quiet laughter. "The only thing you'll be climbing tonight is me. You knew that at that stupid dinner, which just dragged on and on, and while we danced, which I honestly enjoyed. So, why are you in such a rush now?"

They were finally at the end of their journey and had so little time. In a very few hours, everything would be over. Not that Tess wanted to think of that now. Running her fingers over the soft hair at the nape of his neck, she murmured, "Once you're exhausted I swear I'll go slow. I don't want to kill you."

"You are too kind." He playfully slapped her butt, then eased away. "Let's go."

Once Tess had removed her heels and they were on board, Josh took off his shoes and socks, then brought her into an area he called the pilothouse. To her surprise, he left the lights off, got into the captain's seat and started the thing.

Tess stopped looking at the leather bench to the right that might have worked for making love. "We're leaving?"

"You do want to be alone, don't you?"

She went to his chair and sat on the arm. "You'll be there, right?"

Josh lifted his gaze from her right breast resting on his shoulder. "Wouldn't miss it for the world. What I meant by alone is without the possibility of paparazzi or anyone else."

Tess nodded, even as her heart started to fall. Since the publication of that other guy's picture, there hadn't been any paparazzi. Since that shopping trip at Kiki's, there hadn't been any obnoxious fans. As Alan had predicted, Josh was yesterday's news and a dethroned hunk.

A little over a month ago, before they had met, Tess wouldn't have believed that she would have missed the paparazzi or that she could feel so sad. "Good idea." She cleared her throat and made her voice light. "Do you want me to drive?"

He smiled. "I want you to relax and conserve your strength for what's to come."

"You should be doing that. You're an old fart, remember?"

Josh laughed, then slipped his arm around her waist, keeping her steady as he steered the boat away from the dock. "You really want to help?"

Tess ran her fingers under his collar. "I can't let you do all the work." She leaned over and traced his ear with her tongue.

He trembled, then sighed. "You need something to keep you busy."

"Okay." She ran her other hand down his flat belly to between his legs, then cupped and fondled his balls.

Josh inhaled so sharply, he briefly choked. "Not that—not yet."

"You're making this awfully hard."

He slid his gaze to her, then pulled Tess onto his lap, holding her around the waist with one strong arm, while steering the boat with the other. "See that screen to the left?"

Tess looked. "Yup. You need cable or a satellite dish, the reception's lousy."

"It's a night vision display, not a TV. I use it so I don't hit anything."

Tess looked from that grainy black-and-white picture to the outside, surprised at how much detail the display had picked up, clearly showing that this area was fairly deserted.

"Cool." She wiggled her butt into his erection. "Do you have X-ray vision, too?"

His breath was hot against her ear. "Will I need it?"

She turned her face into his and murmured, "Not tonight."

Josh kissed her cheek, then got right back to business. "Now this is what I want you to do."

He wasn't talking sex, but as his voice rumbled in her ear and his stiffened rod pressed against her buttocks it seemed pretty damned close. She was to be his first mate, watching the screen to make certain they "didn't bump into anything."

"But each other," he finally added.

"Then I'll have to watch you."

"You want to get there or not?"

"Where?"

"You'll see."

Tess looked from him to the display, then outside as they cleared the slip and headed across the water. The sea was a rippling black mass with no end in sight, the sky sprinkled with stars, the air a heated caress.

As intimate as the club had been, packed tight with all those dancers and lovers, Tess felt swallowed by the night, protected by the dark.

"How you doing?" he asked.

"I could be more comfortable."

Josh loosened his arm. "Better?"

Tess turned her torso into him until her right breast caressed his chest. "Much."

Josh flicked his gaze at her, then looked back to the instruments, mastering the boat as easily as he had mastered the land.

He really belonged here, while she was no more than a temporary visitor.

Still, Tess was grateful for tonight as she simply gazed at him.

"You're supposed to be watching that screen, not me," he said.

"You're more interesting."

Josh worked his mouth around so he wouldn't smile. "Okay, you win." He brought back his arm, releasing her. "Go ahead and play, I'll do all the work."

Tess got off his lap and hunkered down by the chair. "I'll do some of it later."

"Promises, promises; what are you doing?"

"Do you really have to ask?"

She had already unbuttoned his trousers and unzipped his fly, and now worked her fingers past the opening in his briefs to his hot, stiffened rod.

"Holy shit, stop!" Josh inhaled deeply, then nearly moaned. "Tess, I mean it! You're going to have to stop!"

"But you said I could play."

"Not with me. At least, not until we're anchored."

"To each other?"

He laughed, then moaned, then begged, "Behave, please, at least for a little while."

Tess stroked his cock one last time, loving its stiffness and heat, then pulled her hand out of his briefs and zipped him back up. "Okay." Pressing her fingertips to her face, she inhaled deeply, then moaned to his musky scent.

"Are you going to wait for me or not?"

"Sorry." She sniffed until his scent was gone, then sat in the chair next to his and looked out at the water.

As the minutes ticked by, the area became increasingly deserted until Tess finally saw that they were the only ones on this part of the water. At that point Josh cut the engines. A short time later, he announced that they were anchored.

"We're here?" she asked, getting out of her chair when he left his.

"Yup." He took one last look at the instruments, then hauled her into his arms, letting her kiss him, since Tess already had her tongue in his mouth.

When she was finally through, she asked, "Where's here?"

Josh leaned against the back of his chair, momentarily

limp from her kiss, then gave her the location in longitude and latitude.

"Oh, right, now I see."

"No, you don't, but you will. No more playing around. From here on in it gets serious and you get naked. Come on."

Taking her hand, he went to a cabinet and got a beach towel.

She asked, "What's that for?"

"You'll see." He led her onto the deck that barely moved with the gentle flow of the water.

Okay, this was unexpected. Tess turned into the soft, warm breeze, letting it pull her hair away from her face. "We're not going to one of the rooms downstairs?"

"You mean the cabins that are below?"

"Probably. We're not going there?"

"When we can make love up here?"

Tess followed his gaze to the forward deck, then lifted her face to the moon. It hung heavy and low in the sky, sending gauzy threads of light to the water that slapped gently against the boat.

That was the only sound. It was so very quiet, Tess felt compelled to speak in a lowered voice. The shouting and moaning would come later. "This is a nice surprise."

"You like?"

"Oh, yeah. It's— What's that?" Her gaze had paused on a fire on a beach that was only a short swim away. "I thought you said we were going to be alone."

"Wouldn't have it any other way."

She pointed at the fire. "They might."

"That's for us . . . later."

She looked over her shoulder at him. "You own that fire?"

Josh smiled. "And the beach and the land beyond it."

"How'd you do that?"

"Just negotiated a price that I thought was—"

"No." She laughed. "I meant, how'd you get that fire going? You've been with me the entire—" Tess abruptly stopped, then thought back to that dinner, the call he was on while she was dancing with every guy at their table. "You called someone while we were at that dinner to set this up."

"It pays to have a good staff."

She arched one brow. "And confidence that this would happen."

"I could say the same for you and our night of dancing." Josh held the beach towel to his chest, then put out his other arm as he gently swayed his lean hips.

Hmmm. "You're still not as good as me. But don't you worry; I fully intend to teach you a thing or two in the next couple of hours."

Before Josh could even think to comment on that, Tess turned and padded toward the forward deck. As she did, she unzipped her gown and pushed it off both shoulders.

That garment fluttered in the breeze as it slid to her waist, then over her hips.

At last, she stopped, allowing it to puddle at her feet.

Holy shit. Josh locked his knees so he could keep standing. She was nude, except for a frilly garter on her left thigh. A red garter that made her taut, moon-washed flesh appear even paler.

He moistened his lips, but forgot to swallow as his mind kept dancing around the same thought.

She had been fucking nude beneath that dress all night? She hadn't even worn a thong?

His gaze followed the curve of her calves, the perfect lines of her thighs, that unbelievable garter, her plush buttocks and sleek back, and finally her face as Tess looked over her shoulder at him.

Her honeyed eyes sparkled in the moonlight. The breeze played with her hair. Her smile was seductive.

Josh finally swallowed, then looked back at her garter. Was her weapon in the front of it? Had she carried it that way all night? How had he missed feeling it?

"Something wrong?" she asked.

He swallowed again, then pointed. "You're actually wearing a garter."

"Until you take it off."

His gaze snapped up as she stepped out of her dress, then tied it around the railing so the wind couldn't blow it away. With that accomplished, she padded to the forward deck, her naked cheeks bouncing.

Josh liked that. He followed, holding the beach towel between his teeth as he unbuttoned his shirt as fast as he could, then tore it off himself and tied it to the railing. By the time he reached Tess, he was bare-chested, the towel was under his left arm and his hands were heading for his fly.

"Uh-uh," Tess said, turning to face him. "I'll do that."

His gaze fell to her hands on his trousers, then to her garter and what she had slipped beneath it on the inside of her thigh. Not a gun, oh, no. "You brought cuffs?"

She finished unzipping him, then pushed his trousers to his thighs. "You sound surprised."

"Pleasantly. Where's your weapon?"

"In my purse." She went to her knees as she pulled on his trousers until they were at his feet.

Josh stepped out of them, then waited as she tied them to the railing. "Why didn't you wear it in the garter?"

Her shoulders shook with suppressed laughter. "Not even those babes on *CSI: Miami* could carry a gun in a freakin' garter." Tess looked up and smiled. "What's the matter? Did you want to hold my weapon?"

He grinned. "No, but you better hold mine."

"Yes, sir, Mr. Wyatt. Whatever you want." Tess worked her fingers beneath the brief's elastic, pulled those suckers down, then cradled his thickened cock in both hands.

Aw, damn. Josh liked that so much his head hung between his shoulders and his toes curled.

"Oh, baby," Tess said, running her forefinger over the blunt head, "you are so cocked."

"I know." His voice was strangled. "So, just give me a minute, before we—"

"Absolutely." Tess released him and pushed to her feet.

Josh frowned at his abandoned cock, then gave that frown to her. "You didn't have to completely stop."

"Relax. It's only for a moment." She took the beach towel from him, then said, "Follow me, please."

That "please" and her bouncing buttocks did it. Josh stepped out of his briefs, stuffed them in his trouser pocket and joined her on the platform on the forward deck.

She had already tied one end of the towel to the railing so it wouldn't blow away. "Go on, lie down."

His breathing really picked up. He slid his gaze to her. "You first."

"Uh-uh. First time, I'm on top."

No way was Josh going to argue with that. Once he was sprawled across that towel, hands behind his head, legs spread wide to flaunt his equipment, he arched one brow. "What now?"

Tess moistened her lips as she stared at his stiffened cock that pointed straight at her, and his tightened balls beneath. "You are so beautiful."

Before Josh could offer his thanks, she pulled out the cuffs, sank to her knees by his side and sat back on her feet.

He stared at the moonlight sparkling on that metal. His heart pounded wildly. "Did I ever tell you that I like it when you're mean?"

"You will tonight." She smiled. "Give me your hands."

"Uh-uh. Not so fast. If I let you cuff me now, do I get to do you later?"

"No."

Josh laughed, then inhaled sharply as Tess ran her free hand down his chest to his navel, then to his groin, playing with the hair above his cock. "How fair is that?"

"It's not at all fair to me." She lowered her hand to his balls, cupping them in her palm, then spoke above his prolonged moan. "But then, I'll have the pleasure of knowing that you're too tired to do anything at all once I'm finished loving you."

Josh swallowed hard. He pulled his hands from behind his head and offered them to her.

Tess smiled. "Thanks."

"My pleasure."

"It will be," she murmured, determined to make this a night he never forgot.

Pushing to her knees, Tess quickly straddled him, working her butt against his cock as she snapped the first cuff on his left wrist.

Josh didn't notice. His gaze had fallen to their joined bodies, remaining there, until Tess leaned over him to run the empty cuff around the railing.

His gaze jumped up; he watched her breasts sway above his face, then lifted his head and licked her left nipple.

Tess smiled, then snapped the other cuff around his right wrist. "Now, don't move."

He was momentarily silent. "What happens if I do?"

"You won't get this." Tess moved down him until she could cover his mouth with her own. As she kissed him deeply, leisurely, taking her time, driving him nuts, she ran her fingers down his arms to his pits, then stroked that thick, dark hair.

His chest heaved beneath her.

Tess hadn't even started. Pulling her mouth from his, she whispered in Spanish her need of him. Those lilting words were finally muffled as she pressed her mouth to his neck, suckling that flesh even as she moved her hips so that she was stroking his flat belly with her furry mound.

His legs tensed; he lifted his ass as if he could barely stand the pleasure she was giving.

He would have to. Tess was determined that he never forget this night. She kissed his shoulder, then the underside of his left arm, before moving to his pit. She filled herself with his scent, then buried her face in that hair and licked it.

Josh moaned. His head moved from side to side. "Shit, that feels good. I've never had— No one has— It's something I never—"

Tess finally interrupted his babbling. "No one's ever loved you here?" She found that hard to believe. What was the matter with those other women? As Josh swallowed, then heaved air, she murmured, "To hell with them. You're with me now."

He sighed. "Did I thank you for that?"

"You will."

He moaned as she continued licking until his body was taut beneath her and his breathing was strained.

Poor baby. She was working him too hard and too fast. She smiled. Too damned bad.

Moving to his chest, Tess licked the flat disk of his left nipple even as she roughly fondled his right pec and rocked her hips so that her mound was teasing his cock.

Josh made a strangled sound. He tightened his jaw and lifted his chin.

Tess moved to his navel, circling that depression with her tongue, before licking that thin line of hair beneath it that arrowed to his groin.

There, she prepared to worship him, settling between his legs that were again bent at the knees, though that still wasn't enough. Placing her hands on the insides of his thighs, Tess spread him even further.

Josh squeezed his fists. His chest pumped with his ragged breathing.

Tess listened to that male music as she buried her face in this hair, licking it as she had the other, while her right hand cupped his balls, gently cradling them, working them as Josh gasped, then panted.

Tess gave him a moment's peace, but only so that she could lift his cock in her hands, then run her tongue up his full length.

His voice was agonized, his words incoherent.

She murmured to him in Spanish, telling him again of her need.

It was in her touch as she cradled his cock and swirled her tongue over the blunt head.

Josh cried out.

She licked him again and again, flicking her tongue over the back of his rod, that uneven skin where the feeling was the most intense. When his head thrashed from side to side as if he couldn't stand it any longer, Tess took him fully in her mouth.

"Aw, damn!" he shouted.

She hadn't even started. As Tess worked his cock in and out of her mouth, she played with his balls, loving their moist weight in the palm of her hand, loving him.

For this man, no act was forbidden. Honoring his body, pleasuring him to completion was what Tess had been born for. She knew that now and that she would never love another as she loved him.

When his beautiful body finally convulsed with his climax and his roar of pleasure broke the heavy quiet, Tess kept her head lowered as she continued to serve him, to bring him all that he required.

She was kissing his balls when he finally begged her to stop. The feeling was just too intense; he couldn't endure it any longer.

Tess lifted her gaze and smiled to how he was trying to raise his head to look at her, but could not. She had taken all of his strength and replaced it with joy. "What?" she asked, as her fingers continued to stroke him.

"Stop!" he shouted, then nearly cried, "At least for a few seconds, please!"

Tess looked on either side of herself as Josh tried to close his legs, but could not . . . she was in the way. "What?" she asked again, as she stroked the insides of his thighs.

He swore, then with great effort, finally lifted his head. "Stop. I mean it. It's too intense, I can't stand it. And don't you dare say what again."

Tess sat back on her feet. "Relax. I didn't hear you. You really want me to stop?"

"Hell, yes!"

"Too bad."

"Tess!"

She licked the insides of his thighs and balls until Josh was wiggling like a fish drowning in air.

At last, she straightened. "Okay, okay. I've stopped."

He opened one eye and glared at her.

Tess ignored that as she pushed to her knees, then turned until her back was facing him. Bending forward at the waist and lifting her butt in the air, she lowered her head to kiss his right foot.

It was a long moment before he wiggled his toes.

Tess looked around her shoulder, seeing that his gaze was on her butt. Good. As long as he was distracted, she could do whatever she wanted.

Pressing her left foot against his balls and cock, she licked his toes.

He laughed. "Stop it!"

She pulled her foot away from his groin.

"Not that," he complained.

Tess straightened and looked over her shoulder at him. "Talk about hard to get along with."

He shook his hands until the cuffs clanged against the railing. "I let you do this to me, didn't I?"

"It was a good idea, wasn't it?"

His expression softened, then hardened once more. "You nearly killed me just now."

"Aw, poor baby." She turned around to face him. "I told you you had to take baby steps before you could run."

He laughed. "Fuck that. Open these cuffs."

"When I'm through." She looked at his weary cock. "I figure in another hour or so, when you're hard again, we can finally make love and then I'll be able to open those—"

"You are so going to pay for that."

She met his eyes. "Not as long as you're cuffed."

Josh dropped his head back to the platform. "Give me a minute."

"No rush." Tess pushed to a standing position.

He frowned. "Where are you going?"

"You'll see."

She moved from between his legs to his side, then straddled his lean hips.

His eyes immediately grew hooded. "You like being on top, don't you?"

Tess looked over her shoulder at his cock. That baby was getting hard fast. "The question is, do you like it?"

Josh wasn't certain what to say when Tess met his gaze. She seemed genuinely concerned that she might not be giving him pleasure.

My God, didn't the woman know what she did to him?

If Josh hadn't loved her before this moment, not only would he have been a fool, she would have surely captured his heart after what she had just done. Never in his life had a woman enjoyed his body as much as she seemed to.

The joy that gave him was amazing, though quickly overshadowed by fear.

If she had been anyone else, Josh might have believed she was falling in love with him. But she was an ex-cop and a bodyguard who had been surrounded by cops all her life.

Tess hadn't been sheltered; she lived life like a man. Free. Uninhibited. Even reckless.

Maybe that's why she made love like this. Maybe he wasn't so special to her, after all.

"Hey, you all right?" she asked.

Josh knew he wasn't going to be all right ever again after

this night. He was going to be in love and in lots of pain when this ended.

Oddly enough, that didn't stop him from moving forward. At this point, nothing could. "I do like it," he said, finally answering her first question. "I like everything that you do."

She looked briefly thoughtful, then arched one brow. "I haven't done everything to you."

Josh couldn't help but smile. Damn, he loved her. "Then what are you waiting for?"

She put up her finger as if she needed a moment, then looked over her shoulder at his cock.

"It's already hard," he said.

Tess turned back to him. "Do you always brag like this?"

"Only around you. Now, be nice."

She gave him a look that said *bite me,* then pushed to her knees and wrapped her fingers around his stiffened rod.

Josh threw back his head and so did she as her body lowered onto his, forcing him deep inside.

In that moment, Tess knew what it was like to be completely filled, to have her flesh stretched by a man for his pleasure. Josh was large and knew it. He thrust his hips upward until their bodies touched and he was completely within her heated sheath, and then he flexed his cock, forcing her flesh to accommodate his.

Tess relaxed her body so that it gave him what he wanted and what she needed. Inhaling deeply, she finally lowered her head and opened her eyes.

Josh was already watching her; his gaze was all male and completely dangerous.

It made Tess bold. It made her want to please him as she had no other man. Lifting her hands, she cupped her breasts because he could not. She flicked her thumbs over the taut nipples and squeezed those soft globes; she tightened her muscles around him, holding his cock prisoner, before relaxing, then tightening, again.

His nostrils flared, his fists clenched.

She continued. Her body was relentless in the pleasure she was bringing to them both. Her lips parted in a quiet sigh.

Josh wasn't as delicate. He growled; he even swore as he tried to maintain control of a situation that was in her hands, not his.

At last, Tess released her right breast and lowered her hand to her clit. As she slowly stroked it, while lifting herself off his cock, Josh's eyes closed. When she lowered herself back onto him, he raised his chin to the sky.

Her movements became faster then, more assured. She stroked his thickened shaft with her body, while teasing her erect nub with her hand.

The feeling was too intense, nearly unbearable. Still Tess worked her body against his in this dance that was like no other. The moves belonged to them alone; the lapping sea, the whispering wind was their music.

It was an act of love that could not be denied and one that brought a primal growl from Josh and a moan of delight from Tess as they both reached climax.

In the following moments, the breeze cooled her damp flesh, while her muscles continued to convulse around his cock.

At last, though, only their mingled sighs remained to remind them of what had just happened.

Moistening her lips, Tess lowered her head and looked at Josh.

His lids were heavy, he looked as sleepy as she felt, while his expression was pure contentment. "Come here."

Tightening her muscles to keep him inside, Tess leaned forward, draping her body over his.

Josh smiled, then closed his eyes as she gently kissed his mouth.

"Nice," he said.

"There'll be lots more," she promised, "after you rest."

Josh ran his tongue around his mouth as he shook his head.

"No. I'm fine." He paused to yawn. "I don't need to rest."

"Sure you do." Tess gently kissed the side of his mouth and his cheek. "Old farts always do."

That got him cooking. His eyes immediately opened; he looked more alert than Tess did after ten hours of sleep. "What?"

"I'm just trying to avoid killing you, Josh."

"Fuck that."

"Oh, baby, I want you to do that to me, but are you really up to it?"

He laughed. "When in the hell are you going to be nice?"

"Not now." With as much grace as she could muster, Tess pushed to a sitting position, then off of him.

Josh frowned. "What are you doing?"

She looked from that fire on the beach to him. "Were you planning to cook us something over there?"

"Stuff's already made. It's in a cooler. Why? You hungry again already?"

Tess ran her tongue over her upper lip, then slipped it back inside. "I'm always hungry."

He arched one brow. "Good, now get back—" Josh paused, then shouted, "Hey! Where are you going?"

Tess looked over her shoulder at him. She pointed to the back of the boat. "There's a platform there where I can go into the water and swim over there." She swung her arm to that fire."It looks nice. See ya."

"Hey!" Josh shouted again. "Wait!"

Tess spoke over her shoulder as she continued to that platform. "What is it now?"

Was she kidding? He shouted, "What about these damned cuffs?"

Tess had just reached the area above the swim platform. Turning to him, she shouted, "They're not real, Josh. Did you actually think I'd bring real cuffs?" Her laughter was musical, filling the night air. "Just pull them apart really hard and they'll fall right off." That said, she went down to the platform and dove into the water.

Josh heard that splash, but couldn't believe it. Tightening his fingers into fists, he clenched his jaw, then pulled the cuffs apart as hard as he could.

"Damn!"

Just as Tess had said, they fell right off, sending his hands smacking into the other rails because he had used too much force.

"You are so going to pay for this!" he shouted, rubbing his banged-up wrists as he pushed to his feet, then padded off the platform to the side and dove into the water.

As he swam hard to the beach, Tess had already reached the shallow water. Her naked flesh glittered beneath the moon and then in the firelight as she went to it. Turning, she finally saw him and waved, as if she hadn't just left him cuffed to that damn rail.

"Don't you dare move!" he shouted.

She immediately stopped waving, looked over her shoulder at the cabana, then went into it.

He growled, "You are so going to pay for this."

By the time Josh finally crawled out of the water and onto the beach, he was panting like a man who had just had two orgasms and no rest.

Not that he recalled his fatigue as Tess came out of the cabana patting her hair with a large beach towel.

Water continued to glisten in those thick, dark waves and in her triangle of hair. The firelight turned her flesh to gold. She looked unbelievably dewy and ripe.

When Tess saw him, she smiled. "Josh. You made it."

As if he wouldn't?

Her gaze lowered to his wrists. "I see you got the cuffs off, too."

As if he would be here if he hadn't? Inhaling deeply, he put out his hand for the towel.

Tess gave it to him.

Josh dried his face, then spread the towel over the sand.

"Still tired?" she asked. "Gonna take a nap?"

He looked at her.

Tess gave him a sweet smile, until he grabbed her arm while also wrapping his leg behind hers. Just like that, she lost her balance and he had her on that towel. Before she could recover, Josh was holding her hands above her head as he straddled her. "Quit wiggling," he ordered.

Her brows drew together. "When you get off of me."

"Aw, baby, you really want that?"

A smile tugged at the corners of her mouth. "Damn right I do."

"In time."

"What are we going to do?"

He arched one brow. "Shouldn't you be asking what I'm going to do?"

"Sure, if you're going to be playing alone."

He laughed. "I'm not." He sobered. "And you're going to do as you're told or I swear you'll be walking home."

"I'll be good."

That remained to be seen. He released her wrists. "Put your hands behind your head and don't move them until I tell you, understand?"

"Whatever you want, Mr. Wyatt."

Josh looked down. Her hands were on his pecs. "Tess."

"Sorry." She put them behind her head and arched her back.

His gaze fell to her naked breasts. They were so luscious, he got slightly dizzy.

Shaking his head to clear it, Josh pushed to his feet, then went to her legs. "Spread 'em," he said.

Tess's eyes were hooded, her lips plush and parted as she

opened her legs, bending them at the knees, fully presenting herself to him.

It was a moment before Josh remembered to breathe. When he spoke, his voice was thick with desire. "Don't move."

She did not as his gaze touched each part of her, awed by her beauty and the ease with which she endured his scrutiny, but then, she hadn't been sheltered. She lived life like a man. Free. Uninhibited. Reckless.

That reckless part and her desire to keep putting herself into danger as a cop, bodyguard, careless driver, or what-have-you was definitely going to have to change after tonight.

Josh sank to his knees. Slipping his hands beneath her ass, he lifted his gaze.

Hers was already softened, turned inward, as if she was anticipating the pleasure.

He liked that. "Don't move," he ordered, then lowered his head to her clit, licking it, then suckling.

Tess let out a ragged moan.

Josh flicked his tongue over that hard nub, until she started wiggling. When she tried to close her legs, he moved his hands to the insides of her thighs and used his strength to stop her.

She swore in Spanish.

He smiled, then returned to pleasure, licking her swollen lips and clit, alternating between the two so that she wouldn't come quickly, so that she would have to wait.

As the pleasure intensified and her clit became increasingly sensitive, Josh slipped two fingers into her opening.

Tess immediately lifted her ass, she moved her hips from side to side, she tried to close her legs, but Josh was far stronger and did exactly what he wanted until she was at the edge.

"Ready?" he asked.

She whimpered, then shouted as he allowed her climax, but no peace.

As Tess's chest heaved with her strained breathing, Josh removed his fingers, then lifted his cock and drove deeply inside.

She cried out in Spanish, she pushed her fingers through her damp hair, she finally moaned as Josh brought her close to this newest completion, at which point he stopped.

A moment passed as she breathed hard and seemed confused by his actions. At last, Tess forced her eyes to open. She frowned, then whined, "What are you doing?"

Josh continued to pull out of her until he was free. His stiff cock was slick with her moisture and scented by her flesh. Lifting it, he asked, "You want this?"

Tess gave him a look that said he was nuts. "Of course I do."

"How much?"

She arched one slender brow. "Enough to use my martial arts training on you to get it."

"Not your gun?"

She did not return his smile.

Oh, she was ready for anything now. "You want this," he said, "then it's on your knees, back to me, and don't forget to lift your ass, and spread those legs really wide."

She looked like she wanted to slug him. She also looked intrigued.

As that won out, Tess quickly got into the position he wanted, then shouted loud and long as Josh plunged inside, riding her as she wanted.

Freely. With no ground rules.

Until everything but their shared pleasure faded away and they were finally one.

Chapter Sixteen

They made love twice more in the glimmering light of the fire before Josh surrendered to fatigue, admitting at last that he was an old fart.

"You'll get your second wind in a day or so," Tess said, as she stroked his tattoo. It was so damned virile her toes curled. She wanted him again and again, only that wasn't going to happen right now. He was sprawled naked and facedown over three of the towels, leaving her only one. "Maybe you'll do better then."

Josh slid his arm away from his eyes so he could see her. "Better?"

She nodded. "I wrote it all down in the sand. There's a column for you and one for me. By my count, I had three orgasms to your ten. Not fair, I admit, but then, I can wait to be satisfied. I don't want to kill you."

He laughed until he quickly ran out of steam. "I hope you know the tide's going to wash that away, then where's your proof that I've been unfair to you?"

That was easy, it was in her heart. It would be a long time before Tess forgot that he hadn't been able to love her as she loved him.

Not that Josh seemed to notice or care. He yawned lustily, then snuggled his body into those towels, rather than into her.

Tess suppressed a sigh. "Our totals are way up here," she said, arguing her point to at least keep him awake. "The tide's not going to reach them."

Josh slid his arm back to his eyes, keeping her and the rest of the world away. "Then the wind will."

"Not if I cover them."

"If you do that, you'll mess them up, which proves my point—they're not permanent."

Neither was tonight. Neither was love. Even her parents' devotion to each other hadn't kept her mother alive. Still, out here by the fire, beneath the moon and the stars, Tess just wanted to hope for the impossible. She knew she was acting like a fool, but she didn't want to face the coming days and years without him. "So, they're not permanent," she finally mumbled. "So, I'll just keep working on them whenever something happens."

"Do what you want. But once we're gone, they're gone."

"So, maybe we'll just stay," she argued as he stretched, then yawned. "We've got that food in the cooler. It'll stay cold for a while." They could stay here until that stuff ran out. If his people came by to restock, they could stay that much longer. This might never have to end.

Josh finally finished his yawn. "What?"

Hell. "Nothing."

"No, tell me. I caught the part about you getting cold, but missed the—"

"The cooler's stuffed with food, all right?"

Josh moved his arm and looked at her. "No need to shout, I can hear fine; I'm just a little tired."

Tess continued to kick sand over her foolish tallies, destroying them before the tide, the wind, or his indifference did it for her.

"You're hungry, again?" he asked.

"No."

"But you're still cold?"

"I'm not cold, all right?"

"Sure." He rolled over onto his back and lifted his hands in surrender. "I just thought I could warm you up."

Of course he could, but for how long since nothing was permanent, especially them. "I'm fine, but your fire's going out."

Josh looked at the stone enclosure, then groaned. "Oh, hell, we have to go back."

Huh? "Because the fire's going out? Can't you just fix it?"

"I could add wood to it, yeah. But in a few hours it'll be dawn. We still have to go back to the marina, then there's that ungodly long drive to my place. Even if we start now, even if you drive the boat and my car so damned fast that you break the sound barrier, it's going to take forever."

Tess didn't mind.

Josh obviously did. Despite his fatigue he pushed to a sitting position, then grunted to his feet.

When he offered his hand, Tess didn't take it. "Shouldn't we clean up?"

"One of my staff will be by in the morning to get everything. We can just go."

"Why leave work for them?"

"Tess, that's what they're being paid for. Just leave it."

"Won't the tide wash it away, too?"

Josh looked as if he couldn't care less, but finally picked up the towels and threw them at the cabana, then again offered his hand. "We've tidied up, let's go."

She pushed to her feet without his help.

Josh lowered his hand. "Believe me, my staff won't mind. Okay?"

"Whatever you say."

He hesitated, then sighed. "You're tired. You can sleep on the way back."

Tess leveled her gaze on him.

"Or not," he quickly said. "Whatever you want."

She wanted to stay. She didn't want this freaking night to end.

Josh lifted his brows as if he hadn't a clue what to say next. At last, he turned and trudged towards the water. When he finally noticed that she wasn't following, he called out, "What are you doing?"

She was stalling. "Give me a minute; I'm looking for my garter." She kicked listlessly at the sand.

Josh finally returned. "Are you sure you lost it here?"

She had lost it after swimming here and he hadn't even noticed. She had made a special trip to buy the damned thing and already it was forgotten. "No. Let's go." She ran past him to the water.

Once they were back on the boat, Josh seemed afraid to say anything and that suited Tess just fine. He had said far too much on the beach.

They dried off and dressed in silence, then went to the pilothouse for the trip back.

It was finally over.

As Josh steered the boat back to the marina, Tess sat on the bench to the side, her face turned to the window, her eyes filling with tears.

Uh-uh. You are not going to cry.

She had no right to be sad. This conclusion had been inevitable from the moment she had walked into Josh's office—against her father's wishes—then let him kiss her after they had known each other for two seconds.

After that, it went downhill fast with their picture being published in that tabloid, followed by her father's shouts.

This is how you get us a contract? By kissing the clients during the interview?

Josh is the first.

Tess smiled at that memory, then lowered her head and held back tears, because he would definitely be the last.

No way was she kissing clients anymore; it was too damned painful. And the worst hadn't even happened.

She still had to tell him her news. Even Peg didn't know it yet, because she would have just blabbed and blabbed. Tess had gotten her father's promise that he would let her handle this.

So far, she had managed it badly. She had made her plans on the day that football player was exposed in the tabloid, but had said nothing to Josh.

She had been selfish, wanting to go to that dinner, wanting to dance, wanting to make love.

Only that was all over now; time to move on.

She sighed.

"Tired?"

She rubbed tears out of her eyes and looked at him. "What?"

"Are you tired?"

No. She was in love and scared, and she wanted to tell him how she felt, but no matter how great her dad thought she was, no matter how great Tess knew she was, she wasn't from Josh's world.

Her gaze lowered. He was wealthy beyond anything she could have imagined for herself. He was young and good-looking and surprisingly sweet-natured—at least when he wasn't being a jerk and bossing everyone around. With even half of those good qualities and a lot more of the bad, he could have any woman he wanted.

Even if he wanted her, how long would it last without a deep and abiding love when there were so many others willing and eager to take her place?

"Tess?"

She looked at him and finally recalled his question, then decided to lie. "I am a little tired."

"I'll have us there as fast as I can." He took a prolonged look at the night vision screen. "Once we're at my place, I'll put you to bed." He turned back to her and grinned. "My bed. I'm moving your stuff into my room first thing in the morning." He returned his attention to the instruments.

Tess looked at them, then the side of his face as her heart started to pound.

Had he just asked her to move in with him?

She thought back and decided that he had not. He had simply stated that he was moving her stuff into his bedroom.

For how long? And to what end, other than sex, of course?

Josh started to whistle as he looked outside at the sea.

Tess wasn't certain she'd ever whistle again. As depressed as she had been just a few seconds ago, now she was as pissed. Did he just assume she was going to be his bodyguard or pretend public girlfriend forever, or, at least, until he got tired of it? Did he think he could play at this relationship when what she wanted was something more than just being his live-in lover?

Given the way he was now whistling up a storm, probably so.

After tonight he probably figured he could pretty much have whatever he wanted. Of course, she had enjoyed this night with him and had slept with him because she loved him and because she knew she wouldn't be seeing him again, not because she was looking for some fast fun.

So what would happen if she didn't give him that fun? There were dozens, maybe hundreds, of other women who would jump at a chance to move in with him.

Tess knew they were nuts or didn't know what love was. She did and no way could she open her heart and allow herself to be vulnerable, then have it all come crashing down when Josh met someone else, someone he would truly adore and commit to. That would kill her.

Tess wanted what her parents had shared. The security that on each and every day of their marriage there would be a commitment. No matter how bad things got, no matter how bored they got, they would stick it out.

Josh didn't have to do that. He had enough money and success to keep the good times rolling with as many lovers as he wanted only she wasn't going to be one of them. "No."

He stopped whistling and looked at her. "What?"

"I can't. I won't."

He seemed confused. "Can't what? Won't what?"

"Move into your bedroom."

Josh looked stunned, then quickly grinned. "Will you quit playing with me? Come on, I'm excited about this." He wiggled his brows. "And you will be, too, when you see my bedroom."

Tess wondered if he was listening to what was coming out of his mouth. *My bedroom?* Not *ours,* but *my*? "Where I'll formally begin living with you?"

His smile faded. "I don't know if I'd use the term formally. But yeah, what else?"

A commitment would have been nice. Being told he loved her, in addition to wanting to sleep with her, would have been pretty damned great. The possibility of marriage somewhere on the horizon would have been a joy. But no. Her place was in his room, in his bed, in his house, in his world, on his planet until he decided otherwise.

"My father could think of a lot of what else's."

Josh stared, then shook his head as if he didn't believe she had said that. "I'm certain he could, but you're a grown woman, Tess."

"And because of that, you think I should make up my own mind."

He started to smile, but didn't, as if he thought better of it. "Of course."

"Then, my mind's made up. I'm not going to be your live-in girlfriend, Josh. And I'm not going to be your pretend girlfriend in public anymore, either."

"What?"

"You heard me."

He seemed thoroughly confused. He turned back to the night vision screen and the rest of the instruments, then looked over his shoulder at her. "You're saying you didn't have a good time tonight?" He shook his head. "You can't tell me that. I wouldn't believe that."

Tess pressed her fingers to her forehead and forced her

voice to remain far calmer than she felt. "Josh, tonight has nothing to do with my not moving in with you."

"You've already moved in with—"

"I'm leaving tonight."

"What?"

Despite his surprise, Tess remained calm. This was no different than her days on the force when everything was falling apart around her, people were screaming, sirens were blaring, and she had to keep a cool head. As tears stung the corners of her eyes, Tess told herself to remember that, because as pissed as she still was, she also felt like she was going to die. "I'm already packed."

"*What*? When in the hell did you—"

"Last night. My bags are in the closet, ready to go."

"Go *where*?"

"My apartment!" she shouted right back, then lowered her voice. "My home. Our contract is over."

"Since when? Look," he said, interrupting her, "if you don't want to move into my room, fine. Keep your room. I don't care. Take the whole upstairs if you like. If you need your space—"

"Josh, this isn't about space. You don't need me to be your bodyguard anymore. You haven't needed that for days, not since that football guy got blindsided by the tabloid."

"Is that what this is about, what Alan said?" Josh shook his head and smiled. "Tess, he doesn't run the show, I do, and—"

"The contract is over when the problem stops," she said, her voice firm. "That was clearly spelled out in it. No," she said, speaking above him. "I have a new job starting the day after tomorrow."

Josh stared at her, then quickly looked out the front window as the boat approached the dock. "A new job as what?"

Was he serious? "A bodyguard. What else?"

"Uh-uh. No way," he said, looking at her. "I don't want

you doing that anymore, Tess. It's too damned dangerous. You're too damned reckless."

"Are you kidding?" Her voice was incredulous. "You think you can tell me where I can work and what I can do?"

"Of course not." He seemed to finally realize what he had said and continued to backpedal. "That's not what I meant. I would never tell you what to do. I'm simply asking you not to be a bodyguard anymore. Please."

Tess's eyes filled with tears. Please? Why did he have to say that? Why did he have to look so damned hurt and worried? Why couldn't he have at least said that he loved her? "I like being a bodyguard, Josh. My father needs me to be—"

"No, he doesn't. He doesn't like this any more than me. He wanted you to be a dancer."

"And I wanted you to respect my work. Looks like nobody's going to get what they want."

"Aw, Tess." He turned back to the instruments and finished docking the boat as he talked. "I do respect your work. I'm amazed by what you can do and what you have done as a cop. All I'm saying is, you don't have to risk your safety anymore, not if you're with me."

"In your bedroom."

He looked at her. "I didn't say that."

"You didn't have to. I can connect the dots, Josh. And even if I were to agree to such a thing, what makes you think I could continue to live with you while I'm taking new jobs? Maybe I'd have to live with my new clients, like that football guy or another guy who—"

"Whoa, whoa, whoa. You'd actually take a job like that?"

"I took yours."

He finally frowned and sounded pissed. "You weren't involved with anyone when you took on this job. I know. I asked."

"Sleeping together one night is not being involved."

He couldn't have looked more stunned.

"Good-bye, Josh."

Good-bye? What the hell had just happened here? "What are you doing—Tess, don't touch—"

She already had, activating the gangway so she could leave.

"Wait!" he shouted.

Tess was already out the door, her shoes in one hand, her purse and his car keys in the other.

"Hell." Josh so quickly moved out of his chair, he rammed his knee into the panel. When he got to the door, he pulled it into his foot. By the time he limped to the deck, she was already leaving the gangway. "Tess!"

She hurried down the dock.

He shouted, "Dammit, Tess, I love you!"

That stopped her.

Thank God. At last, he'd said something right. "Tess, please!" Josh shouted as he limped down the gangway and onto the dock where he finally stopped. "I love you!"

She turned and looked at him. Her mouth was trembling as if she was about to cry.

Josh hadn't a clue what was going on here. Was she about to cry because she was happy he loved her or because she didn't feel the same way about him? Didn't matter. He couldn't let her go. "Tess, please, come on back," he said, gesturing with his arm. "We can talk. We'll go to my place."

Her expression changed. Just like that the tears were quickly replaced by anger. "Your place?"

What the fuck had he said this time? "Yeah."

"Why not your yacht or your island or your car or your—"

"Tess, I love you!" he repeated. "Don't you want that?"

"You love me?"

"Yes!"

There was sudden applause from the side.

Josh followed that noise to two young guys who were

seated on the dock with their feet dangling over the edge and a six-pack between them.

"Get lost," Tess ordered, "this is a private conversation."

"Dock's public," the heavier guy said, then guzzled his beer.

"You heard her," Josh growled. "Get lost. If you don't," he said, interrupting the thinner guy, "she'll arrest you. She's a cop."

"Ex-cop," Tess corrected, frowning at Josh. "I'm a bodyguard now."

The heavy guy belched. "You're a bodyguard? Damn."

"God bless America," the other guy said, and saluted her with his beer.

Tess turned and continued down the dock.

Josh limped after her. "Tess, don't go, please! I love you!"

"You say that now!" she shouted as she turned to face him. "You say that in the heat of this moment, but only to keep me from leaving!"

Huh? He stopped. "What are you talking about?"

"What loves means to you, Josh. You really should think about that. Love isn't telling someone what to do or putting them into one part of your life as if they're something you purchased like your boat or your island or your car or your estate. Something that can be tossed aside when you get bored with it."

"Now you're doubting my sincerity?"

"I wonder about your level of commitment when you're used to getting your way."

Used to getting his way? Was she kidding? "You think because of what I have I always get my way?"

"I think you've become used to the concept. Money gives you a right to expect a lot."

"Apparently not from you."

She cried, "I don't care about your money, Josh! I've never

cared about it! I will never care about it! It can't give me what I need from a man! The kind of love I want and deserve!"

"Haven't I been telling you—no, don't go!" he shouted as she ran to his car. "Tess! Wait!"

She did not. She got inside his car and drove away, leaving him at the dock.

Chapter Seventeen

Forty minutes later Josh was in the passenger seat of Alan's car with his cell to his ear listening to the phone in his Mercedes just ring and ring.

Any other woman would have answered by now to hear what he had to say and to possibly apologize for ditching him; or to at least hang up. Not Tess. Josh had been calling since she left and not once had she picked up.

She was either the most stubborn woman he'd ever known or she thought all the calls were from someone trying to reach him on business.

Sure. Still, that gave him some hope. Josh tried his house again. "Come on," he complained after the twentieth ring. "You're probably there by now. You drive like a maniac. You have to at least suspect that all calls aren't business-related. Pick up." She did not. Josh called her cell again, but it was still turned off.

"Who're you trying to reach?" Alan finally asked.

"Can't you drive any faster?" Josh asked.

"Not on a two-lane road with cars in front of me."

"Just pass them."

"There's oncoming traffic, Josh."

That was the least of his worries. His cell just went dead. Shit. "Give me your cell," he said to Alan.

"I didn't bring it."

"Why not?"

"Well, excuse me," the attorney finally said, "but I wasn't expecting you to wake me from a sound sleep to pick you up at a marina when you should be at home, and you apparently got to this marina without a car, and apparently no cabs were available to pick you up, and apparently even Tess wasn't available to pick you—"

"She's got my car."

"So why didn't you call her to pick you—"

"Because she left me at the marina when she took my car, isn't that obvious?"

Alan flicked his gaze at Josh's wrinkled shirt and trousers. "What's wrong with your foot?"

He stopped rubbing his bruised toe. "Nothing."

Alan's brows lifted as his gaze noted that Josh was wearing only one shoe.

"You can pass now." Josh pointed.

Alan looked, but didn't pass. "You know, you could just call the security company to have them check to see if Tess got to your place yet."

"I'm not calling her father, Alan."

"Does he answer his own phones at this hour?"

"As soon as his help hears Tess's name, you can bet they'll call him. And I don't want him sending Bonnie and Clyde out to my place to shoot me."

"What did you do?"

"What did *I* do? I told her I love her, that's what I did."

"No kidding? And she left you stranded at the marina? I thought she liked you."

She had while she was cuffing him to the yacht and when he had mounted her repeatedly on the beach. "Everything was going great until I said that we should live together."

"You're already living to—"

"You know what I mean." Josh sighed. "After that, I don't know what the hell happened. I finally told her I love her, but did she listen?"

Alan didn't comment. When Josh looked, the attorney's brows were arched. "What?"

"You told her you loved her after you asked her to live with you?"

"It's not like I planned it that way. She was tired and I told her I'd put her to bed when we got back to the estate, and it seemed like the perfect time to mention moving her stuff into my room."

Those brows didn't lower.

"What?" Josh asked.

Alan finally passed a slow-moving vehicle. "You didn't even ask her to move into your room, you just assumed she—"

"I thought she wanted that, Alan. It didn't occur to me to formally propose the matter to her."

"Uh-huh."

"What's that supposed to mean?"

The attorney looked uncomfortable. "I don't know too many women who'd be thrilled about shacking up with a guy who's got a whole slew of other women after him without any hint of what might happen in their own future."

"I should have spelled out our future? Alan, she wouldn't let me get past the part about moving her stuff to my room. After that she told me she's through as my bodyguard, because she's already got another job. I asked her not to do that. I tried my level best to explain that it's too dangerous of an occupation, and that if she and I were together, as a couple, she wouldn't need to do it anymore."

Those brows were shooting up again.

"Alan, her dad doesn't want her to be a bodyguard, either. I'm not the only one."

"She's a grown woman, Josh. She can do whatever she wants."

"Okay, let me ask you something. If you were in my shoes and Tess insisted on being a bodyguard and putting herself at risk, what would you do?"

Alan didn't even hesitate. "Become a bodyguard so I could

go on jobs with her to protect her, and so she couldn't hurt me when she got pissed about that."

"See!" Josh said, pointing his finger at the man. "She'd drive you crazy with worry, too!"

"Isn't that a big part of love?"

"Have you ever loved a woman who carried concealed weapons in the back of her boxers and handcuffs in her garter?"

Alan looked from the traffic to Josh. "She carries handcuffs in a garter?" He grinned. "That sounds so cool."

He had no idea. "She could get hurt; that's all I was trying to tell her. But did she thank me for my concern? Did she even try to see my point of view? Oh, no. She as much as accused me of trying to run her life and everyone else's because I have a little dough."

"A little?"

"The point is she kept shouting at me that she didn't want my money, she would never want my money, and that the only reason I get my way all the time, which is a huge joke by the way, is because of what I have. Like money has changed me or something."

"Well, of course it has."

Josh looked at him. "What?"

He passed another slow-moving vehicle. "Nothing."

"Alan."

"I don't want to be critical."

"You should have thought of that before you told me I did everything wrong tonight."

"Not everything. Okay, okay," he said when Josh swore. "You didn't call a cab tonight, did you? You just expected that when you called me I'd pick you up."

"You could have said no."

"I did. Three times. But you kept interrupting saying that you needed to get back, and that your toe hurt, and that you had taken dancing lessons and still it all went to hell." He shrugged. "At that point I finally gave in. I figured this trip was worth it to hear about those lessons."

Josh muttered, "I was upset. I don't usually act like that."

"Well, not at this hour."

"Meaning?"

Alan sighed. "I'm more than willing to do whatever it takes to protect you and your business from any legal action even after business hours. But you demand a lot, Josh, and you keep forgetting that I do have a life of my own. Not as good as yours, I'll admit, but it is a life."

Josh frowned, ready to argue that he was a reasonable person and that money hadn't changed him, but did not. For the first time since Alan had picked him up, Josh noticed that the man was freshly shaved and wearing an immaculate Polo shirt and chinos.

He could only wonder what Alan wore to bed, or if he had left a woman in his bed to make this trip tonight, or if he was even dating anyone.

They had worked together for years; Josh even considered Alan a friend and yet he had never thought to ask about things that were important to him. Maybe Tess had been right.

"Did I thank you for picking me up?"

Alan waved his hand as if it was no big deal.

"Do you have a girlfriend?" Josh asked.

Alan looked at him, then back at the traffic. "What?"

"Never mind." Josh pulled out his cell and tried calling Tess again, until he remembered his cell was dead.

"Want me to stop at a pay phone?" Alan asked.

"No, just keep driving. Maybe she's still at the house."

"If she hasn't burned it down."

"She wasn't that pissed."

"What did she say before she left?"

"That I better think about what loves means to me."

"That's not so bad."

Tell that to his pounding heart. A short time later, when

Alan finally dropped Josh off, his car was in the drive and Tess's stuff was completely gone.

It was as if their time together had never happened. Not even her powdery fragrance remained.

She had taken it all; she had walked out of his life without as much as a backward glance.

If she had been any other woman Josh would have just said to hell with it.

But she was his woman, whether she realized that or not, and by God she wasn't going to get away with this.

"Hon, do you think it's safe to leave?"

Tess couldn't have cared less if it was, but forced herself to sound interested. "Everything looks fine so far." She continued scanning the thin crowd in the bookstore. Her newest client was a fifty-something romance author who wanted protection, during her book signings, from a conservative group that didn't like all those steamy sex scenes in her stories.

When Tess had read those scenes and the romantic interludes that followed, she couldn't stop crying. Of course, that was nearly two weeks ago. She was okay now, just as long as she concentrated on her work, which included listening to all those snotty messages that had been left by that group on the author's answering machine and reading the equally snotty e-mails.

As supposedly bad as that was, it was the rotten reviews posted on all the Internet sites that was the straw that broke the author's back.

"They're after me," the woman had said. "Who knows what they'll try next?"

Tess figured nothing would be tried, but having a bodyguard accompanying her made the author look important and was getting press. Not in *Keys Confidential,* of course, since that was reserved for bad boys like Josh.

Uh-uh. You're not going there.

Tess had thought of him far too much these past days, and kept second-guessing what she had said that last night.

Maybe Josh wasn't being a rich, bossy jerk for expecting her to move in with him. Maybe he was just being a man. The other guys Tess knew weren't exactly known for their sensitivity.

Of course, she hadn't loved them. They couldn't hurt her.

Josh could and had.

From the moment they had met, the man made her behave in ways Tess never dreamed possible. She had kissed him when he was still a stranger, she had moved in with him when he was supposed to be nothing more than her employer, she had taken over a press conference to tell the world she was his girlfriend, she had worn handcuffs in a garter, and she missed all of that so much she wanted to die.

"Hon?"

Tess brushed tears from her eyes and looked at her client. The woman seemed worried, though it was hard to tell since all that Botox in her face wasn't allowing her to frown. "Yeah?"

"Did you see something that concerned you?"

Only her future without Josh. "No." Tess scanned the bookstore one last time. Everyone had behaved themselves during the signing, except for a few teenage boys who kept giggling as they read those steamy sex scenes. "Everything's all right."

"Then you're ready to escort me to my car?"

"I'll go first," Tess said. "Keep fairly close to me, all right?"

"I understand," the woman said.

When Tess got out to the mall and saw that no one even looked in the author's direction, she turned to tell her client the coast was clear.

The woman was still in the bookstore. When Tess went back inside, that nitwit was raising her arm in a lavish farewell. "I'm leaving now!" she said in a raised voice as she swung her arm. "I'll see all of you at my next signing!"

The store clerks stared at her from behind the counter.

"I think that went well," the woman said as she joined Tess. "I appreciate you keeping me safe."

Right. This time Tess told the woman to walk ahead of her, rather than behind.

"Is that wise?" the woman asked.

If they ever wanted to get out of here it was. "You'll be fine," Tess assured, not letting the woman out of her sight.

By the time they had reached the parking lot, Tess noticed that in addition to a face full of Botox, this lady had had her butt and thighs seriously overhauled.

Maybe her dad would find this woman interesting. Maybe then he wouldn't date Peg anymore since that only reminded Tess of how much she missed Josh.

Will you just stop it?

"Here we are," the client said as she reached her jet black Jag.

"I'll follow you home," Tess said.

The woman glanced around the lot to see that there were no fans or press in the vicinity. She sighed. "I'm sure I'll be just fine all by myself." She patted Tess's shoulder. "And I'm sure you have big plans for tonight."

Only if that included making food for her father and the rest of the guys at their weekly poker game that had turned into a wake. At last week's game everyone was real quiet, watching her like she was going to break down and sob. When Tess hadn't, they couldn't compliment her food enough, as if that was going to make her feel any better about Josh.

"Yeah, I do," she said. "Thanks."

As the woman finally pulled away, Tess sighed. "Big plans. Right."

Tonight was going to be brutal.

The truth of that was in the way no one came out to her car even though Tess sat in it for twenty minutes after arriving at her father's house.

They knew she was here, Tess saw them pulling back the front curtains to sneak peeks at her. Maybe they were hoping she'd drive away and they wouldn't have to eat her stuff. Maybe they were afraid she had finally started crying and they hadn't a clue how to make it stop.

She wasn't crying, but a sadness so deep that it could no longer be ignored had gripped Tess on the drive here. She kept wondering what tonight would have been like if everything hadn't gone so bad with Josh.

They might have gone skinny-dipping in his pool or run naked over the grounds of that golf course or kissed like crazy in hijacked elevators or took turns cuffing each other to his boat or started a journey they would share for the rest of their lives.

She would have loved him forever if only given the chance. She would love him forever and he'd never know it.

Sighing deeply, Tess finally hauled ass and left her car.

When she got to the porch she heard everyone hurrying away from the window where they'd been watching her. Tess gave them a few minutes to get to their chairs, then went inside.

Everyone started talking at once, trying to act natural. Vic and Hank and her dad were ganging up on Sammie and Peg, who was now considered one of the usual suspects.

"Hey," Tess said.

"Oh, look," Sammie said, "Tessie's here."

"That she is," Peg said. "Hi, hon."

"Hey, Tessie," Hank said, then spoke to Vic who was sitting right next to him. "Tessie's here."

"Hey, Tessie," he said.

She wanted to run. She pointed over her shoulder. "I'll be in the kitchen."

"Sure, go on," Vic said, "we're getting ready to play and we all really liked those little pizzas you made last week. Right, guys?"

Everyone nodded in agreement.

Tess wondered if she should tell them about the extra fiber she had put in the sauce, but decided against it.

"Go on," her father said. "We can't wait all night. We're hungry. Right, guys?"

Everyone nodded again.

Tess turned, then went down the hall to the bathroom to have a good cry.

"Where's she going?" her father asked.

"Bathroom, I bet," Sammie said.

"You want me to get her?" Peg asked.

Vic called out, "Tessie, are you going to go into the kitch—"

"Okay, just stop it," Tess said as she came back down the hall. "I'm going into the stupid kitchen, okay? And if any of you say my food's good tonight, there will be hell to pay, understand?"

They all nodded again.

Damn. Tess went into the kitchen, rounded the counter, and stopped dead.

There was a guy on the floor with his head under the sink.

Uh-uh. Couldn't be.

Tess checked out those long, blue-jeaned legs and that snug black T-shirt before her gaze settled on that lovely bulge behind his fly.

Oh, my God. She was so quickly dizzy she had to lean against the counter for support.

At just that moment Josh finished whatever he'd been doing, then pushed out and looked up at her. "Hey, you okay?"

Tess didn't think so. Her ears were ringing and her mouth was unbelievably dry.

He was really here. It had been so long since she'd seen him that his eyes seemed darker than she recalled. His hair seemed lighter, too. Tess was about to sink to the floor so she could touch it and his bristly cheeks and every other part of him when she thought better of it. "You're here?"

His brows lifted. He pushed to his feet and wiped his hands on a rag. "Sure."

Sure? As if being in her father's house and under her father's sink was the most natural thing in the world when her heart was still pounding out of control. "Why?"

Josh seemed uncertain how to answer, then finally shrugged. "It's poker night."

That was not what Tess had expected or wanted to hear. She frowned at him, then looked over her shoulder as Hank and Vic laughed about something. Those goons had known all along that Josh was in here fixing the sink, that he would be here for nothing more than poker, and hadn't warned her?

She wanted to yell at them . . . and maybe kiss them, too. Now, she would at least be able to see Josh every single week during these games. She would be able to watch him as he played. She would be able to hear him talk about his life that might possibly include another woman.

She turned back to him. "And poker's the *only* reason you're here?"

Josh seemed surprised by her tone, not to mention a little uneasy. "Well, the guys gotta eat, too."

Tess suddenly noticed the serving dishes on the kitchen table. She frowned, then looked over her shoulder at more laughter coming from the living room.

"But I'll be here a lot more than just poker nights," he said.

Another surprise. "You're going to start cooking for my dad?"

Josh smiled. "He would like that, wouldn't he? But no, I'm not cooking for him. Lots to fix around here, though." He took a tool out of his back pocket and put it on the counter.

Tess looked at it, then him. "You're going to fix stuff around this house for my dad?"

"I'd like to keep him as happy as possible since he's armed." His gaze dipped to her shorts as if he was looking for her gun. "But even if he weren't, it wouldn't be wise for a guy to piss off his future father-in-law."

Her ears started ringing again. "What?"

"If you'll have me," he said.

Tess could barely breathe. She started to cry. "You're proposing to me?"

"He finally did it," Sammie called out to the others.

Tess looked over her shoulder just in time to see a wavy image of the older woman hurrying back to her chair while everyone else, even her father, gave each other high-fives.

Maybe she was in the wrong house. Tess looked back at Josh as he called out, "Hey, guys! Can Tess and I have a minute?"

"Let's go outside," Freddy said.

As the screen door banged shut, Josh gathered her into his arms. "Are you okay?"

Tess nodded as she continued to cry.

"Sure?"

"You're really proposing to me?"

"Yeah. I finally got up the courage."

Tess threw her arms around his neck. "Oh, my poor baby!"

"Huh?"

"You're still scared of commitment, huh?"

Josh pulled her arms away and eased back. "No, I'm scared of you."

"What?"

"Holy shit, Tess, what man wouldn't be? You didn't exactly do backflips when I told you I loved you at the yacht on what I considered one of the best nights of my life. After that, it took me until today to get up the nerve for this and to get your father on board. He's almost as bad as you are."

Tess heard him and the others talking in the front yard. She wiped her eyes with the backs of her hands. "But he finally agreed?"

"He had no choice. I told him I wasn't giving up."

She started crying again. "You fought him for me?"

"Are you kidding? I'd fight the world for you. You're my

woman; you've been my woman from the first moment we met."

"Your woman?" She threw her arms around his neck again. "Oh, I like that."

"You're also a snob."

That wasn't so nice. This time, Tess pulled back. "What?"

"You think you're morally superior to me because I've made a lot of money. You think you have a corner on honor, integrity, feelings, and what it takes to be a good marriage partner, to honor a commitment, or to simply be in love. Well, let me tell you something; you're not the only one who's had a couple of lousy weeks. I've never been so damned miserable in all my life. And it's all your fault."

Her cheeks and throat were hot. She mumbled, "I just wanted you to know what I need."

"You told me what you needed and then split because you just figured someone who has my dough isn't only morally hopeless, but no good."

"I never said that, Josh. I'd never say that. But you were insensitive and bossy."

"So I didn't sing you a love song, is that any reason to run away? You couldn't have stayed and continued to criticize me at least until we worked things out?"

Even her scalp felt hot. "Was I that bad?"

"We both were. Let's start over. I don't want you being a body—"

"You call that starting over?"

"You didn't let me finish."

Tess cupped his face in her hands. "Sorry, but baby, I do like being a bodyguard."

"Yeah, I know." He sighed, then continued, "That's why I'm supporting you fully in it, even though I don't particularly like it. I worry about you. And if we have a daughter, no way is she being a cop or a bodyguard. She is going to be a dancer."

"A daughter? Oh, I like that."

He smiled.

"But it'll be up to her whether she wants dancing, Josh. We don't push. We don't choose. We don't bitch. Please."

He sighed, again. "Maybe we'll have all boys."

Tess wreathed her arms around his neck. "Josh, there's no reason for you to worry about me. I would never put myself in danger without discussing it with you first."

"Gee, thanks."

She smiled, and she cried, and then she smiled, again. "With most of these jobs I'm just a glorified babysitter like I was with you."

He arched one brow.

Oh, how she loved playing with him. How Tess had missed that. "With others, I run errands. You know, pick up stuff at the pharmacy or the cleaners. I never dodge bullets, throw myself on bombs, or taste food to see if it's poisoned. I'm watching my weight and my limbs, so I have to draw the line somewhere."

He laughed.

It was so rich and free, Tess fell in love with him all over again. "The client I'm working for now is this middle-age lady who writes romances and wants me around as a status symbol."

"Yeah, I know. Your dad told me," Josh said, before she could ask. "Thank God he's running the show. I'm expecting him to keep you in line at work."

Her brows lifted.

"And," he added, "for you to keep yourself safe for me."

Tess smiled. "I would never choose danger over you, never."

Josh ran his hands to her butt. "Good to hear. So, what else?"

She shook her head. "That's it. I'll be safe. You'll be happy. And our daughter, if we should have one, will be whatever she wants even if it's not a dancer."

"I love you, Teressa. There, I've said it again. Don't you have anything to say to me?"

What was she thinking? Cradling the side of his face in her hand, Tess spoke from the heart. *"Yo le adoro."* I adore you. Words her mother had always said to her father.

Words Tess repeated to Josh again and again in between their kisses.

"Ah, guys?" Freddy finally called from the living room. "We're hungry. You two through yet?"

"Not for a very long time," Josh murmured.

Tess smiled, and then she cried a little, too, because the truth of that statement was in his eyes; she felt it in his touch. They wouldn't be through for a lifetime.

It was more than she had ever hoped for and exactly what she needed.

Someone to watch over me.

Susanna Carr does it again!
Here's a sneak peek at
LIP LOCK
available now from Brava . . .

She scurried back into the closet, begging—absolutely begging—for him not to enter the closet. It was midnight, after all. On a Saturday.

But time meant nothing to Kyle.

She heard him enter the bathroom and hit the lights. Molly dove for the very back rack in the closet and squatted down.

Her heart pounded. Her tongue felt huge and she couldn't swallow. She kept her eyes glued on the door, but she didn't want to look.

This was why she could never play hide-and-seek as a kid. She couldn't handle the idea of being found. Couldn't tolerate the wait.

She knew she was going to get caught. She couldn't shake off the feeling. Or bravely meet the inevitable.

No, instead she was huddling in the corner, images of her work record flashing in her head. *Terminated because she was hiding in her boss's closet.*

Yeah, let's see how long it would take her to get another job with that kind of reference.

She drew in a shaky breath, ready to have that door swing open. For Kyle to find her. The interrogation that would follow. She'd have come up with a good reason why she was here. Something brilliant. Irrefutable. Logical.

So far, she had nothing.

And why wasn't he opening the door? She couldn't take much more of this.

Molly craned her neck and cocked her head to the side. All she heard was the shower.

The shower! Molly sat up straight as a plan began to form. The bathroom would get all hot and steamy. The glass would fog and she could sneak out. Perfect!

But that would mean getting out of her hiding place. Maybe she should wait until he left.

So that he could what? Go to his desk and spend the rest of the night working on the computer? Leaving her stuck here?

This was her only chance to escape. She needed to take advantage of it. Now.

Molly reluctantly crept to the door. She winced and cringed as she slowly opened it a crack. She was so nervous that Kyle might see the movement. Or that he would spot her. Look right at her. Eye to eye.

Instead she got an eyeful.

Kyle grabbed the collar of his white rugby shirt and pulled it over his head. The bright lights bounced against the dips and swells of his toned arms.

Molly ignored the tingle deep in her belly as she stared. She already knew that guy was fit, but oh . . . my . . . *goodness . . .*

Kyle's lean body rippled with strength. He was solid muscle. Defined and restrained.

She memorized everything from the whorls of dark hair dusting his tanned chest to the jutting hip bone. Her heart skittered to a stop as his hands went to the snap at his waistband.

Oh . . . The tingling grew hotter. Brighter. She shouldn't look. No. She really shouldn't. Not even a peek.

He drew the zipper down.

She should turn her head away.

Her neck muscles weren't cooperating as the zipper parted.

Okay, at least close your eyes! She forced herself to obey and her eyelids started to lower.

Until the jeans dropped to his ankles.

Molly's eyes widened. *Oh . . . wow.*

He was long, thick and heavy. There was nothing elegant or refined about his penis. It looked rough. Wild. And this was before he was aroused?

She could imagine how it would feel to have him inside her. Before he even thrust. Molly pressed her legs together as the tingling blazed into an all-out ache.

Kyle turned around and she stared at his tight buttocks. *Oh, yeah*. She could go for one of those, too. She could imagine exactly how it would feel to hold onto him as he claimed her.

He stepped out of her field of vision. A shot of panic cleared her head. Where did he go? She caught a movement in the mirror and saw Kyle step into that sinfully decadent shower. She watched the reflection as he stepped under the water.

Great. Just what she needed. A hot, naked, and *wet* Kyle Ashton.

The shower stall didn't hide a thing from her. Water pulsed against body. It sluiced down his chest and ran down Kyle's powerful thighs. She wanted to lick every droplet from his sculpted muscle.

Molly pulled at the neck of her sweatshirt. How hot was that shower? It was getting really warm in here.

The scent of Kyle's soap invaded her senses. Sophisticated. Expensive. It usually made her knees knock on everyday occasions, but this was concentrated stuff. It knocked her off her feet.

The steam wafted from the shower stall and began to cloud the glass. Molly had to squint as the fog slowly streaked across the shower glass. She was half-tempted to wipe the condensation from her view when she remembered this was what she was waiting for.

Sure she was.

She glanced at the door. It was closed, but not all the way. That was her escape. She'd better get moving before he was finished. Molly glanced back at the mirror.

His head was tilted back and water streamed down the harsh angles of his face. She fought the fierce urge to join him and press her mouth against the strong column of his neck. To run her hands along his body as his hands remained in his drenched hair.

That was never going to happen. She could fantasize about that later. Right now, she had to get away from Kyle.

She slowly opened the closet door, thankful it didn't creak. Hoping Kyle was like the rest of the world and closed his eyes when rinsing out the shampoo, Molly got on her hands and knees. She gathered up the last of her courage and began crawling along the bathroom floor.

Her heart was banging against her chest. Nerves bounced around inside her. She couldn't breathe. When she had to pass by the shower, she got down on her elbows and shimmied her way to the door.

Almost there . . . She wasn't going to look at Kyle, no matter how tempting. Her focus was solely on the door, and once she got it open, she was making a run for it.

Molly reached out and grabbed the edge of the door and slowly, oh so slowly, opened it enough that she could squeeze through. She could feel the cool air wafting in from the other room.

Home free! Molly exhaled shakily.

"Hey, Molly," Kyle called out from the shower. "Could you grab me a towel while you're at it?"

It was funny how life turned out. Who'd have thought that a girl who'd been forced to buy her clothes in the Chubbettes department of the Tots to Teens Emporium, the very same girl who'd been a wallflower at her senior prom, would grow up to have men pay to get naked with her?

It just went to show, Emma Quinlan considered, as she ran her hands down her third bare male back of the day, that the American dream was alive and well and living in Blue Bayou, Louisiana.

Not that she'd dreamed that much of naked men when she'd been growing up.

She'd been too sheltered, too shy, and far too inhibited. Then there'd been the weight issue. Photographs showed that she'd been a cherubic infant, the very same type celebrated on greeting cards and baby food commercials.

Then she'd gone through a "baby fat" stage. Which, when she was in the fourth grade, resulted in her being sent off to a fat camp where calorie cops monitored every bite that went into her mouth and did surprise inspections of the cabins, searching out contraband. One poor calorie criminal had been caught with packages of Gummi Bears hidden beneath a loose floorboard beneath his bunk. Years later, the memory of his frightened eyes as he struggled to plod his way through a punishment lap of the track was vividly etched in her mind.

The camps became a yearly ritual, as predictable as the return of the swallows to the Louisiana gulf coast every August on their fall migration.

For six weeks during July and August, every bite Emma put in her mouth was monitored. Her days were spent doing calisthenics and running around the oval track and soccer field; her nights were spent dreaming of crawfish jambalaya, chicken gumbo, and bread pudding.

There were rumors of girls who'd trade sex for food, but Emma had never met a camper who'd actually admitted to sinking that low, and since she wasn't the kind of girl any of the counselors would've hit on, she'd never had to face such a moral dilemma.

By the time she was fourteen, Emma realized that she was destined to go through life as a "large girl." That was also the year that her mother—a petite blonde, whose crowning achievement in life seemed to be that she could still fit into her size zero wedding dress fifteen years after the ceremony—informed Emma that she was now old enough to shop for back to school clothes by herself.

"You are so lucky!" Emma's best friend, Roxi Dupree, had declared that memorable Saturday afternoon. "My mother is so old-fashioned. If she had her way, I'd be wearing calico like Half-Pint in *Little House on the Prairie*!"

Roxi might have envied what she viewed as Emma's shopping freedom, but she hadn't seen the disappointment in Angela Dupree's judicious gaze when Emma had gotten off the bus from the fat gulag, a mere two pounds thinner than when she'd been sent away.

It hadn't taken a mind reader to grasp the truth—that Emma's former beauty queen mother was ashamed to go clothes shopping with her fat teenage daughter.

"Uh, sugar?"

The deep male voice shattered the unhappy memory. *Bygones*, Emma told herself firmly. "Yes?"

"I don't want to be tellin' you how to do your business, but maybe you're rubbing just a touch hard?"

Damn. She glanced down at the deeply tanned skin. She had such a death grip on his shoulders. "I'm so sorry, Nate."

"No harm done," he said, the south Louisiana drawl blending appealingly with his Cajun French accent. "Though maybe you could use a bit of your own medicine. You seem a tad tense."

"It's just been a busy week, what with the Jean Lafitte weekend coming up."

Liar. The reason she was tense was not due to her days, but to her recent sleepless nights.

She danced her fingers down his bare spine. And felt the muscles of his back clench.

"I'm sorry," she repeated, spreading her palms outward.

"No need to apologize. That felt real good. I was going to ask you a favor, but since you're already having a tough few days—"

"Don't be silly. We're friends, Nate. Ask away."

She could feel his chuckle beneath her hands. "That's what I love about you, chere. You agree without even hearing what the favor is."

He turned his head and looked up at her, affection warming his Paul Newman blue eyes. "I was supposed to pick someone up at the airport this afternoon, but I got a call that these old windows I've been trying to find for a remodel job are goin' on auction in Houma this afternoon, and—"

"I'll be glad to go to the airport. Besides, I owe you for getting your brother to help me out."

If it hadn't been for Finn Callahan's detective skills, Emma's louse of an ex-husband would've gotten away with absconding with all their joint funds. Including the money she'd socked away in order to open her Every Body's Beautiful day spa. Not only had Finn—a former FBI agent not charged her his going rate, Nate insisted on paying for the weekly massage the doctor had prescribed after he'd broken his shoulder falling off a scaffolding.

"You don't owe me a thing. Your ex is pond scum. I was glad to help put him away."

Having never been one to hold grudges, Emma had tried not to feel gleeful when the news bulletin about her former husband's arrest for embezzlement and tax fraud had come over her car radio.

"So, what time is the flight, and who's coming in?"

"It gets in at five thirty-five at Concourse D. It's a Delta flight from LA."

"Oh?" Her heart hitched. Oh, please. She cast a quick, desperate look into the adjoining room at the voodoo altar, draped in Barbie-pink tulle, that Roxi had set up as packaging for her "hex appeal" love spell business. Don't let it be—

"It's Gabe."

Damn. Where the hell was voodoo power when you needed it?

"Well." She blew out a breath. "That's certainly a surprise."

That was an understatement. Gabriel Broussard had been so eager to escape Blue Bayou, he'd hightailed it out of town without so much as a good-bye.

Not that he owed Emma one.

The hell he didn't. Okay. Maybe she did hold a grudge. But only against men who'd kissed her silly, felt her up until she'd melted into a puddle of hot, desperate need, then disappeared from her life.

Unfortunately, Gabriel hadn't disappeared from the planet. In fact it was impossible to go into a grocery store without seeing his midnight blue eyes smoldering from the cover of some sleazy tabloid. There was usually some barely clad female plastered to him.

Just last month, an enterprising photographer with a telescopic lens had captured him supposedly making love to his costar on the deck of some Greek shipping tycoon's yacht. The day after that photo hit the newsstands, splashed all over the front of the *Enquirer,* the actress's producer husband had filed for divorce.

Then there'd been this latest scandal with Tamara the prairie princess . . .

"Guess you've heard what happened," Nate said.

Emma shrugged. "I may have caught something on *Entertainment Tonight* about it." And had lost sleep for the past three nights imagining what, exactly, constituted kinky sex.

"Gabe says it'll blow over."

"Most things do, I suppose." It's what people said about Hurricane Ivan, which had left a trail of destruction in its wake.

"Meanwhile, he figured Blue Bayou would be a good place to lie low."

"How lucky for all of us," she said through gritted teeth.

"You sure nothing's wrong, chere?"

"Positive." She forced a smile. It wasn't his fault that his best friend had the sexual morals of an alley cat. "All done."

"And feeling like a new man." He rolled his head onto his shoulders. Then he retrieved his wallet from his back pocket and handed her his Amex card. "You definitely have magic hands, Emma, darlin'."

"Thank you." Those hands were not as steady as they should have been as she ran the card. "I guess Gabe's staying at your house, then?"

"I offered. But he said he'd rather stay out at the camp."

Terrific. Not only would she be stuck in a car with the man during rush hour traffic, she was also going to have to return to the scene of the crime.

"You sure it's no problem? He can always rent a car, but bein' a star and all, as soon as he shows up at the Hertz counter, his cover'll probably be blown."

She forced a smile she was a very long way from feeling. "Of course it's no problem."

"Then why are you frowning?"

"I've got a headache coming on." A two-hundred-and-ten pound Cajun one. "I'll take a couple aspirin and I'll be fine."

"You're always a damn sight better than fine, chere." His grin was quick and sexy, without the seductive overtones that had always made his friend's smile so dangerous.

She could handle this, Emma assured herself as she locked up the spa for the day. An uncharacteristic forty-five minutes early, which had Cal Marchand, proprietor of Cal's Cajun Café across the street checking his watch in surprise.

The thing to do was to just pull on her big girl underpants, drive into New Orleans and get it over with. Gabriel Broussard might be *People* magazine's sexiest man alive. He might have seduced scores of women all over the world, but the man *Cosmo* readers had voted the pirate they'd most like to be held prisoner on a desert island with was, after all, just a man. Not that different from any other.

Besides, she wasn't the same shy, tongue-tied small town bayou girl she'd been six years ago. She'd lived in the city; she'd gotten married only to end up publicly humiliated by a man who turned out to be slimier than swamp scum.

It hadn't been easy, but she'd picked herself up, dusted herself off, divorced the dickhead, as Roxi loyally referred to him, started her own business and was a dues paying member of Blue Bayou's Chamber of Commerce.

She'd even been elected vice-mayor, which was, admittedly an unpaid position, but it did come with the perk of riding in a snazzy convertible in the Jean Lafitte Day parade. Roxi, a former Miss Blue Bayou, had even taught her a beauty queen wave.

She'd been fired in the crucible of life. She was intelligent, tough, and had tossed off her nice girl Catholic upbringing after the dickhead dumped her for another woman. A bimbo who'd applied for a loan to buy a pair of D cup boobs so she could win a job as a cocktail waitress at New Orlean's Coyote Ugly Saloon.

Emma might not be a tomb raider like Lara Croft, or an

international spy with a to-kill-for wardrobe and trunkful of glamorous wigs like *Alias*'s Sydney Bristow, but this new, improved Emma Quinlan could take names and kick butt right along with the rest of those fictional take-charge females.

And if she were the type of woman to hold a grudge, which she wasn't, she assured herself yet again, the butt she'd most like to kick belonged to Blue Bayou bad boy Gabriel Broussard.

Mayhem. Men. And buried treasure.
Here's a look at
WHO LOVES YA, BABY?
by Gemma Bruce.
Available now from Brava . . .

The night was suddenly still. Cas peered into the woods again. He would swear someone was standing just inside the ring of trees, out of the moonlight. He rolled tight shoulders and cracked his neck. What the hell was he doing in Ex Falls, chasing burglars through the woods?

He snorted. His just deserts. He'd chased Julie through these woods more times than he could remember. And caught her. He smiled, forgetting where he was for a moment. He'd been pretty damn good at Cops and Robbers in those days. He'd been even better at Pirates.

A rustle in the trees. *Wind? No wind tonight.* Another rustle. Not a nocturnal animal, but a glimmer of white. All right, time to act, or he might still be standing here when the sun rose, and someone was bound to see him and by tomorrow night, it would be all over town that he had spent the night hiding behind a bush with an empty gun while the thieves got away.

Cas said a quick prayer that he was out of range and stepped away from the bush. He braced his feet in the standard two-handed shooting stance he learned from *NYPD Blue,* and aimed into the darkness. He sucked in his breath.

A figure stepped out to the edge of the trees. There was just enough light for Cas to see the really big handgun that was aimed at him.

The "freeze" he'd been about to yell froze on his lips.

"Freeze," said a deep voice from the darkness.

Hey, that was his line. He froze anyway, then yelped, "Police."

"Yeah. So drop the weapon and put your hands in the air. Slowly."

Cas dropped his gun. "No. I mean. Me. I'm the police."

"You're the sheriff?" A sound like strangling. "Why didn't you say so?"

"I did. I was going to, but you—Who are you?"

"I'm the one who called you." The figure stepped into the moonlight. Not a thief, but an angel. Not an angel, but a vision that was the answer to every man's wet dream. A waterfall of long dark hair fell past slim shoulders and over a shimmering white shift that clung to every curve of a curvaceous body. His eyes followed the curves down to a pair of long, dynamite legs, lovely knees, tapering to . . . a pair of huge, untied work boots. He recognized the boots—they were his—but not the apparition that was wearing them.

He must be dreaming. That was it. It wouldn't be the first time he'd dreamed of Julie coming back to him. Her hair long and soft like this, hair a man could wrap his body in. A body that he could wrap his soul in. Mesmerized, Cas took a step toward her. She stepped back into the cover of the trees, disappearing into the darkness like a wraith. He took another step toward her and was stopped by a warning growl. His testicles climbed up to his rib cage. *Stay calm. It's just a dream.* Strange. He'd imagined Julie as many things—but never as a werewolf.

He barely registered the beast as it leapt through the air, flying toward him as if it had wings. *Time to wake up,* he told himself. *Now.*

He hit the ground and was pinned there by a ton of black fur and bad breath. The animal bared its teeth. Cas squeezed his eyes shut and felt a rough, wet tongue rasp over his face.

"Off, Smitty."

Cas heard the words, felt the beast being hauled off him. He slowly opened his eyes to find himself looking up at six legs: four muscular and furry; two, muscular and sleek—and definitely female. He had to stop himself from reaching out to caress them.

Her companion growled and Cas yanked his eyes away to stare warily at the dog. He was pretty sure it was a dog. A really big dog.

"Never lower your firearm on a perp who might be armed." She waved the muzzle of her weapon in Cas's direction, then leaned over and picked up his .38 from the ground. She looked at it. "And maybe, next time, you should try loading this." She dropped it into his lap and heaved a sigh that lifted her shoulders and stretched the fabric of her shirt across her breasts. And Cas forgot about the dog, as he imagined sucking on the hard nipples that showed through the silk.

She stomped past him, shaking her head. The dog trotted after her.

Cas watched them—watched her—walk away, her hair trailing behind her, the work boots adding a hitch to her walk that swung her butt from side to side and set the fabric, shifting and sliding against her body. And he wanted to touch her, slide his fingers inside the shift, and feel warm, firm flesh beneath his fingers. But mostly he wanted to touch her hair.

Halfway to the house, she paused and looked over her shoulder. "They're getting away," she said and continued toward the house.

After a stupefied second, he pushed himself off the ground. What was happening to him? He never thought about groping strange women, even magical ones like this one. He licked his lips, stuck his .38 in his jacket pocket and followed after her.

When he reached the porch, she was at the front door. So was the dog.

"Uh, miss . . . ma'am? If you'd call off the dog, I could take down some information."

He saw a flick of her hand and he had to keep himself from diving for the bushes, but the dog merely padded past her into the house.

"Well, if you're not going to chase the thieves, you may as well come in," she said and turned to go inside.

"Wait," he cried.

She stopped mid-step.

"You might want to leave those boots on the porch."

She looked down at the work boots, sniffed, then wrinkled her nose. "Oh." She leaned over to pull them off.

Her ass tightened beneath the soft nightshirt, and Cas had a tightening response of his own. He shifted uncomfortably and stared at the mailbox until he got himself under control.

This was ridiculous. He should be used to this. For three months, women called him in all sorts of getups at all hours of the night. He was, after all, the town's most eligible bachelor. Actually he was the town's only eligible bachelor. None of them had the least effect on him. But this one knocked him right out of his socks. Made his dick throb, just looking at her. She might not be Julie, but she looked pretty damn good. He might as well find out who she was and what she was doing here—and how long she planned to stay.

"Coming?" she asked and let the screen door slam behind her.

Oh yeah, thought Cas, *I'm coming.*